Praise for

'A brutal, brilliant tal   : is a terrific creation'

'A highly enjoyable ride through a story rich in detail. Bale takes the reader from the terror of battle where a crown is lost and won to the sparkling jewel that is Venice, teeming with intrigue and treachery. Loyalty tested, love for a woman reclaimed, a quest beckons to reclaim the English crown. Great storytelling'

'An absolute gem of a novel. I was taken aback by Bale's skill and talent. Meticulously researched, with a totally authentic medieval feel, the novel fizzes with action, romance and intrigue. A gripping yarn'

'This character-driven plot holds the interest to the end. Hawker is an ageing, flawed character and it is in his description of the man's inner turmoil, his bursts of energy and, above all, loyalty that the author has created a living soul. Compelling, authentic characters, a tight narrative which drives the story with verve; dialogue which is neither mock Gothic nor anachronistic, all allow the reader to feel part of the sounds and sights of the late fifteenth century. The novel deserves high praise'

The Lost Prince

Ethan Bale was a defence journalist in both Washington and London before he turned to writing historical novels, non-fiction and short stories. Despite covering modern military technology for much of his professional career, he was always passionate about times past, particularly the Renaissance and early modern Europe. Indeed for many years he donned full medieval armour to participate in fighting tournaments in the US and UK. These days, he is usually found wielding a pen and not a sword.

Also by Ethan Bale

The Swords of the White Rose series

Hawker and the King's Jewel
The Lost Prince

The Lost Prince

ETHAN BALE

CANELO

First published in the United Kingdom in 2023 by

Canelo
Unit 9, 5th Floor
Cargo Works, 1-2 Hatfields
London SE1 9PG
United Kingdom

A CIP catalogue record for this book is available from the British Library.

Print ISBN 978 1 80032 970 6
Ebook ISBN 978 1 80032 969 0

This book is a work of fiction. Names, characters, businesses, organizations, places and events are either the product of the author's imagination or are used fictitiously. Any resemblance to actual persons, living or dead, events or locales is entirely coincidental.

Cover design by Black Sheep

Cover images © ArcAngel, Shutterstock

Look for more great books at www.canelo.co

Printed and bound in Great Britain by Clays Ltd, Elcograf S.p.A.

I

MIX
Paper from
responsible sources
FSC
www.fsc.org
FSC® C018072

For Pauline and Mike

Prologue

Before they had even reached the place, the joyous laughter of crows told Pedja that there had been a great slaughter.

He glanced across the road to his friend, who returned his grim scowl, and slowly drew his slender, reverse-curved sword from its scabbard, circling it over his head to signal the riders behind to catch up.

'Doesn't bode well. Our lads should have made it back to us last night.'

Pedja nodded emphatically at the Turk's obvious deduction. 'Yes, and *whose* plan was it to split us up yesterday and have the hotheads ride ahead to raid? I told you we should stay together.'

Orkan didn't bother to look him in the eye but stood up in his stirrups. He pushed back his fur-rimmed conical helm and gazed up the road. The thatch of house roofs was visible through the bare trees. 'Since when did a lazy garrison hanger-on like you become an *akinci*?' He wiped his sword arm across his thick black beard, kicked in his spurs, and moved ahead.

Pedja shook his head and spurred his own horse, the rest of the Ottoman raiding party, some two dozen men, but just five of them his own, coming up alongside him. He was already regretting his decision to accompany the *akincis* on their raid out of Zvornik two days before. But the boredom of garrison life was grinding him down, his brother too. Orkan's offer to take them along for some excitement on a raid into the Hungarian lands had seemed a welcome adventure. Pedja Jankovic had served the

I

Ottomans for several years, as had his father. He was a *martolos* – a Christian soldier under the command of the Bey of Zvornik. He'd met the swaggering Orkan Ozdemir over a game of backgammon outside the fortress. A few games and a fistfight later, they'd become friends over a bottle of *raki*. It was an unlikely pairing: him a pudgy but pugnacious Bosnian and Orkan the blustering Ottoman raider, but their friendship had survived and prospered for over two years now.

Martaloses rarely got the chance to do much beyond garrison duty. Orkan had made some excuse to his commander, saying he needed a party of them to guard prisoners and to translate. The bey had allowed it and here Pedja was, practically on the banks of the Sava River, deep in Hungarian territory. But his over-ambitious younger brother had joined the advance raiders and now Pedja was regretting his decision that had allowed it. He drew out his heavy, single-edged sword from his saddle scabbard and clicked his tongue. The horse quickened to a trot, Pedja's small round metal shield clanking against its crupper.

They cleared the woods and entered a broad river plain, a large village off to the left. A flock of crows wheeled near the first few houses at the edge of a shorn grain field. On the ground, they strutted and pecked at some heaps arranged in a long row. Corpses.

Orkan's mount was already trotting ahead and Pedja caught him up. Some dozen bodies were laid out neatly. Pedja recognised the clothing and armour of several – *akinicis* and *martaloses* both; mud- and blood-stained breeches and tunics, cloaks lifted up to cover their faces in death.

'Holy Mother of God,' Pedja mumbled.

Orkan made a deep rumbling sound, but he didn't reply. His eyes scanned the row of houses, peasant dwellings by the look of them. There wasn't a soul to be seen. He still had his bare sword in hand, tapping it against his boot. He looked over to Pedja. 'They didn't fall like that. Someone's dragged them over here and laid them out. So, where are they?'

The loud creak of a door drew their attention. An old man emerged, his dark red woollen cap clutched in both hands. He walked out and over to them, bowing and squinting, no doubt terrified that he would be cut down at any moment. He stopped a few feet in front of Orkan's mount, bobbing up and down, and then started to speak.

Orkan pointed at the man with his sword. '*Allah kahretsin!* What's this fool saying, Pedja?'

'He's Croat, not Bosnian. He's saying he is sorry for your men. He says others came. There was a fight.'

The old man looked to Pedja now, as he continued to speak, the words dripping out, laced with fear.

'And he says his people here did nothing. They have only just pulled the bodies in from over there across the field.'

Orkan swore again, gesturing with his blade. 'So where are the others? Who did this?'

Pedja asked the old man and waited while the fellow squeaked out a reply.

'They were another band of raiders, he says. Maybe Hungarians. Stradiotti were with them. He thinks they moved on. Across the river. It all happened early this morning.'

Orkan shook his head and looked north towards the wide Sava. Pedja dismounted and walked over to the corpses. Already his chest was tightening with anxiety for his brother. He turned to the old man. 'Did you find any wounded?'

The old man followed at a respectful distance, still crushing his tattered bonnet in his spindly hands. 'Yes, my lord. There is one. He is being tended in my house.'

Pedja didn't reply. He had spotted a thick leather belt and brass buckle on one of the bodies. A belt he recognised. He bent down and gently pulled away the man's rough-spun blue cloak from his face. Pedja sank down to his knees in the cold, straw-strewn mud. Davud's eyes were closed, his face bluish grey, lips white as a snow-drop. Pedja's hand drew across the young man's forehead, smoothing a black forelock back. He then placed his hand on his brother's bloody chest and with lowered head, said a quiet prayer. He became aware of someone standing behind him, then a hand gently placed on his shoulder.

'Come, Tombik. We grieve later. We have to find out who did this.'

Pedja nodded. Orkan had always called him 'Fatty'. A ribbing at first, but later a nickname he didn't really mind. It was better than what Orkan called most of his comrades. Pedja carefully pulled Davud's cloak back over his face and rose, brushing a mud clod from his breeches and the hem of his dark woollen tunic. He had killed his headstrong brother by not being the older brother he should have been: a protector. Despite the rough comfort of his friend, his stomach sank and a cold emptiness overcame him.

Orkan reached forward and gave a light tug at this elbow. 'Come on.'

Pedja turned to him. 'Let's find our comrade.' He strode to the old villager and hauled him up straight by the back of his tunic. 'Show us the wounded!' He shoved the man forward towards the clutch of houses and ramshackle outbuildings.

Orkan set the raiders to guard outside as the old man scurried ahead to his door, then followed, sword in hand. Pedja halted at the open door and turned back to glance at his band. Some had wide eyes, tensed for what might happen next. A few were still staring from their saddles at the corpses on the ground, their faces set hard. All were on edge, having seen the handiwork of the unseen enemy upon their comrades. Pedja knew *akincis* were brave, but they were not renowned for open battle. They favoured hitting an unsuspecting village or town then leaving as fast as they had come, dragging away as much loot, women and children as they could manage. Horsemen. Ruthless, yes – but lightly armed. He followed Orkan into the dark hovel.

It was a single room with a floor of packed earth. In one corner a round hearth surrounded a small fire, the smoke rising up to the hole in the rafters above. Lying next to this was a man. It was one of Orkan's lads. The Turkish captain knelt down and narrowed his eyes, trying to see what wound had been sustained. The man stirred, groaning, and then recognised Orkan. He struggled to raise himself but Orkan gently placed a hand on his shoulder and guided him back down.

In the gloom, Pedja could just see the shine of wet blood covering the top of the man's chest.

Orkan leaned over his man, smiling. 'Ahmet, you fell off your horse again. What have I told you about larking about?'

The man swallowed hard, eyes blinking. Orkan bellowed for water in the Slav tongue and the old man hurriedly brought over a clay vessel. Orkan tipped it towards the wounded man's lips, cradling his head. 'Now, Ahmet, tell me what happened. Who attacked you?'

Ahmet swallowed again, water dribbling down his chin. 'Infidels. Strange ones. We were rounding up horses here. No money in this place. They rode straight in and hit us hard.'

Orkan pushed the man upright, almost in a sitting position. The man groaned in pain. 'Think, Ahmet! Who were they?'

'Hungarians. Stradiotti... maybe Venetians. Speaking languages I did not know. They had a *woman*, Orkan. A woman who *fought*. I saw her cleave Ibrahim before he could even raise his arm.' Ahmet shook his head. 'She led the stradiotti. She gave the orders.' His head drooped onto his chest.

Orkan gave him a gentle shake. 'Ahmet, how many?'

Ahmet opened his eyes wide as if startled from a nap. 'Many. Armoured men. A dozen maybe... I don't know.'

'Banners?'

Ahmet shook his head. 'No banners. They rode off. Didn't stay.'

'Where?'

'East. Following the river.'

Orkan looked up at Pedja but said nothing. He lowered his man back down to the stinking straw mattress and then got up, retrieving his sword from the floor. He gestured with it towards the old villager. 'He dies, you die,' he hissed in Turkish.

5

Pedja translated. The Croat, resigned to what fate had brought him, nodded. Orkan harrumphed, pushed past Pedja, and went outside.

'You know who they were, don't you, old man? They helped you. You will tell me or I will burn this place. All of it.'

The Croat looked at Pedja, for the first time showing some defiance in his eyes. 'She was Hungarian. A lioness. She commanded them all. The Albanian stradiots. The Frankish knights. All of them. They saw your men attacking us and they came in like wolves. Saved our lives. Our winter stocks. Our herds.'

Pedja stared back. 'Maybe I'll burn you down anyway.'

The Croat shrugged.

'Tell me about the Frankish knights. Explain.'

The old man's lips curled in the faintest of smiles. 'Venetian… English… French. I don't know. I heard many foreign tongues. But they are on a quest. Searching for someone. I heard what she said. What she told me after they fought. She tried to reassure us and said they're looking to find Prince Vlad, son of Dracul. The Dragon – or the Devil as they called him. I am old enough to remember when he passed this way once, going south to wage war on the Ottomans.' His smile widened. 'The Turks call him the Impaler. The lioness said he yet lives.'

Now it was Pedja's turn to smile. 'You are either a very stupid old man or a very gullible one. Perhaps both. But you're still bold enough to try and fob me off with a wives' tale. The Wallachian is dead. Has been for years.'

The Croat looked downwards and Pedja had half a thought that he was trying not to grin. After a few seconds the old farmer spoke again. 'The dead man you knelt by. Was he kin to you?'

Pedja bristled and pushed his shoulders back. 'He was my brother.'

The old man nodded. 'I am sorry. It was the lioness. I saw her strike him down when they fought.'

Pedja glared and spat on the man's floor. But he said nothing more. He turned and went outside into the chill air, which was

6

threatening to turn to a misting drizzle. Orkan had put a group of villagers to digging graves and the *akincis* were beating those that were not working hard enough.

'Well, what more did you learn from that damned *soysuz*?'

'There were strangers among them. Frankish knights. They are searching for Vlad the Impaler.'

Orkan folded his arms across his chest, brown eyes opening wide. '*Kaziglu Bey*? That Wallachian's head rotted away a long time ago on the gates of Constantinople. Should I go back into the house and tear out the old fool's tongue to punish him for telling tall stories?'

'You can do what you like, my friend. I am going to bury my brother. Then I am taking my men and going after the Hungarian and her soldiers.'

Orkan's arms dropped to his sides. 'You and your *five* men are going to invade Hungary? And you expect my men to come with you too, I suppose?'

'I'm going to avenge my brother. And – if God wills it – then I'll bring back the Impaler for the sultan's pleasure as well.'

Orkan Ozdemir let out a very audible sigh. 'You have a way of shaming me into doing things I do not wish to, Tombik. But blood is important. And so is honour. We'll go – and see how far we get. And if it gets too hot, we cut and run, understood?' He sheathed his sword and walked to his horse before turning again. 'But it *would* be worth it just to see the sultan's face when I present Vlad the Impaler to him!'

Pedja nodded. Something told him that Orkan was only half-joking.

Part I

BRIGANDS

1

Ten days earlier...

Sir John Hawker's gloved hands gripped his reins tightly. He felt as if all the eyes of the world were upon him as he and his men rode up the steep hill that led to the old Gradec quarter. In front of him, by a few yards, rode the woman he and his men had agreed to serve under, surrounded by her Albanian mercenaries – *stradiotti*. Theophilius, her young Greek servant or slave, Hawker wasn't quite sure which, rode at her side laden with her belongings. Gradec was the oldest part of the free imperial city of Zagrab, a place that anchored the southern fringe of the Kingdom of Hungary in the Croatian lands. And Hawker had been here years before.

Jacob de Grood, Hawker's long-time man-at-arms, hadn't failed to notice his lord's tightened posture and twitchiness. 'Why so worried? We can get ourselves the best meal we've had in a week!'

Hawker glanced over to his comrade. 'If no one knew of our arrival before, then they do now. We don't exactly look like a party of Venetian merchants, do we?'

Jacob shrugged. 'This is a free city still. No questions. Everyone minds their own business.'

'We are what we look to be. Brigands.'

They were certainly not attired as knights. Not anymore. Behind Hawker rode Sir Giles Ellingham, the young knight and bastard son of the fallen king, Richard the Third. And next to him the Burgundian enigma who was Gaston Dieudonné, a *sieur* of a noble house and a mercenary who had made his escape from Bosworth Field like the rest of them. Riding at Hawker's left was his squire, Jack, a boy of fourteen years who looked to be much older after the trials of the past four months. They had all barely escaped alive from Venice, the blame for which Hawker placed firmly upon his own shoulders. They had their weapons, but the rest had been abandoned in the headlong flight from the Serene Republic. Now, their pitted and rusting open-face helms, greasy leather brigandines of riveted plates, and tall mud-stained and cracked leather boots all told a story of loss and ill fortune.

Jacob shrugged again. 'Brigands? Maybe, my lord. But who would dare tell us so?'

Hawker had to smile grimly at that. 'Let us hope Mistress Maria knows the city better than I remember it. This is her expedition after all, not ours.'

They rode on up the hill into the depths of the old city, the tall Cathedral of the Virgin rising up to meet them. They were still in western lands – just – but beyond the city lay the East and the old Christian Orthodox kingdoms, most now under the hand of the Ottoman sultan and the banner of the Crescent Moon. They were headed for the debatable lands, the fringes of the Hungarian kingdom now under attack by the Turks, who were forever probing for weakness. As unpredictable as their circumstances were in Zagrab, Hawker knew full well that once they reached Wallachia, now a tribute state of the sultan, they would be in a land with few friends.

Hawker watched as Maria Hunyadi, the Hungarian noblewoman and their saviour in Venice – now their paymaster – rode confidently up the wide street, surrounded by her loyal but menacing *stradiotti*. They rarely spoke and seemed content to glower at all passers-by, their tall felt hats, forked beards, curved blades and small square shields marking them as Albanian men of the sword, sworn to their mistress. The only clue to their better side was a long slender mandolin that one of them had slung behind his back. Maria had promised a good inn this night and a meal to go with it. She had also promised they would be joined by more mercenaries she had hired. Hawker knew that, where they were going, they would need them.

Jacob spoke again, his eyes remaining focused on Ellingham and Maria. 'You could have talked him out of it, you know. He would have listened to you.'

'He is his own man now. I served his father and gave my bond to watch over his son.'

Jacob snorted. 'He's a boy yet. And he's had a whiff of her charms and bought her tale like some gullible peasant.'

'He's made his choice. And I'm not sure I could have argued him out of it. Where would we have gone, anyway?'

Jacob shook his head. 'You were sulking, my lord. Wounded in the heart. I understand.'

Hawker tightened up his rein, jerking his mount's head. 'Keep your sentiments to yourself, Jacob de Grood!'

The price of their salvation from the clutches of the Doge of Venice had been a jewel of great worth in Hawker's keeping, one of the Tears of Byzantium, but they had also been offered service and payment in gold if they would help Maria in her quest. Something that King Richard's bastard had eagerly signed on for, and that he had acquiesced in. It was to be the search for her father, an infamous prince of Wallachia who had dared challenge the sultan. Vlad Dracula – son of Vlad Dracul – known as *Ţepeş* – the Impaler. He had long been thought dead but Maria claimed to know that he lived still. Now, Hawker's little band was to join the quest to find him and free him in a land beset by enemies. As far as Hawker was concerned, Maria told a good story, but it was one that Sir Giles had devoured and now pledged his sword to. And since Hawker had sworn service to *him*, one of the last Plantagenets, the die had been cast.

Maria and her men turned left down a side street and they came to a large, ochre-coloured house and its paved courtyard: The Inn of the Dancing Bear. The *stradiots* dismounted along with Maria and she stood before Hawker, her sword hanging at her side and her dark red tunic cinched in tight across her waist by a great leather belt. She pulled her woollen cloak up around her shoulders and beckoned him to come down from the saddle.

'We are here! And you've earned a rest, Sir John, after such a long ride. We've done well to make good time given the cold. Come! This place will give you a steaming bowl of *gulyás* to warm your bones.'

Stableboys emerged from the other side of the courtyard at the sound of hooves. Hawker smiled, noticing their reticence to take the mounts from the *stradiots*. It took just a word from Maria to her men and they obeyed, patting their horses with affection and handing over their reins to the wide-eyed Croat boys.

'I would pay good money for even cold stew and a flea-ridden bed after such a journey, my lady,' said Hawker. 'I am glad you know this house.' He trusted her. He had to. And she had kept her word so far. The jangling purse of gold at his belt was part proof of that, even if the source of it was still a mystery. He dismounted and Jacob did the same, taking both their mounts and leading them off to the stable.

'Come, Jack Perry!' called the Fleming over his shoulder. 'You're not getting your stew just yet!'

Jack nodded towards Hawker and then pulled his horse by the bridle, following Jacob.

Ellingham and Dieudonné were untying their bedrolls and leather portmanteaus from their mounts as Hawker walked up to them. 'Well, my lords, the first leg is at an end. From here we will have to earn our pay.'

Ellingham slung his satchel down, but his eyes followed Maria when she went inside the inn. 'I'm eager to hear what she next proposes,' he said, not a trace of irony in his voice. 'And to learn who is joining us here.'

'As are we all,' replied Hawker. 'Isn't that right, my lord Gaston?'

The Burgundian gave Hawker a thin smile and a nod, but no reply. Hawker thought it odd that he had grown quiet in the last days, no longer the wise-cracking cynic he had been before. The three followed Maria, her servant and the *stradiots* inside. It was a large hostelry, and they descended a short flight of wide stone steps into the hall where long tables were arranged before a great blazing hearth at one end.

They were eyed by a few Croat merchants who were eating and drinking, and some others whom Hawker thought looked to be tradesmen. No militia, which reassured him a little. Maria spoke quietly with her seven men who then bowed and went off to their own trestle, the one closest to the door, Hawker noted. She then sat near the fire and called out, 'Sir Giles, join me that I may tell you a story!'

Hawker looked at Ellingham and raised an eyebrow. Ellingham smiled and went to her without even a pause. It was then Dieudonné who raised an eyebrow to Hawker.

'Let's get a drink, shall we, Sir John?'

They took a table near the back wall and close to the heavy oak staircase that led to the mezzanine. They had not sat for long before serving women came out with platters and wooden bowls. Another followed with a pitcher of red wine and cups. Dieudonné grabbed the pitcher and a clay vessel, filled it, and passed it to Hawker before filling another.

His quiet French only just reached Hawker's side of the trestle. 'Sir Giles is in love, I think. But heart and head do not often go together.'

Hawker sipped his wine, savouring its burn, but did not answer. Jacob came in and joined them, sitting next to Hawker.

'Horses are watered and fed, Sir John. The locals have covered them for the night and the lad should be in presently.'

Hawker nodded. 'Good. Fetch yourself a mug and some food.'

'I see Sir Giles is in good company.'

'He is his own man,' said Hawker. 'He may do as he pleases.'

Hawker watched Dieudonné as he in turn watched Ellingham. The Burgundian shovelled in the brown, fat-strewn *gulyás* that had been placed in front of each of them without taking his eyes from Maria or her companion. His spoon was soon noisily scraping the bottom of the wooden bowl.

'I begin to worry,' he said, 'that he falls under her spell. He is young after all.'

Hawker's face was a mask, expressionless. 'I remember it was you who urged him to take this course. To come here rather than return to Flanders.'

Dieudonné reached for his mug again but did not look at Hawker. 'Yes, that is true. I do not deny it.'

'Then why are you concerned now? It is the path that was chosen.'

Dieudonné drained his mug and reached for the jug. He filled it again, slowly, his eyes looking into the middle distance. 'I do not regret my counsel, Sir John. But I have questions still. Questions big and questions small.'

Jacob looked at Hawker but the knight kept his focus on the Burgundian. 'Go ahead,' said Hawker quietly. 'Lighten whatever load it is you carry.'

'Why has she proposed a route south after you advised a northerly one? Why do we not journey through Buda? She had promised us that on the ship, no?'

Hawker's fingers entwined around the cool clay of the wine mug. 'She gave her reasons. It is a more direct route to Wallachia. Time is of the essence, she says. For her father.'

Dieudonné, frustrated, shook his head rapidly. 'No! No! You *warned* her we will now stray into Ottoman territory if we follow the Sava River. Still she insists on going there. I must listen to you as I do not know these lands. But you *do* know them. And I think you don't believe her.'

'Don't believe her? She has paid us thus far. Are you already losing faith?'

Dieudonné swore under his breath. 'I say, why does she not gain the aid of her royal uncle to help her? More men and more gold. Instead, it's just us and her little pack of wolves. If she is who she says she is, she could have raised an army in Hungary.'

Hawker returned a small, bitter smile. 'Then go and ask her yourself.'

Dieudonné mumbled another oath and reached for a piece of bread. Hawker inwardly admired the Burgundian's reasoning, even if he wasn't about to tell him so. He himself already suspected that Maria's route south was dictated by the fact that her uncle, the king of Hungary (if she was to be believed), didn't know of her plans, nor did she want him to. Hawker remembered that it had been King Matthias's decision to let Vlad's enemies in Wallachia defeat him nine years earlier, for Matthias never sent an army to aid him. It was late December of 1476 when the Turks and their Wallachian vassals finally defeated the prince's dwindling force near Bucharest. Hawker didn't know the reason why the king had sold Vlad out, but he believed that maybe Maria did. Matthias had imprisoned Dracula once before, in Buda, for more than a year. His loyalty was fickle. Something the Impaler should have remembered.

Jack had come in and taken a seat on the bench next to Jacob, wiping his sleeve across his face and then his hands on his short blue tunic in readiness for his meal. He cast a quick eye over to Jacob before addressing Hawker.

'Can I eat with you, Sir John?'

Hawker clapped him lightly on the shoulder. 'Well, if the horses are fed I suppose we should feed you, too.'

He was proud of his young squire. Too young, really, that he knew. But the boy was in his care and needed upbringing. He would one day make a competent squire, of that Hawker was certain, even though he himself had never felt the need to have one or had time to find one. For the moment, Jack would need training and guidance. He was growing fast, and Hawker saw that the down on the boy's upper lip was now darker and thicker than even in the summer just past. Rogue chin hairs had sprouted, too, reminding Hawker of a puppy dog's muzzle.

But this boy had already been thrown into the world of men. He had slain. Proved himself during the weeks of their flight out of England, across Flanders, Burgundy and into the Italian lands. And it was in Venice that he had killed to save Hawker's love, Chiara. A woman now lost to Hawker, nonetheless. As the weeks had progressed, their flight from Venice to the shores of Dalmatia and across the hills of Croatia, Hawker sensed that Jack's worries of dealing out death had diminished. He knew that Jack was coming to a crossroads; the crossroads where one accepts the mercenary life or rejects it, and where possibly – and more darkly – one doesn't just tolerate it, one enjoys it.

Dieudonné shot Jack a brief look of disgust as the lad noisily dived into his bowl of stew, starving after the long day's ride. He then turned back to Hawker. 'I think we should learn more about where she is taking us next on this pilgrimage of faith. Perhaps Sir Giles could gain it from her. And while he is at it, he could ask where the rest of her hirelings are.'

Hawker took in another mouthful of stew and chewed it, slowly. The arrow had been loosed. There was nothing he could do to change that. They were in the hands of the fates.

What was more, he didn't really care. Half of his soul remained in Venice.

Dieudonné grew frustrated again, slicking back his long dark hair, still damp with sweat. 'Listen to me, Hawker! We are supposed to be met here aren't we? She promised more men.'

Jacob, whose French was good, chuckled. 'Would have thought, my lord, that you'd have no need for any help. Nor any desire to share the rewards.'

Dieudonné flew to his feet, the bench screeching backwards on the tiles. His hand went to his dagger but Hawker held up his palm, his last two fingers curled downwards, like a bishop giving benediction. 'Sit. Now.'

Dieudonné swore but sat down again, simmering in silence.

-

Giles Ellingham sat next to Maria Hunyadi, both facing outwards and looking into the chamber. She had thrown off her cloak and with elbows on the table had begun tearing off chunks of black bread before placing them into her mouth with a sense of delicacy. The slender, effete Theophilius refilled both their cups.

Ellingham could feel the heat coming off her thigh, so close was it to his.

'Your comrades pay close attention to you,' she said. 'Was it always so? Do they not trust you?'

Ellingham laughed lightly, still not quite believing how Maria dressed like a man: a belted and pleated russet *giornea* tunic, green hose, and brown leather boots that went up to her knees. Far different than the finely dressed lady of the Venetian court he had first set his eyes upon a month earlier.

'They trust me. And I them.'

She leaned in towards him. 'Then perhaps it's me they're staring at.'

'I imagine they have not been on a march led by a woman before. Nor have I. And we all have questions about where we're going. How to find your father, how to free him...' He found it difficult to avoid her large green eyes, which demanded his attention.

'There are women among the Wallachians, and the Moldavians... and others further east... who fight alongside their menfolk. And I am half Wallachian.'

She smelled of cinnamon and sweat and he found it not unpleasant. 'Then that must be the half of you I saw on the deck of your galley when we escaped. Fire in your eyes and a sword in your fist.'

She smiled. 'You seem far older than you are.'

Ellingham smiled in return. 'It's been a difficult year.'

She laughed at that and then a silence fell between them. He did not know how old she was. Young, but older than he, he believed. Ellingham drank of his wine and then lowered his head a little. 'Tell me, my lady, will others be joining us like you promised? I think that is why Hawker seems worried these last days. You've said little, and we still have far to journey.'

She reached for her wine vessel and drew it closer. 'I thought they would be here to meet us, but they will come. Tomorrow or the day after. It has been arranged and I know their captain well.'

'Hawker thinks the route south to Bosnia risks encountering Turkish raiding parties. Aren't you worried too? We're not a large force.'

Her dark brow furrowed a little. 'You don't trust me, son of Richard? Have I not proved myself these past weeks? We will just skirt the sultan's lands then break north for Belgrade on the Danube. Castelbianco, as the Venetians call it – the White Fortress. It *is* the fastest way to Ultra Silvam, Ultrasylvania – the Siebenbürgen as the Saxons name it. And then to Wallachia.'

Ellingham nodded. 'I believe you. But I don't understand why your uncle has not lent you his aid. Provided men.'

'He's provided the gold that is already in your purse. And there is more to come.'

He could not doubt that. She had paid them all, and paid for food and fodder at every halt, keeping farmer and innkeeper happy. She also had a fortune in rubies in her possession and if she chose to part with them she could buy an army. That, he believed, would never happen, for they seemed to have a magical and holy significance for her. Still, it bothered him that their swords were few and their goal both elusive and vague. She had still not explained how they would free Vlad Dracula from his prison while avoiding the soldiers of Prince Călugărul, Vlad's half-brother, the vassal of the sultan, and current ruler of Wallachia. But he had a dark suspicion that it would be up to Hawker to meet that end of the bargain.

Maria gently swiped at the tip of his nose with a bread crust. 'You *do* believe. We are destined for this quest. You and I both.'

Ellingham smiled again, trying to tamp down his doubt, worried her luminous eyes could see deep into his heart.

'And… here's something I have not told you. We have others in the mountains – near Făgăraş – others who are waiting to join us.'

'Who are they? You did not tell me of this before.'

She tilted her head and gave him an indulgent look. 'Sir Giles, you worry needlessly. God is with us in our endeavour. The men

I speak of were retainers to my father. They still are loyal to his name even after nine years have passed. I will share more when the time is right.'

Ellingham frowned at this new revelation. Half-truths and intelligence that dribbled out, spoon-fed encouragements... this was sure to anger Hawker and the others. And it disconcerted him more and more despite his attraction to her. 'It would be better if you shared what you know with Sir John now. We all deserve that... if our necks are on the block.'

She suddenly went cold, all the previous allure vanishing from her face. 'It is *I* who have rescued *your* company – saved *you*, Sir Giles – and it is *I* who leads this expedition. You would do well to remember that you have agreed to my offer and my gold.'

The large oak door swung in noisily and admitted a new arrival. Ellingham stood. It was clearly a man of worth, a knight wearing a mirror-like breastplate of the best Milanese harness with tassets and pauldrons, black riding boots, and a fine red cloak of heavy wool. The man stepped into the hall, armour jangling, saw Maria, and gave her a curt bow of recognition. His shoulder-length black hair was set off by sky-blue eyes and a fair complexion despite a few days' growth of beard stubble.

Before Maria could open her mouth, Hawker was on his feet and rushing towards the new arrival. Ellingham's hand went to his dagger but he froze when he saw Hawker envelop the man in a bear hug.

'Christ's nails! Bartolo Faldi! You're still alive!'

Bartolo Faldi let out a joyous roar of recognition, returned the hug and lifted Hawker clear off his feet. 'Hawker, you English devil!' he shouted. 'The Wallachian lady is full of surprises!'

Ellingham broke into a grin, not sure if he was more surprised by the coincidence or that the man spoke English.

'By Jesus,' swore Hawker, 'if I had known it was you we were waiting upon here... my God, it is good to see a man of Milan such as you. We will have need of your sword arm, you may be assured of that.'

'Ser Bartolo!' Maria Hunyadi reared up and smashed her wine mug on to the table. 'You would do *me* the service of making your greetings *first*!' she barked in Venetian.

Faldi set Hawker down and moved forward a step, arms spread wide. He bowed his head again. 'My lady, I meant no dishonour. It is just that my heart is full! Full to the brim to see an old friend and comrade-in-arms.'

Her anger seemed to diminish, and she nodded at him. 'It gladdens my heart also to see you have arrived. And the four lances that you promised. We will find room for them to bed down, here or out in the stable block with my stradiotti – if your men are brave enough.'

Ellingham saw Faldi gaze downwards, not meeting her eye.

'So, how many of your company have you brought, Ser Bartolo?' Maria asked.

The knight of Milan threw up his arms, grinning, his pauldrons clanking. 'You have Ser Bartolo Faldi! There is no need for more!'

Ellingham, who had learned enough of the tongue to understand what had been said, immediately caught Hawker's eye. The old knight winced. But when Ellingham turned to Maria, he could see that the Hungarian's comely visage had transformed into a gorgon's glare.

2

They were seven days out of Zagrab, heading east. The company weaved through the valleys between the mountains and entered a low-lying plain along which the great Sava snaked its way towards the even greater Danube. Hawker rode with Jacob at his side and watched Ellingham again riding with Maria, but this time also with Faldi. He had noticed in the past week that the youth had become quieter than before. Certainly quieter since the arrival of the Milanese mercenary. Maria Hunyadi, after a quick burning rage at Faldi's solo appearance, had regained her composure and accepted their limited numbers. They would go on.

Hawker was lost in his thoughts as they rode, his mind filled with a jumble of scenes from the past. His curt, leaden saddle conversation didn't go unnoticed.

'You should unburden yourself, my lord,' said Jacob. 'I have seen you like this before. Many times. It leads to nothing good. Your pot is boiling, so tell me what you're thinking.'

Hawker smiled thinly and glanced over to Jacob. 'What am I thinking? I'm thinking how I've ended up here. How I lost Chiara… again. How I lost my contract with the Doge. My house. My gold. There seems to be little left save my honour and *that* I am determined to hold on to.'

'Then that is why we are here in this place, my lord. To find honour again. And to honour our comrades we lost. Our poor Jan Bec. And Sir Roger, braggart that he was.'

Hawker wasn't quite sure what to say in reply. To be sure, he mourned the loss of his loyal Flemish man-at-arms, but in the weeks since they fled Venice, he could still not bring himself to tell

Jacob or the others of Sir Roger's treachery. His dark mood was bad enough. To tell them they had been betrayed to the Doge's men by Beconsall would make them low. It also would cast doubt on him for having trusted Beconsall in the first place.

'You are right, Jacob. And that is what we must do.'

The six *stradiots* led the column, arrayed in their light armour, pantaloons, tall black felt hats, and wielding spears. On one raised spear was a small banneret with the royal arms of the Hunyadis: a raven with a gold ring in its beak. Maria rode in their midst. Hawker's first intimation that all was not what it seemed had been when they disembarked at Senj after the run from Venice, the banner of Dracula folded and concealed in her baggage. There she had abandoned her galley and its crew, Hawker discovering that she had merely hired them. Half the dozen *stradiot* warriors then went south into Dalmatia, headed for home. That left his small party, Maria, her servant, and her bodyguard of six. And of course, with the addition of one bombastic Milanese *cavaliere* who Hawker well remembered thrived on risk, they now numbered fourteen.

Faldi's arrival had enlivened things, though. Every night he regaled them with stories of his exploits and of his service in the Neapolitan League fighting against Venetian and papal troops over the Duchy of Ferrara. Ellingham and Jack had been transfixed by his tales, Dieudonné, less so, seemed to sulk. It was after one of Faldi's performances one night where they had taken shelter in a small village on the Sava, having crossed the river the previous day, when Hawker and Ellingham found themselves outside alone, relieving themselves before bedding down.

They were now in the debatable lands of Bosnia and Serbia; still nominally under Hungarian rule but in reality a chessboard of never-ending struggle with the Turks. The air had seemed to grow colder with every passing day, the chill of the night ever deeper. They wrapped their cloaks tightly about themselves and wandered to the edge of the hamlet, the way illuminated by a moon not yet set.

'You knew him well, then?' offered Ellingham as he laced up his hose.

Hawker nodded. 'Aye. But we never did fight on the same side. Until now.' The older knight laughed to himself. 'The fool even managed to talk his way into leading a parley with us when we fought against the Milanese at Molinella, just so we could meet to drink together!' They watched as another figure approached them. It was Faldi.

'Gentles, are you so eager to resume the march on your own and not take rest?' His good-natured voice boomed out across the field.

'Won't sleep without a good piss first. Come, walk with us, my friend,' replied Hawker. 'I have need of your counsel.'

'Counsel? It is time we were all abed! What more would you know from me?'

Hawker's voice became quiet. 'To find out why you came. A man such as you could find a more reliable patron I'm sure. But here you are, on our little quest.'

Faldi smiled and shrugged. 'What would you like to know? I met her in Buda after the Feast of the Presentation, February last. She was looking for soldiers. I liked her spirit. We journeyed to her house in Temesvár and then she sent me to Zagrab, where I have carried gold for her and letters drawn on Lombard banks.'

Hawker looked down at the broken stalks at his feet. 'But your men like her less, it seems.'

'Bah! They were not willing to come down here. Were barely willing to take service in Hungary at all. What of it? The woman has argued that we need a small party that can move quickly. I agree.'

'Just who is she?' It was Ellingham who asked, tension in his voice.

Faldi's cheeks puffed once. 'Who is she? *Allora*. She is who she says she is. A niece of Matthias Corvinus, the king. A Hunyadi.'

'And a daughter of Vlad Țepeș?' said Hawker. 'How is that?'

'It is complicated... these things should best come from her.'

'Bartolo, if we are going to fight together – and by God, there will be fighting – then you will be the one to tell us what you know. Now.'

Faldi let out a loud sigh. 'My lords, you have cut me to the quick. But I will tell you what I know. Maria *is* the daughter of Vlad Țepeș. But she is a bastard. She was born in Ultra Silvam, the Siebenbürgen, to Dracula's concubine who herself was the daughter of one of John Hunyadi's concubines a generation ago. Therefore, King Matthias is her half-uncle.'

Hawker looked at Ellingham.

'So... she is illegitimate?' stuttered Ellingham. 'How can she be recognised by the king? She is not even the Dragon's daughter, by the law.'

'Things work differently in this land. As the Wallachians say, she is "of the bone". Legitimacy counts for little. Besides, she says she has a pension from the royal court and I know she does not want for coin. But in Buda she kept to the shadows. Vlad Dracula's widow, a Szilágy, and also kin to the Hunyadis, lives there with her young son. Life at court would be... awkward.'

Hawker swore under his breath and shook his head. 'Vlad Dracula's widow? Apparently not, or why else are we here. Does King Matthias know what she is planning?'

Faldi raised his chin slightly, looking at Hawker. 'No.'

Hawker swore again. 'So, you're telling me that we could be on the run from the Wallachians, the Turks *and* the Hungarian militias?'

Faldi moved his hand to his heart and bowed slightly. 'I cannot tell you we are not.'

'Then what are our chances of making it deep into Wallachia, to Târgoviște?'

Faldi shrugged. '*Allora*... the chance of a coin toss?' He then threw his arm out towards Hawker. 'But you and I, Hawker, we change the odds in our favour!'

'You are mad, Faldi. And I'm having doubts about Maria's sanity, too.'

Faldi gave Hawker a mischievous little grin and cocked his head. 'You are here. Sir Giles is here. We must all be a little mad, no?'

–

The road they followed the next morning barely looked like a cow track. The River Sava, wide and brown, lay off to their left, and they rode strung out across undulating open fields and pastureland. The pace was a slow trot and Jack felt his balls begin to ache from bouncing in the saddle. The *stradiots* were in the vanguard, as usual. If a hamlet or farm came into view, one would kick in his spurs and go ahead to scout for danger. He didn't dare even lock eyes with them, even though he could not quite believe Jacob's remarks that they were infamous baby eaters.

Maria rode just behind them, confident and bolt upright, an obvious horsewoman. Jack had never seen a creature like her in his life and though she had never acknowledged him even once since they had arrived in Croatia, he found her bewitching nonetheless. As did Sir Giles, a fact that he wasn't hiding from any of them.

The front of Jack's quilted arming cap kept working its way down over his eyebrows from the horse's movement and the weight of the open-face barbute helm that Hawker had given him. He slowed, shoving the helm up higher and grabbed a fistful of rein again, kicking to catch up with Hawker and Jacob. The helmet had the remnants of the previous owner's lining and Jack couldn't get used to the stink.

Behind Maria rode Ellingham and Dieudonné. Jack admired them both and hoped that one day he would be as good a swordsman as they were. But he could only dream that he would one day become a knight and only then if Sir John would continue to train him and call him his squire. The Italian knight, Sir Bartolo, rode in lockstep with Maria – had been all morning – and he laughed to himself that Sir Giles was probably nursing a grudge about that. Jack didn't quite know what to make of the new mercenary. Not that his opinion mattered worth a fig, but what the other comrades thought about Faldi did matter a great deal, that he knew.

He was bringing up the rear along with the Greek, Theophilius, someone who appeared older than he – perhaps the same age as Sir Giles – but looked like he could be knocked over by a feather. Mistress Maria's two great leather sacks balanced on either side of the Greek's mount. He wondered if that was where she kept her treasures. Jack knew he was stationed in a not-unimportant position on the march, as Sir John had told him, and every so often he would glance behind him and search out the way they had come, looking for riders. He had been lost in a daydream about having a suit of plate armour like Bartolo Faldi when he heard shouting and looked up to see the *stradiots* galloping out ahead, with Maria and Faldi right behind. Sir Giles and Dieudonné, after reining in for a few seconds, kicked their own mounts and followed. He couldn't yet see what they had seen but he managed to draw his arming sword out of its scabbard just as Hawker circled back to him.

'Jack, stay close! And keep your wits!'

Hawker then yanked his reins and bolted after the others. Jacob had now ridden up alongside Jack and they cantered forward. 'Boy, stay with us! Keep sharp!'

Jack nodded and leaned forward as the horse gathered speed. They were riding down across a fallow field, a long gradual slope that led to a small village, and it was now that he saw other riders, some with long spears or lances, trotting between houses and barns and chasing people. It seemed to take a long time for him to get there and already the *stradiots* were way ahead. His eyes began to take in what was happening, catching glimpses of helms, spears, swords and shields. Strange-looking riders with tall hats, fur hats or conical helmets milled about the village while they pursued its inhabitants. As he drew closer to the enemy, Jacob pulled out slightly ahead, his sword in his right hand held out low.

Jack watched as the *stradiots* hit the enemy in their flank, spears knocking two of the strangers from their saddles. He felt as if he was somewhere else – or dreaming – not actually in the thick

28

of it himself. But he knew now that these were Turks, Ottoman raiders on the attack. A few had odd-looking little square shields and curved swords. He saw Sir John ride up close to a warrior, his horse making a funny little quick stop just as he reached the man's left side. Hawker's blade swung out and down on the man's helm and then Hawker converted the swing of the blow immediately with another to the man's face, the Turk desperate to bring up his own sword to ward off the attack. They began trading blows, the sounds of steel ringing loud enough for Jack to hear. But his own horse was still moving forward, leaving Theophilius behind him. And suddenly, he was no longer a spectator but into the fray himself.

The Turks, still mounted, had moved beyond the houses and into another fallow field beyond. Maria and her men ploughed into them, hacking with their blades after they had thrown or thrust their spears. Jack wasn't even sure he was guiding his horse, it was just following the others straight in. He caught a flash of movement on his right and twisted in the saddle to see a warrior bearing down on him just a few yards away. He raised up his sword and turned his horse in to meet the attacker, just as Hawker had taught him. The Turk's blade skidded off his own and flew up, clattering against his helm, jarring him. Jack saw the man's face: wide dark eyes, black beard, a turban wound about a conical helm. But then he was hacking away himself, raining blow after blow with his blade, the Turk's little square shield rising up to deflect his wild attack. Jack wasn't thinking or planning his fight, just windmilling frantically, landing blows only on the man's shield.

He then feigned a swing, causing the Turk to move his shield, and followed up with a crossing blow which caught the man in the head, staggering him a moment. But not for long. The Turk's narrow sword slid in a cut across Jack's coat of plates, scoring it. He could hear the man's grunts and breathing as he twisted himself around, trying not to lose his reins. A blur of armour and cloak came from beyond the Turk and Jack saw it was Jacob, engaging from the opposite side. A few furious blows, and the Turk was knocked from the saddle.

'Move!' shouted Jacob as he cleared the dead man's meandering horse. 'Don't sit still!'

Jack cast about, looking for another opponent. The melee had spread out and some of the fighting was now on foot, with the *stradiots* pursuing Turks who had been unhorsed but not injured. He saw Ellingham and Dieudonné fighting almost as one, still in their saddles, warding and striking blows. Bartolo Faldi engaged two men, their slender swords glancing off the Italian's glistening plate armour with no effect. Bartolo was roaring – with what sounded like laughter. Hawker seemed to fight in a tight, controlled style, keeping his movements restrained and precise, hitting out when he knew he could land a killing blow. Jack watched him size up a Turk as Hawker's mount came up alongside. The knight snapped out a vicious sideways blow, and dropped the man in a spray of blood.

Four Turks tried to cut and run, whipping their horses' flanks. Maria chased after them with a *stradiot*, Faldi close behind. Jack kicked in his spurs and rode hard towards them. He saw the Turks slow and close together, realising that they would not be able to escape. The sound of steel on steel began again. Jack singled out his man and rode straight at him. This time, he found himself in the fight on his own. It was a large man, a drooping moustache running down to his chin, and he was armed with a mace. Jack had a momentary glimpse of him as he drove in, the man wearing what looked like an entire dirty-white sheepskin instead of a breastplate. He had just enough of his wits to lean back as his blade *tinged*, numbing his wrist, deflected by the swinging iron mace. The mace whizzed past his face and Jack raised his blade to ward off the next wild swing. The man yelled at him continuously, the curses of an unknown tongue.

Jack caught the mace on the haft and quickly twisted his sword and drove it up the shaft, lifting it and thrusting it into the unprotected neck of the Turk. Jack saw the blood gushing from the man's throat, soaking the sheep's-fleece armour, and the man fell forward clutching at his neck. Jack didn't give him the time to do anything else. He followed up with all his might, a downward blow that cut into the back of the man's neck. The Turk leaned to the far side and tumbled out of the saddle, one foot still in the stirrup. Jack guided his own mount away, sword raised up, and watched as the Turk was dragged away by the confused beast.

His field of view opened again. He saw Maria hack a man down with her light curved sword. In that instant, he thought the Turk was as young as he, or maybe Sir Giles. The fellow was wide-eyed with fear and his raised blade did little to deflect Maria's savage and repeated blows. He missed his third parry and her slim, light sword slashed his throat. From the other side, a *stradiot* appeared to deal the killing blow, a thrust down into the Turk's collarbone that went deep. He toppled over and fell, one foot still in a stirrup. The man's now aimless mount dragged him away.

And then it was done. There was only the sound of pounding hooves on the ground, horses circling about themselves. No yelling or cursing. No cries or screams. He could feel his heart pounding away in his chest and both hands were shaking. But he wasn't frightened, he was fired with power, an exhilaration he had never known before. Sir John trotted up and met him, his face sweat-streaked and red with exertion.

'Are you whole, lad? Did they cut you?'

Jack shook his head but couldn't yet find his voice.

Hawker reached out and tilted his head back, then grasped his shoulder. 'Aye then, not your blood by the looks of it.' He smiled. 'Good lad!'

Jacob came trotting up. 'Young Jack Perry! I saw you topple that Turk out of his saddle! You've learned well, like I taught you.'

Hawker nodded. 'He did well.'

Jack finally found he was able to speak. 'I just kept swinging, Sir John. That's all.'

Hawker reached over and gripped the boy's shoulder. 'Whatever you did, it kept you alive. Let's find the others and see what has happened.'

They trotted back towards the edge of the hamlet. Bodies lay on the ground, at least a dozen, thought Jack. Riderless horses wandered aimlessly or stood stone still in the field. Theophilius had dismounted and was walking his horse towards Maria. They reached the others who were gathered and still mounted, and as they arrived Jack heard Dieudonné talking in French, a language he was still struggling to comprehend.

'I tell you, my lady. That was rash beyond belief. You had no call to gallop after them and attack. We've made an enemy now.'

Maria patted the neck of her horse, skittish from the smell of blood. 'They were already our enemy,' she shot back. 'And not one got away to tell their friends. These were akincis – raiders. They're nothing but murderers and robbers who have free rein from the local bey to harry these villagers. We did our duty.'

'Then let's hope their friends don't miss their company,' said Dieudonné.

Bartolo Faldi laughed.

'It's done,' said Hawker, roughly. 'I suggest we don't linger about too long in case there is another squadron of Turks patrolling nearby. My lord Gaston has a point.'

'I agree,' said Maria, her eyes scanning the village. 'We take some water here and move on.'

Ellingham spoke up. 'Sir John, look!'

Jack turned to where Ellingham was looking. He saw three villagers led by what appeared to be an old man, coming towards them.

Maria gestured towards them, giving a flourish of her gloved hand. 'See, we are being thanked!'

The three reached them and began bowing and clasping their hands in front of their breasts. They all wore long ragged tunics and loose, baggy hose. The old man, his thinning wisp of white beard flapping in the breeze, started speaking. Maria grinned. She answered in what Jack thought must be the Magyar tongue, Hungarian. He had been frustrated for months at listening in ignorance to the tongues that surrounded him. He, alone, spoke only English. It felt like being the only one not in on the joke, and maybe being the butt of it. It also made his entire world even more uncertain than it was and necessitated him pestering Hawker or Jacob for explanations. He resolved to learn at least one foreign tongue before he died. But which?

Maria turned to Hawker and Ellingham. 'They are grateful we came when we did. The akincis had only just started their raid. He tells me that only one of his neighbours was killed and that we have saved their womenfolk from slavery.'

Dieudonné shifted in his saddle and harrumphed loudly. 'At what cost to us? I don't suppose these people even have a pot to piss in never mind a reward to give us.'

Maria shook her head slowly, scolding him. 'Being a Frenchman, my lord, I would have taken you for a Christian who defends his faith and those who follow it.'

'Burgundian,' muttered Dieudonné darkly.

Maria turned back to the old villager and spoke again. Jack didn't know what she was saying but he had to admit she looked magnificent as she did so.

'We may water our horses – feed them if we wish from their stores, he says. I suggest we take a few of the better of these akincis' mounts that haven't run off.'

'And what about our stomachs?' said Faldi, smiling.

'They say they will share with us what food they have,' said Maria.

Hawker surveyed the treeline that lay a few hundred yards to the south. 'No feasting for us, my lady. Rest the horses a bit and then we should push on. The day is only half done.'

Maria nodded. 'We push on.'

Jack's hands had by now stopped shaking. His mind was again seeing his short, sharp fight with the Turk, his ears again hearing the grunts and heavy breathing of the struggle. The memory of the acrid smell of sweat and the metallic scent of freshly spilt blood. He was still holding his naked blade across his saddle bow. It glistened with blood, the colour transitioning from orange-red to dark claret as it dried on his blade. The sight of it did not sicken him at all. It made him feel powerful, unafraid. He had cried himself to sleep after shooting a sheriff's man at Hawker's house in England months before. A lifetime ago. And later, in Venice, after he had stabbed Luca Contanto in the back, it had given him nightmares and cold sweats. He knew that he had saved Hawker's mistress from death at the man's hands, but it had tortured him for days nonetheless. That feeling was suddenly gone now, dissipated on the Balkan winds. And he did not miss it.

Jack edged his horse up to Hawker's and thrust his chin towards the effete Theophilius, who again guided his mount into position, its nose near the cruppers of his lady's horse.

'That fellow was no great help, Sir John. Where did he run off to when we were in the fight?'

Hawker crossed his wrists over the saddlebow and looked at Jack with a trace of a smile. 'Some have other means of defence, my lad. They use what God has given them and know what they can and can't accomplish. I'm told that he has already slain three men in Venice. Two by poison and one by a dagger thrust. Be not quick to judge those you know nothing of.'

3

Gaston Dieudonné smiled to himself as he sat and listened to Maria spin her tales to Hawker and the Milanese knight at the far end of the long table: all about her illustrious father. As someone who prided himself on his ability to spin tales and twist truths, he knew a liar and a charlatan when he heard one. He was even beginning to believe that he actually was Burgundian, a ruse the Frenchman had adopted when joining Hawker's company. They had made it to Belgrade without getting killed though. Lucky that, he thought, as the needless fight on the Sava was foolhardy and could have gone very badly. His fingers tightened around his pewter wine beaker. Maria had ensconced them in a run-down house, one of several tall creaking buildings rammed together and facing a small courtyard just inside the town walls. It was not an inn, it was not inhabited, and he wasn't even sure it was hers. But she had led them straight to it and laid on a banquet for them. He wondered who she had paid for it all.

He glanced over to Ellingham, who sat next to him. The youth, he knew full well, was enraptured by her voice and the tale she told. To be fair, the woman had transformed from warrior to maiden, now in a long Venetian dress, high-waisted bodice, her hair wrapped by a linen veil. He was losing Giles, he could tell, slipping through his grasp like sand through his fingers. Bewitched by her boldness as much as her beauty. He chewed on his lip for a minute and then leaned a shoulder gently into Ellingham's.

'That Italian is tupping her. I would bet you a ducat on it. They are as thick as thieves, surely you can see that.'

Ellingham turned his head and narrowed his eyes. 'You dishonour her with such words.'

Dieudonné moved his eyes to Maria sitting across the table, a smile on his lips while he whispered, 'More than words, dear Giles. I have seen things.' He hadn't, of course, but he *believed* they were lovers – or had been. It was only a matter of time before they would give themselves away but, for now, he had only to plant the seed in the youth's mind.

'You are just jealous she does not fancy you, my friend,' replied Ellingham quietly. 'If you have spied them together then tell me when and prove yourself.'

Dieudonné snorted softly. 'Time will tell, Giles. They are *old* friends. You will see.'

Maria's raised her voice higher. 'My lords, does my story bore you?'

Dieudonné clasped his hands together and bowed his head like a penitent monk. 'My good lady, I do apologise. I was merely remarking on the fame of your father in the Burgundian lands.'

Maria's dark eyes blinked and she raised her chin towards him. 'His deeds were spoken of throughout Christendom. But I do not recall that the Duke of Burgundy ever sent an army to his aid.'

Dieudonné's head bowed a bit lower. 'Sadly, no, my lady.'

Such a noble table gathering, mused Dieudonné, as de Grood and the boy squire had been banished to eat on the other side of the room with the sullen *stradiots*. This was a feast for the high-born and knights of good birth. He belonged there.

'My father is a survivor though,' continued Maria, her attention moving back to the other knights. 'He has always done what was necessary to go on, to return to fight another day. I know he survives even now as we sit here, feasting. Did you know he was a hostage for several years to the great Sultan? When he was a boy. He and his brother both. He learned the language, the customs, feigned loyalty to the sultan to preserve his life and that of his father. He knows the Turk very well and now – all these years later – the Turk knows him.'

Hawker nodded thoughtfully. 'Aye, he impaled enough of them over the years. That does tend to keep you mindful of Vlad Dracula.'

Maria laughed lightly. 'It is a singular form of punishment. One he reserves for traitors as much as Turks. Tell us, Sir John, of your service with my father in these lands.'

Hawker plucked at the leg of roast chicken on his plate. 'Nine years ago, it was. I was with the Venetian contingent sent to aid your uncle Matthias in his crusade to retake the Bosnian lands from the sultan.' He gestured towards Maria with the drumstick. 'Your father, Vlad, was appointed a general of the Hungarian forces because of his knowledge of the country and the enemy. We took many places that summer and the Turks fell back to the silver-mining town of Srebrenica. A walled town with a large garrison.'

Maria nodded. 'Go on, tell them the rest.'

'I tell you this as a soldier who was there, but I was not in command nor a confidante of Vlad. Just a poor mercenary captain with a few Venetian men-at-arms. And Jacob over there! The tale is told though, that Vlad saw no point in battering the place down knowing it was almost impenetrable. He did something I later found out he had tried before in Wallachia: he dressed some of his own men – Wallachians and gypsies in the main – in the Turkish fashion and then sought entry on the market day. It had to be men who knew the tongue. There were not many I think, perhaps twenty or thirty.'

Dieudonné began to listen more closely. He enjoyed tales of subterfuge, and he had himself heard many tales of Dracula as a youth – stories to scare misbehaving children with tales that usually involved boiling people alive or flaying them, then serving them up to their relatives. He took a swig of wine and wiped his lips.

'These men,' said Hawker, 'talked themselves past the gates and the guards and spread through the town. They waited until the sun set and then attacked the garrison soldiers, set fires, and opened the gates. Vlad's army poured in and took the place in an hour. By the time I got there, the place was in the hands of the Hungarians and they had captured nearly a hundred prisoners plus the local bey.'

'And I imagine their fate was not a good one,' said Ellingham solemnly.

Hawker nodded, then looked again at Maria. 'It was not. When I rode up to the gates we were met by a grisly welcoming party. At least forty Turks, all set upon ten-foot stakes planted in the ditch around the gates. And the bey, still in his best silks, was set up highest of all.'

Bartolo Faldi, who had been content to stuff his face throughout Hawker's retelling, shook his head. 'Impaled alive... No way for a man to die. Even if he is an infidel.'

Maria frowned at that, which amused Dieudonné greatly.

'You would judge my father? Then you do not know what struggle we have made here. And such executions are our custom. Ours as much as the Turks', who practise such punishments themselves. One must set an example if one is to rule and keep the peace.'

'Oh, I surely agree, my lady,' said Faldi, smiling. 'Sometimes harshness in war is a necessity. I seek not to judge, but even as we speak my arse tightens at the thought!'

Ellingham looked into his beaker and then at Dieudonné. The Frenchman raised an eyebrow in return and shot him a sly smile.

Maria laughed lightly. 'Ser Bartolo, you need not fear. Such punishment has fallen out of fashion among my people. But do not let yourself fall into the hands of the Turks. They still practise impalement and a few other tortures that would curl your toes should I regale you.'

Faldi laughed and briefly laid his hand over hers before removing it to take up his cup again. Dieudonné watched with approval and saw that the gesture had not gone unnoticed by Ellingham either. The youth's whole visage had suddenly gone blank with the realisation he had competition for the affections of Maria Hunyadi.

Hawker placed both forearms on the table and straightened his back. 'I think the time has come, my lady, to confide to us your planning for the remainder of the journey. I do not question your decisions; you've gotten us this far. But here we are, skulking just inside the walls at the riverside – not in a hostelry, not in the upper town – and you, you of noble family.'

Maria opened her mouth, eyes beginning to flash, but Hawker cut her off with a raised hand.

'You will allow a belted knight the courtesy of finishing his piece.'

She closed her mouth and gestured for him to continue.

'I have seen much war in many a place. I have little to show for it except my honour, and I mean to keep that. My company serves you true, that was our agreement. But I am not so calf-headed as to not realise when we are keeping to the shadows, avoiding attention and avoiding officials of the crown. *Your* crown. That raises more than a few questions.'

'Are you finished, Sir John Hawker?'

'No, I'm not. Your business and your quest is your concern. But getting my men there and back is mine. Is that not so, Sir Giles?'

Ellingham nodded after a few seconds of hesitation.

'We need a ruse – a cover – from this point forward, and I don't mean a fig leaf. It must be something that is believable. Whether we are merchants or mercenaries, I don't know. But we need something. Something that won't smell like a rotting fish for officials to sniff out and question.'

Maria looked at Hawker, and slowly, her wide mouth broke into an admiring, if restrained, smile. 'I would have thought less of you if you hadn't questioned me, Sir John.'

Dieudonné smiled too. The old fox had neither lost his wits nor his suspicions. At least he realised there was more to Maria Hunyadi's motives than she was willing to admit to. Dieudonné didn't like having to depend on Hawker for wisdom or answers, but for the moment he had to. He knew not the Hungarian lands or Wallachia, nor could he speak anything but French and poor merchant's English. There was promise ahead, he could taste it, but he would not be able to reach it without the help of his companions.

'Very well,' said Maria, placing her palms on the table. 'You have surmised that my uncle either does not know, or approve, of my intentions. That is true. And to put the matter to rest I will tell you that he does not know. He and my father have had a tempestuous friendship over the years.'

'He put your father in a prison,' said Hawker. 'I'd say that was more than tempestuous.'

'And he released him shortly thereafter. Gave him a cousin's hand in marriage. Supported him to retake the Wallachian throne. Which he did.'

Hawker shrugged. 'And then turned a blind eye and let him lose it again. After that glorious campaign nine years ago.'

Maria's demeanor went cold again. 'Do not mock me, Sir John. Matthias *did* send a force to relieve him but did not make it in time.'

'That is in the past now,' said Hawker, leaning towards her. 'Tell me what you propose to do.'

'Very well. King Matthias fights against the Holy Roman Emperor. He has taken Vienna and continues his campaign there. He has bought off the Turks for a while and turned his attentions westwards. That is why I have decided that now is the time to find my father.'

'That is the why, but not the how.'

'If we are challenged as we ride north, I am on a diplomatic mission. I have a letter and seal. It will not be questioned. You and your men – and of course, Ser Bartolo – are my escort. We will tell any enquiring officials that we are en route to join Matthias and the Black Legion and that I am raising a force in the Siebenbürgen to go to Austria.'

'What is this Black Legion?' asked Ellingham.

Faldi let out a good-natured laugh. 'Why, it is the largest collection of mercenary rogues to be found in the known world!

You won't find a baker, a butcher or a vagabond pedlar among them. All veteran men-at-arms.'

'It is a shame King Richard did not hire them,' mused Ellingham. Dieudonné clapped him on the shoulder in consolation.

'Once we leave Belgrade tomorrow or the day after, I do not anticipate any trouble to Temesvár. All the way there is open plain, small villages and towns. We should make it in two or three days if the weather and horses hold out. Once there, I will outfit you all in proper harness as befits your station. Ser Bartolo is already equipped.'

The Italian smiled and inclined his head. 'And, if I might add, Donna Maria, would it be too much to ask that your stradiotti lose their ridiculous hats? Much too obvious, no?'

Dieudonné stared into his half-drained cup. He doubted that Maria's ruse would fool anyone for very long.

–

The next morning, early, Hawker ventured out of the courtyard and into the street, wrapped full in his woollen cloak.

'Sir John!' It was Ellingham, following him out of the warren they'd stayed in overnight. 'Where are you off to?'

Hawker hunched and drew the cloak higher up around his neck. A freezing fog had rolled off the Danube and infiltrated the town. 'Getting some fresh air.'

Ellingham joined him and they began walking up the street towards the upper town. In front of them the steeple of a great church rose up and beyond that, higher still, the grey walls and towers of the inner fortress at the top of the hill. As they trudged up the hill, they saw traders busying themselves at their stalls. The houses here were already of better quality: tall and with many windows, roofs topped in bright clay tiles the colour of dried blood. Ellingham was ill at ease, now knowing that they had no sanction for their journey into the Hungarian empire. Two Englishmen wandering around the streets of Belgrade might start a ripple of gossip that would carry on up the hill to the fortress and the governor. Ellingham, too, pulled up his cloak, more an effort at disguise than to shield from the cold.

They had not gone very far when Ellingham touched Hawker's arm. 'Perhaps we should head back again, break our fast with the others. There's bread and cheese. God knows what else besides.'

Hawker stopped and looked down at the cobbles. 'What is the matter, Giles?'

Ellingham let out a sigh of frustration and drew his cloak even tighter. '*Did* I make the right choice? To join with her and her quest? You gave me the choice on the ship. But now… I question myself.'

Hawker put an arm around the youth's shoulders and slowly turned them both the way they had come. A short, heavyset fellow in a frayed cloak coughed and walked closely past, avoiding their gaze. Hawker became aware that English was probably rarely heard on these streets and it was probably unwise to roam. They resumed a slow pace, down the glistening wet street back towards the ramshackle warren. 'The point is, you *made* a decision,' said Hawker, his voice quieter than before. 'That is something that many men find they cannot do. Whether you have made the right choice, I do not yet know. But we go forward and meet what comes – as English knights and men of our own destiny.'

'I should have more courage… and confidence. Why have I so much doubt?'

'You are King Richard's son. I have seen your courage already in abundance. Trust in yourself. I am at your side until I fall.'

Ellingham nodded. 'I am heartily glad you stand with me, Sir John. I will not fail you.'

Hawker slowed his walk further then stopped and half-turned to face the youth. His eyes searched Ellingham's. 'Do you desire her?'

Ellingham said nothing.

A rumble emanated from Hawker's throat, the words having trouble coming together in his head. 'I say only this. She is… for the moment… your paymaster. We are in her service. Do not let your heart overrule your head.'

'I hear you, Sir John.' And he said no more.

They reached the straw-strewn courtyard again to find the others gathered and wearing their armour except for helms. Maria was again dressed as a fine lady but, jarringly to the eye, she carried a sword. She pushed it into the brass-studded leather roll that lay tied to her horse's cruppers. Hawker looked around, brow furrowing.

'Mistress, where are your men?'

She turned and placed her hands on her hips. 'I sent them away to their homes as soon as the gates opened at dawn.'

'That is half our force. Why in God's name did you release them?'

She stepped closer to him. 'Because my agreement with the stradiotti ended at Zagrab. It was only out of loyalty – and their initial distrust of *you* – that they came this far. They are returning to the Dalmatian lands.'

'Halving our strength is a foolish gamble,' growled Hawker.

'We are in *my* country now, Sir John. I told you there will be others, and there will be. When we need them. Do not challenge my decisions.' She gave him a bow of her head, exaggerated to the point of insulting, and turned to tighten her mount's bridle.

Bartolo Faldi gave Hawker a sheepish look. He walked over to him and placed a hand on his shoulder. '*Allora*, Don Falco,' he said quietly, calling him by his old moniker from the Italian wars. 'Don't question it. Her bite is every bit as harsh as her tongue. I have learned the hard way.'

–

Dieudonné had finished strapping his own bedroll to his saddle and was watching the young Greek struggle to buckle the straps of the leather bags on his own mount at the far end of the stalls. He walked over, stood close at the youth's left side, and then reached up to help pull taut the strap so the Greek could fit the tongue of the brass buckle into a hole. The hardware seated home with a dull pop, and the bag sagged down.

Dieudonné was intrigued how this tall, darkly handsome lad, legs as thin as bulrushes, had cozened the great Doge of Venice out of his treasure. He had cleverly swapped the real Tears of Byzantium, those blood-red rubies, for near worthless – but perfectly formed – pieces of cut Murano glass. Being the catamite of the old Doge had enabled him access to the jewels and Dieudonné reckoned that was a small price for a slave to pay to obtain such a great prize. Servants and slaves knew things, *secret* things. He wondered now whether the youth knew more of Maria's secrets. Things she was concealing from them all. And he knew he had to find out before Giles was ensnared by her. Finding out secrets was something that he excelled at.

He pulled his hand away slowly, running it down Theophilius's back, past his wrist, and up his forearm. He leaned in close to the youth's ear. 'Let me come around to your right that we may do up the other strap.' Dieudonné knew that the youth spoke some French from their journey across the Adriatic. He then shifted across, his body rubbing against the youth's back and cloak. Dieudonné then reached up with his left arm, looping the strap through the buckle, and began to pull it taut. He leaned in and whispered.

'You are a pretty thing. But you say so little. Why is that?'

Theophilius's fine-featured face turned towards him, noses nearly touching. Dieudonné looked into the large, doe-like almond eyes but could not discern any emotion in them. He then felt a firm prod in his belly. Dieudonné glanced downwards and saw a thin iron stiletto, held in the youth's left hand, sticking into the links of his chainmail. The light, padded arming doublet he wore underneath pressed further into his belly as the point of the stiletto probed deeper.

'Thank you, my lord, for your help. I can do the rest.'

Dieudonné's lips slowly parted into a smile and he pulled his torso back, extracting the needle blade from the chainmail. Such is the gentle, sweet struggle of courtship, he thought.

4

'That's as close as I'm willing to get, Tombik.' Orkan Ozdemir leaned forward on his saddlebow and contemplated the sprawling white fortress that lay a mile distant: the city of Belgrade. 'We should have hit them hard and fast from behind when we had the chance yesterday. Now they're going in *there*. I can still just make out their horses ahead.'

'Are you calling me a coward?' said Pedja, jerking his reins and guiding his mount in front of Orkan's.

'No one is calling you anything. But that was our best chance at taking them.'

'You don't know that. Better to track them and take them while they sleep at some place. You've seen their armour. Look at us – oxhides, a few shirts of chainmail, rusty swords, two spears and a mace you stole from a janissary. You really fancy a fight on open ground like this?'

'I don't fancy being here at all, my brother. But we've missed our chance. It is Allah's will. We'll pay them all back another day and the sultan is bound to lead another campaign come the spring. You can join in on that.'

Pedja scowled. Not at Orkan, but at his situation. He knew Orkan spoke the truth. They weren't equipped to deal with heavy horsemen, being only light cavalry themselves, more accustomed to burning and stealing from villages guarded by old men and boys with pitchforks. And he himself was just a garrison soldier with pretensions of greatness. He stared off into the east, watching the hulking stones of Belgrade that appeared almost luminous in the winter sun. The longer they lingered, the greater the chance of encountering a party of Hungarian militia or mercenaries. It was madness to remain and he knew it. But, deep down, his anger and grief still burned, and he desired revenge on the unnatural woman who had taken his brother from him.

He remained motionless in the saddle, agonising over the choice he faced. Orkan was tolerant but Pedja knew the Turk was mindful of his men, all of whom were twitching in their saddles, grim-faced.

'Tombik…'

Pedja looked at his friend and nodded. 'You are right. This was no plan. But I cannot go back and look my father in the face and tell him I lost his youngest son. And I couldn't live with the dishonour of it either.'

'*Orospu çocuğu!* You can kill a different Frank in a few weeks and that can even the score! But we go back – now.'

Pedja choked up on his reins and his mount skitted sideways. 'Take your men – and mine – back to Zvornik. I have to stay and find out about that woman. I will slay her if I get the chance, but I must find out who she is and where she is going.'

Orkan's eyes widened. 'It is madness. If you go in there you won't be coming out. Don't make me beat you up and tie you to your horse. We're turning back – all of us.'

'God go with you, my friend,' said Pedja quietly, a trace of a smile on his lips. He watched Orkan's face go blank for a second and then saw a pained look in the Turk's eyes as the realisation sank in that he was determined to go on alone.

'Allah protect you, Tombik.' Orkan nodded at him solemnly then turned in his saddle and called to his men, and Pedja's.

Pedja watched as they trotted away and then broke into a canter, headed west again. He then turned his own mount and started towards Belgrade at a walk, thinking about what he would do. What he *could* do. He had a bag of silver, his weapons, and he could speak his own tongue – that of Bosnians, Croats and Serbs – plus a reasonable amount of Hungarian. But that was all he had. What would he say if he was challenged?

The south gate had many people jammed up against its barbican, some poorer folk selling wares near the ditch, other more prosperous merchants, mainly Serbians, arguing with customs men and soldiers about fees. He worried that he might be stopped, looking as he did – obviously either a brigand or a militiaman – but, keeping his bare head down, wearing a long, dark woollen cloak, he attracted little attention in the crowd and the commotion of the gate. Before he knew it, he was inside the walls, a *martolos* in the service of the sultan and now in the great city of the enemy.

He was not quite prepared for the cacophony around him nor the throngs of people, a mix of folk from across the Hungarian empire and even a few Bulgar and Greek travellers from the looks of them. It was far larger than Zvornik, the largest town he had ever been in. How could he even hope to find the woman and her Frankish knights when he did not even know what they looked like? If she wore a sword though, that would be as clear a sign – for how many women were so armed? He remembered what the villager had told him. Different tongues were spoken: French, Venetian and *English*. That tongue he had never heard in his life. Perhaps his ears would provide the intelligence that his eyes could not.

He stumbled upon a mean-looking hostelry and stable and left his horse and equipment, his sword too. He kept his long dagger tucked up under his cloak and left on his shirt of chainmail as well. There seemed nothing for it but to wander the town, stop by other inns, and look for folk who clearly appeared not to belong. He cursed his own foolhardiness at the thought of the task he had set himself. For hours he walked, first trying to understand the layout of Belgrade, mainly the lower town which seemed to present the best chance of finding his quarry. The high town and its citadel was for the wealthy and for nobles. A place best avoided. He saw men who were clearly mercenaries or militia, all speaking Hungarian, Slavic or German, but nothing more. The afternoon wore on and as the winter sun sank, so too did his spirits.

It was a great city, he thought, filled with churches, and huge houses of whitewashed plaster, stained glass windows, and proper roofs of clay tile — no straw or thatch to be seen. The quarter near the south gate was less salubrious, with ramshackle wooden dwellings packed tightly together and dark alleyways that were a robber's paradise. People shouted and argued, crockery smashed, babies howled. Despairing, he retreated to his hostelry, making sure his own meagre possessions had not been thieved, and made his way into the tiny common room and its blazing hearth fire. He slammed down a few silver *denar* and called for some wine and some food. To his amazement it arrived quickly, a good-sized *börek* meat pie, but containing what animal he could not tell. He was starving though, and he devoured it, washing it down with the dark and tannic wine.

He was left unmolested. A few other guests as dubious-looking as him wandered about, sitting at the trestle tables or buying a jug of wine to take elsewhere. It was late in the afternoon and now getting dark outside. He wondered if Orkan and the men had been waylaid and he already felt guilty for dragging them this far into Hungarian lands. He thought of his own men. What would they think of him for abandoning them instead of leading them home? He consoled himself with another large *börek*, no doubt adding to his visible paunch. He'd always loved his food and since he was a boy had always rewarded himself with it whenever he had trouble — if it was to be found. So he sat, with no plan and no hope, relishing the taste of the pastry and its oozing filling. The landlord, seeing that Pedja actually had some money, offered a bed for the night and so he waited, half-hoping the Hungarian woman would walk in to escape the cold. At length, as his head filled with wine fumes, he decided he would sleep and decide in the morning what his choices were.

Five Hungarian *denari* bought him a low, rope-slung pallet in the eaves of the hostelry and a mattress the thickness of an unleavened loaf of bread. A few other travellers snored away across the loft in similar beds. If it had not been for the wine, he probably wouldn't have been able to drift into sleep. As it was, his head swirled with not just drink, but with memories – memories that now brought pain and a sense of guilt.

I would show you up. That's why you won't help me. I'm better.

He could not drive his brother Davud from his mind and the memory of his brother's desperate demands to be allowed to join the *martaloses* at Zvornik.

'You would not be happy,' he had told Davud. 'You're better off here with Father working the land. You're good at it and besides, you'd be bored at the fortress. It's just rousting beggars and drunks, cleaning the stables and feeding the prisoners in the bey's dungeon.'

'More likely you would lose favour with the bey's captain. Once they compared you and me. I'm faster – and a better fighter.'

'Maybe you should have been dragged off by the Janissaries. Then you would have gained what you crave. Father would probably have bribed them to take you.'

Davud had laughed at that jibe. 'If only father had given me up to them! I slave away here for nothing. Nothing. While you amuse yourself in the town.'

Five years' difference in age seemed a lifetime to Pedja then. His brother was cocky, headstrong, and did not understand what lay beyond the village, beyond the Bosnian lands. Davud was jealous of him, that he knew for sure. Jealous that he had been allowed to join the *martalos* just as their father had done when he was a young man.

Davud then tried a different tack. 'You're ashamed of me. Ashamed because I farm and slaughter chickens instead of men. And you will not give me the chance I deserve as your brother to prove myself as a soldier. Prove myself as you did.'

Eventually, Pedja relented. Their father agreed that Davud was unhappy and would not take to the land. He deserved a chance to serve the sultan as he once had. Pedja took Davud to Zvornik and gave him an introduction to the garrison captain. The Turks believed deeply in tradition and that service to the empire from father to sons – and brothers – should be encouraged. Davud joined up and learned the ways of a soldier. He did not become bored with garrison life and worked hard. After a year he was competing with Pedja for advancement and favour – just as he had taunted – and Pedja slowly came to regret his decision. The advent of Orkan Ozdemir and his band of *akincis* gave Pedja the opportunity to teach a lesson to the little brother who was nipping at his heels.

So it was that anger and jealousy overrode brotherly affection and Pedja said nothing when Davud pushed himself into service with the *akincis*. He had thought he could keep an eye on his brother before he would find danger, but Davud was fired with raw enthusiasm and the promise of bountiful booty and female slaves, and the prospect of reward by his superiors. And Pedja soon found he had no influence on him anymore at all. The afternoon when Orkan had split their party into two and sent a dozen men to scout ahead to the bank of the Sava, his brother had been the first to the front. That was Pedja's final memory of him. A loud telling-off by him, a rude gesture in reply by Davud, and the sight of his brother riding off never to be seen alive again. Their petty rivalry played out to a sordid end, one that did him no honour either as a brother or a man. He was ashamed.

–

Pedja awoke to a grunting sound. Weak light shone through the opaque yellow rosined window at the far end of the garret room and Pedja saw a couple tussling under a blanket a few beds away from him. It was very cold and his breath condensed in a cloud as he lay on his back, staring at the rafters. He still didn't have a plan, but he did have a headache.

All things considered, he had not slept too badly and his heavy cloak had kept the worst of the night chill out. He pulled it off and threw his legs over the side of the bedframe, which practically touched the floor. He undid his leather belt, dagger and money pouch and then dragged his padded coat and chainmail out from underneath the pallet and pulled them both on, jiggling the mail until it fell into place, with difficulty, past his midriff. The grunting on the other side of the room had abruptly stopped. He pulled on his tunic and buckled on his belt and pouch again. Lastly, he threw his cloak over his shoulders and set off down the stairs. Wet wood in the hearth had created a dull fog of smoke in the chamber. He coughed and went outside into the morning light. The cold, fresh air felt good. He started walking out of the tiny courtyard and into the nearest street.

There were not many about at that early hour, but he quickly spotted two men walking side by side, up the street towards the inner walls of the fortress. One had long, dark blond hair, while his companion was shorter and older with a bowl haircut and streaks of grey. They looked Frankish to his eyes, but he could not tell. He quickened his pace and caught up, keeping a careful distance behind. They were speaking a foreign tongue. At first Pedja took it for German but he quickly realised it was not. Something else, similar. Not French either. After just a few minutes they stopped and then turned around. Pedja, surprised, stumbled a bit and coughed. He passed them by, looking at the cobbles. They took no notice of him and continued back the way they had come.

The tall one looked handsome, with angular features that bespoke high birth. The other, not so at all, but still with the manner of a western man-at-arms or a knight. His hard, line-scored face all but proclaimed he was a veteran of many wars. Pedja turned and feigned interest with the wagon of a street pedlar to give them some breadth. After a moment, he followed them, stopping only to pick up a woven rush basket that someone had left in front of a house. It contained half a dozen rotting apples. He slung it over his shoulder and carried on. The two men entered the courtyard of a hostelry that lay next to the south gate, the same gate he himself had entered from the day before. Holding back and keeping his head down, he saw others come out of the inn and greet the two. One was a woman with jet hair, a woman of worth, dressed finely. He saw she carried with her a thin, scabbarded blade, cradled in her arms as if it were her own babe. Something important to her. His heart leapt at that.

In his time, he had heard French spoken by Turkish officials in the bey's retinue at Zvornik. A musical tongue, he thought. This was what they were all speaking. Then another came outside, a knight in full plate, cloak thrown over one shoulder. He was clearly a Frank, loud and full of humour, long dark hair and bright blue eyes. And when he spoke it was Venetian. That he would swear by. Pedja slowly carried on past the group bearing his basket and went into the adjoining stables, his heart racing. Once his eyes had adjusted, he saw a boy forking hay into the enclosures. He approached the lad, probably no more than fourteen and with a shaven pate, and gave him a big smile.

'Would you have need of apples, young man? I am selling. How about your master?'

The boy stopped and sneered. 'Piss off.'

At least he understood what was being said. Pedja threw the basket off his shoulder and made a show of looking inside. 'Oh well, seems I have but only a few and even those a bit soft. Something better for the horses maybe.'

The boy shook his head, pursed his lips, and began forking hay again.

'Who are those Franks outside? They look important.'

The boy shrugged. 'They are foreigners. That's all I know. Got money though.'

'And where might they be heading?'

The boy paused and leaned on the pitchfork. 'I heard them say Temesvár. At least that is what the woman told my master.'

Pedja nodded thoughtfully. 'They don't look much like merchants. I wonder who they are.'

'Mercenaries,' said the boy. 'That's what they are. I seen enough of them here before. This be a strange lot though. Northern knights, a few Albanians, and this woman. She has a look with her eyes that'll turn you to stone.'

'Reckon they're heading out this morning? Weather's cleared.'

The boy sneered again. 'Why do you think I'm out here feeding their nags?'

Pedja hefted his basket again and slung it. 'Then I'll be going on then.'

He again passed the party of mercenaries as he left, taking in what details he could. It was hard to tear his eyes away from the woman. She was striking, with big eyes, and her long hair tied up and back. This time he noticed her gown was more than that. It was slit at the front and back and she wore Ottoman-style breeches and boots underneath. She would not be riding side-saddle – she would be riding like a warrior. He hurried on, back to his own hostelry, and prepared to leave after first breaking his fast with hard cheese and a hunk of rye bread. He bought a wineskin and paid to have it filled by the landlord. He decided that he would wait an hour or two to let the Frankish knights leave, then he would follow. He knew Temesvár lay many miles to the north on the far side of the Danube, but he did not know how to get there. That he would have to ask. He could always say that he was a soldier looking for employ with anyone who would pay. Could probably claim he was a Serbian as he knew many Serbs served the Hungarian crown. Rascians, as the Hungarians named them. And he would pray that God would keep him safe on the journey into the unknown.

He asked the landlord where to cross the great river and was told that there were two ferries going across from outside the city. One was a westerly crossing that led to the road to Petrovaradin and Buda, and another further east of the city that put one on the road to Pančevo, Padina, and eventually Temesvár. He tipped the landlord two *denari*, retrieved his horse and sword, and left via the south gate. It was still madness to pursue the foreigners, he was in no doubt of that, nor did he know how he would confront the Hungarian woman if he ever got close enough. But for now, the pursuit of them was all he could think of.

He was just beyond the south gate and trying to follow the wagon traffic on a tiny road that snaked around the outer curtain wall of the city when he saw him. Or rather, he saw the great black beard of the lone rider who was stationed on a low hill just above the road and observing all the travellers that passed. Pedja grinned and kicked his horse into a trot.

Orkan Ozdemir spotted him and broke into a smile. 'Merhaba, Tombik!'

'Maybe you are the one who is mad,' said Pedja, his head shaking in wonderment. 'A Turk sitting outside the very same walls that the last Sultan couldn't break. A Turk just watching the world go by.'

Orkan shrugged. 'An Ottoman army gets attention. One old Turk on a horse gets none.'

'You waited for me, my friend.'

'I did. Froze my balls off, too. But I have sent the others back. They will tell the captains at Zvornik what has happened. That we're pursuing some Franks to settle a blood debt. And to find out if the Impaler still lives. That bit I'm sure they won't swallow. So... you didn't find them then?'

Pedja shot him a big-toothed grin. 'I did find them. They're a group of northern knights, all right. Mercenaries. Who the woman is I don't know, but they're journeying to Temesvár.'

Orkan's eyebrows raised. '*That* is a fair old distance, Tombik. Are you ready to ride that far to become an assassin?'

'I am. Or at least take my chances trying.'

Orkan nodded slowly and sighed. 'Come on then, let's find out where to cross this river. I'm coming with you.'

'You don't have to do this, Orkan. Even I don't know how I'm going to do this.'

'Good thing we're not janissaries, otherwise we'd be court-martialled and executed for desertion if we make it back.'

Pedja moved his horse up alongside. 'You do speak some Slavic, my friend. We can pass as Serbian mercenaries looking for work with the Hungarians in the north. But... you look *too* Ottoman. We'll have to shave off that great beard of yours.'

Orkan pulled up on his reins and leaned back. 'What?' he said, his voice betraying quiet alarm.

5

Hawker had never journeyed this far into the Hungarian lands before. All as flat as the skin on a custard. They rode north by north-east along an ancient road, one that deviated from the great road that ran north by north-west to Buda. On the first day, between the towns of Kovacica and Padina, they encountered a squadron of militia heading south. Maria, confident as ever, with Faldi at her side, charmed her way through and they were allowed to carry on. Hawker had to admire her boldness; she did not even have to produce the pass of free conduct she claimed to possess. They spent the first night in a barn, although Maria was given the best bed of a prosperous peasant after introducing herself. The peasant slept in the barn too.

The second day, the land continued flat and featureless, all fields, farms and hamlets, its peasants digging up their winter crops of parsnips and cabbages. The sun shone brightly across an azure sky, but the flat plains drove a fierce cutting winter wind from the east. And from the east, Hawker could just make out the ridge of dark mountains that rose up, beyond which lay Wallachia and Transylvania. He already dreaded having to cross them in the grip of the dead months. Maria had mentioned her guides knew the passes between the mountains, but even so, the way would be treacherous and bitterly cold.

Jacob and Jack rode either side of him. Ahead, Giles and Faldi flanked Maria, Theophilius following close behind. Alone, Gaston Dieudonné rode at the rear. Hawker thought he had grown sullen and dissatisfied with his lot. A far cry from his stand in Venice when he had urged Giles to follow the Hungarian into the east. Hawker could only think that the rash Burgundian either felt cheated of a fortune or that the earning of this one was proving too difficult, too slow, or both.

He glanced over to Jack. The lad was taking to soldiering without complaint. Not surprising since that was all he had known for the past two years. And he was mastering his profession, not afraid to practise and not afraid to fight when he had to. His arms were stronger now, chest and back too, and Hawker was proud that he had made the right decision in keeping the boy and in making him a squire, if in name only. Indeed, he was not a boy anymore. He was a newly minted man.

It was Giles that Hawker worried more about. The young knight's ardour for the journey seemed to be flickering as doubts about Maria's quest multiplied. He himself had sworn to protect Giles in whatever path was chosen. That was still his aim. He had confided his true thoughts to no one, but he believed that a choice would have to be made soon: follow Maria into the east or part ways at Temesvár and find a different patron. Maybe even Matthias Corvinus. That king's war against Austria dragged on and the need for mercenaries had not lessened any. But could he trump the Dragon's daughter's persuasive charms to win back the confidence of the youth?

Most of all, he worried for himself. The long hours in the saddle had made it easy for his mind to drift, to contemplate what had gone before. He could not rid his thoughts of Chiara in Venice and whether she even still lived. She might be alive but penniless, maimed by the Senate for being an adulteress. She might even be dead. And it was the second time that he had not taken her away when his heart told him he should have. He had always bowed to her wish to remain, come what may. This time, it may have cost her life.

'Sir John?'

Jack called to him again and he roused himself. 'Aye, lad?'

'Have you been to this place? This fortress?'

Hawker looked over to him and threw him a strained smile. 'No. I soldiered far south of here in the kingdom of Bosnia, where we had our little battle with the Turks a few days back.'

Jack digested that for a moment. 'Do you believe what she is telling us? That she has friends who will join us… up ahead?'

'I believe that she believes it.' He wasn't about to lie to the boy. He was a man-at-arms now in the service of a knight. Truth was more important than the false comfort of wishful reassurance.

'I believe in *you*, Sir John. That's enough for me.'

They rode on into the afternoon and entered an area of low hills of grassland where the road ran deep and narrow, twisting and turning. The party slowed its pace and Hawker drifted off once again into disquieting thoughts.

—

Pedja and Orkan heard the clash of steel at the same moment. They'd been shadowing the Franks and their mistress at a distance, not allowing themselves to be seen. Without saying a word, Pedja kicked his heels in and moved forward, Orkan, cursing away in Turkish, followed him. Pedja lifted his little round shield from behind his saddle and hastily pulled it up his left forearm before drawing out his sword. Orkan fumbled at his saddlebow to free up his dangling iron mace. Riding parallel to the road across the fields, they went over a rise and saw what was unfolding below. Both pulled up smartly, horses neighing in protest.

The Franks were under attack by a band of horsemen, most armoured, and double their number.

'Allah favours you, Tombik!' yelled Orkan. 'Your work is being done for you.'

The Franks had circled onto themselves, off the road and into the grass, fending off the repeated charges of their attackers. Pedja watched as one of the Franks – the gleaming one – struck his attacker full in the head, snapping it and sending the man tumbling down. The woman was violently jerking her reins, circling behind her men, trying to free up something from behind her saddle. She was weaponless and even her expert horsemanship wouldn't save her for long.

'No! Not this way. I will decide when to kill her. And now is not that time!' Pedja raised his blade and kicked his mount forward again, shooting towards the fray. Orkan's jaw dropped and he shouted for him to stop, but the Bosnian ignored him. Orkan swore a stream of oaths and slapped his horse's flank, plunging into the skirmish.

Pedja pelted down the gentle slope, aiming for the Hungarian noblewoman. She had managed to free her blade and had just blocked a blow from her attacker, a fellow in blackened plate armour but without a helm. Pedja readied his sword arm and pulled up only as he reached the man's left flank. He swung a full horizontal blow, catching him in the ear and taking off half his skull in a spray of blood and brains. As Pedja recovered, he momentarily locked eyes with the woman, savouring for an instant the look of utter surprise in hers. There was nothing more as a second man-at-arms was upon him and he raised his shield to ward off the incoming blow.

The next moment he glimpsed Orkan on the far side of the soldier taking a mighty swing of his mace. It collided with the man's shoulder, nearly knocking him out of his saddle. Falling forward, the soldier spurred his horse away. A few feet away he saw one of the Franks, a young lad, knocked out of the saddle by a glancing blow to the helm. The horseman moved to trample the lad but Pedja interposed his own horse and engaged the soldier. There was a flurry of traded blows and he thought his shield arm might be broken when a sharp pain rode up his arm to his shoulder. He caught the next blow with his sword blade and twisted his horse around to get to the man's left side. Somehow he managed, and this time he tried a thrust straight on. It rode up the soldier's breastplate and on into his neck, opening his throat. The man fell back, jerked his reins and pulled away.

Orkan flailed away at another soldier, his chainmail and thick oxhide jerkin protecting him from an attack. The mace swung again and its small but heavy iron head took the soldier full in the chest, unhorsing him. Pedja disengaged enough to get a view of what was happening. The Franks had beaten the attackers back without a loss, it seemed. The remaining band of attackers had ridden off, no doubt confused by his and Orkan's timely arrival. The Franks were calling out to one another in a confused babble of differing tongues and had only just realised that there were two strangers among them. Two who had come to their defence.

One of the Franks, an older knight, dismounted and ran to the young lad who had been struck down. The Hungarian woman guided her horse towards Pedja and Orkan, her sword at the ready, her comrades at her flanks.

'Who are you?' she called out.

Pedja knew enough of the Magyar tongue to understand her. He lowered his bloody sword, and stroked the quivering neck of his nervous mount. 'We are poor travellers on the road to Temesvár. We saw you come under attack. Those men could have come for us next so better to even the odds.'

The woman stopped a few feet in front of them. 'You are as much soldiers as you are travellers. I ask you again. Who are you?'

Pedja glanced over to Orkan, whose face was set hard, furious at him, the haft of his mace lying across the saddle in a clenched fist.

'We are soldiers of fortune. Looking for new service. We are Serbians… loyal to the crown of Hungary.'

'So, *Rasciani*. Then your arrival was by the grace of God.'

Pedja could not tell if she was being ironic or not. His Hungarian wasn't that nuanced. And luckily, Orkan was being wise enough to keep his mouth shut for the moment. The Franks behind her looked as tense as Orkan. Pedja was beginning to hope his impetuousness in aiding them wasn't going to be something he would come to regret in the next minutes.

Pedja nodded at her. 'It is the mark of a Christian in these times. Who do you think they were?'

Two of the Franks rode forward and skirted him and Orkan, slowly. They were being studied: dress, armour, saddles. Pedja smiled at them and saw Orkan wetting his lips. The Turk's face was red and raw, even a few cuts, from where Pedja had hacked at his beard with some dull scissors he had found. All that remained was a drooping black moustache. He knew that Orkan would likely beat his brains out if they got through the next hour alive.

Her gaze continued to drill through him. 'You might be deserters. Deserters from my uncle's army up north.' She had switched to Slavic.

Uncle's army? Then she *was* a woman of worth. A family of wealth and influence perhaps. But she had slain his only brother. He would have to become the fox among wolves. He nodded again, this time replying in Slavic. 'Perhaps we should stay together, at least until we reach Temesvár. The brigands might return.' He prayed that Orkan was understanding it all. Pedja saw the older knight raise up the younger one whose helm he had taken off. The lad was much younger than he had first thought, almost a boy. The lad began to retch while the knight supported him. There wasn't any blood to be seen; he'd been knocked badly though. Another young man, dark-haired and slim, hurried to the fallen soldier, knelt and offered up a wineskin to him.

The woman didn't take her eyes off Pedja but she began speaking French for the benefit of the others. Translating, he supposed. There was a brief exchange. The older knight looked at him and then the woman before joining in. Pedja watched the shining one – a Venetian, perhaps – shrug and stick out his lower lip, signalling doubt.

The woman nodded slowly towards Pedja. 'I would hear more of you and your comrade.' She didn't smile even once. The woman rode closer to Pedja's mount and studied his tack. 'This is an Ottoman harness. I am sure there hangs a tale of how you came to possess it.'

'There is much Turkish harness south of the Sava,' replied Pedja. 'Easy enough to find and buy. Or steal.'

Now she smiled and, he guessed, turned to translate for the others again.

'So what are you both called?' she said, again turning to Pedja.

'I am Pedja Jankovic. My comrade is Orkan... Orkan Nikolic.'

She looked across to the Turk. '*Orkan*? That is an Ottoman name. Not a Christian one.'

'He ran away from the Janissaries when he was a youth. Escaped from their army and found his way back to free Serbian lands. But he kept the name they gave him. He has fought the Turks since he became a man.'

'Is this true?' she asked Orkan, still smiling. Pedja swallowed and it felt like a stone had travelled down his gullet.

'That is true, mistress,' said Orkan, haltingly, tripping over the Slavic. Pedja had already arranged the ruse earlier in the day in case Hungarians would challenge them and he had not been sure that the Turk would be able to carry it off. He still wasn't.

The woman nodded slowly. 'You must have had a hard life. It shows on you and you wear it well. And now, here you are. With us. Sent by God.' She tugged on her reins and called to the others in French. She then turned to Pedja again.

'Very well. You may join us on the road. But you will ride in front of us.'

6

Jacob de Grood and Hawker each took an arm and gently raised up Jack Perry to his feet.

'Christ above! That's one goose egg on your thick skull, boy!' said the Fleming, giving Jack a good-natured shake of the shoulder. Jack promptly bent over and cast up the remaining contents of his stomach.

'We'll get him back on his horse and I'll take the reins,' said Hawker. 'I don't fancy staying out here in the middle of nowhere. We'll tend to him at the next halt.'

Maria showed little concern for their only wounded man. 'Fear not,' she said flatly. 'We ride on until sunset and the next village.'

'I can ride,' said Jack, staggering a little.

'Perhaps,' said Hawker, 'but right now you can hardly stand. Jacob, get him mounted again.'

Jacob wrapped an avuncular arm about Jack. 'I will take him under tow, Sir John. He's made of stern stuff. Aren't you, lad?'

Jack somehow managed to nod.

Hawker's eye caught Ellingham's. There was quiet concern there. More doubts. He would have to get better answers from Maria in the next day otherwise he might consider a different course of action for them. Hawker knew that from Temesvár they could ride north-west for Buda and volunteer with King Matthias's forces or even push on westwards back to Flanders. But once they had committed to entering the mountain country of Ultra Silvam, they would be entirely dependent upon Maria and whatever men she claimed to have at her disposal. The amount of trust he had in her at the moment wouldn't fill a thimble.

The arrival of the Serbian mercenaries had been timely and he was grateful for two additional swordsmen given the lawlessness of the road north. Maria announced they would make it to Temesvár – God willing – by midday on the morrow. They formed up again and this time Hawker rode at the rear to prevent a surprise return from the band of deserters. Dieudonné took up a position next to him on the deeply rutted road, still unfrozen despite the November chill.

Dieudonné kept his eyes on the track ahead. 'How much would you wager, Sir John, that those two decided to change sides a moment before we were attacked? I sniffed out some measure of desperation upon them.'

Hawker looked over to the man he believed to be Burgundian. 'To what purpose then? To seek reward?'

Dieudonné smiled to himself. 'Fighting men often make such decisions on the toss of a coin. I've seen it myself.'

'To risk their very lives on the decision of a moment's chance? In my experience of soldiering, men take the safest path open to them.'

'Many different demons – and angels – drive the choices of men. I keep an open mind upon such things.'

Hawker chuckled lightly, giving him a look of near contempt. 'By God, you're wise beyond your years. I'm blessed that you share it with me. So then, my lord, what demons drive you? Are you thinking about tossing a coin yourself? I remember it was you who advocated the path we find ourselves on. And that is what you counselled Sir Giles.'

'And I am still for staying this course unless we find out that Prince Vlad is dead. Maria Hunyadi offers us – offers Sir Giles – the best chance of fortune. And a future.'

Hawker detected uncertainty in Dieudonné's voice. Just a hint, but it was there. 'Even if her royal uncle doesn't want Vlad found – or freed?'

Dieudonné didn't reply for a few moments, the only sound the jangling of harness and thump of hooves in the mud of the

63

road. 'We don't know that is the case, Sir John. She has not said that.'

'She has said little of anything.'

Dieudonné finally turned his head. If he was stung by Hawker's barbs he did not show it. His face remained serene. 'I'll grant you that. But I am willing to believe her as far as Temesvár. And I am sure Sir Giles feels the same.'

'We will need more than encouraging words, my lord. Or wisdom from you. We'll need gold and we'll need good intelligence of what lies ahead.'

That evening, they paid an elderly farmer to tend to Jack's bruising and to supply them a place to bed down for the night, and shelter and fodder for their horses. Maria was afforded the bed of the farmer and his wife while all others made do with hay and blankets near the hearth of his large house. The old man had no doubt seen much strife in the wars of the Hungarians and Turks over the years and he took their arrival stoically, probably even a little surprised by the coin that was proffered. His two adult sons looked on, sullen and distrustful of the unwanted guests. The wife would not look any of them in the eye and instead peeled parsnips, carrots and onions for the stew pot.

They were all tired and on edge after the fight. Jack complained about the stink of the poultice on his head but fell asleep as soon as he lay down. Hawker kept to himself and his thoughts, watching his companions in silence. The two Rascians asked to sleep in the barn near the horses and no one suggested anything to the contrary. He didn't believe Dieudonné's claim that they were part of the band of deserting mercenaries that had attacked them, but he wasn't sure they were all they claimed to be either. He knew that Rascians served the Hungarian crown in great numbers but just as many served the Ottomans. He didn't care enough to worry, but the farmer certainly did. He sent his sons to sleep in the barn alongside them.

The next morning, they resumed the march north. This time Hawker rode next to Jack, making sure that he had recovered sufficiently of the knock to his head. He seemed cogent enough, thought Hawker, but the bump was still so big that Jack could not wear his helm.

'I won't let that happen again, Sir John,' Jack rasped, his body loose and rocking as the horse negotiated the rutted road. 'I would have had him. I know it. But I'll split the skull of the next man that I come up against. I swear it.'

Hawker heard the anger in Jack's voice. The urge to kill for revenge and the shame of having been bested and nearly slain. At times, he was still reluctant to admit that the servant boy who had been Jack Perry was now gone for ever. A killer was in his place and he himself had put him there. Hawker felt he didn't have a choice. Not after the house fight when they had all fled Bosworth. Jack had drawn first blood there with just one crossbow bolt, and the rest followed on from that. Still, it made part of him sad to think how the lad was now corrupted. His tutelage had soiled Jack's pristine soul. For ever.

By midday, just as Maria had predicted, they sighted the fortress town of Temesvár. It squatted on the flat plain, surrounded to the south by marshland and thousands of tall reeds swaying in the stiff wind. Hawker saw a river flowing through the place, right to the walls, and then realised that Temesvár sat between two rivers, strategically situated to make the most of such a natural moat. The fortress itself sat on its own island, connected by a drawbridge to the palisaded town beyond. Long banners of red and white rippled atop each of the four slate-shingled towers. It was a large town and even from this distance looked to be a prosperous one.

Maria must have caught Hawker studying the tall, white-washed walls of the stronghold, which stood out strongly in the cloudless blue sky beyond. She grinned broadly.

'Behold, the gateway to Ultra Silvam and Wallachia.'

'And what awaits us in there?' said Hawker, unimpressed. 'Tell me you have ten lances, ready to fight. And that we won't be arrested by the town guard.'

'Don't worry. The Count of Temeş is away fighting in Austria with my uncle. There is only a small garrison remaining. Besides, we won't be paying the fortress a visit. We stay at *my* manor.'

She gave him a prideful look, the look of a noblewoman who was returning home. They rode on, Maria guiding them to one of the town gates over westernmost river. The bridge and gates were open, and Hawker watched wagons and traders coming and going, seemingly without impedance. He was hoping Maria would not be challenged either, if this was indeed the place of her estate. He already suspected that her pass and seal were a forgery.

'Then I hope you can offer us the comfort of a feather bed after such a journey,' Hawker replied, inclining his head.

Bartolo Faldi patted the neck of his chestnut mount. 'I can assure you Donna Maria provides her guests with worthy accommodation, Don Falco. I have been her guest here before.'

Dieudonné and Giles exchanged a quick glance with each other. To Hawker, Faldi's offhand remark added more questions to those that were already piling up over the past week. 'I have no doubt of Mistress Hunyadi's hospitality. It is the hospitality of Temesvár that worries me the more.'

Maria laughed. 'I cannot believe these English knights fear for their safety *inside* the walls when they've already faced a fight outside them! Come, we're riding in to take food and rest.' She turned her horse again onto the road.

'My lady, what about the Rasciani?' asked Faldi.

Maria guided her horse around Faldi's mount and approached Pedja. The Bosnian's face was impassive, his eyes locked onto hers.

'Yes, our Rascian saviours,' she said. 'We are grateful for your aid.' She pulled a gold coin from the purse at her waist and flipped it over to Pedja. His arm shot out and he caught it in his palm as quick as a striking serpent. 'I wish you well in finding good employment in the days ahead. Will you journey onwards to Vienna?'

Pedja bowed his head. 'We go where we find a worthy captain to serve. Wherever that may be.'

Maria nodded. 'Then fare you well in Temesvár. Perhaps our paths may cross again.' She looked over to Orkan who did his best to avoid her deep gaze. 'This one has a story to tell, that I can see. Perhaps one day we shall hear it.'

She nodded at Pedja, lightly prodded her horse, and turned to lead the column. Faldi followed. Hawker looked at Ellingham. 'Well, are we going in?'

Ellingham didn't reply but gave a quick kick with his spurs and moved forward, following Maria Hunyadi. Dieudonné shot Hawker an arched brow and then clicked his tongue. His mount stepped forward, following the others. Jacob came past next, Jack in tow, and the Fleming shook his head as he looked at Hawker. That was hardly a measure of confidence coming from his brother-in-arms. Hawker turned to the Serbians who were sitting rooted on their mounts, silent.

'I give you my own thanks,' he said, speaking Venetian, and hoping that they had some knowledge of that tongue. 'If you are looking for a war, just ride in any direction. One will find you. Fare you well!'

The one called Pedja nodded at him and Hawker returned the acknowledgement then trotted after the others.

-

Side by side, Pedja and Orkan watched the Hungarian and her men make their way to the city gate. The only sound was the furious rustle of marsh reeds in the gully next to the road, a chill wind stirring the air.

Orkan shifted his weight in the saddle. 'Last night, Tombik, while you slept... I thought about strangling you. And I must tell you it was more than a passing thought.'

Pedja turned to look at his comrade. 'You think I'm mad?'

'I know you are mad. Mad dogs get put down. Sometimes people, too.'

'You saw those Franks. Men of worth, some of them. That woman is up to something. Something important. I believe what

67

that old goat of a Croat told us. They're after the Impaler and they believe he lives still. When they find him, I mean to steal him. And kill her.'

Orkan groaned loudly and dropped his head to his chest. 'You may be mad, but I'm the fool. For letting you lead me this far.'

'So leave. I will go on alone.'

Orkan muttered a dark oath. 'You bastard, you know it's too late for me now. If I made it back to Zvornik the bey would say I had run away from my command. And I wouldn't be able to argue the point.'

Pedja smiled at him. 'But… if you returned with the Impaler on the back of your horse, trussed like a pig, then what would they say?'

'You're dreaming, Tombik. This won't end well. I feel it in my bones. But there's no going back now. Thank you, you miserable *dhimmi*.'

Pedja inhaled the crisp air into his lungs. 'Well, are we going in? They're getting ahead of us.'

Another groan issued from Orkan's hairy unshaven throat. 'I don't like the look of that old Frankish warhorse… the one they call Hawker.'

Pedja clenched his jaw, loosened his reins, and gently gave his mount a prod. 'Then I will take *him* and you can deal with the others. But not the woman. She is mine.' Pedja raised his head and watched Hawker and his men enter the gates unchallenged. That was promising at least. If Hawker wasn't stopped, they wouldn't be either.

'Come on, we have to follow them to see where they stay.'

'What if they turn on us? Ask *why* we're following them.'

Pedja threw his arm up in the air, at once a gesture of insouciance and impatience. 'We tell them we want to work for them. They need mercenaries, don't they?'

Behind him, Pedja heard another groan emanate from the Turk.

Part II

ULTRA SILVAM

7

The house of Maria Hunyadi was full of shadows and clearly long forgotten. The tall, narrow windows were opaque, coated with the grime blown from a dozen autumn storms. The walls of dull white plaster were unadorned, not a single painting, mirror or tapestry to be seen. Along the oak ceiling beams, strands of cobwebs shivered in the draught. The only saving grace seemed to be the large stone hearth as high as a man, in which two great logs blazed away, crackling in the eagerness of the licking flames.

Hawker took a seat along with Ellingham, Dieudonné, and Faldi at the long trestle table, the only furniture in the room. Wine in large pewter ewers was brought in by the ever-silent Theophilius and Maria's other servants, another little surprise in itself. They were gypsies. A people that Hawker knew had a status lower than serfs, many still slaves under the laws of Wallachia and Hungary. Hawker held out his brass goblet while a woman poured his wine. Her face was weathered, brown as a walnut, black haired, with eyes that were not afraid to meet his. Her gaze seemed to linger as she moved to Ellingham and then filled his goblet. Bartolo Faldi rattled away about the quirks of the city but the others remained silent. An air of foreboding sat heavy upon the chamber.

Hawker had dismissed Jack and de Grood upstairs in the strange house; Jack still sullen and ashamed after his near-death the day before. Hawker had seen to his lump and ensured the lad's skull was not broken. De Grood had seen to the rusting old chainmail and brigantine armour they had worn thus far, stacking it in the hallway. Now the party were in *cioppas* and tunics. Even

71

so, Hawker made sure to buckle on his sword belt and the others, except Faldi, had followed suit. Their employer – and host – after ushering them in and showing them where they might sleep, had disappeared, but the refreshment had come anyway.

The little manor sat in the northern part of the city, surrounded by other dwelling places of metalworkers, weavers, potters and other artisans. A neighbourhood of industry, not nobility. Hawker had noted that they were on the far side of the fortress, which sat on a little island all its own. The fortress had great stone walls while the rest of the city made do with tall wooden palisades. It was almost as if Maria had chosen to be as far away from the Hungarian officials as possible. Like other mysteries concerning the woman, he was not even sure that the house actually belonged to her.

The minutes went by. Ellingham and Dieudonné conversed in low tones and Hawker seemed to be the only remaining audience for Faldi's tales of Temesvár. Theophilius hovered, pouring wine, his large, dark brown eyes attentive to empty cups, and Hawker suspected his ears were just as attentive. He sipped his wine, lost in his own thoughts, nodding politely to the Italian from time to time.

Maria entered the hall, dressed in a dark green gown bordered with golden trim over a brown kirtle. Her long hair was coiffed high and draped by a black velvet hood embroidered with golden thread. Hawker pursed his lips and sunk his head slightly into his shoulders. It appeared that Maria Hunyadi was about to hold court again. She looked upon her four knights and smiled.

'I hope the wine refreshes you,' she said in her strangely accented French. 'I have much to tell you all. And no doubt Sir John will be glad of it.' She waved a scolding finger at Hawker. 'I have seen your disapproving looks over the past days. You are a most direct soldier. One who demands answers. I will give you some of them now.'

She slowly walked around the table as she spoke, pausing briefly behind the bench where Faldi sat clutching his goblet. Her hand gently brushed across the back of his shoulders as she passed him. 'Sir John wonders – worries even – where my army is for this quest we have set upon. I can tell you that what we must do, and will do, does not require an army. It only requires you.'

'You have a very high opinion of us, my lady,' said Hawker flatly.

Gaston Dieudonné giggled.

Faldi raised his hand just above the tabletop and patted the air. 'Give the donna a chance, Don Falco. Let her speak.'

Hawker inclined his head, a gesture of respect. But he shot a glance to Ellingham, who was looking anxious at the revelation.

Maria continued her circuit of the table, passing behind Hawker and then taking the seat at the head of the table. It was an ornate chair and not a rough-hewn bench as the others sat upon. She spread the folds of her satin gown as she positioned herself and then pulled her goblet closer to her. The gypsy woman behind her filled it and then took a few steps back.

'I did not intend to recruit you in this venture when we met in Venice. My task then was to obtain the last of the Tears. But I judged your mettle to be what I needed. That is why I offered you service.'

Hawker smiled. 'After you abducted my squire and threatened to kill him. Wounded my man-at-arms.'

She frowned. 'I would never have killed him, Sir John. And the Fleming attacked my stradiotti first. Besides, you all entered freely into my service. I told you that you could go where you pleased when we reached Dalmatia. You and the son of Richard *chose* to remain. To join the quest. Did you have another means of escaping Venice?'

Hawker ignored the question. 'The way we have slunk across these lands over the past weeks, avoiding the well-travelled roads and dodging curious eyes, tells me that your quest does not enjoy the support of all quarters. Am I right?'

Her chin elevated slightly. 'You are right. I will not lie to you. My uncle does not know of my task, nor does his oafish captain here – the Count of Temeş – Pál Kinizsi. My purpose to any who

73

ask is that I seek to raise troops for King Matthias in his war against the Austrians. You are my captains in that effort. My pass and seal from Buda attest to this.'

'Forged, no doubt.'

Maria smiled demurely.

'And if the king of Hungary finds out?' It was Ellingham.

Maria looked at him squarely. 'He will try to stop us. It suits him to believe that my father is dead. Vlad had always been an unpredictable vassal. That is why he imprisoned him for ten years, then unleashed him on the Ottomans one last time when it suited. Are you having second thoughts, son of Richard?'

Ellingham shook his head slowly. 'No, my lady. But we deserve to know what we are facing. And the odds.'

She sipped her wine and dangled the cup loosely in her slim hand. 'Agreed. And you shall.' Her gaze moved to Dieudonné. 'The Burgundian is silent, it seems. To what purpose?'

Dieudonné shrugged. 'When I hear something that concerns me, I will speak.'

Maria laughed lightly. 'Would that your comrades had the same spirit!'

Hawker shifted on his bench and tugged down his *cioppa*.

'These are strange lands to you, as northern men. Not just customs and tongues. I speak of political arrangements, fealty and divided loyalties. Ser Bartolo knows of these things.'

The Milanese gave a slow, sage nod of agreement.

'Wallachia has always been a vassal state to the crown of Hungary,' said Maria. 'My father accepted that fact when he ruled a decade ago. It is Vlad Călugărul – the Monk – who is kissing the sultan's feet and making Wallachia kneel to the Ottomans. It was he my father went to for help after he escaped his last doomed battle. The Monk shielded him in secret while Basarab took the throne again, with Ottoman help. Then the Monk decided *he* wanted the throne. He imprisoned my father and with the help of the Moldavians he gained Wallachia. He has kept it by bowing to the sultan. My father has been rotting away, forgotten, ever since.'

74

She played with her goblet, moving it in a circle upon the table. 'Then, there are the Saxons. German settlers here for over a hundred years. They run the towns of Transylvania – the Ultra Silvam in the Latin tongue. Merchant folk in the main, and wealthy. They live under Hungarian rule but must accommodate the prince of Wallachia at the same time. My father had to bring them to heel on several occasions.'

Hawker smiled at that. Vladislav Dracula had brought the Saxons of Brasov to heel by impaling outside their city walls any who opposed him. Including those who sought to have him overthrown and place his brother Radu on the throne instead. Dozens had been impaled, boiled, skinned alive, or beheaded. The terror crushed outward rebellion but Dracula still had enemies. He knew that King Matthias had imprisoned Dracula for years when the Wallachian went rogue and, after letting him regain the throne a third time, Matthias was content to see him fall to his Wallachian foes.

Hawker could tell she was irked by his amusement. 'I see you recall those times,' she said, her voice becoming cold.

'I'm still trying to puzzle out just where your sire fits into your plans for the future, my lady. It appears that neither the king of Hungary, nor Vlad the Monk would have him back.'

'There are others, Sir John. Do not forget that King Stephen of Moldavia is my father's kinsman. He has supported him before and would do so again when he finds that Dracula is not dead.'

Ellingham leaned forward, elbows on the table. 'So... we are to find and free your father and then take him east to Moldavia?'

Maria raised her chin. 'Yes, if that is what my father wants. The border is but two days' ride from where we will find him prisoner.'

Ellingham nodded but Hawker suspected the youth was just being polite and deferential. He had heard nothing to instil the slightest glimmer of hope in their bizarre quest.

It took Dieudonné's raw candour to say what needed to be said.

'My lady, what gives you *any* certainty that your father still lives? You've told us nothing to prove it. You ask that this company risk life and limb on a quest that may lead us to an empty cell. One that we will find ourselves occupying. Until we join the impaled who are rotting on stakes.'

Maria slowly rose up from her chair, fixing Dieudonné with a basilisk's glare. Hawker saw the Burgundian begin to flex his shoulders and then pull his goblet in closer to himself. Seeing the fire in Maria ignite, the old knight at that moment began to truly believe her claims of parentage. Next to him, Faldi took in a long inhalation of breath.

Maria's expression, colourless and hard, remained unchanged. 'I *know* that he lives.' She clapped her hands, twice.

A man entered the chamber and walked to her side. He was as old as Hawker – maybe even older – and of average stature. His curly, salt-and-pepper hair fell to his collar and the cords of his thick neck stood out proud on skin like saddle leather. His features were sharp and angular but it was his eyes that proved the most disconcerting. Iris matched pupil in blackness, giving the man an unearthly look. His eyes instantly commanded those they looked upon. He wore a strange pied-cowhide jerkin over a gauze-like, embroidered shirt, secured with a wide belt and brass buckle. His black woollen hose were baggy and his feet were shod in wide, flat-heeled shoes of rustic fashion. At his side hung a long, thin Turkish blade.

Maria gave him a nod of respect and turned to the company. 'This is Tokár. He was one of my father's armaşi, a retainer and man-at-arms. He is a free peasant even though he is of gypsy blood. And he has never given up on his master. Nor has his clan. These are the folk that I can call upon. And who will guide us.'

From the time he had served in the Venetian expedition to Bosnia a decade earlier, Hawker remembered the stories of how Prince Dracula had beaten down the power of his fractious and rebellious Wallachian nobility – the *boyars* – by recruiting an army of the dispossessed. Comprised of peasant Wallachians and Hungarians, gypsies and even Turks, these *armaşi* had carried out

Vlad's orders with ruthless efficiency. These were the men who put people on stakes.

Maria addressed Tokár in Wallachian, he nodded and then drew out a large, folded piece of paper and placed it open upon the table. It was a map. Hawker and the others all stood and leaned in to get a look. Tokár eyed each of the knights and spoke, looking to Maria to translate from Wallachian.

'The prince has been taken out of Târgoviște,' said Maria. 'Taken north, to the mountains. To the castle of Argeş on the river. It sits at the top of a mountain. One road in and out. Tokár says the garrison there probably numbers fifty men, mainly local militia and a few mercenaries. All loyal to the Monk.'

Hawker pulled the map closer and began tracing a finger along the roughly sketched terrain. 'The fortress lies south of Sibiu. One has to get across the Carpathian ridge to get there.'

Maria nodded. 'That is right. We will take the trade route along the Turnu Roşu Pass. Once on the other side it is hill and valley country eastwards, until we reach the Argeş. Three days' ride out of Sibiu. Hermannstadt, as the Saxons name it.'

'And from here to Sibiu is four days' ride,' added Faldi helpfully.

Hawker looked over to Ellingham. 'And my lady, how many men does Tokár offer us?' He watched Ellingham swallow and turn to Maria.

'Tokár's band numbers a dozen men, possibly fifteen,' she replied.

'And the castle. Walled in stone? Towers and gatehouse?'

'Yes.'

'My God,' said Dieudonné softly. 'Do you expect us to sprout wings and fly over the walls?'

Maria pulled back the map from Hawker and tut-tutted. 'And here I thought my Burgundian was made of sterner stuff. I do not expect you to fly. I expect you to rise up from beneath. Tokár knows of a cave, a cave that leads to a tunnel. Up from the mountainside and into the fortress.'

77

Dieudonné folded his arms across his chest. 'Perhaps flying might be easier.'

'And how does Tokár know of this cave under the fortress?' asked Ellingham.

'Because he was with my father when it was built. Dug out and braced up like a mineshaft. And those slaves that did the digging were put to death afterwards. Only a few surviving armaşi know its location. It was used for escape by my father when he was laid siege there by his brother Radu and his Janissary army twenty-five years ago. We shall use it again to get him out.'

'And Tokár knows the location of this cave and its entrance?' asked Hawker.

'He knows someone who does.'

Hawker shook his head slowly, sat down, and reached for his wine. He put the cup to his lips and drank. 'You have a great love for your father, my lady, to undertake such an adventure. Truly great for a daughter who could never have even remembered him.'

Maria's smile was like a crack in a windowpane. 'You seek to draw my ire, my lord? It is true he was captured and taken to Buda when I was but a small child. That does not lessen my loyalty or my duty. I will save my father. The time is right. King Matthias is distracted. So are the Turks.'

'Her *father*.' It was Tokár, speaking broken Venetian. 'Her father lives. I have seen him.' The gypsy slammed the flat of his palm hard upon the oak table. 'You Frankish knights! You owe him a debt if you be Christian men.' The grey-haired gypsy pointed a gnarled finger straight at Hawker. '*You* serve Dracula once. You remember.'

Hawker's brow raised and Faldi smiled faintly.

'I remember,' replied Hawker quietly. He looked at Maria again and switched to French. 'Do you propose we take on and defeat the entire garrison? Or do you want us to take him by stealth if we can? Neither will be simple.'

Maria leaned forward, arms braced on the table. 'That is why I have chosen *you*. All of you. Each a soldier of fortune and a captain. And each blooded in battle. Vlad Călugărul's peasants are no match for you. And Tokár's clan will fight like lions to free their prince so long as he lives.'

'And Tokár has to find us the man who knows where to find the cave,' said Hawker flatly. 'Already this venture hangs upon a man whose whereabouts are unknown and who may not even still be alive.'

'We *know* where he lives,' shot back Maria. 'And Tokár met with him before he arrived here. The place lies on the road that we will take. Near to Deva. He will need little convincing to join us, I assure you.'

'And the money?' It was Dieudonné, hunkered forward on his elbows and with a sly grin on his face. 'When do we see that?'

Maria reached into a slit along the side of her gown and pulled out a small leather pouch she had pocketed underneath in her kirtle. She tossed it onto the table, its contents jangling. 'There are forty ducats. Ten for each of you. More than enough to equip yourselves in good armour before we set out east. I will again pay you ten ducats at Hermannstadt. If you free my father there will be a hundred more – for each of you.'

Dieudonné sucked in his cheek and gave an almost imperceptible nod.

Hawker exchanged glances with Ellingham and set down his goblet. 'That is a princely sum. You either have a trove of treasure hidden or a very generous but simple banker. Or do you intend to sell the Tears of Byzantium?'

Maria inclined her head. 'You've seen what resources I have at my disposal these last weeks. I am not lacking.' She made it sound like she was talking to a fool. She then spoke in Wallachian to Tokár, who bowed and left.

'You have your wine, now let us have some food and break bread together. Tomorrow, we prepare for the journey.' She raised her hands over her head and clapped loudly, twice.

–

Giles Ellingham was not feeling quite himself. He wondered if it was because, deep down, he might be frightened of what was to come. Because he was in denial of his own mortality. Because Maria's grand quest was a dangerous and possibly fatal delusion. He felt embarrassed when he recalled his earlier enthusiasm on her ship sailing out of Venice, a boyish excitement that was badly misplaced. Even so, part of him did believe in her quest, even that they could accomplish such a daring task. He believed in Hawker and he believed in Gaston. De Grood was a powerful man-at-arms and Bartolo Faldi seemed to know no fear. Perhaps they could succeed. And he recalled the words of Gaston many weeks before. That the future of York and his own fortune might be aided more by helping free Vlad Dracula than by simply offering himself as fodder for some half-baked uprising.

They had feasted that afternoon, de Grood and Jack joining them. The company even joked, Maria sitting among them, almost regal, beautiful. He had forgotten his worries then. Now, evening having settled over the cold house, the lingering doubts were creeping back. He had been outside in the small courtyard to relieve himself before retiring. He came back in, passed the scullery where two gypsy women cleaned pots and trenchers, and went up the stairs to the long hallway that overlooked the main chamber below.

Maria had placed his company together in one large bedchamber, extra mattresses strewn upon the wide planks of the floor. He did not know where the Milanese was sleeping, nor Tokár. The servant Theophilius was never usually far from Maria but now he was nowhere to be seen. As he reached the top of the dark-stained, rustically carved staircase, Maria was waiting for him. Without hesitation, she looped her arm in his and began a slow walk down the corridor.

'You said little this afternoon at our parley,' she said to him quietly. 'Have you lost your faith in me? In our quest?'

He focused on a wall sconce and its single, guttering candle. 'No, my lady,' he lied. 'I have just been melancholy a little. So far from everything that is familiar.'

She nodded at that and squeezed herself closer to his shoulder. 'We have come far, I know. And there is further to go, I admit. But we will prevail. I have *you*.'

He could feel her body heat against his side, a feeling that aroused him. She was so unknowable, it seemed, and that, he knew, was part of the attraction. They reached the end of the hallway and came to a large door, one that Ellingham assumed was her chamber. She turned him towards her and her arms encircled his waist.

'We are much alike, we two,' she whispered. 'We are of the bone. Children of kings. Of princes. That does not change even though we carry the stain of bastardy. I told you this, in Venice.' She raised up her chin to him and he found himself kissing her. A kiss she returned heartily. Their lips separated but their faces nearly touched still.

'I will see us through this, son of Richard. Stand by me. We will all be rewarded for our loyalty.' She kissed him full again, this time longer, and Ellingham felt his heartbeat quicken in his chest. As she gently pulled away from him he, looking down, caught sight of her bosom and spied something nesting between her breasts. A dark ruby in a golden setting peered upwards. He knew it was the Tears of Byzantium, the gem-encrusted crucifix inverted and somehow secreted on her chest. He quickly looked up at her and she beheld him with her large, dark green eyes for a moment before turning to open her door. Ellingham didn't think that she had noticed what he had glimpsed. She slipped inside, flashing a smile to him as it closed.

Ellingham wasn't quite sure how he felt. Her ardour seemed real, unfeigned. But she was still a cipher to him. He turned to make his way back to his bedchamber. Ten feet away stood Tokár, motionless, his craggy face and inky eyes fixed upon him. Ellingham had not heard a sound of his approach up the stairs.

'I bid you good night,' he said to the gypsy, awkwardly, and in French. Tokár remained silent and unmoved, his gaze still locked upon him. After a few seconds Ellingham walked past, half expecting a dagger thrust in his back. He felt the hairs of his nape rise up as he approached his door. When he glanced back along the hallway, there was no one there.

-

Despite the questions and contradictions that cantered through his mind, and regardless of the deep, rippling snores of Jacob de Grood, Ellingham drifted off to sleep quickly. The fatigues of the day's ride and the revelations of Maria had finally exhausted him. And he slept well for the first time in an age. With the weak light of sunrise coming into the chamber, he had become half-awake. For some time, he drifted in and out, the light gradually growing stronger. But he bolted upright when the walls reverberated with the sound of someone banging on the door of the house, a distinctive clanking of metal accompanying each knock.

Hawker and de Grood were up in an instant, both of them throwing their *cioppas* over their heads and fumbling for their sword belts. Hawker's face, while not showing alarm, was set hard, as if he had been long expecting trouble. Hawker was out of the room before the others, barefoot, and charging down the staircase. Ellingham, his sword belt girdled about his waist, leaned into the doorframe to pull on his second boot. More pounding ensued. By the time Ellingham reached the great hall below, the door had been opened by Theophilius.

Three men in armour pushed past the gypsy servants and entered. Ellingham glimpsed at least four more beyond. Maria, hair loose down her back and clad in a heavy brocade robe, barefoot like Hawker, stepped forward to challenge the intruders. Ellingham saw that Hawker and de Grood both had their hands on their hilts, poised to draw steel. Someone pushed in from behind him. It was Faldi, bare-chested and in only his braes, huffing with exertion.

The soldiers were clad in plate, wearing barbute helms, and bearing halberds. One of them barked at Maria in Hungarian. It was clearly a command.

82

She half-turned to address the company, translating. 'They are from the fortress. They say that the Count of Temeş demands my presence. Immediately. He returned to Temesvár last night.'

Ellingham thought for the first time that her voice lacked its usual cold confidence. Maria replied to the guards, her tone conciliatory, and the captain gave her a curt bow and retreated to the threshold with his two companions. When a gypsy tried to close the heavy oak door, a gauntleted hand slammed it open full.

Maria turned around and sought out Hawker. 'Sir John, I would be grateful if you would escort me.'

Hawker's reply was sonorous and measured. 'I was coming along, my lady, even if you hadn't asked me.'

'I must dress,' she said, pushing past Ellingham and Faldi, the skirts of her robe flowing behind her. She called for Theophilius to follow and the youth hurried behind her, after casting a worried look towards the knights. Ellingham turned back to the doorway and the stone-faced veterans of King Matthias's Black Legion. It seemed that even Maria Hunyadi could sometimes be surprised.

8

Orkan Ozdemir peered dubiously at the wedge of hard cheese he held in his hand. 'This is not what we would call cheese back home. I'm not even sure it can be called cheese anywhere. It's only fit to be a doorstop.' He poked it delicately with his knife a second time, almost as if he expected it to jump out of his hand.

Pedja frowned at him. 'Eat your bread, then.'

They had spent a cold night in a flea-infested hostelry on the eastern palisade of the city, where no questions were ever asked and no explanations were ever expected. They had shared a bed in a room with eight other travellers. Even with the window open, the miasma was nearly choking. Pedja had welcomed the cold blasts of wind that periodically blew through, clearing the stink for a while. Now the two sat side by side in the hostelry's brick-paved courtyard, the building leaning drunkenly into the one next to it.

'You know,' said Orkan, between mouthfuls of black bread, 'last night I dreamt I had strangled you after all. And after that, the sultan had sent for me a gift of a fine white stallion and a polished Iberian leather saddle with golden studs.'

Pedja warily eyed a house guest taking a piss in the trough at the back of the yard. 'I doubt my head would be worth that prize. But I'm pleased that I can provide reward for you if only in your dreams.'

Orkan took a bite of the cheese, his eyes squinting. 'It is still suicide, Tombik. You know it. You must. Picking a fight with them and killing her won't bring back your brother. We'll end up joining him in death, that is all. Search your heart. We must go back.'

Pedja looked down at his boots. The last thing he wanted to hear, sitting there chilled to the bone, was the truth. He had wrapped himself tightly in a desire for revenge and he wasn't about to discard it now. Not after coming this far. 'Then you will have to return alone. I have little to lose by staying.'

Orkan's shoulders sank. 'Only your life, you foolish dhimmi,' he said, affectionately.

'Is it not worth the prize?' asked Pedja. 'Not some fantasy in your dreams. A real prize. Worthy of the sultan's praise and reward. I know that the Franks and the Hungarian are on the scent of something. Why would four knights join her for no good reason other than to fight somebody else's war? They smell gold.'

Orkan leaned closer to the Bosnian. 'The only fantasy is that the Impaler still lives,' he hissed. 'And that is yours alone.'

'You never knew my little brother. Pestered me for months to let him come to Zvornik to serve the bey. Said that raising chickens and geese for my father would kill him. I understood that he wanted to get away. I tried to tell him that the garrison was no path to glory. Instead of chicken shit he'd be sweeping horseshit in the stables. He said he didn't care. Said I was jealous that his star would outshine mine.'

'But you let him come anyway.'

Pedja nodded to himself. 'I did. Because I knew what it was like to slave away on the smallholding of a peasant. I wanted adventure. And war booty. Women. How could I sentence my brother to a life of drudgery? Why should it only be me to see the world?'

Orkan scratched at his face, his new growth of whiskers itching. 'So what? It was his choice in the end. The Prophet tells us that our free will is a test from Allah.'

'You don't have a brother, do you?'

Orkan grumbled. 'Aye… well, not that I know of. I left home when I was a boy.'

'I failed Davud. Failed him because I wanted more than the life of a martalos. More than being a gaoler at the garrison. That

85

is why I went with you. To become like an akinci. And that is why my brother followed. He thought I was guiding him.'

'Tombik, we can still go back.' His voice was now just a whisper. 'Pretend we learned things about the Hungarians. Maybe they will reward us and not throw us in the dungeon. But every day we stay and follow that evil woman and her little army, we are closer to getting found out.'

'We've come this far, so I'm staying. Yesterday *you* said that there was no going back. Now you tell me you are.'

'I've thought better of the situation. In between my dreams of killing you.'

'You can go back if you like, Orkan. I will take God's test. Exercise my free will.'

Orkan raised his eyes upwards, as if imploring Heaven. 'Now you give *me* a test. Of *my* own free will. Whether to abandon you to the Franks or stay and fight with you.' He hurled the remaining lump of hard yellow cheese across the yard. He then looked over to Pedja and slowly shook his head, a slightly grim, ironic smile on his lips. 'You know... I passed Allah's latest test last night, Tombik. I didn't strangle you while you slept.'

–

Hawker and Maria walked side by side, four soldiers just a pace ahead of them. Two more followed close behind, Hawker listening to the racket made by the jangle of their harness and weapons. Townspeople stopped and gawped as they made their passage, distrustful eyes following them, studying what they wore. Puzzling who they were. It was clear to anyone that they were under escort: either high-ranking visitors to the count or else his new prisoners. Hawker didn't like it either way. He was exposed. They all were.

They passed through the outer gatehouse to the palace and then over a drawbridge into the fortress itself, sandwiched between the meandering courses of the river Bega. Hawker was sanguine about his chances; for days he had half-expected that they would be apprehended. Maria's carelessness seemed to make it inevitable. He glanced at her. Her face was as tight as the skin of a drum and just as white. He hoped her clever brain was calculating a believable lie to get them out of whatever trouble they were in.

'What reception do you expect?' he asked her.

She kept looking straight ahead. 'Don't worry. I will talk us out of it. Just follow my lead and remember you are my captain. We're here to raise a company for Matthias. *That* is our mission.'

Hawker scanned the wide courtyard, filled with horses, men and wagons. It was a well-defended place, high stone walls and four turret towers plus the main fortified keep to which they were headed. Puffy, mist-swollen clouds scudded over the red roof tiles, driven by a strong breeze from across the plain. They were ushered into the keep and towards the heavy wooden staircase that wound its way to the upper floors. By the time they reached the top and the royal receiving chamber, Hawker could feel the sweat prickling his armpits. His hand rested upon his *cinquedea* dagger, a long-serving companion from his time in Venice. Grasping the hilt gave him some measure of comfort but he knew if it came to a fight, it would buy him little time against sword and halberd. On the second floor, they halted at the landing while a soldier knocked on a double-planked and studded door. It opened and they were led inside.

At the opposite end of the room, its stone walls draped in massive tapestries and battle flags drooping from poles, were two great gilded chairs. Sitting on one was a short man, wearing heavy crimson robes, and a Hungarian velvet turban trimmed in rabbit fur upon his head. A long thin black moustache drooped down either side of his mouth, reaching the bottom of his square, cleft chin. A bodyguard of armoured soldiers stood off to one side, clenching the hafts of their pole arms.

The sergeant who had led them in barked an order.

'Make your obeisance to the captain-general,' Maria said quietly.

She took a step forward, brushed back her woollen cloak and then grasped both sides of her brocaded gown and gave a curtsey. Hawker took a step, extended his right leg, and bowed his head curtly.

Pál Kinizsi, the Count of Temeş, leaned forward, resting his arms on his knees. He broke into a smile, one that Hawker thought more derisive than welcoming.

'Maria Drăculeşti.'

Maria replied in Hungarian and Kinizsi smiled. Maria spoke again, this time to Hawker. 'I told him you do not speak the Magyar tongue.'

Kinizsi then addressed them in something between Florentine and Venetian, but understandable nonetheless.

'This Maria, one who calls herself a Hunyadi. Now returned to our domain once again. And who is this Venetian with you?'

Hawker bowed. 'I am Sir John Hawker, liege man to King Richard of England and of late a captain in service to the Republic of Venice.'

Kinizsi smiled broadly showing a full set of teeth. 'So, an Englishman. I have not met many of your compatriots in these lands. Not enough war in your own kingdom?' He looked at Maria again. 'And what brings you back here? I did not think we would be seeing you in Temesvár again. You and the dark cloud that always seems to follow you. Like a pet.'

'I am raising a company in the service of King Matthias, my noble uncle. Sir John is assisting me to recruit men.'

This time the smile quickly blossomed into a laugh. 'A company? Of soldiers? You are very late to the revel, mistress. The war is nearly over. We hold Vienna.'

Maria bowed respectfully. 'There is still fighting, I am led to believe. And desertions. We encountered brigands on our way here. I am hoping to serve the kingdom by giving you more who will do service in the king's name.'

'Is that so? How many do you have?'

'We have just begun. I have my captains only.'

Kinizsi nodded. 'Yes. Four knights and two men-at-arms. A veritable army.'

'We will work our way east, recruiting in the German towns, at least as far as Sibiu and Brasov.'

The count leaned forward on his throne, his voice descending into a growl. 'You were warned – in Buda – about using the royal name. Now, woman, I find you doing it again. The king acknowledges your blood – barely – and he tolerates your presence. But you are still the daughter of a whore. Dracula's whore, who was the daughter of a whore herself. Don't force my hand. You will stop referring to His Majesty as your uncle. Is that understood?'

Maria bowed her head.

Kinizsi leaned back, his velvet-covered throne creaking. 'I suppose you do need to call yourself something. Aye... well, you could call yourself a Drăculeşti. Or a Dăneşti clanswoman.' He leaned forward again. 'But there is also the matter of your finances. I understand you've come into some money during your sojourn to Venice. That is of no concern to me. I remind you that the king's chancellor still harbours doubts about you. The matter of some treasure missing from the palace. There were rumours about you and your mercenaries in Buda last year. Questions were asked. You are lucky that these came to nothing. But I am watching you so long as you remain in the Banat and in Transylvania.'

Maria curtsied. 'I am in your debt, your Grace. When we next meet I will have a hundred men ready to do service in the king's name.'

Kinizsi pursed his lips. 'You will pardon me if I do not hold my breath upon that score, mistress.' He waved his hand to shoo them away. 'You may go. But keep in mind what I have said.' He raised a forefinger towards Hawker. 'And you, Englishman. You had better keep an eye on this one. She has a honeyed tongue but she is as slippery as an eel. It is a family trait, I'm afraid.'

Hawker wasn't quite sure which family the count was referring to. But it was more than likely he meant Dracula and not Hunyadi. He bowed again, Kinizsi gave an order to the guards, and they were led outside. Maria's face had flushed the colour of Kinizsi's robes and she said nothing as they made their way back down the stairs. Out in the courtyard, and led as far as the inner gates, they were then abandoned to their own devices.

Maria avoided his eyes. Hawker knew that rage was stoking in her, that she was embarrassed by the tongue-lashing she had just received and stung by the insults. Stung too, that now Hawker knew her reputation.

Hawker pivoted to face her. 'How is it you own a house here? Or maybe it isn't even yours.'

She looked up at him, eyes blazing. 'It *is* my house. Given to me by the king. A bribe so I would keep away from Buda and the court.'

Hawker shook his head slowly, like some disapproving priest. 'So then, mistress, what now? Do you choose to continue in your quest? Because I owe it to my comrades to tell them we go against the will of the kingdom of Hungary if we continue.'

'I give up nothing. That trumped-up Rascian peasant Kinizsi has done well enough for himself. He'll not deny me my fortune nor my birthright. We go back to the house and prepare for the journey east. I promised you decent accoutrements, Sir John, and those you shall have this day.'

'That is something at least, because we're going to need good armour. Before long we shall be fighting either the Wallachian militia, the king's Black Legion, or Saxon mercenaries in Sibiu. Maybe all of them.'

'We will slip through them like shadows in the night, I swear it to you. And we will free my father.'

Hawker's mouth curled up in a thin smile. 'You have more fight in you than many a man I have known. But blind courage will get you killed as easily as walking off a cliff. We must think this one through – and carefully. You understand me?'

She started walking forward, forcing Hawker to shift to one side. 'That is precisely why I have employed you. So let's begin!'

They returned to find a household on the verge of battle. For an instant, Hawker had spotted Jack in the upstairs window, probably sent up there by Jacob as a lookout. Then, the door creaked open, revealing Bartolo Faldi standing in his full suit of polished plate, naked sword in hand. Behind him, Hawker's company stood also, fully armoured.

'*Beata Vergine!*' shouted Faldi, seeing them arrive alone. Hawker saw they had dragged benches into the entrance hall to reinforce the door if it came to it.

'Back inside, my war dogs!' said Maria, laughing. 'The count received us civilly, but he did not provide a very warm welcome.'

Ellingham sheathed his sword and gave Hawker a nod of relief. Jacob just stood where he was and sucked in his scarred cheek, a look of annoyance on his face. Dieudonné raised his eyebrows towards Hawker, practically begging to be told the story. Perhaps it was Faldi who seemed most relieved at their safe return. He grasped Maria's hand and stooped to kiss it. She smiled and covered his gauntleted hand with her palm.

'A false alarm, Ser Bartolo,' she said, looking to each of them. 'The Count of Temeş only wanted us to know he is watching. But we are not staying for long anyway. We have business in the Siebenbürgen to the east. How is your German tongue, Sir John?'

Hawker didn't answer her. He walked down into the large hall where the hearth blazed. 'Jack! Go find that gypsy woman and get me a cup of ale. And someone get me a bench to sit my arse on. Wait, hang a moment.' He grabbed him by the shoulder and parted the lad's hair to inspect the lump underneath. It had shrunk down, leaving only a discoloured mark on the scalp. He nodded and gently pushed Jack away. 'Ale.'

'You men may all take off that old armour,' said Maria, walking closer to Ellingham and touching his arm. 'Today I pay you in the finest plate that Temesvár has to offer. And then we shall prepare for the journey.'

Faldi beamed at her and Ellingham smiled and bowed. She threw the young Plantagenet a particularly long glance before climbing the stairs to her chamber. Faldi bowed to the others and then followed her.

Jacob began carrying back the benches to the long table while Ellingham and Dieudonné joined Hawker.

'So then, we are out of immediate danger?' asked Ellingham. 'Just what happened to you?'

Dieudonné placed his rusty brown barbute on the table. 'The count does not know what she plans, does he?'

Hawker shook his head. 'I suspect he does not. But neither does he trust her.'

'My question is why did she take you with her and not Faldi?'

Hawker looked up at Ellingham from where he sat. 'I would wager it was because if it *had* gone ill for us, then Faldi would escape capture. She wanted to save him from joining her fate. So it was me that went with her.'

Ellingham's brows knit upon hearing the words. 'Are you implying they are…?' His words trailed off.

'Partners in some arrangement? I don't know. Faldi is a good soldier with a stout heart, I will give him his due. Loyal to his employer until his condotta is at an end. I think she has known him a few years. Perhaps she is fond of him. Or fonder of him than she is of me.' Hawker chuckled to himself.

'Ser Bartolo was here before us. Hired before us,' remarked Dieudonné archly. 'We don't know the terms of his condotta with *her*.'

'Then what is your counsel, Sir John?' said Ellingham quietly.

'Count Kinizsi seems to accept that she is here to raise mercenaries for King Matthias, even if he doubts she can accomplish it. We'd better make the count at least *think* we're recruiting a company for the Austrian war, before he figures out we're doing something else. Because he will be watching.'

Jack pushed a brimming cup across to Hawker, his ill-fitting armour noisily scraping the table edge. 'What if she doesn't want to do that, Sir John?'

Hawker smiled at his young squire and hefted the cup. 'Then we shall have to convince her of the wisdom of it. She dismissed her stradiotti and then we were nearly hammered by those brigands on the road. We might not be so lucky to escape next time.'

Ellingham nodded. 'This is a lawless place. But she seems determined that we need no more help. Her gypsy army is an invisible one so far. Maybe she will listen to your reason.'

Hawker looked over to Ellingham. '*My* reason? No, Sir Giles. She is more inclined to listen to *yours*. You are the son of Richard. The son of a king.'

Dieudonné nodded at Hawker's words but Ellingham broke into a frown of indecision. 'How am I to convince her of this?'

Dieudonné grinned. 'With your considerable charms, my friend.'

9

The armourer, a Saxon from Braşov, eyed the five men and one woman, literally sizing them up. Hawker saw that his crossed arms were completely hairless, red and covered in numerous round white scars the diameter of a farthing. The splatter of molten steel wasn't kind to flesh, and this man had been working the forge for quite some time by the look of it. He was stocky and ham-fisted as befitted his trade, long black hair gathered and pulled back tight into a topknot which crowned his wide head. A long moustache, well-oiled, draped either side of his mouth.

He wiped his hands on his stained leather apron and smiled broadly at Maria. 'Fitting out your retinue, then? I was wondering when you would turn up.' He spoke in Venetian, something Hawker found surprising. The power of Venice extended far. Unless perhaps he believed Maria had come from there.

She had brought Hawker and the company directly into the workshop and they were surrounded by the din of metal being pounded and riveted by half a dozen apprentices. A great wooden wheel revolved beyond the armourer, driven by the river that flowed along the back of the building. The wheel powered a huge trip hammer which rose and fell like the rhythmic working of a tower clock.

'You doubted me, sir?' said Maria, returning his smile. 'These three good knights and their two men-at-arms require new harness to replace that which was lost. And you are the most skilled in Temesvár, able to equip soldiers on the day so they say.'

The armourer nodded and wiped his brow with the back of his arm. 'Let's go across the way, then you can tell me what you need. And I can tell you what it will cost.' He smiled again mischievously.

He led the way out and across the tiny alley into another house, Maria right behind him. Hawker looked at Ellingham dubiously. He knew that good plate needed to be fitted to the man, something that required measurements and weeks, if not months, to fabricate. Hawker pulled a gawping Jack away from the great wheel and they followed Maria into the other house. The ceiling was high, rafters bracing the sloping roof and the white walls adorned with all manner of breastplates and backplates, shields, pole weapons and swords.

Ellingham stood alongside Hawker. 'A tailor's shop – for killers,' he muttered in English.

The armourer went from man to man, studying arms and legs, each time taking a few steps back to view the entire figure. He got to Jack and shook his head. 'This boy, too? He will outgrow what I give him in less than a year.' He shrugged. 'But it is your money. No matter.'

He turned and shouted into another room. A lad about Jack's age scurried in and the armourer spoke to him in German. The boy bowed and ran back.

'We will get these fellows fitted with arming doublets first, then move on to finding some plate to fit them.'

Maria nodded. 'Harness to the satisfaction of my English knights here. They will pay you directly for their armour. And they will decide on what to equip their three men with. You and I will settle up afterwards.'

Hawker saw Dieudonné visibly bristle at being lumped in with Jacob and Jack. He glared at Maria but kept quiet.

The armourer beamed. 'I will find the Englishmen suitable harness, have no fear. What were they wearing before?'

'Harness that my grandfather would have worn,' said Hawker, speaking up for the first time. '…and would have been ashamed of for the rest of his days.'

Jacob de Grood sniggered.

The armourer laughed. 'Well, I have supplied half the king's army these past two years. I will have something you can agree on, my lord.'

'But no white harness that I can spy here,' said Hawker archly.

The Saxon guffawed. 'White harness? No one has time to buff and polish around here, my good knight! It's generally blued steel or blackened all around. That's what the count prefers for his army and anything else will rust to buggery in a fortnight in these parts.'

Maria wiped her hand along a blue annealed breastplate lying on a bench. She rubbed her fingers together absently. 'And you will honour the undertaking to give me credit for the armour we are discarding?'

The armourer bowed to her.

'Good. Then let us begin.'

First came the bleached linen doublets, quilted with wool. Hawker saw that these were newly sewn and with sleeves attached to the shoulders by leather laces so they could be adjusted somewhat for length. Amazingly, and after the boy had brought out a dozen garments, all of them were passably fitted. As for the armour plate, it was all second hand or base quality. Serviceable, but Hawker regretted losing his fine armour in the headlong flight from Venice. None of them would be able to compare with Ser Bartolo's fine Milanese suit of plate. Jacob picked up a black-lacquered breastplate and stuck his forefinger through a hole that had been made by a spike or an arrow. He waggled it for Hawker and raised his eyebrows.

The Saxon did his best for Hawker though. A fine blued breast and backplate that even had some gold etching, mail skirt, cuisses and greaves, vambraces that actually fit his forearms and floating elbows that tied to the doublet. They found him a gorget that didn't strangle and pauldrons that he could move with. It was all a mix of styles: Nuremburg fluting on some armour – probably scavenged from a dead man – and plain, serviceable pieces probably forged by the Saxon himself. It would do. Hawker chose a fine German sallet helm with an open face and two raised

96

ridges which cascaded down to the tail of the back. The Saxon had blued it and installed new padding of linen and horsehair with a leather chinstrap and brass buckle.

When the Saxon's assistants got to Jack, Hawker watched with pride. The lad stood, arms outstretched, unable to supress the grin that suffused his entire face. They buckled on his first proper breastplate and back and did their best to find pieces that fit him. They added gussets of chainmail to protect his exposed armpits and a pair of old spaulders instead of pauldrons. Jack windmilled his arms and swung his hips, Hawker nodding as he checked the degree of free movement. They found the lad an Italian *barbuta* helm that fit snugly and when placed upon his head, Hawker saw the boy become the man.

Two hours passed. An apprentice brought in mugs of beer for them and some black bread and cheese. Dieudonné argued with the Saxon in a mix of languages, determined to get the quality of armour he felt he deserved. Sir Giles had Maria to harangue the Saxon on his behalf, kitting him out to befit his station as a prince of the blood. The armourer did his best to comply, running back and forth to bring out his best wares from storage in hay-lined oak chests and knowing that the strange noblewoman would pay for the luxury. Jacob didn't complain, content to find armour that, despite being pitted and blooming with a patina of rust, fit him the better, knowing his life would depend on moving inside it without hindrance. He, too, chose a *barbuta*, one with a heart-shaped cut-out for the face.

Jack pulled off his barbute, face still aglow, and Hawker took it from him. 'Satisfied?'

Jack nodded. 'I won't go down so easily next time, Sir John. I promise you.'

Hawker started helping him out of the armour, unbuckling the straps for the spaulders and then the breastplate. 'Good armour is only half the fight, lad. You better keep up your practice with Jacob.'

'I will, Sir John. I won't fail you.'

Jacob, listening to it all, gave Hawker a wink.

'I know that you won't, my lad.' Hawker could see the boy was changing fast. Maybe not in height or weight but in outlook, developing a more sanguine view of himself and the world he found himself in, one to match his increasing prowess at self-defence. Such a confidence would help keep Jack alive, Hawker knew, but part of him was saddened, too. He was witnessing the slow death of a boy and the birth of a man, a man who would probably know only battle and risk in his service. And it was a path that he himself had set Jack upon.

The sudden musing was interrupted when the armourer re-entered the room. 'Englishman! This is for you. A gift from the mistress who says you are in need.'

It was an *espee bâtarde* – a bastard sword – of fine workmanship, with a silver fishtail pommel, a grip long enough to be used with both hands and a blade a bit longer than his old arming sword. Back home, he had been fond of the German style of half-swording, with the left hand gripping the blade itself, the right hand holding the leather-wrapped grip. It was deadly in a close, tight fight. Hawker hefted the weapon and wrapped his fingers tight. Flexing his wrist and arcing the sword, he found it balanced a hand's width above the hilt. It was a noble's sword and of fitting quality. The Saxon handed him the scabbard.

'I do not know what task your employer has in mind for all of you, but something tells me you'll be needing a good blade.'

–

Ellingham followed Maria into another one of the rooms of the seemingly endless house of the armourer. It was a spartan study, or library of some sort, its centre table littered with large parchment sketches of armour. Maria went to stand on the far side of the table near the leaded window. She turned and locked her eyes on him, as if knowing all along it was he that followed her. Ellingham saw that she was cradling a scabbarded sword to her breast.

He moved to her and she pointed the sword towards him, hilt first. 'My gift to you, son of Richard. The first of many such rewards for your aid in my cause.'

Elllingham took it from her grasp, smiling. He turned it in his hands, admiring its golden wire-wrapped grip and the silvered wheel pommel, finely etched. The blade was long and slim, designed to pierce gaps in plate armour. 'I thank you, mistress. It is a generous gift.'

'You deserve nothing less,' she replied, looking at him intently, as if she was trying to divine his very thoughts, his heart.

He looked down and pretended to study the sword, withdrawing an inch from the leather scabbard.

'I know that Sir John doubts me,' she said, her voice soft. 'Doubts my strategy, my plan. Maybe even my parentage.'

Ellingham cast his eyes downward for but a second.

'Don't worry,' she said, 'I would imagine he has shared what was said at the fortress by Count Kinizsi. That my mother was a courtesan.'

'I think the word was whore,' said Ellingham. He regretted the word as it left his mouth but Maria only laughed lightly at hearing it.

'Yes, that is what the count said. And that I am a bastard.'

'Like me. My mother was a miller's daughter… I am told.' The last words trailed off quietly.

'We share that bond of shame. But we still carry royal blood. You believe in me, don't you? Believe that my father lives? That I – and he – will help you in turn once he is freed? There are many ways to die in this world and they are easily found, by both design and by accident. But we share a bond in this quest, one that is worth the risk. Much more than a mercenary's condotta.'

'I do not think that Sir John sees things that way. But he left the decision to me and we're here. And I share some of his doubts.'

She raised her chin, brow furrowing momentarily. 'My leadership?'

Ellingham set the sword upon the table. 'Your strategy.'

He watched her eyes narrow ever so slightly, shoulders stiffening. 'You question my planning? You don't think I have put the elements of my strategy in place, everything thought through?'

Ellingham stood practically toe to toe with her. He shook his head. 'I question why you released your stradiotti when you did. That we had to face a skirmish with so few of us that we could have been killed then and there. That even before that, your impetuosity led us headlong into a fight with raiders before we even had time to prepare.'

A smile crept across her long, alabaster face. She reached up and stroked his chin. 'My little lion has teeth.'

Ellingham snatched her hand away. 'I have fought in far more battles already than you have even dreamt of. I am not your pet.'

She tried to pull her hand away, her face clouding in anger, but Ellingham held her wrist fast.

'You should heed Sir John. You should heed me. We need more men-at-arms. Now. You desire to keep the confidence of this company? My confidence? Then make it happen.'

She did not seek to pull away from him, content for him to hold her wrist. Her anger melted into an emotionless expression, her eyes on his. 'You are less pliable than Ser Bartolo, that is most certain. More determined. I judged you well I think… from the moment I first saw you.'

It was all Ellingham could do to resist leaning in and kissing her. She saw his rising desire and pressed herself against his breastplate. He loosened his grip on her and inhaled, straightening his frame. 'You keep a servant – a useless slip of a man Theophilius – yet dismiss several swordsmen from your service. You must hire more swords to give us the chance to succeed in this quest. Even you are not infallible.'

Maria placed a palm flat on his breast and slowly stood back, nodding ever so slightly. Ellingham saw equilibrium return to her face, suffused with confidence. 'Very well. I yield to your experience of battle. And of men. We will recruit a few more. *Only* a few more. A large force will only attract attention and there are places that we must pass through that will be unavoidable. And dangerous. Theophilius will remain here in Temesvár. And he has been far from useless, if you remember how I obtained the rubies from the Doge.'

'I accept that,' said Ellingham, wetting his lips.

'And make no mistake,' she said, 'Where we are journeying it will be hard to tell friend from enemy. It is a place of deceit and hidden hatreds. Our company must remain true. True to each other. True to me.'

She reached out and touched his forearm.

He lifted her hand and brought it to his lips. 'Agreed, my lady.'

'Let us return to the others. I must settle with the Saxon and that will take some skill.' Ellingham detected a flush to her cheeks. She turned, lifted his sword up and handed it to him. 'Use this well, my lord.'

—

They returned to Maria's house wearing their new harness: Jack chattering like a magpie to Jacob; Hawker escorting Maria by the arm; and Dieudonné at Ellingham's side pestering him about his exchange with her.

'What undertakings did you get from her?' the Burgundian pleaded.

'She knows the concerns of this company now,' said Ellingham flatly. 'Ask her yourself if you wish to know more.'

Dieudonné swore at the reply, a flash of anger showing before he put a comradely arm about Ellingham's shoulders and gave him a shake.

Walking from the walled gate of the house into the court-yard, Ellingham saw Tokár loading heavy wicker baskets onto a donkey. As they passed, Tokár shot them all a suspicious look, his distrust or disdain unhidden. The glare didn't linger though, and he continued buckling up the pack animal. Ellingham wondered just how well Maria knew the gypsy and his men and how deep the trust ran between them. Inwardly, his heart sank a little at the thought of having to keep one eye on their backs.

Faldi met them at the entrance, exclaiming about their magnificent new harness, his arms windmilling with excited compliments. Once inside, they set about taking off their new armour, one helping the other and even Ser Bartolo willing to play the squire while prattling away. Jack, still grinning, insisted on remaining in his, the better to become accustomed to its weight and feel. Ellingham smiled, not at Jack, but at Hawker upon seeing the almost fatherly pride in the old knight's eyes.

Maria stood regarding them, hands on hips. 'See, I have delivered what has been promised. You have no need to doubt me.' Ellingham smiled at her, wrapping his sword belt about his scabbard.

Theophililus glided into the room, bearing a cup for Maria which she took and drank from. As the servant began to withdraw, she pulled him back gently by his sleeve. 'I have decided that Theophilius will remain here at this house while we proceed.'

The youth glanced downwards, a clear sign to Ellingham that he wasn't pleased with the arrangement.

'I don't trust the Count Kinizi not to dog our trail and Theophilius will be able to watch the garrison and get word to us should we be followed.' She reached out and gave the nape of his neck a squeeze. 'He will be our rear guard. One we can depend upon.'

'I seek only to serve you, my mistress,' the youth said quietly in his heavily accented Venetian, his eyes searching and resting briefly upon those of the company, as if it were some warning for the mercenaries to honour their own promises. Ellingham gently exhaled in resignation: their numbers were dwindling. Something Maria seemed to care little about for reasons she kept to herself. Theophilius was no man-at-arms to be sure, but might have been useful upon the road. Now they would never get the chance to find out how.

Tokár came bursting in, speaking loudly in what Ellingham thought might be Wallachian. Maria turned and addressed him in the same tongue, her own voice just as urgent.

She turned to Hawker. 'Tokár says there are men outside. Armed men.'

Hawker swore loudly and drew his blade. Everyone stopped for a moment, eyeing one another, but it was Hawker that led the way with Maria at his side.

Two men stood side by side at the far end of the courtyard. They were strangely attired, both shaggy and unkempt, one with a sword on the hip, the other wearing a mace slung off his wide red leather belt.

Ellingham saw who they were. He nodded to himself, thoughtfully. Things happen for a reason, all in the Lord's good time.

Maria put her hands on her hips and called across the yard. 'You again! What business do you have with me?'

Pedja Jankovic bowed low and then slapped Orkan Nikolic's backside to induce him to do the same. 'Noble mistress, we have been sadly unsuccessful in finding an employer. But I have always believed it is better to serve with those you have fought alongside before. We are here to offer our blades to your cause. Will you take us? We will follow wherever you lead.'

10

Maria reined in and the others of the party did the same.

Hawker's eyes scanned the strange-looking, single mountain that lay ahead. It was shaped like a sugarloaf, a cone of green topped by a circular fortress sprouting narrow red-tiled towers. Maria gestured towards it.

'Deva.'

Hawker looked over to Jacob, who was riding next to him. The Fleming shook his head slowly. 'I pray to the risen Christ that the fellow we're looking for isn't up *there*.'

Ellingham, mounted on the other side, kept silent.

Maria urged her horse over to Hawker. 'The town lies at the foot of the mountain. Tokár says that the armaşi Vilkas lives near the edge of settlement. Closer to where the river is. He is a cobbler now it seems. Keeps to himself.'

'Who rules this place?' asked Hawker, his voice not much more than a growl.

'This is Hunyadi territory. There was a time when the last king stayed here but Matthias rarely visits. One of his lords rules up there now in his stead.'

'I trust he will turn a blind eye to a band of mercenaries coming in and abducting one of his townsfolk.'

Maria's laugh trilled across the wide road and into the meadow beyond where the Mureş river flowed past. 'Sir John, these days there are more mercenaries than townsfolk. We'll all be fish in the same pond! And Vilkas knows where his loyalties lie. He will come along gladly when he finds out why we're here!'

She tugged her reins and moved off, rejoining Faldi and Tokár at the front of the column.

Jacob gave Hawker a knowing look.

The old knight smiled thinly. 'Loosen your blade in the scabbard, my friend.'

When they reached the town, Hawker grunted to himself seeing that Maria's intuition had proved correct. No one bothered to look at them as they rode in. Townsfolk kept about their daily business, wagon-loads of hogsheads and bushels kept rolling slowly along, and vendors sang their wares. Tokár led the way on his donkey, Maria at his flank. The rest followed two by two with Dieudonné, Jacob and Jack bringing up the rear. It was the strangest procession Hawker had ever been in: led by a gypsy on a pack animal. He smiled to himself. It was like Christ returning to Jerusalem but with no palm fronds to meet them.

Tokár led them through the main street, and down to the edge of town. Ramshackle cottages of marsh reed thatch lined the now deeply rutted road down the centre of which ran a gutter filled with rotting cabbages and the slops of the previous day. They could see the row of settlement coming to an end, fields opening beyond. The gypsy raised a hand to signal them and then turned to the left. Without waiting, he dismounted and walked through the mud to a hovel that sagged against the adjoining cottage.

Ellingham called over to Hawker. 'Do we dismount, Sir John?'

Hawker didn't answer but instead dismounted himself and followed the gypsy, his hand on the pommel of his *cinquedea* dagger. A few peasants had now begun to watch them from their windows in the way that fearful peasants always did, their eyes drifting away the moment yours met theirs. Tokár emerged from the house, face set hard. Maria called to him in Wallachian and he shook his head in reply.

A peasant, obviously braver than the others, emerged from his house, his apron smeared with the gore of whatever he had just slaughtered. He said something in the Wallachian tongue, gestured to the hovel, and put his hands on his hips defiantly. Maria's face hardened and Tokár scratched vigorously at his greying mop in frustration at whatever was being said.

'Enlighten us, my lady!' called out Hawker.

She wrapped her hands once around the reins, pulling them tauter. 'He is gone. Taken. A band of soldiers he'd been gambling with.'

The peasant pointed towards the blanched yellowish meadows beyond and spoke again.

Maria translated. 'Deserters and brigands. They make camp down there.'

Hawker bit his lip and then let out a mumbled curse. 'Let us hope they haven't flayed him yet.' He strode back to his horse and mounted again.

'Here we go then,' said Jacob, voice rich with foreboding.

–

They rode into the fields, making for the group of mildew-stained bell tents that were pitched there. Smoke rose from several cook fires and men in various garb lolled about eating, drinking, and laughing. A few women tended to the fires, hair bound under turbans and long skirts hiked up and tucked into wide leather girdles. It was a camp the likes of which Hawker had seen many times in his life and a place where life could be extinguished in the blink of an eye. He ordered Jacob to stay at the rear with Jack, Dieudonné and the Rascians while he and Ellingham joined Maria, Faldi and Tokár in the lead. 'Keep a distance,' he said, 'let us negotiate, but keep an eagle eye for something going amiss.' Jacob nodded grimly but Dieudonné's lips parted in a smile that almost spoke of eager anticipation.

At first their advance into the camp seemed not to be worthy of attention, but when the captains spotted Maria they stopped their chatter, stared for a moment, then came forward with their hands on their sword pommels.

'State your business!' said one, in German, turning his gaze from Maria to Hawker. He was helm-less and hat-less, his long, stringy blond hair to his shoulders. He wore a breastplate and back, a red gambeson showing underneath down to his thighs.

His green hose was holed at both knees and the only thing that looked of worth on him was his fine leather boots.

Maria answered his challenge straight away while Hawker kept his eyes on the small band that was now rapidly gathering around them.

'We search for a comrade,' said Maria. 'One called Vilkas. A Balt.'

The mercenary smiled then looked down at his boots. 'Vilkas. Damn good cobbler. But a very poor gambler.' His companions broke into some scattered laughter. 'And why would you be looking for Vilkas? If he's your comrade then why is he here in Deva?'

'A *former* comrade. One we wish to rejoin our company. May we see him?'

The captain folded his arms across his chest. 'He owes me a lot of money. He is here to work off his debt. I'm not sure he needs to see any old friends just yet.' He turned to his companions, grinning widely. 'And he's not much use to anyone most of the time anyway.'

Hawker caught sight of a man sitting on the ground, chained at the ankle to a large tree stump. His head of long unkempt greying locks kept lolling from side to side, legs sprawled. He looked to have been badly beaten.

Maria leaned back into her creaking saddle. 'All the same. We would speak with him.'

The captain moved closer and stroked the nose of her mount. 'Hungarian? Back from the Austrian wars? So are we.' He gestured around him. 'Life is good here even in winter. And the local Hunyadi noble up there,' he said, pointing to the castle on the mountain, 'lets us keep the peace down here.' He looked up again, studying Maria. 'Rare to see a woman leading a band. Something one sees more of in the eastern lands than here. But you would be welcome to join our little free company.' His smile changed to lascivious. 'I am called Melchior.'

Hawker gently kicked in his heels and his horse inched forward, closing nose to nose with Maria's. Bartolo Faldi then urged his mount a little wider as if he was flanking. The mercenary stepped back. 'But I see you have these fine knights to ride with.'

Hawker counted the soldiers. There were sixteen. Most were dishevelled and unarmoured, some already drunk. But others lay beyond in a second encampment, though for the moment none ventured closer. If they were to fight they might have an advantage initially, but numbers would tell if things got bogged down. He called over to Maria in French.

'I suggest you tell him you will pay the Balt's debt. And then some.'

Maria glanced at Hawker, considering his counsel. She looked down at the mercenary and smiled. 'We have no bone to pick with you and we can soon be on our way. Just let me pay what Vilkas owes. I will sweeten it with a florin as well.'

The captain puckered his lips and tilted his head in mock deliberation. He then moved behind one of his men and grasped him by either shoulder, giving the soldier a gentle shake. 'Stefan here was saying how bored he is. Me too. What say you we have a little wager? We play some cards. You win, you may take old Vilkas. You lose, Vilkas stays and we take your horses. Fair enough?'

'Very well. Name your game.'

'Do any of your men know Karnöffel?'

She hesitated. Hawker waited a moment and then spoke up for her. 'We know it.' He then spoke quietly to Maria. 'Be damned sure you need this old Balt. If we lose they'll try and take more than our horses. Even if we win I don't trust them not to murder us. Every single one is a rogue.'

Smiling for Melchior's benefit, she replied, 'They're Black Legion runaways. Swiss, Germans, Bohemians. A few Wallachians I spied as well. But we *need* Vilkas. We do this thing.'

Hawker nodded. 'Then I shall fetch my player.' He turned his mount and trotted back to where the others had held. 'Jacob! We must gamble for the life of the prisoner. The game is Karnöffel. Something you know well.'

The Fleming shut his eyes tight for a moment and shook his head with resignation. 'Aye, my lord. Too well.'

'Karn-awful?' said Ellingham, his eyes wide. 'What game is that?'

'It means something like ball-buster, in German,' said Jacob.

Ellingham's mount twitched under its rider's agitation. 'This is madness, Sir John!'

Dieudonné, listening intently at his side, let out a cackle of amusement.

Hawker pointed a forefinger at Ellingham. 'We play. Stay on your guard, both of you! You too, Jack!'

The boy nodded solemnly.

'Jacob, with me.'

—

'Is he dead?' Hawker stood back from the man Vilkas, still sprawled and manacled to the stump.

Jacob bent down and raised the man's head by his long wiry forelock. He let it drop again and then he stood up. 'Dead? Yes. Dead drunk.'

Faldi, who was standing next to Hawker, made a tut-tutting sound. 'At least you know you won't be risking it all for only a corpse.'

Hawker glanced over to Maria who had remained mounted, looking beautiful and imperious, commanding the scene and ever aware of the role she had to continue playing. 'Bartolo,' he whispered, 'remount and stay close to the donna. Bring the others up just behind. But all of you: stay in the saddle.'

'Fear not, Don Falco. If any of these rats draw steel on you, I'll ride them down before they can raise the blade.' He moved off, waving his hand towards Melchior with a flourish.

Melchior came forward, looked down at Vilkas, and put his hands on his hips. 'It is a wonder how he can even sew on a sole when he can hardly stand up most of the time. Still, he did well enough with my boots. But there are two things he can't live without: the grape and the dice.'

Hawker's German was slowly coming back to him. 'Unchain him. He sits where we play.'

Melchior shrugged. 'If you wish it. He's not running anywhere.' The captain signalled to a few of his men and they duly released the old man, dragging him to where a large wooden chest sat outside the largest of the tents. 'Now, is your man ready to play cards?'

Despite the cold, sweat was already beginning to bead on Jacob de Grood's brow as he sat on an upturned tub on one side of the ornately carved camp chest. Hawker stood at his shoulder, arms folded across his chest. The lieutenant named Stefan had seated himself opposite the Fleming, fanning the deck of tall playing cards. Hawker's gaze shifted to his comrades. Ellingham seemed to be protesting to Faldi and Hawker prayed the youth would not overreact to what was unfolding. Maria stood like a statue though, her eyes fixed on Jacob and his opponent.

A loud belch sounded from Vilkas as he pulled himself upright, swaying on his backside. 'Perkunas will take your souls! His almighty hammer will crush you all!'

A soldier standing behind Vilkas lifted his boot toe and shoved the old man over. Melchior laughed. 'He is always spouting his pagan nonsense. Pay him no heed. So… Fleming… we are agreed on playing one hand. Best of five tricks.'

Stefan smiled at Jacob and fanned the deck again. 'Low card deals, yes?'

Jacob lost the cut and Stefan reshuffled and dealt them each five cards, the first face up. 'Ah,' said Stefan dramatically, 'the chosen suit is Bells.'

Jacob studied his hand and played his first card, the King of Hearts. Stefan laid down the six of Bells. 'The Pope trumps your king.' Jacob chewed the inside of his cheek while Stefan swept the cards to his side. Hawker remembered that the game had been banned in some cities in the Holy Roman Empire, it being an insult to the ruling classes and the Church because it inverted the order of things: the low trumped the high.

Stefan then played the four of Acorns which Jacob beat with the three of Acorns. That made it one trick each. Hawker swallowed, moving his gaze to the others of the mercenary band who began to crowd in. Hawker slyly shifted his left hand to the grip of his *cinquedea*.

Stefan won the next throw which meant that Jacob needed to take the following or lose the game. He managed it with the Jack of Leaves which bested Stefan's Queen of Acorns. Laughter and hooting rang out.

'Perkunas take you all!' bellowed Vilkas, eyes rolling, his cheek lying in the filthy, mud-churned grass.

Hawker laid his hand lightly on Jacob's right shoulder. The next trick would determine the game. Hawker tensed. No one was going to take their horses – or their lives – without a fight. He looked up and caught Ellingham's eyes a few feet away. Making sure that Ellingham had seen him, Hawker nodded once. And Ellingham did the same.

Jacob took his last card and Hawker could feel the Fleming's muscles tense under his hand, ready for whatever came next. The card was the Devil of Bells. It trumped all cards save one. Stefan's face went blank for an instant. He then grinned broadly and gently placed his card on top. It was the Jack of Bells – the Karnöffel. The ball-buster card.

But before Hawker could draw his blade, Vilkas had – fast as lightning – arisen from the dead, tackling Melchior with the roar of a raging bear. And then all hell was unleashed.

11

Hawker pommeled the soldier next to him, struck another with his gauntleted left fist, and then pulled Vilkas off the bleeding mercenary captain who was now missing most of his nose. A horseman thundered past: the half-Turk, one hand seizing the nape of a mercenary and propelling him into a group of his comrades, sending all tumbling. Hawker saw his own comrades riding in too amongst the confused mercenaries. All was chaos, and with Melchior and Stefan downed, the others in the band lost cohesion. Hawker dragged Vilkas out of the melee and waved for Jack. The boy reined in, Tokár on his donkey close behind, and Hawker threw the now comatose Balt over the back of Jack's saddle.

'Move off! Hold on to his belt and don't lose him!'

Jack nodded vigorously and jerked his reins, his horse hopping and stamping with excitement until Jack got the gelding under control. He trotted off across the field, Tokár following, and Hawker turned back into the fray, long dagger in hand.

The company's mounted charge had scattered the disorganised deserters who were now mainly trying to defend themselves in ones and twos. Hawker dragged Jacob out of a tussle in the mud and kicked away the half-drunk mercenary who had latched onto Jacob's leg.

'We must remount!' he yelled.

Jacob nodded, wiping blood from his lip. They ran to their mounts, with three soldiers pursuing. But Faldi and Maria rode in, knocking the Black Legion men to the ground. Once Hawker and Jacob were on horseback, they rode in again, this time cutting tent lines and collapsing the camp. Hawker saw Melchior had regained his feet, clutching his face and screaming to his men, but no one paid him heed. Then Gaston Dieudonné appeared, calmly trotting up to the mercenary. With a broad smile on his face, Dieudonné hauled his right arm back and brought his blade down, nearly severing Melchior's head with one blow. The head flopped to the side at an unnatural angle, a fountain of pulsing blood erupting.

Hawker swallowed, his mouth dry. The Burgundian enjoyed his killing a little too much. He had hoped that they might make an escape without too much death-dealing: causing a blood debt would make it much more likely they would be pursued for vengeance. But then he saw Ellingham compound that problem: the youth found himself in a fight with a mercenary who had managed to find a horse. The two circled each other trading edge blows, but after only a few exchanges and warded blades, Ellingham's blade bit deep into the man's bare neck, dropping him motionless over the saddlebow. Ellingham, holding aloft his sword, then skirted around his opponent to trot to rejoin the company.

Hawker and Jacob reined in to where the others had assembled, out of distance of the shambles created. 'We must fly now!' warned Hawker. 'Jack has the Balt with him. Your gypsy is there too.'

The Rascians joined them, sweating, and looking grim-faced. The one called Pedja said something to Maria in her tongue.

She replied curtly and then turned to Hawker. 'I'd hoped to take lodging in Deva this night. That is out of the question now.'

'Does that surprise you, my lady?' Hawker was incredulous, his eyes darting to where the enemy were calling others to arms. 'We should get well away – at speed.'

Dieudonné rode up calmly, both hands resting on his saddlebow, his sword sheathed again. 'My lords, I cut the head from the snake. The rest will fall away.'

'Not worth another gamble, Gaston,' said Ellingham, irked by his friend's carefree tone. 'Sir John is right. We must leave now and ride at speed.'

'I know where we can make for,' said Maria. 'We go east, remain this side of the river. There's a town called Broos. We can get there before dark.'

–

They tied Vilkas over the back of the spare mount and Jack pulled him along at a fast trot. The old Balt had not regained his senses and he bounced and swung like a slaughtered stag as they rode along. They reached the town of Broos after a few hours, the sun dipping low and night descending. Hawker's seasoned eye noticed houses and a church had been recently built, the wood still fresh and bright. Others lay in ruins.

'The Turks burned this place seven years ago,' said Maria, noticing Hawker's interest. 'A great army under Sultan Mehmed pushed through. Many thousands. But the Hungarians destroyed them a few miles east of here. They've not been back since.'

'Not yet, anyway,' added Hawker, still melancholy over the earlier melee and the fact that their new comrade with a vital secret was a hopeless sot.

They found a small inn, the Saxon keeper grateful for their custom in these hard times, and the company took their ease. Jacob and Jack carried Vilkas to the stables so that he could be attended to. Tokár found no wounds on him and after a few minutes the man was conscious again, confused as to his surroundings. He looked ancient – probably far older than he truly was for the hardness of his life. His filthy long hair hung lankly on his skull, the skin of his face was sallow, and a drooping, grey moustache still held traces of red and blond bespeaking of his youth. The old gypsy spoke with him softly in broken German and soon Vilkas began to focus enough to ask for wine.

'Get your man to ask about the cave!' demanded Faldi, leaning in. 'If he doesn't know then we have no need of extra baggage like him.'

Maria shushed him angrily. 'He needs food. And a little more time. He will remember.'

Hawker rubbed his palm across his forehead. The day's trials had tired him. 'He needs a drink. I've good experience of men like him. You don't deny them the grape or grain. If you do, they'll sicken more and likely die. You give just enough to keep them going.'

Maria pursed her lips and considered that. 'Very well. I'll have Tokár fetch some from the innkeeper.'

'My lord Ellingham and I will go make sure the wine is drinkable,' said Dieudonné sarcastically, tugging at Ellingham's elbow.

Hawker ordered Jacob to take some food and then keep watch. There had been no signs of their being followed on the journey across the flat, open valley, but vengeance was a strong driver of men. He would take no chances.

By the time they had all taken refreshment, the hour growing late, Vilkas had recovered enough to make himself understood. The hall of the inn was deserted of any other guests and Hawker and Maria listened intently to Tokár's gentle questioning of the Balt. He was from the Lithuanian lands, had drifted south through Poland during the wars, and found employ under Vlad Dracula. Tokár said he had served with Vilkas years before and Hawker found it difficult to square the gypsy's recollections of a brutal *armaşi* henchman with the wreck of a man who slouched before them.

When Vlad had been defeated, ten years ago, Vilkas had drifted west, working first as a skinner and tanner where he put his torture skills to use on animal hides. Later he repaired shoes, ending up in Deva with nothing to his name but a bag of knives, catgut, needles, and a hammer.

Tokár gave Vilkas another shake of the shoulders when his question went unanswered. Faldi leaned in and dangled a wine flask in front of him. Vilkas sat up and blinked rapidly. Then he began to talk.

Tokár burst into a grin. 'He says he remembers the cave! Says he will serve the master again if it is true that he yet lives.'

Ellingham stood back and folded his arms. 'He would no doubt say anything we wanted if a drink was at the end of it.'

'In vino veritas, son of Richard,' said Maria softly. 'We have no choice but to believe him.'

Vilkas snatched the flask from Faldi and gulped the red wine until Faldi pulled it away. The Balt wiped his mouth, head lolling, and then focused his wayward orbs on Maria. 'Tokár says you are the Dragon's daughter. I will serve you.'

Maria answered him in the same Saxon dialect of Ultra Silvam. 'Take us to the prince and you will be handsomely rewarded. I swear this.'

Hawker gently tugged Ellingham away from the table and walked him to another in the tap room. Dieudonné followed. Hawker sat on a bench and retrieved his wooden cup of wine, still half full. 'Sit, my lords,' he said, voice deep with weariness.

Ellingham was quiet but Dieudonné seemed jovial for the adventure of it all. 'Well, Sir John, be of good cheer. We have found our truffle pig. And if his nose is as good as the old gypsy says, he will lead us to our prize.'

Hawker wrapped his thick fingers around his cup and leaned forward. 'Only if he stays alive long enough to do so. It will be no easy task.'

A loud thump sounded beyond followed by an exclamation from Maria and a guffaw from Bartolo Faldi. Vilkas the Balt had slipped under the trestle table flat onto the floorboards.

Part III

LADY AND LORD

12

They were two-thirds the way to Hermannstadt – or so Maria told them – once they had made a halt for the day. They had ridden through the wide, meandering valley of the Mureş, flanked by mountains on either side. The landscape was umber, copper and grey in the grip of Father Winter, the only green remaining was in the scattered forests of pine at the higher reaches of the hills. The wind that blew from the north, sharpened with biting cold from its passage down the high mountains, enveloped them as they rode, the chill penetrating through cloak, armour and doublet.

Maria and Faldi, side by side, reined in, and Hawker trotted up to them. Faldi's armour had begun to blossom with rust, having no one with him to polish it. But he still looked the part of a *condottiere* in his burgundy wool cape and gilt chain and brooch. Maria was dressed as an Amazon, as she had been since they had left Temesvár. Under her mulberry red cloak she wore a black leather breastplate and back, moulded to the contours of her youthful figure. Her gown discarded and packed away, she now wore baggy woollen hose and tall black boots, sitting astride her horse as a man would. The vulgarity of it she either did not realise or did not care about.

'We have but one spare mount,' said Hawker, tugging tightly at his reins. 'We should not push our horses further. Where is this place you said we might find shelter?'

Maria pointed to a fork in the road up ahead. 'There is a village just beyond sight, off to the right.'

Hawker smiled. 'And you know this. Without a map?'

She returned his grin. 'I do. I was born in these parts. In Hunedoara.'

Ellingham had followed in Hawker's wake. 'Why did we not make for Hunedoara, then? Surely, we would have found a welcome reception there if it was your home.'

The smile slowly evaporated from her face, replaced by a wistful twist of her lips. 'Yes, it is the domain of the Hunyadis still. I was born in the great fortress, built by my grandfather. But I have not been there in many years nor had cause to. Besides, it lies south of Deva. We are many miles past it now, much further east. This place will suffice.'

Hawker nodded slowly. More mystery to fuel the fire. It had long been clear to him that she concealed much of her past, but if that meant enemies lurked in their path then that was something he wanted to know. He knew she was right about a village though. He could smell the smoke of wood fires already. 'Then lead us there, my lady,' he said, flicking his reins and turning back to the rear of the column where Jacob and Jack rode. 'I, for one, could use a warm meal.'

It was hardly a village; Hawker thought it generous even to call it a hamlet. It was two houses and a long barn and animal pen. The stockade held half a dozen horses and the larger of the two reed-thatched houses belched a comforting pillar of smoke through the roof hole. It looked to be a small hostelry run by some enterprising peasant who took advantage of its situation near the crossroad. Maria dismounted and beckoned the party to do the same.

'Wait while I go inside and see what we might procure!' She beckoned Tokár to join her. The old gypsy tied off his donkey's lead to a fence and followed her inside.

Hawker watched as the men assembled and led their horses to the stockade and hitching rail. Old Vilkas stood looking gormless, eyes casting about, no doubt looking for where he might find a wine flask. His hands shook. The two Serbians looked ill at ease, and had done so since they had joined the company two days before. Hawker could spot desperate men a mile away and these two were clearly on the run from something. Still, they had proved their worth at Deva in the fight at the meadows. The

Serbians talked only with each other and with Maria when she addressed them. He suspected they knew only the Slavic tongue and a few words of Hungarian. He once thought he had heard the taller of the two utter a Turkish word. Still, he thought, they could just be desperate for coin, outcasts from wherever they had come from. Even so, he had already told Jacob to keep a sharp eye upon them.

Maria quickly emerged from the house and approached the company.

'We may stay the night, sleeping near the hearth. The man and his wife are glad for the custom. They oversee this place for the Saxon owner, some merchant of Melnbach. But they are Wallachian and not Saxons so you should expect warm hospitality. They will stable the horses for us, too.' Her eyes moved to each one of them and then she turned to Hawker. 'Sir John, make sure your men speak nothing of our true quest. We are here to raise a company for the king, to fight in the west. That is all.'

'And what did you tell them your station was in all this?' asked Hawker.

'That I am a Hunyadi cousin and you are my bodyguard of the road. I am joining family in Sibiu.'

'And they do not think it suspicious that you are an unmarried woman in the company of soldiers?'

She didn't hesitate in her reply. 'What makes you think that? Here is my husband whom I have wed in Venice.' And she gestured to Ellingham.

Ellingham's eyebrows rose almost to his hairline. Before he could speak she had looped her arm in his and begun walking towards the house. 'Come, husband. It will be an amusing deception.'

Bartolo Faldi looked at Hawker and shrugged. 'The donna commands. We obey. I'm used to this now.'

Dieudonné tugged at this cloak and hunched his shoulders. 'She is reckless.' The French poured from his throat in a low growl of displeasure.

Hawker barked a short, sharp laugh. 'From the man who nearly got us all killed in Venice.'

'And who saved your life there.' Dieudonné shot back. 'More than once.'

'My lords,' said Faldi, calming the waters, 'it matters not in a place such as this. The donna knows what she is doing and I trust her.'

Dieudonné glared, turning his ire to the Milanese. 'And what is your role in this grand deception, sir? You are much too accommodating to my mind. And too familiar with the lady. And you haven't convinced me of how your paths crossed.'

Faldi shook his head, aggrieved. 'My French – as you can hear – is poor. But if you are questioning my loyalty then I take that as an affront. I have been hired just like you and, like you, she found me by chance. No more and no less. I serve her so long as she pays.'

Dieudonné gave a thin smile laced with derision. 'And she has all those little rubies, too, doesn't she? Well, my friends, time to get warm and to eat!' He turned to his horse to retrieve his clothes roll.

Hawker gave Faldi an unsympathetic look. He was loath to admit it, but he wasn't completely convinced of the man's blissful ignorance either. His eye caught Jack, the dutiful squire, bearing his leather portmanteau roll into the house and, without a further remark, he followed the lad into the hostelry.

They were, for the moment, the only guests. Maria was received with great respect and a large degree of fawning, as was Ellingham. She was ushered up a creaking, black lacquered staircase to the bedchamber while the rest of them found space in what served as the great hall. The blazing hearth was some consolation for the bone aches of the day's ride. Jack helped Hawker out of his armour, neatly piling it in a corner in the order it would have to be donned again. Hawker buckled on his belt and slung his *cinquedea* dagger while making sure he saw where his sword lay propped.

Jacob grinned and nodded to Hawker, who winked.

'Come lad,' said Jacob to Jack. 'I'll play squire to you.' He set about unbuckling Jack's harness.

Jack sighed audibly as the breastplate and back came off. 'God's nails, I feel I could fly away now!' He straightened up and stretched, laces popping on his padded doublet.

The diminutive Wallachian innkeeper gestured for them to be seated at table and he soon had brought in bread, cheese and beer followed by his wife – tall and thin as a birch – balancing wooden bowls and spoons in her hands. She set about ladling some dark stew from an iron pot that hung from a hook on the roasting spit over the fire.

Ellingham sat on a bench, looking sheepish because of the deception that Maria had thrust upon him. He said nothing but reached for a cup of beer and then spent more than a moment just peering into its depths before putting it to his lips.

After a few minutes, Maria reappeared, wearing her brocade gown which Hawker couldn't help but notice was stained with road mud along the hem. As she descended the stairs, Faldi stood to meet her and was quickly followed by the others. Hawker grudgingly rose to his feet. He was fast tiring of treating Maria Hunyadi – or Maria Drăculeşti – like some queen. He noticed that even Ellingham looked uneasy, trying to avoid his gaze.

She bowed her head in recognition of their courtesy. 'Gentles, please do not interrupt your repast. We have ridden long this day.'

The innkeeper bowed to her and said something.

'He is asking,' said Maria, 'whether the men-at-arms are breaking bread with the knights or should they be fed elsewhere.' She made a point of looking at Hawker as she translated.

Hawker didn't hesitate or look to Ellingham. 'This company eats together, high and low.' And he sat down. It would be foolish to divide themselves by station on such a risky venture and when their numbers were still so dangerously small.

'Very well,' said Maria, nodding, and she spoke to the innkeeper in his tongue. He bowed again and then rushed to bring her a chair to sit at the head of the rough-hewn oaken table. Faldi threw a sour glance at Hawker, waited until Maria had seated herself gently, and then took his seat again.

'Our knights are generous. Gentles all. More the benefit to the men-at-arms, yes?' She then lifted her head and called down the table in Slavic to where the Rascians sat.

The one called Pedja smiled and nodded but his eyes did not follow, thought Hawker. His companion, equally rugged and hale in appearance, after a quick cryptic glance to his comrade, looked into his bowl and began shovelling in stew like a pig at a trough. The Serbs were still a puzzle, but he was now bone-tired and eager to pull more intelligence from their secretive taskmaster. 'My lady, I shall continue to speak in French for I think that the safest tongue for us here. I ask for Ser Bartolo's indulgence.'

Faldi scowled but gave a nod of assent. Maria smiled at Hawker.

'Speak your mind, Sir John.'

'Very well. You know your father's history in these parts. I worry about the reception we will receive in the Saxon towns. Both before and *after* we find who we are looking for.'

'Vlad was prince of Wallachia, ruler of the duchies of Amlaş and Făgăraş, which lie in the midst of the German burgs. And as a captain of the king of Hungary, he had every right to enforce royal law in Ultra Silvam.'

She had dismissed his concern as if he was a child, but he wasn't yet finished.

'Which he did rather too well. What do you think the good burghers of Hermannstadt and Kronstadt will think about your quest to restore your father? *Their* fathers remember the hundreds of townsfolk he impaled outside their towns. Left to rot on tall stakes, food for the crows. A dozen villages razed and every man, woman and child killed.'

Ellingham leaned back and Jacob's spoon froze in his hand even as it touched his lips.

A cloud fell across her face as she listened. She held up a hand towards Hawker. '*Their* fathers rebelled against the prince of

Wallachia,' she said, her voice dripping venom. 'They sought to overthrow him and put others on his throne. To interfere in the affairs of his land – *Tara Românească*. Wallachia is a foreign name given by others.'

Hawker nodded. 'Yes, others. It is the Saxons who supported Vlad the Monk against your father, isn't it? The same Vlad who rules now.' He could see the colour rise up her long neck, suffusing her pale face.

'Do not lecture me on the history of my land. The Saxons learned their lesson and Vlad Dracula showed great mercy when he resumed his throne. They flocked to his standard for the last campaign. He restored all their privileges. Kronstadt begged King Matthias to bring him back as prince! The Monk only rules now because he hides my father, crushing his memory across the land.'

Hawker shook his head slowly. 'You say you know the history, but you don't even remember your father. How could you?'

Maria slammed her palm on the table, rattling the crockery. 'Do not seek to tell me my life! I remember him and he will remember me! I was there when he assembled his host nine years ago at Torda. His quest to rid the kingdom of Basarab – that slave who ruled Wallachia for the sultan. I was sixteen. And all of Ultra Silvam rallied to his cause. They will again!'

Hawker sipped his beer and put the wooden tankard down. 'But it is Vlad the Monk who has an army now. Where is yours?'

A slow smile spread across her face which now glowed red like summer cherries. 'Ah, Sir John, you seek to draw me out, to make mockery. To rile me.' She waggled a finger. 'I know you mean well though. And I tell you, we will find our army once the Dragon standard is raised.'

Dieudonné jutted his chin forward. 'To my mind it makes little sense to win over enemies through mercy. It just encourages them further. Your father, my lady, was right to use a heavy hand. It is a universal language, one that everyone understands. And it only has to be spoken once.'

Maria appeared to ignore the Burgundian's words of support. She turned back to Hawker. 'I do not live in some fantasy of my own mind. I know there are Romans, Hungarians and even Saxons who will follow Dracula. Because he will free them from the yoke of the Ottomans.'

Hawker nodded. 'God willing, my lady. But the immediate question for us is where will we go when your father is delivered into our hands? Do we make for Buda? Will he be received by King Matthias? Do we hide out here in the Saxon lands while we wait? Because if you mean to drive south for Târgovişte and seize the throne you will need more men than what you see here.'

He could tell she was biting the inside of her lip while he spoke.

Faldi spoke up in his halting French. 'You are *condottiere*, Falco! One does not question their paymaster. It is for her to decide.'

Ellingham lifted his face up from his cup. 'I think, Sir John, that it was you who deferred to me the decision of undertaking this journey. And I made that decision. It is to serve this honourable lady in her quest to free her father. To question that now would be to dishonour all of us.'

Hawker sat back on his bench at the words, his crow's feet creasing deeper. His hands gripped the edge of the table. He had not expected Sir Giles to come to her blind defence, not after even he had raised his own concerns back in Temesvár. He held his tongue for a few moments even as he could feel the eyes of the company settling upon him. A collective held breath hung over the table.

Hawker then leaned forward, his eyes upon the young knight. 'Sir Giles, it is no dishonour to talk of strategy. Or tactics. Are you content to rush headlong into the unknown? Have you forgotten that it was Maria who tasked *me* with planning this assault?'

Maria raised a hand. 'I tasked *both* of you in this quest! As knights and men of battle. Sir John is correct and so are you, Sir Giles. But I will decide what is to be done after my father is freed. I alone.'

Hawker said nothing but moved to wrap his hand around his cup and then raise it to his lips. His ears began to burn with the realisation that the fabric of their company was beginning to rend, a curtain torn.

–

The company bedded down for the first sleep. Precedence mattered as they took their places around the burning hearth: Hawker closest to the fire, Faldi opposite, and then Dieudonné, Jacob and Jack. Pedja and Orkan sulked further back upon the large flagstones, wrapped in their cloaks and lying upon sheepskins provided by the hosteller. The gypsy, Tokár, was nowhere to be seen. Whether any of them would rise to take refreshment at midnight would depend upon how cold the chamber would be.

Upstairs, Maria Hunyadi and Sir Giles Ellingham eyed each other from opposite sides of the rough-stained elm bedstead.

'You stood up to the old war dog,' said Maria. 'It was your right to do so. You are the son of a king, not he.'

Ellingham folded his arms and looked down to the bed. 'I will sleep upon the floor.' He was desperate for her but he knew full well the danger that would pose for both of them.

She laughed. 'Did you think it would be otherwise?'

He smiled, tension breaking. 'One can hope.'

Maria looked at him thoughtfully. He felt awkward as soon as the words had left his mouth. But only days earlier she had played coy with him, confusing him against his better nature. He was her *condottiere*, her captain. Paid to serve her, not to become her lover. Already he was ashamed of how he had spoken to Hawker. But something had risen up in him, the desire to stand his own ground. Hawker had stepped back from them all upon the ship at Venice, giving over to *him* the destiny of the company. A faintly ridiculous company at that, broken men and outlaws all. Maria's offer seemed a chance at least. A chance to find their fortune again and maybe, further along, to aid the cause of the White Rose.

'I propose we divide the territory.' She gestured towards the coverlet. 'We shall both remained clothed. You on one side and me on the other. I will go under the blankets and you will remain above – wrapped in your cloak.'

Ellingham held himself tighter. 'I am not sure, my lady, that will satisfy—'

'Satisfy Hawker? And the others? They will already assume the worst. They did so the moment we ascended together.'

Ellingham stuttered, awareness of the trap he had fallen into just settling upon him. 'It was all a ruse… as you said. To remain seemly for the benefit of the hosts… an unwed woman travelling without chaperone.'

She nodded. 'It is no more and no less.' She pulled off her head scarf and set it upon the nightstand.

'Why this ruse now? In Temesvár you saw no need to play husband and wife.'

'We are now in my old lands, my home. And we will be watched more from this time onwards.'

He admired her cleverness. And she was beautiful, he thought, watching her let down her raven tresses and flouncing them about her shoulders. 'You want the others to think we are lovers now, don't you?'

She gave a small shrug and pulled the coverlet and woollen blankets back. 'It may give you more command over them. Hawker, too.' She sat and began to pull off her riding boots, a jarring contrast to the brocade gown and heavy chemise she wore. It was an obvious example of the strange, conflicted creature that she was. A woman who chose combat to the dance, and foreign adventures instead of the safe seclusion of the Hunyadi court.

'We two are equals, Giles. Of the royal bone and blood. It is time for you to lead with me. At my side.' She leaned over and pulled the coverlet from the bottom of the bedstead. 'Look! They have given us some hot coals in a copper pan to warm our feet.'

Ellingham sat upon the floor and pulled off his own boots, hips aching from the day's ride. 'You forget. I am on top of the bed, not in it.'

'You'll still feel the benefit, and besides, there are some sheep-skins to do service as a blanket.' She slipped into the covers and pulled them up over herself, keeping close to the edge of a bed that Ellingham thought much too narrow for two. He got up, wrapped his cloak tighter about himself, snatched up a gamey-smelling sheepskin, and then lay down upon the bed. His head sank into the pillow and he flapped the sheep's wool over himself. She was right. He could still feel the heat of the copper pan. And he could smell her next to him, the scent of rosemary upon her hair.

'Snuff the candle,' she ordered, staring up at the ceiling.

He leaned over to the table and pinched the wick. Weak silver moonlight cast a faint glow as it penetrated the narrow window at the end of the bedchamber. He could still just make out the contours of her face as she lay.

For a few minutes nothing was said and the silence of the chamber became notable, a humming of the blood coursing through his own head.

'Why have you not married?' he asked quietly.

She didn't even hesitate with a reply. 'Because it has not suited me thus far.'

'Even though you court attention and risk by your conduct? You are a noblewoman among mercenaries. The only woman on a galley of cutthroat Dalmatians. An adventurer who negotiates with dukes, buys weapons and armour, and commands a secret army of gypsy peasants.'

This time, she did not answer him immediately. It seemed an age before she did, and Ellingham heard every creak of the roof over their heads while he waited.

'And do you think if I had a husband he would let me do any of those things?'

The answer was obvious, and he lapsed into silence.

'Would a husband want me to find my father and release him? To set Dracula upon his throne again? An act that would diminish his hold over me as his wife and chattel? What man would tolerate that?' She tittered and turned her head towards him. He could see the glow of her eyes even in near-darkness. 'No, I shall remain my own master for as long as God allows it.'

He swallowed hard. 'You are a wonderment to me. I thought so from the moment I saw you in the candlelight of the church at San Silvestro. An age ago, it seems.'

'A wonderment, you say? You do not think me low and wanton? A whore? A fallen virgin on travels without her abbess in tow?'

In truth, Ellingham did not know what to make of her. For he had never met a woman like her. 'I do not think any of those things, my lady. And I would never seek to tame you or dampen your fire. That you must believe.'

Silence descended again, Ellingham was not sure what to say nor did he know if the conversation was at an end. Finally, she spoke again, her voice quiet.

'How does one bear the shame? Of being a bastard. That is what I had to decide. My father was never married to my mother. I am sure that Hawker told you as much.'

'He told me what Duke Kinizsi called you back in Temesvár. He didn't say he believed it though.'

'It is true. Most of it anyway.'

'Yet you are acknowledged by King Matthias... and your father.'

He thought he could almost feel her frame sink a little into the mattress, a small, almost inaudible sigh emanating from her lips.

'And you... When did you learn who your father was?'

'I think I always knew I was a bastard even though I did not know for certain until... until Hawker told me. My whole life I have been an Ellingham, believed I was an Ellingham. *Lived* as an Ellingham. But I was a cuckoo in the nest all along.'

'You are the son of Richard Plantagenet. The king of England. I am the daughter of Prince Vlad, Dracula, son of Vlad Dracul, rightful ruler of Wallachia and Duke of Făgăraș and Amlaș. Those things can never be taken away from either of us.'

He knew she believed what she was saying. But still, it rang of false bravado in a raging storm. He knew full well his own bloodline was little more than a target upon his chest, enemies abounding. For the moment, at least. He prayed that it would not be the case for her too but, from all she had told them, Dracula had, in his time, made many enemies.

'Maria... Will your father remember you? Accept you? Tell me.'

He heard her head rustle on the pillow as she turned to him again. 'I have to believe that. It is all I have.'

'Then I will pray it is so, my lady.'

Ellingham heard the floorboards outside their door creak, then silence. He pushed himself up on his elbows and began to reach for his sword, which lay alongside the bed. Suddenly, he felt her hand upon his arm.

'Fear not,' she whispered. 'It is only Tokár, keeping watch. You must remember, Giles, that we have friends in the shadows, too. You will see.'

Ellingham relaxed and sank back down, pulling the sheepskin over himself. Friends in the shadows. Enemies in the shadows. He could never admit it, but Hawker's reticence about their journey now seemed the wisdom of an old war dog and not the nervous fears of some old man. But they had come too far now to go back with nothing. He tried to clear his mind of doubt and shut his eyes, listening to the slow, steady breathing of the mysterious alluring creature who lay next to him. Finally, exhausted by the exertions of the saddle as much as by worry, he drifted off into a fitful sleep.

13

They took to the road the next morning, rested, but a few still nursed doubts deep in their breasts, Hawker among them. It was an ill omen that Sir Giles had decided to play husband to their patron, an act that overnight had drawn an invisible barrier between him and the rest of them. It didn't make sense to Hawker that Maria required the mantle of a respectful wife when she hadn't previously and, more to the point, when she'd swung a sword as gustily as any of them. It had been clear to him for weeks that Maria Hunyadi had no qualms about drawing blood.

The weather, grey and low like a vast, dirty coverlet, held firm as they made their way eastwards. Hawker brought up the rear of the column with Jacob, Jack riding just ahead. In the van rode Maria with Ellingham and Faldi on either side. The further they rode the hillier the terrain became. Flanked on their right by the great range of the Carpathians, the tallest peaks crowned in snow, they followed the rutted road through the valley.

Off to either side they would pass fortified hamlets and small villages built upon hillocks and guarded by wooden palisades twenty feet high all around. Within, clusters of houses sheltered around squat, square church towers and Hawker felt uneasy at the picture it painted: villages brimming with fear and distrust, nervously shielding from the threat of rapine and pillage. A land whose bounty invited invaders from all sides, and now it was the Ottoman sultan who coveted it.

'You have said little this morning, Sir John. What are you thinking?'

Hawker looked over to Jacob and threw him a pensive smile. 'I was reflecting upon the beauty of this place. And also why I have the feeling that its denizens reach out one hand with the clasp of friendship while the other conceals a dagger.'

Jacob nodded. 'Christ alone knows, we're well on our way to Cathay now. And leagues further from anywhere either of us have travelled before. That is always a good reason to be cautious. But I'd feel better if we had a hundred with us, not eight men and a woman who thinks she is a queen.'

Hawker noticed for the first time how drawn Jacob's face appeared. Jacob was younger than him, that he knew, but he had also been through much in the last weeks, all of it far from the normal soldiering they both were used to. More to the point, a certain sullenness had entered him since the debacle at Venice and his battering at the hands of Maria's *stradiotti*. Or perhaps it was, as in himself, a certain world-weariness rearing its head.

'At least you will understand the language. You know well enough the German tongue they speak hereabouts.'

'It is not Flemish, but it will suffice,' Jacob mumbled.

'What do you make of the Slavs?' Hawker asked, jutting his chin forward to indicate where they rode up front, side by side.

Jacob shook his head slowly. 'Probably bandits themselves. Threw in their lot with us just for the ready coin. I've been keeping an eye on them. I'm not worried yet – unless they get a better offer from someone else.'

Hawker smiled again. 'That is encouraging.'

'But I am uneasy about Sir Giles. You have appointed him our captain and he in turn is being led by his nose... or his cock.'

Hawker frowned. 'Captain?'

'At Venice. You told him he was now the captain of the company. That it was his decision to go east or back to the west.'

Hawker craned his neck upwards and squinted. 'Aye, well... it was more I gave him the choice of *direction*. Not command. At least that is how I see it.'

'Very well, my lord.' Jacob's voice carried the dullness of a lump of lead when dropped on a goldsmith's bench. 'But how does *he* see it? Or the Hungarian... Wallachian... whatever she is. Sir Giles has a stout heart, I will give him that, but he is no commander. Not yet. And that Milanese jester who worships her? What does it say about a knight who lost his own squadron?'

Hawker didn't reply. His heart had been sick over the past weeks and he knew he had been content to drift with the current they found themselves in. And as for losing a squadron, had not he lost the same at Bosworth? Jacob's words stung, but the Fleming was right and he knew it. After an awkward silence, Hawker spoke up.

'*She* understands. And she knows she cannot do without me… or you. Or even our mad Burgundian.'

Jacob managed something between a cough and a weak laugh. 'Yes, they will turn to the grandsires when the time comes! May God make it so.'

They made a few halts in the course of the morning and early afternoon to take food and drink and to rest and water the horses. Hawker watched Maria speaking with Tokár and Vilkas. The old gypsy then had a few words with the sullen Balt and offloaded some of the donkey's satchels onto his own mount and then took off alone, riding ahead. Maria then circled around to the rear and trotted up to Hawker.

'If we press on, we can make Hermannstadt by nightfall. I have sent Tokár ahead to make preparations.'

'Preparations for what?' said Hawker, leaning forward on his pommel.

Maria looked confused a moment and then smiled. 'Why, a hostelry of course. You would prefer a bed tonight rather than a haystack, I presume.'

'I'm pleased the gold is holding out, my lady,' replied Hawker. 'I hope there will be enough left to pay us, too, when the time comes. And I trust we won't need what Tokár has just carried off with him.'

She laughed, a full-throated bark that would have rivalled a grizzled veteran of the Calais garrison. 'Consider it an incentive to quicken our progress, Sir John! The horses will stand the pace! Plenty of meat and drink when we reach the Saxons!'

Hawker's jaw clenched a little. 'We are but your servants, my lady.'

She reached out and touched his vambrace, giving it a little shake of insistence. 'Stand by me and we will honour our promise to the White Rose you so fondly speak of.' She gathered up her reins, gave her mount a kick, and trotted back to the head of the column where Ellingham and Faldi had been watching the exchange. Bartolo Faldi gave a loud whistle, waving his shining arm like the blade of a windmill, and they started down the road once again. The Rascians followed after, then Dieudonné by himself, with Jack behind him towing the donkey and Vilkas, who looked half-asleep. Jacob pushed back the brim of his sallet helm and shot Hawker a look of pure weariness of heart.

Hawker adjusted his weight in the saddle, snapped his reins, and the horse responded with a reluctant drooping of the neck and a slow walk forward. 'At least we're not starving yet,' he said as he moved off. Jacob, unable to suppress a grin, swore an oath in Flemish and followed the knight down the rutted, mud-spattered track.

The hours passed, light receding fast given the low ceiling of dirty-white cloud, and Maria made a good pace as was her wont. The company went at a trot when the road was uneven and in those places where it was still firm and wide, the Hungarian would put her spurs in and force them all to canter for a time. The donkey brayed loudly at every tug of the halter and it was all Jack could do to keep the beast moving with the rest of them while keeping Vilkas in the saddle.

His banter with Jacob aside, Hawker had been running through his mind potential strategies for storming the Castle Argeş. He liked none of the options. They did not have the numbers for a frontal attack, a siege was out of the question, and the supposed cave at the base of the castle could still be nothing more than a wives' tale despite Tokár's and the Balt's insistence that it was there. Even if it was there, who was to say it had not collapsed into rubble over the past twenty-five years?

The lamps had been lighted by the time they arrived at the gates of Hermannstadt. Maria cajoled and charmed her way past the gate tower captain despite the lateness of the hour. Hawker, still at the rear, his horse stamping on the planks of the bridge, supposed she was telling him that she was a noblewoman with her escort, all the way from Buda. After a brief exchange, the captain bowed to her and waved them through.

Hawker saw that Hermannstadt was the same as the smaller villages they had passed: surrounded by sharpened palisades. But it was much larger. The guards, all in velvet brigantines and barbute helms, polearms poised, eyed them intently as they rode past. Hawker looked down at them and raised a gloved hand to his helm in salute. Once inside the deep stone gate, he spied a great church spire and nearby a high square tower with an onion-domed roof. Whitewashed houses clustered closely together like sheep in a storm.

Maria led the way, obviously knowing where she was going. They rode into the centre market square having passed through the walls and towers of the inner fortifications. Two iron braziers on the cobblestones cast flickering light onto the walls of the houses that lined the square. Maria led them down a side street and to an inn at the sign of the White Hart. They all dismounted and were soon met by an innkeeper and his grooms bearing torches.

'We've been expecting you!' bellowed the man in German. 'Your Romany servant was most insistent we stand ready for you tonight. But I am surprised the guard let you through once darkness fell.' Hawker remembered enough of the tongue from his days of fighting the Swiss alongside the Bavarians, though here it was of a strange lilt, some words different.

Maria handed her reins to a groom as she eyed the innkeeper with studied hauteur. 'We shall need the room above the stable for my men-at-arms. These gentle knights here will take lodging inside your house with me.'

Jacob shot Hawker a look of annoyance and slowly shook his head. 'Jack Perry!' he called. 'Bring along that braying beast and your horse that we may put them to bed.'

Hawker smiled and nodded at the boy and Jack yanked the halter and followed Jacob, his armour clanking. He turned to Maria and Ellingham. 'You know this place then?'

Maria nodded. 'I have stayed here before. It is a good house for us to take our rest in. And to make our plans.'

'And is your ruse still in play, my lady?' he asked, nodding towards Ellingham.

'It eases our way,' said Ellingham before Maria could reply. 'Fewer questions for us all.'

'Sir Giles is right,' Maria said. 'We two serve as the contracting party and—'

'And the rest of us are your retainers,' added Hawker, smiling.

Bartolo Faldi looked uncomfortable, his sweaty face glowing in the torchlight. He turned and untied his baggage from his horse's cruppers.

'It is for the sake of appearance, Sir John,' said Maria soothingly. 'Surely that is what is best for us all, no?'

'We are in your employ, my lady. But all ruses eventually come to an end. And one has to remember not to become entangled in the web that one weaves.'

Dieudonné let out a cynical chuckle from where he stood and Maria sent him a poisonous glance in return.

'Come, Sir John,' said Ellingham. 'We are all road-weary and tempers grow frayed. Let us go in and take refreshment while we may.'

'Aye, you are right.' Hawker clapped Ellingham lightly on his shoulder. 'And I could eat my horse just as soon as stable it. Let's go inside.'

–

Hawker slept well thanks to the wool-stuffed mattress and heavy coverlet of his bed. The innkeeper had bowed and scraped to

Maria – and to Ellingham – and given them the best chamber in the house as he proclaimed. The inn was all dark wood, heavy carved beams, and leaded windows filled with coloured glass. It was a comforting place and Hawker had drifted off easily, the worries of his road reverie momentarily forgotten.

In the morning, the company convened in the great hall in front of the roaring, crackling hearth. Although Jacob and Jack had slept above the stables, they both looked the better for it and told Hawker that an iron brazier filled with red-hot coals had kept the night chill at bay. The trestle groaned under the weight of bread, cheese and sausage that the innkeeper had brought to them along with pewter pots of weak beer. Tokár – now the warder of Vilkas – had rationed him wine the night before, admonishing the Balt not to search for more. Vilkas picked at his food, eyes scanning the table for drink instead. The Rascians tucked in with the gusto of the starving, nodding and smiling to Hawker and the others. They were an uncomplaining pair, almost strangely vacant, thought Hawker. Still, want drove men to undertake most anything and here these two had found a generous billet for the time being.

Maria, as usual, held her court as if she ruled a kingdom.

'Today, we rest,' she said, in French. 'For this will be the last place of comfort for us all for some time to come. I will send Tokár out today to plan our next halt where the mountains begin. And to meet our friends.'

Hawker leaned over to Jack, seated on the bench at his side, and translated quietly. No one did any such thing for the Rascians however and they merely watched the woman speak, brows crumpling occasionally in consternation.

'My lady,' interrupted Hawker. 'Perhaps you might enlighten the Rascians of your words.'

Maria froze for a second but she then smiled and addressed them in Slavic. The one named Pedja nodded as she related her intentions; his comrade, the black-moustachioed and rugged Turkish deserter, remained as unreadable as ever. He watched

Maria with an almost detached look on his face. Whether he was a dullard or a man who just didn't care, Hawker could not tell.

'Do not wander far in the town,' Maria warned, in French and then translating again. 'Saxons are a distrustful lot at the best of times. We are here only to resupply and to take rest, as I have said.'

'And do you wish to recruit more men?' asked Hawker, reaching for a loaf. 'We are still lean in numbers for the enterprise you have planned... despite your friends to come.'

She looked at Ellingham first and then Hawker. 'No,' she said. 'I do not. They are not necessary, as I have told you. From this point forward we need allies who are to be trusted. You will meet them tomorrow, God willing, at our next stop to the south. Before the Pass of the Red Tower.'

Hawker nodded, looking to Ellingham. Ellingham glanced away. 'Well, my lady, I have need of a few particular weapons and this town would seem the best place to obtain them. Do you know of an armourer or ironmonger nearby?'

She tilted her head slightly. '*More* weapons? I thought you now had the weapons of your choice.'

'If I am to be your strategist then you will indulge me in what I think this company needs. Can you grant me that?'

Jacob's right eyebrow raised, no doubt curious as to what he had in mind.

'I will find such a place for you, Sir John,' said Maria. 'Be at ease.'

'That all sounds very mysterious,' said Dieudonné at the far end of the trestle, stroking his chin archly. 'What wheels are turning in your clockwork, then?'

Hawker gave him an indulgent smile in return but said nothing.

'Sir John has been a captain longer than even me,' said Faldi. 'I trust his judgement as to what he thinks we need.' He grinned wider. 'Can you tell us, Sir John?'

Hawker leaned back and broke the loaf of bread in half. 'In good time, Ser Bartolo. And only if I can find what I seek.'

'Fair enough,' said Faldi, his voice falling a little.

A quiet descended and they set to, eating the food laid out for them. Hawker watched Dieudonné watching Ellingham. The Burgundian seemed petulant of late, as if he was jealous of Ellingham's involvement with Maria. He knew that Ellingham and Dieudonné had become firm friends since the summer and it was clear that a distance of some sort had now set in between them. Bound to happen, thought Hawker, with a woman as their ultimate captain and employer. As for Ellingham, Hawker wasn't sure that the free rein he gave – or disinterest, as Jacob considered it – had had the desired effect on the young Plantagenet. He had given Ellingham the choice of their future and the youth had made it. But Hawker now realised he had perhaps expected too much of someone so young and lacking in experience of the world of men, politics, and battle. Worse, Ellingham seemed to have changed his personal counsel: from him to Maria. Even more now since this ruse of marriage Maria played upon them all.

While Jacob playfully teased Jack and Ellingham and Faldi spoke quietly with Maria, the Rascians remained watchful, and Dieudonné picked apart his black rye bread, seemingly in another sulk. Hawker heard raised voices at the front and a moment later the innkeeper came in, red-faced and breathless. He bowed towards Maria and Ellingham and Hawker caught the gist of his words: the council demanded their presence at once.

The company looked to one another and Maria slowly rose, Ellingham and Faldi following her lead.

'This is becoming rather predictable,' growled Hawker.

Maria showed no alarm, her face a mask of studied calm. 'Sir Giles and Sir John shall accompany me. You too, Ser Bartolo. I shall need all my knights around me.' She looked over to the Saxon. 'Is there an armed escort waiting?'

The innkeeper nodded.

'Very well. Let us make ready.'

'And I'll finish my breakfast,' mumbled Dieudonné, a look of bitterness on his long, vulpine face.

Jack helped Hawker strap on his breastplate over his quilted doublet, cinching up the buckled straps as he had done countless times before.

'I should be going with you. I'm your squire.' It wasn't petulant in tone, it was sincere devotion to what he believed was his duty and Hawker knew it.

'I need you and Jacob to get the horses ready. Just in case. Put on your arms and armour. If I am arrested then you both must get out of the town any way you can. Dieudonné will probably fend for himself but I'll leave it to Jacob to decide what to do with him.'

'We will free you if that happens. I swear it.'

Hawker gripped Jack by his shoulder, pausing him. 'No, boy. You won't. I haven't trained you to be a simpleton. If we are thrown in the prison we are not coming out alive anytime soon. You must get out of Hermannstadt. Head for the west. Jacob will get you home.'

Hawker had decided to make the breastplate his only armour, leaving the rest along with his helm. Finally, Jack buckled on Hawker's *cinquedea* dagger and his new bastard sword, then threw the heavy madder-red woollen cloak over his master's shoulders.

Hawker turned around in a circle, arms outstretched. 'Do I look fit to see the burghers of Hermannstadt?'

Jack smiled, nodding. 'That you do, my lord.'

Hawker looked at the youth, his gaze lingering longer than a moment. He then unbuckled the hangar of the dagger from his wide leather belt. The *cinquedea* came loose in his hand and he handed it to Jack. 'Watch this for me. I'll be asking for it from you when I come back.'

Jack took it from his hands, reverently. 'Aye, my lord. That I will.'

Hawker could hear loud German voices outside and imagined the guard was growing impatient with the wait that Maria had inflicted upon them. 'I best be going down there now,' he said.

He laid a hand on Jack's shoulder as he passed by him, moving for the doorway.

Outside, the innkeeper was doing his best to prevent the town guard from pushing their way inside and dragging Maria out. Hawker emerged, hand on hilt, and the guardsmen relented. He was followed by Ellingham and Faldi, both accoutred as he was, wearing the barest of protection but carrying swords. Then Maria emerged, hands daintily lifting both sides of her brocade gown as she walked, her white cambric headscarf hiding her coiled black locks, a shining mark of her modesty. The captain of the guard nodded curtly at her and bid her to follow. The party set out at a walk, across the cobbled square: the lady and her three knights, two halberd-toting guardsmen leading and three more behind.

The Council Tower was a great hulking square fortification, rising up high over Hermannstadt. It was built into the inner ring of the town with a great gate at its base. Hawker saw it was built for defence with but few windows. They entered the gaping maw of the stone archway and were ushered through a heavy, nail-studded oak door which led to a staircase taking them up to the first floor and the council chamber above.

They were led into a cavernous room, the air far colder than outside, with a large, half-moon-shaped leaded window at each end to let in the light. Both floor and the high ceiling above were built of dark-stained wood while the bare walls were adorned with tapestries and a few ancient, painted triangular shields. They were marched to the middle of the chamber and then the captain slammed the butt of his halberd to announce them. Hawker saw that the only furniture in the chamber was a long, covered table at one end, at which sat three worthies, undoubtedly burghers of the council.

He wasn't surprised about the immediate morning summons. At least the authorities had let them all have a good night's slumber. How Maria believed they could simply bring an armed party of men into such a place and not be called to task made him doubt Dracula's supposed daughter all the more.

The burgher in the middle – a man in a black skullcap and crimson robes – leaned towards them and adjusted the large round spectacles of horn clamped upon the bridge of his prominent nose.

'Well, you've kept us waiting for you long enough. Bring forth your pass if you indeed even have one!'

Hawker watched as Maria gently shoved Ellingham forward, then followed at his side, half a pace behind. The captain's halberd swung down fast as a bar to them, causing Ellingham to pull up.

'Disarm, sir!' said the councilman.

Hawker heard Maria whisper to Ellingham urgently and then, slowly, the youth drew his sword and handed it hilt-first to a heavyset militiaman who strode forward to accept it. Hawker tensed and Faldi must have sensed it.

'She knows what she's doing, Don Falco,' whispered Faldi in Venetian. 'Stand firm.'

Hawker kept his eyes on the guards but did not move a muscle. Ellingham and Maria proceeded forward, their footsteps clunking on the wide, grit-strewn floorboards. They reached the table and Maria handed over the now well-worn vellum pass. The bespectacled burgher reached for it even as one hand held his lenses to nose. He pored over it for half a minute and then passed it to the man at his right.

'Raising a company for the king then?' he said, having taken in its contents. 'And you, mistress, purport to be Maria Hunyadi, kin to Matthias?'

'That is just so,' Maria answered, chin held high. 'You see the royal seal there affixed. I have permission to raise men for the war in Vienna. I seek worthy, experienced men-at-arms and the Siebenbürgen have supplied those in times past.'

The man leaned back into his ornately carved chair and wiped a forefinger under his nose. 'Mercenaries we have, my lady. But I find it strange that a woman is in the business of recruiting them. And who is this fellow with you who obviously doesn't speak our language? Your escort?'

Maria translated quickly for Ellingham and then she turned back to the burghers, eyes flashing. 'This is my husband. Giles Plantagenet, a prince of England and son of King Richard. We together run this enterprise for my uncle. And you would do well to allow us to continue unhindered.'

The bespectacled burgher smiled. 'Must keep your hands full teaching him German... and Hungarian too?' He looked Ellingham up and down for a moment, considering.

'With respect,' said Maria, 'your only concern is to allow us passage. Something I hope you will grant without delay.'

The burgher on the right slid the vellum across the table and over to the man on the left, who began perusing it.

The burgher in the middle took off his lenses and gave Maria a cold, hard stare. 'It is this council's duty to preserve the peace and safety of this town. Even as we speak, the Great Turk and his army lie not fifty leagues from here, laying waste to Moldavia. You think we would spare fighters for Matthias's ludicrous campaign against the Austrians when such a danger is on our doorstep? And while the Wallachians sit on their hands and let the Turks come and go as they please? You have found barren ground here for your entreaties, mistress, despite your royal kin.'

The vellum made its way across the baize table cover yet again, ending up in the ink-stained hands of the bespectacled man.

'Matthias has won his war in the west with his Black Legion,' said the man on the left, a tiny fellow with grey hair and a wandering left eye. 'To what purpose is your company now?'

Maria turned to the man, annoyed, as if he were an interfering child. 'The campaign goes on, I assure you. We have just come from the west.'

The burgher on the right reached over with his velvet clad arm and tapped the vellum pass where it lay. 'The seal *appears* genuine. But why does the signature of the chancellor look to me... awkward? Even careless. I have seen his documents before this.'

Maria bristled. 'Perhaps he was ill. How do you expect me to know such things?'

Hawker could feel the sweat pouring down his armpits despite the chill in the chamber. He was just about following the twisted, eastern German they spoke and he was growing worried. Next to him, Faldi stood like a statue, unflinching, his gaze locked onto the quiet drama unfolding a few paces in front.

Maria had once again rapidly translated for Ellingham's benefit. As she finished, he moved forward and leaned on the table with both palms splayed flat.

'Do you accuse us of some base crime? Do you know who I am?' The English words rang through the chamber, reverberating loudly. 'We are of royal blood! Of the royal bone!'

The guards shifted uneasily but held their ground.

'He is asking what crime you would accuse a prince of the English crown of,' said Maria, solemnly.

'Prince no more, I should think,' said the bespectacled one, his face taut. 'We heard the sad news of King Richard in this very chamber a month ago.'

Maria held her steely gaze. 'The pass is genuine, my lord. And I demand that you grant us free passage.'

The burgher pursed his lips and turned to each of his fellow councilmen. The burgher on the right merely shrugged. The one with the squint pinched his nostrils briefly, then whispered his counsel.

The bespectacled burgher grunted a little and pushed his skullcap back. 'You are not to recruit mercenaries inside the town walls. And I expect to see you and your company leaving Hermannstadt tomorrow. Of that we will make sure.' He pushed the vellum towards Maria and waved his hand as if brushing off a fly. 'You may go now.'

Maria curtsied and Ellingham merely gave a quick nod and reached for Maria's wrist to guide her away from the table. Hawker exhaled a long breath and looked to Faldi.

The Milanese winked at him. 'Tutto bene, Don Falco!'

14

Gaston Dieudonné sharpened his dagger. For the second time in an hour. It was a soothing exercise and one that allowed him to take stock of the situation he now found himself in. Deeply in.

'Keep that up and you will find you have a toothpick,' quipped Jacob de Grood in French as he walked past the long table of the inn's hall on his way to the door.

Dieudonné shot him a smile that could kill at six paces and went on grinding the whetstone, slowly and rhythmically.

Jacob smiled back. 'As you are busy I will check and see what mischief the Rascians are up to out in the stables. The drunken sot Lithuanian, too.'

Dieudonné gave only a shrug in reply.

Jacob shouted up the staircase. 'Jack Perry! Where are you?'

The lad came pounding down the wooden stairs, armour jangling. 'I'm here, Jacob. But I'm not *your* squire. I should have gone with Sir John.'

'To do what? Show off your new harness? You need to get your arse outside and look to the horses. You think that fat innkeeper gives a damn about whether they're fed and watered?'

Dieudonné's eyes followed them even as his hand scraped the blade with a long, full stroke. Only just a month before, he felt sure that he was going to have to kill the Fleming. There was always distrust in his eyes and he did not want that distrust to spread and find its way to Sir Giles or Sir John. He had almost gotten himself killed in Venice with his rages and had nearly given the game away with Hawker. He'd since learned to restrain his impulses but had thought about knifing de Grood at night and pushing

146

him overboard when they were sailing towards Dalmatia. It was an assassin's technique he had used on de Grood's little comrade Jan Bek when they had fled England and *he* was about to tattle. No body to be found. But, since leaving Venice, Jacob de Grood seemed to have lost interest in him and that was all for the greater good.

Now though, his bigger worry was the young Plantagenet. For days, as they had travelled into the east, he had felt his hold on Giles slipping. And the reason was clearly Maria Hunyadi. She had impressed Giles with her power, her beauty, and her wiles. But she had not impressed him. There were too many unanswered questions.

He finished with his dagger, wiping it down with a cloth and then putting his whetstone away in his belt pouch. A serving girl laboured at the fire and he absently watched her as she toiled with a stack of wood. He flipped the dagger over in his hand, caught it, and sheathed it. It was time for a baring of the soul to Giles, he thought to himself. He had opened up to the youth before, in the early days of their Venice debacle, and had been repaid in confidence and trust. That gave him influence. He needed to re-establish that before it all slipped away to nothing.

Two merchants came in, stamping and shaking in their heavy cloaks. They nodded towards Dieudonné and made their way into the hall. He acknowledged them with a nod in return but had no desire to engage them. He stood and went outside. The late morning air was crisp and heavy with the smell of wood smoke which seemed to hang low around the houses and stable. But the winter sun shone strongly in a sky of azure. It cheered him. He watched the alley that led to the main square, waiting for the company to return. Part of him worried about just what the town council was telling Hawker. If he saw an armed party coming then he would know it had not gone well and that he would have to flee or fight, or both.

When he saw Giles and Maria come around the corner, Hawker and the pompous Italian right behind, he nodded to himself in relief. They had somehow talked themselves out of arrest. He met them as they entered the courtyard and made a dramatic bow before Maria.

'My lady, you have assuaged the worries of the burghers, then? Or have they kept open a dungeon for us just in case?'

Maria smiled at him tolerantly. 'They have told us to leave in the morning, which is no matter. I expected as much from them. A gaggle of worried old fools, trusting no one on either side of their walls.'

'A sign of the times, my lady,' replied Dieudonné, shaking his head. 'I expect you told them nothing of your intent?'

'I told them what they needed to hear and that was enough.'

Dieudonné caught a glimpse of Hawker standing a few paces behind. The old knight's face had a grim cast to it, clearly unimpressed by the Hungarian's words. Young Ellingham was smiling at her though, like a besotted calf.

'Where are the others?' asked Hawker.

'Why, I believe they are attending to the horses in the stable, Sir John.'

'Then I shall repair there. I think we should be prepared to depart on a moment's notice. A feather would weigh more than the amount of trust I have in that council.' He walked off to the stables, hand on hilt, leaving them looking at each other a bit awkwardly.

'I for one would take some refreshment,' said Maria, 'before we must again face the road tomorrow. Let us go inside.'

'A good suggestion,' said Faldi, beaming. 'We must appreciate the comforts we have here and now. It will be harder going when we reach the mountains. You will need all your strength for that, *Frenchman*!'

Dieudonné lips formed a twisted smile. He ignored the jibe. 'Sir Giles, will you walk with me to the town square? I must stretch my legs.'

Ellingham looked slightly confused at the request but nodded and Dieudonné stepped forward and put an arm about his shoulder, gently turning him away from Maria and guiding him towards the alley. Faldi looped his arm through Maria's.

148

'Then we two shall take some sweet wine, my lady.'

–

'In truth, dear Gaston, I was in some thirst and now you drag me off for a walk.'

'Well then, let us find a wine shop in this place. We can take some hot spiced wine to warm our bones.'

Dieudonné had spotted the timber lean-to earlier, and he guided the youth to it now where it lay on the edge of the cobbled square. The shop's front shutter was open and propped and a few mean benches and upturned barrels provided a place to sit and imbibe. Dieudonné pointed to the little black cauldron that steamed away inside the tiny shop over a brick-built hearth. 'You see? They are ready and waiting for us!'

Dieudonné bought them two wooden mugs of spiced wine and they sat upon a bench watching the townsfolk pass: merchants with their hand carts loaded with goods, a group of joking clerics of the Latin church, some high-born woman and her demure attendants, a few swaggering men of the town guard, and two boys whom Dieudonné rapidly surmised were attempting to cut the purse strings of passers-by while they feigned begging. Dieudonné saw Ellingham wrap both hands about the wooden mug, warming them, and then raise it gingerly to his mouth.

'Not too bad, eh?' he proffered, raising his own mug.

Ellingham smiled weakly. 'What is on your mind, Gaston, that you feel the need to speak in confidence such that we steal away?'

Dieudonné sniggered a little. 'Am I that obvious in my desires? You know me well, my friend.'

'We've already been through much together. That we are even both alive seems more a miracle of God than our own designs. Our adventures have given us wisdom of each other, no? I *am* your friend, Gaston, and you may speak plainly. What is it that vexes you?'

Dieudonné took another swig. 'Do not think ill of me. I speak as your friend, your comrade. And I grow worried about your

149

tryst with our beautiful patron.' Ellingham opened his mouth to protest but Dieudonné cut him off. 'Nay, I judge you not. She *is* beautiful. And she is clever. But we are here to accomplish her quest and to be paid for it. Bedding her makes our contract all the more... complicated.'

Ellingham laughed and shook his head. 'Gaston, what you observe is only for the sake of appearances! We're both as chaste as clerics.'

Dieudonné rolled his eyes. 'Not the clerics I've known.'

'Last night I slept upon the truckle bed in the chamber! Not her bed, I swear it. I admit the first night I was tempted but it was she who made the matter clear to me.'

Dieudonné wasn't sure what to make of that. She had set the youth's loins on fire, but believed she was using her chastity to keep him all the more ardent for her. It was a power that he knew well and had exercised over both sexes in his time. Chastity was a weapon and Maria knew that very well.

'I am relieved, dear Giles, to hear you say that. It's caused a few mutterings within the company as I'm sure you must understand.'

'It's awkward for me, too, but the ruse has made things easier for us all. Fewer questions.'

Dieudonné scowled. 'Fewer questions? Maybe from the burghers and innkeepers but I still have a few. For one, what is her hold over Bartolo Faldi? And how did he manage to lose all his men before we even met him? We had little choice in joining her peculiar quest you might remember, but what about him?'

It was time now for Ellingham's forehead to crease up in puzzlement. 'Faldi? I had not given it much thought.'

'He either seeks her love or her gold. That is clear to me.'

Ellingham leaned back a bit, tilting his head. 'That is rather cynical, dear Gaston. Perhaps he's just loyal. And romantic for the quest to free her father.'

Dieudonné smiled thinly. 'Yes, the quest. That is another mystery to me. She is treated like a leper in every town we pass through, yet wants to free a father she has probably never known. A father who may have never even acknowledged her as his own.'

'As my father did not?' growled Ellingham.

Dieudonné waggled a forefinger. 'Nay, Giles. Your father did acknowledge you, even if he didn't in his court. He knighted you. He gave you a protector in Sir John. As for Maria, daughter of Vlad, she claims to have met him once when she was sixteen! That is a filial love most rare indeed.'

Ellingham took another drink and looked off into the square. 'You hold a cynicism that is most rare, Gaston.'

'And it's kept my head on my shoulders these past years.'

'Have you forgotten that it was you who advised we follow her? On ship. That my fortune would be better served by finding and freeing this prince of Wallachia than by skulking back to Flanders and begging for alms.'

'I did. And I've not changed my counsel to you. I only ask that you trust my judgement and start asking questions yourself. For the moment, our fortune is best served by keeping the company together under her banner. But one must always have choices. Other paths.'

'You mean routes of escape.'

'Exactly so, my friend.'

Ellingham shook his head. 'So then, what would you have me do?'

'Put your trust in me and what I counsel. Ask Maria about her plans when you lie abed. Ask her more about her father and what plans she has for him. I fear that Sir John has lost interest in our quest because of his broken heart. Tragic, alas, but we risk running adrift, rudderless.'

Ellingham didn't reply.

'Giles, in the coming days we'll enter the lion's den. We will need to know who is the enemy and who is the friend. And for that, one must think like a spy does. Maria has your ear, but you must have hers, too.' His long fingers gently held the youth's wrist for a moment. Giles tolerated the intimacy and it gave Dieudonné a frisson of hope. 'My dear friend – one who has my affection and loyalty – it is good to give her your confidence, but I beg you, do not – do *not* – give her your heart!'

Hawker strode rapidly down the narrow lane, cloak billowing behind, following the little boy he had paid to lead him to the armourer's shop. At his side was Jack, keeping pace in full armour. He had insisted on wearing his harness to accompany his knight – including his helm – and he held his head high, proud to be so accoutred, a proper squire. Hawker could not restrain a grin of amusement at the sight of the boy, whose pride of station was stamped upon his face.

They soon found themselves on the far side of the town and near the wooden palisade walls, in a district of tanners, carpenters and metalworkers. The place stank so of tanners' vats that Hawker swore under his breath. But they passed these and the air cleared a little by the time they came to the armourer's shop, its location marked by a stack of unpolished glaives and halberds leaning near the entrance.

The street urchin stopped, put one hand on his hip and held the other outstretched. Hawker signalled to Jack to pay the boy and then went inside. It was open at the back, two great barnlike doors, to let in more air and light. A large furnace lay at the centre along with a bellows that was dormant. A bull-necked man was at a work table nearby, tapping the rivets of a vambrace on an anvil. He looked up at Hawker and Jack, put the vambrace to one side, but held on to his hammer.

'Was wollen Sie?' he growled, pushing his bench back and standing.

'Armbrüste,' replied Hawker, the German for crossbow.

The man looked over to Jack. 'Sohn?'

Hawker shook his head and the man gave a small snort. He mumbled something that Hawker thought sounded like 'foreigners' and then turned to wander off into the workshop. He picked up something hanging on a timber-planked wall and returned. It was a large crossbow.

Hawker saw the look on Jack's face and knew what memories the sight of it had summoned up. The lad's eyes focused intently on the bow, so intently that he was seeing beyond it, seeing something else. It was the weapon that Hawker had first taught him to use, and with which Jack had killed his first man only a few months ago. Jack had triggered more than the crossbow when he had sent that bolt flying towards the Tudor sheriff. He had triggered the beginning of their journey and their exile.

Hawker held up his hand as the armourer tried to hand him the crossbow. 'Too big. *Kleiner*. For hunting… die Jagd.'

It was a heavy war crossbow, old by the look of it and requiring a windlass to span it. It was not what Hawker needed. It would have to be smaller, reloaded quickly and by hand. The armourer shook his head, muttered something darkly, and went off again. He returned with two more crossbows and this time Hawker gave him a nod of approval. They too, were a little old, but the wrapped string bundles looked sound. The polished wood of the stocks, inlaid with hart's horn pieces, had aged almost black.

The armourer placed one on his bench and put the other on the floor, placing his toe into the little metal stirrup at its end. He leaned over and in one quick pull upwards had spanned the bow. He hefted it and rummaged through a drawer on the bench. He pulled out a quarrel, placed it into the slot of the crossbow and shouldered it, pointing towards the wall where it had hung. The strings twanged and instantaneously a loud crack sounded. The feathered bolt had pierced the wall and driven in up to its fletchings.

Hawker watched as Jack stared at the wall, reliving his experience. Hawker opened his belt pouch and pulled out four small gold coins, placing them on the bench. The armourer sniggered at the amount and tapped his hairy forefinger next to them. Hawker gave him a thin grin and pulled out another coin, adding it to the pile. The armourer nodded and placed both weapons on the bench top. It took a few more coins for the man to supply a pouch full of quarrels but when they departed Hawker was satisfied.

When they had left and started their way back to the inn, Jack found his voice again.

'You want me to use this, don't you, Sir John?' He was carrying the un-spanned bow as gingerly as if it were a baby.

Hawker hefted the other crossbow over his shoulder, holding it by the butt of the stock. 'That I do, Jack. We're going hunting soon. Jacob will take the other bow. Or Dieudonné, more likely. He says he was a crossbow captain at Bosworth.'

'I don't understand, Sir John.'

'Hunting. But not for game. We need weapons that will give us surprise and stealth. These will do. Do you think you can manage to draw it by hand as the armourer just did?'

'I think so. But I will learn.' His voice was hesitant.

'You're a good bowman. I've seen it. And you will have to be again. Can you do this?'

Jack shifted the crossbow in his arms, shouldering it as Hawker had. 'I can, Sir John. I'm your squire now.'

Hawker listened to the jangle of Jack's leg armour as he walked. He looked over to the lad. 'This is the life we lead. It is now the life you lead, too. Your heart and head must come to accept that truth. And then embrace it. Understood?'

Jack answered, his breaking voice half a boy's and half a man's. 'Aye, Sir John. I understand.'

They crossed the square and Hawker saw that they were now being followed, at a distance, by two of the town guard. They made it down the alley and to the inn courtyard where they found Faldi and Maria in a shouting match with one another in Italian. Barring the stable doors was another detachment of the town guard, bearing glaives and fully armoured. Dieudonné stood in the doorway of the inn, arms folded, his eyes locked onto the militia like a nervous cat poised to pounce or flee. Jacob, standing behind Faldi, suddenly saw Hawker and strode to the knight's side. His face was set hard, his scarred cheek all taut and twisted.

'The Rascians have been arrested. The council say they're spies for the sultan. I fear we're in for it now.'

15

Despite his bulk, Pedja Jankovic somehow sidestepped the thrusting halberd, grabbed the shaft and yanked it backwards, pulling its owner closer to him. His left fist swung wide to connect with the guard's bare head, staggering the fellow. He could see Orkan wrestling on the large carpet stones of the square with another of the town's guardsmen. The Turk was bashing the back of the man's helmeted head repeatedly onto the stones and swearing a stream of Ottoman oaths. Pedja prayed that his fool of a comrade wasn't going to kill the Saxon. There would be no mercy for them if that happened.

He needn't have worried. In the next instant another guardsman smacked Orkan in the small of the back with the butt of his glaive and Pedja actually heard the *oomph* as the Turk had the wind knocked out of him. Orkan, spittle froth covering his face, rolled off his opponent, gasping. Pedja lost sight of that struggle as his own opponent renewed the fight. A fourth militiaman came at him from the right, aiming a blow that would decapitate him. Pedja somehow managed to wrench the halberd off his first opponent – who was still gripping it – and push it upwards just in time to deflect the incoming glaive.

Now it was two against one and the combat became an awkward, brutal, *basse danse* for three. Pedja knew he had to stay close to the Saxons to prevent them from getting the distance they needed to wield their pole weapons. It was all a whirl of blue and green brass-riveted jerkins, barbute helms, stinking breath and flailing hands. While he grappled, pulling them closer in a bear hug, the trio revolving and staggering, a distant part of his mind was already wondering how he and Orkan could ever get out of it all alive. He suspected Orkan had already made his own mind up and was going to go down fighting to the end. Orkan was still cursing and screaming so he wasn't dead yet. If they surrendered, he still wasn't sure they would live even another few hours. A quick trial perhaps, a muddled affair with a veneer of justice, but nevertheless ending in their very public deaths. Maybe Orkan had the right idea after all.

He was close enough – practically nose to nose – with one of the Saxons to get a good look at the man's expression. It was a look of complete bafflement, as if the man didn't quite know what to do next. Pedja didn't have a good view of the other fellow, but Pedja's arm was wrapped firmly around the glaive haft, held tight in the inside of his elbow. He felt the man doing his utmost to tug it away. The little group tottered, Pedja in the middle, but they stayed upright, still swaying. A moment later though, Pedja felt his left leg collapse from under him, agony shooting through him. Someone else had kicked him in the back of his knee, dropping him. As he fell back, he caught sight of Orkan getting hit on the head with the flat of a glaive blade and the Turk dropped like a sack of wet grain onto the cobbles. Pedja felt a boot on his chest and then the cold sting of a glaive touching his Adam's apple. He let out a long, loud breath as he lay there on his back. So then, it would be a public execution after all.

They were both roughly rolled over and had their hands bound. His cheek lying on the cold stone squares, Pedja saw that a large audience of townsfolk had gathered, gaping and jostling to see the sport. Some of them were laughing, others chattering noisily with each other, no doubt eager at the thought of a hanging or, even better, a beheading. Pedja wasn't sure if the Saxons had adopted impalement, Dracula's favourite method. The townspeople themselves had suffered its pains under the reign of *Kaziglu Bey*, but what better way to get even than by doing it for themselves?

Somehow Orkan had regained consciousness and they were both hauled to their feet. Orkan sounded like he was drunk, spewing out more curses at his attackers. Pedja swallowed and called over to his friend in Slavic.

'Stop speaking Turkish, you simpleton! Save your strength!'

'What's the point?' he bellowed back. 'We're dead men now. It is Allah's will.'

He'd warned Orkan about speaking Turkish in the street. But the fool had kept slipping up, lapsing into the tongue when he couldn't find the right words in Slavic. Several times that afternoon Pedja had noticed people taking notice of them and a short time later they found themselves being trailed by the liveried militiamen. It was only a matter of time before they were stopped and challenged. One of the guardsmen had shoved Orkan in the chest and that had set off the big *akinci* like one of the sultan's great siege cannons. It was a brawl there and then, fists flying and then pole weapons swinging.

They found themselves shoved and prodded across the square towards the great Council Tower and the inner defensive wall of Hermannstadt. Pedja watched Orkan in front of him, staggering like he'd had too much *raki*, his legs threatening to buckle at any moment. He shouted over to his comrade to try and keep him from passing out.

'Orkan! Stay awake! Otherwise we lose our commission with the Hungarian!'

Orkan shook his head violently like a dog after a beating, his long, greasy black hair flying. Trying to rouse himself, thought Pedja.

'Very funny, Tombik!' the Turk called back. 'I won't say I told you so... but *I told you so*, you stupid *dhimmi*.'

Inside the wide tower arch, they were driven into a door on the right side that led down spiralling stone steps into a damp underground chamber. Their guards shouted in German to the warders who came out and ushered them into one of the cells behind a thick oak-planked studded door. Knocked to the straw-covered flagstone floor, their ankles were chained to the wall. One of the guards hit Orkan in the face with his steel mitten-gauntlet, splitting his lip wide open. Pedja took a cuff to his ear that sent his head ringing. And then they were left alone in the darkness of the cell, the only light from which was that of a wall torch shining through the door grating.

For a few minutes, neither of them spoke. Pedja's nostrils were assailed by the smell of the urine of the last inhabitants. It was not how he had expected to end up and he now reluctantly accepted that his decision to follow his brother's killers deep into the Hungarian kingdom had been more than just foolish, it had been prideful and headstrong. Just as Orkan had declared at the outset. What would his younger brother say? That his need for revenge was now getting him killed as well? Both brothers are dead then, all is done. But Pedja still felt he had a debt to pay. The one he owed Davud for not protecting him. Or treating him as he deserved. He was not about to admit defeat yet, even if it meant crawling on his knees and begging for mercy from the Franks and the Saxons.

'I am sorry, my friend,' Pedja said softly. 'I should not have talked you into this journey.'

He heard Orkan make a sound like a muted laugh. 'You think you're so clever as to talk me into something I don't believe in, Tombik? Who else was going to look after you?'

'Don't give up yet. I shall pray to the Christ. You pray to Allah. Maybe one will listen.'

The laugh in the darkness was a bit stronger this time.

'*Evet*, Tombik. Don't forget we must find Kaziglu Bey. Our great prize.'

–

Pedja did not know how much time had passed when the cell door finally opened, its bottom screeching on the uneven stones of the floor. It seemed like hours, but in the dark it was hard to tell. Four guards with drawn swords and a torch bearer entered and roughly unshackled them. They were led up and out, crossing the road under the arch of the tower and through to the other side. They were led up more stone steps and into a great chamber decorated with shields and arms. Pedja's eyes blinked rapidly as they adjusted to the light. The room was even colder than the dungeon and he repressed an involuntary shiver.

He immediately saw Maria Hunyadi standing on the far side of the room. The foreigner knights were with her too, Hawker and the younger one. He would have thought that they would be glaring with fury at him. Instead, they just looked tense and sombre. He realised then that the Hungarian was probably in as much danger as he and Orkan were. A guard grabbed the back of his doublet and pushed him forward a few feet then forced him to his knees. Orkan quickly ended up next to him in the same position. He was facing some sort of tribunal seated at a long, covered table. Four dour-looking Saxons looked down on him, dressed in velvets and capes, skullcaps and gloves. The one in the middle wore horn spectacles, making his eyes look monstrously large. Every a one seemed to be dripping with disdain for the two wretches kneeling before them, thought Pedja.

The man in the spectacles said something to Maria in German and she answered him. A bit too haughtily thought Pedja, for someone in her situation. The Saxon spoke again, this time in Hungarian, and now Pedja understood.

'You admit then, these two here are your men-at-arms? Then why were they spying out the town and the walls? Speaking in Turkish?' The Saxon leaned forward and addressed them. 'Do you speak the king's tongue, churl?'

'I do, a little,' said Pedja, pain shooting through both knees. 'But my comrade here does not speak it well.'

'You mean your Ottoman friend here? One in the employ of the sultan, no doubt.'

'I swear to you, my lord, he is not!' lied Pedja. His stomach felt like he would retch at any moment. He knew there was little he could say to save himself or Orkan. Not if the town was intent on their blood.

'Pah!' The burgher waved his hand dismissively at Pedja's protestation. He swivelled to face Maria again. 'You freely admit that these two are in the employ of you and your husband but you say they are *not* Ottoman spies? We have witnesses that will swear they have been observing us and speaking the tongue of the enemy. I have a good mind to have them beheaded now and not waste the time of the council on a trial.'

Maria lifted her hand with Ellingham holding onto it and she stepped forward a few paces, pulling the young man along with her.

'My lord, the tall, shaggy fellow is indeed a Turk. Only a dolt would not notice. But do you accuse me of harbouring a spy? A spy against the king, *my* uncle?'

Pedja looked over at Orkan. His eyes were darting from Maria to Pedja, barely comprehending what was being said.

'So, you willingly employ this Turk. Employ him even as the sultan's army scours Moldavia? And his fellow churl. This fat fellow here on his knees. Both attacked my men in the square, once their game was discovered.'

'My lord, with respect, these two are Rascians, denizens of Hungary – not Ottomans. The tall one is a by-blow of a Serbian mother who was ravished by a Turk. He was later taken into service by the pasha but managed to escape north a few years later. He may be a Turk but he is only half a Turk. The other is a Serb only, both are loyal to the crown. They have already fought bravely to defend our party when we were attacked in the Banat.'

The burgher pursed his lips and puffed out his cheeks, his head shaking slowly side to side.

'Do not Turkish merchants still freely come and go in the Siebenbürgen?' asked Maria. 'Since when is speaking a certain tongue proof of treason?'

The burgher spluttered, tripping over his Hungarian. 'Merchants carry *passes* to sell their wares here! These two brigands are no merchants!'

'But I hold a pass. One you and your council members have already approved. I vouch for this poor wretch and his comrade, both of whom have suffered long under the fire and sword of

Ottoman raiders in their land. And if you do not release them back into my custody then I shall have no choice but to return west to Buda. And to make a full account of what has happened here.'

Pedja watched as one of the other council members leaned over and whispered into the bespectacled man's ear. That man then turned to the one on his left, arm over shoulder, whispering intently. They were debating his fate. But he was still trying to puzzle out why Maria Hunyadi had even tried to save them. She could have thrown Orkan to the Saxons in a gesture of conciliation but here she was, fighting for both of them with steel in her voice. The irony that he and Orkan were the very raiders that she claimed they had suffered under was not lost on him. He might yet be executed, but if he was, he would now go to the block feeling sheepish that the woman he planned to murder had tried to save his life. It was embarrassing.

If it couldn't have become worse for their dignity, in his distress and bent on his knees, Orkan farted loudly enough for the burghers to interrupt their whispering. The Turk lowered his head and mumbled to himself. Pedja shook his head slowly. It was as if God had indeed abandoned them for being impetuous, would-be assassins. The Saxons frowned and returned to their secret debate. After just a minute, the bespectacled man sat upright and focused his lenses on Maria, adjusting them on the bridge of his nose.

'Your company, my lord and my lady, has worn out its welcome. In the interest of keeping the peace and respecting the interests of the kingdom, we will release your two men here. But you are to leave the town this very day – before the sun sets. If you are not departed I will give orders for all of you to be arrested.'

Pedja felt his shoulders slump in relief. He whispered over to Orkan in Slavic. 'They're freeing us.'

Orkan's eyes widened, his jaw dropping. The orders were given in German and they found themselves hauled up and dragged out of the chamber. Pedja swivelled around to see Maria and the knights following, all grim-faced. They were led back out into the square where their bonds were cut. Orkan received one last kick in his arse before the militia turned and went back inside.

Pedja looked at Maria and started to make an apology. She held up her hand to stop him. 'We go back to the inn, now!' She set off arm in arm with the knight called Giles and Hawker followed behind. Orkan just looked at the cobbles. Pedja looped his arm through the Turk's in the fashion of their menfolk. 'Come, we go back and try to explain to them. And just hope they don't want to kill us.'

They were followed at a close distance by a detachment. Pedja didn't look back and he prayed that Orkan wouldn't either for fear of setting it all off again. At the inn, the guards at the stables were told to leave and the company was on its own, but not out of sight.

Pedja quickly told Orkan what had transpired and the Turk smiled forlornly. 'Now what, Tombik? What cleverness have you in mind now that she has freed us?'

The Frankish knights talked excitedly amongst themselves in French and he and Orkan sat themselves in the hall as Maria ordered wine and food from the servants. Pedja thought the Franks looked relieved, but also angry. With him, he assumed. Maria came to them and stood hands on hips, grimacing, and Pedja realised how beat up they must look. His head pounded, his body ached, and Orkan's lower face was covered in dark, dried blood, his lip blackened and swollen large.

She walked over to Orkan and to both of their surprise began speaking the Turkish tongue, haltingly but understandable.

'You think I did not guess your blood?'

Pedja drew a breath while Orkan looked at his boots.

'I heard you both speaking Turkish in the last days.'

'Why did you bother to save us then?' asked Orkan.

She smiled at him, took a cup of spiced wine from the serving girl, and handed it to him. 'You know little of me, Rascian. Turk or half-Turk. I stand by those who serve me.'

Orkan took the cup, a curious look of disbelief on his broken face.

'My nursemaid at Hunedoara was a Turkish slave,' she said. 'I grew to love her and she stayed with me until I grew to be a maiden. She taught me much. Far more than my mother ever did. My father has slain many of your blood, it is true. But he also took many in his service. Not as slaves but as free men. The sultan and the pashas are his enemy, but not all of your people.'

Orkan looked over to Pedja, not knowing how to reply. Pedja gave him an almost imperceptible nod. Orkan looked up at Maria again.

'Thank you, my lady.'

She continued speaking to them in Turkish. 'We set off again soon. I need you to prepare the horses, load up our supplies. Remember, I will reward you well for your service.' She paused, fixing them both with a sterner look. 'But never, *never* disappoint me again.'

She left them there, nursing their wounds and their pride.

'So Tombik, now what?' mumbled Orkan.

'We do what the lady asks,' grumbled Pedja, throwing back the last of his wine and gripping the bench as he struggled to stand again. He looked across the chamber to see that Hawker was observing all. He was sure the old knight hadn't understood their words, but still, he did not trust him. A Frankish warrior with a grey beard meant two things: that the man was good at his profession, and that his cleverness had allowed him to stay alive to become a grey-hair. Pedja knew he would have to be careful in the days ahead even if he did not know what his own actions were to be. But he believed in Maria Hunyadi's faith in her quest: that Vlad Dracula, son of Dracul, Prince of Wallachia, yet lived. He had to believe that, too.

He threw a nod of respect towards Hawker.

The old knight remained as stone, not acknowledging him, then turned away.

16

By the time the company passed out through the town gate, it was already mid-afternoon. The ball of the sun looked small and faint where it sat in the pale sky, wrapped in a halo of spider's silk. Hawker was already worrying again. Although Maria had assured them they would make their next destination by nightfall – if Tokár was to be believed – Hawker thought they still might end up with the horses stumbling in the darkness along a road only one man said he knew. The burghers had made sure of their leaving without any delay, and the town guard, also mounted, followed them for nearly half a mile down the track leading south.

Riding next to Jack, Hawker looked ahead, and for as far as he could see, the Carpathians rose up, sombre brown and grey in their winter garb. A few patches of green clung to some of the slopes where evergreen forest grew. Looking east, towards the higher range of hills, snow caps topped the peaks. It was through this great wall that they would have to travel a winding path along the valley of the Olt River. And John Hawker already smelled acrid rain on the air that would doubtless change to sleet as the temperature dropped.

The line of the column was as before. The Rascians with Tokár and Vilkas led, followed by Maria, Ellingham and Faldi. A short distance behind them Hawker and Jack rode with Jacob and Dieudonné bringing up the rear. Hawker did not trust the burghers of Hermannstadt as far as he could spit and it would not have surprised him for the company to be attacked from the rear before the sun finally set. Better to have those he trusted the most at the back and those the least at the front.

Jack rode tall and confidently and Hawker cracked an involuntary smile, his heart swelling a little. The lad's crossbow was slung over his shoulder by a long, woven strap and rested on his backplate, his pouch of quarrels he slung from his red leather belt over his right hip, his arming sword riding high on his left. Hawker had been concerned that the bow might bring back the unpleasant memories of the boy's first fight, but it seemed that Jack had embraced his future fully and without misgiving. There was a certain hardness, an edge, to him now, thought Hawker, the kind of armour that a man needed on the inside to match what he wore on the outside. Yet, so too, there were mixed feelings in his mind about the lad. He had raised and trained a soldier – a slayer of men – a boy soldier who knew how to kill but who had yet to fall in love. For a moment it made him profoundly sad, only then did he realise he was really thinking about his own lost love. An image of Chiara Contanto filled his mind's eye. With it came the memories of just a few weeks ago: their renewed love, the killing rage of her jealous husband and his death at the hands of young Jack Perry. He felt sick in the pit of his stomach at the thought of what might have befallen her now.

He had begged her to flee Venice with him. She had refused, willing to take her chances in her city. Her home. With hindsight, Hawker now knew she might not be any better off had she come with him. Dragging her on this campaign might have ended her just as quickly as the iron-rimmed wheels of Venetian justice. But it was not knowing her fate which ate away at him each day.

After an hour in the saddle, Tokár signalled from up front, and then turned off the road down a smaller one that was more a rutted track than a road. This wound its way through thickets of hawthorn and hazel, old oak and beech, the track sometimes widening only to narrow again a while later. Through the mostly bare branches, a few amber leaves left clinging, Hawker saw that the sky had cleared a little in the dying light, azure blue to an inky purple. It was then they came upon the place: a hamlet of small wooden houses, cobbled together from old planks with cowhides for doors.

A large open fire blazed away at the centre of the clearing and a group of men and women, children darting between them, came out to greet the new arrivals. Tokár dismounted and began speaking to the menfolk.

'These are gypsies?' asked Jack, intrigued by their looks.

Hawker nodded. 'That they are. And the last recruits to our little army.'

The Romani men looked long hardened to adversity, an aura of dogged resilience about them. All were garbed in similar fashion: jerkins of piebald cowhide, loose baggy hose of browns and tans, and short boots. The womenfolk, dark-eyed and brown, wore linen chemises over which they draped a woollen wrap that tied under the opposite shoulder. Most wore turbans of white wound around their heads, hair tucked up. The children, many of them very young, wore blanket-like cloaks fixed with leather and wooden toggles.

Before Hawker could even dismount, the group had surrounded Maria's mount, bowing and raising their hands. She acknowledged their respect with clasped hands, nodding at them. Hawker understood the significance. They were giving obeisance to the Dragon's daughter. Ellingham turned his head to Hawker, a look of confused surprise on his face. Hawker gave him a slow nod. Faldi dismounted next and helped Maria off her horse with great ceremony. Unnecessary of course, but Hawker saw the game. Then the rest of the company dismounted, Dieudonné wearing a great grin of amusement at the rustic spectacle. A few of the men came forward and took their bridles, leading their mounts further into the hamlet. Jacob called to Hawker that he would go with them to see that things were arranged.

Hawker walked to the fire, feeling the heat warming his damp bones even through his armour. Ellingham joined him, holding out his gloved hands towards the crackling flames.

'Dubious about our new allies, Sir John?'

Hawker stared into the fire. 'I'm hoping that they have the secrets we need to get into the castle. Otherwise, they are only a few more men. A few when we require a hundred.'

'Maria says the garrison is only small. Why shouldn't we be able to defeat it?'

Hawker gave a brief snort. 'Because we have to get inside first.'

'We will, Sir John. We will.'

'God willing, yes. But what do we do after that?'

Ellingham looked down towards his boots and said nothing.

Maria joined them with Faldi in tow. 'Tokár says that the Romani will put you all up in their houses for the night. It may be humble but it will be warm. And he says they have prepared a meal for us. A welcome.'

'I am sure that Don Falco would like to interrogate these Romani about the fortress,' said Faldi. Hawker thought that the Milanese had, over the past days, lost some of his jollity. Certainly after the threats at Hermannstadt. Perhaps the risks had grown too much for him, the promise of reward increasingly less of a certainty.

'If these gypsies hold good intelligence about the place, my lady, then we must get it from them. The odds do not favour us as things stand.'

Maria nodded solemnly. 'We will hold a council this night. Here, around the fire. Tokár and I will translate for the rest of you. Do not underestimate these folk, Sir John. They fight like wolves and have stout hearts. If they know how to get inside the Argeş you will find out.'

Benches were carried out from the hovels and were put around the fire. Jacob reappeared, loosening his cloak as the fire warmed him. 'They have fed and watered the horses. I have tied them securely and the gypsies gave me blankets to cover them for the night. These folk have been generous with what little they have.'

'They serve Vlad Dracula still,' mused Hawker. 'Even if it be through his daughter.'

Jacob's eyes scanned the womenfolk who bustled about the clearing, bearing bowls and beakers. 'Is this all of our help? These dozen men, their wives and their brats? Can we really storm a fortress with what we have here?'

Ellingham didn't wait for Hawker to reply. 'We have come this far and I for one have pledged myself to finish the task. I have fought alongside both of you before. I know we shall succeed. I *feel* it.'

Hawker shot him a wan smile and then nodded. But he said nothing.

They supped around the warmth of the blazing log fire as darkness fully fell upon the forest. One of the gypsies played a long-necked Ottoman lute and a woman danced, an intricate dance of whirling steps, her sinuous arms entwining and her fingers and hands flexing like two snakes in combat. The company relaxed but the boar stew was consumed largely in silence, each keeping to his own thoughts. Maria conversed in low tones with Tokár and with Faldi. After the lute fell quiet, Hawker set down his bowl and spoon and stood.

'My lady, it is time we speak of the fortress. If your Romani friends have news of the place then I would hear it.'

'You are right, Sir John. It is time for us to take counsel. Perhaps it will allay your doubts.'

She exchanged words with Tokár and the gypsy came forward to stand in front of Hawker. He swept back over his ears his long greying locks of once-jet hair and then folded his arms in front of his chest. His eyes, two bottomless pools of blackness, stared into Hawker's face.

'Ask him again about how many man the garrison.'

Maria complied and Tokár called to one of his comrades across the fire. The man answered immediately.

'He says, thirty to forty,' said Maria. 'No more. And that is as of a week ago.'

'Good,' replied Hawker. 'That is a few less than Tokár told us before. But how does he know that?'

When Maria had translated, Tokár's face darkened, as if Hawker was challenging his word. But he answered quickly enough that his clan had set watch on the place for three days straight. One had spoken with an ostler who had brought up

168

bread and meat to the gate and had passed inside. The man was more than happy to tell of the misery of the garrison. Bored and lazy and with nothing to do except look after the Monk's prisoners. Two even got into a fight over dice. One was killed so they hanged the other. Tokár looked to Hawker again and broke into a grin.

Hawker turned to Maria. 'Now ask about this cave leading to a tunnel. Can we reach it without being seen from the walls?'

This time Tokár answered Hawker directly, in his broken Venetian. 'Maybe. But the trees bare now. Night too dangerous. No light. Maybe when sun is low. We come to it on the south side. Vilkas remembers.'

Jacob nodded, understanding. 'Torches would be seen. We would need to find the cave while we still have some daylight. Risky. And we depend upon a drunkard's memory.'

Hawker growled, digesting the information and not liking it. 'Can he find the entrance again?'

Tokár's face remained unchanged, stoic. 'Yes. Ask him.'

Vilkas looked up at Hawker, eyes rheumy and only half-focused. Hawker beckoned with his forefinger. 'Stand up!' he demanded, the German tongue coming back into his mind.

Vilkas got up, wobbling on his feet. His wine ration had already been drunk and it was clear he was feeling the benefit. Hawker addressed him again and asked about the cave.

'I *remember*,' slurred the Balt, digging his own finger into his chest. 'Big rocks near to it.'

'And at the end – inside the tunnel. Where does it lead?'

Vilkas nodded. 'Big square tower – near a cistern.'

'And the prison? Where does that lie?'

'Same place. Square tower.'

Hawker nodded slowly. At least that made it simpler. 'May a man walk upright? How wide?' Hawker spread his arms.

Vilkas rubbed at his jaw. 'I was young then. Long time ago. One must walk like this.' And he demonstrated, crouching slightly. He then spread both his hands a little more than a shoulder width apart. 'Dievas and Perkunas – they will guide us from above.' He smiled, half to himself it seemed.

'You better pray hard to your little gods, my friend,' Hawker growled.

He noticed that Ellingham was following all intently even if he could not comprehend the Balt, his lips pursed tightly together. Was it just dawning on the youth that the raid would be so perilous? Hawker turned slightly to face him. 'He swears it is still there. Passable. But if that tunnel has collapsed in the last twenty years then we must take them by the gate.'

Ellingham winced with that realisation.

Hawker looked over to Maria. 'And, if that be so, then we would have to trick the garrison. Pretend to be ostlers with supplies, food and wine. Get them to open the gate and then take them with the crossbows. We would have but one moment to overcome them before the alarm is raised. But even if we get twenty of us into the gate we're still outnumbered two to one. And it would be in the daylight.'

Hawker looked over to Jacob, his face half in shadow. The half he could see looked haggard. He saw the scarred cheek twitch a little in irritation.

'Sir John,' said Maria, smiling, 'that is why I've made contract with you and your company. You are true men-at-arms. Not like the garrison rats of the Castle Argeş. I believe in you. *All* of you.'

Hawker turned to Tokár. 'And the Dragon Prince. Does he live still? Unless you can swear he still breathes we will not risk our lives on just a wives' tale.'

Maria again spoke to the gypsy. Tokár nodded and turned back to Hawker. He placed three closed fingers of his right hand to his forehead and then touched the centre of his chest.

'The master still lives. I know this. I swear it.'

Hawker looked down for a few seconds and then turned to Ellingham. He spoke in English. 'He says that Vlad still lives. Are you prepared to throw in all upon this quest?'

Ellingham didn't hesitate in his reply. 'I am, Sir John. We have come this far. And it was always about more than just gaining some gold.' Ellingham switched to French so that Maria would understand. 'We are with you, my lady. Your task is ours.'

Maria beamed at him.

Hawker nodded, feeling their future was now sealed, for ill or for better. And he suddenly felt the weight of his years, a weariness of heart.

'And what comes afterwards, my lords?' It was Dieudonné, speaking up from where he stood in the shadows, away from the fire. 'No one has yet answered *that* riddle. Are we to set the old man back on his throne? Or do we take our pay and go home? If Sir Giles even has a home anymore. I seem to remember there was a promise made. A promise of help for this son of Richard here.'

Maria locked her eyes straight upon Ellingham. 'I gave you my word, Giles. That my father will aid your cause if you free him. But we must free him first.'

'I believe her,' said Ellingham. 'And we will find out how in the Lord's good time. For now, we know what we must do.'

None could see Dieudonné's reaction, but no words came from him.

Hawker swallowed the bitter taste in his mouth. Leave it to the Burgundian to speak so plainly. And he could not gainsay the sentiment. It went to the heart of their bargain. They would risk their lives on a promise made on behalf of a man thought long dead. And if he indeed lived, it was a promise he did not yet even know about. It was a dark gamble but if it succeeded, surely they would be in a better place than they had been a few weeks earlier. Hawker glanced down to the bench next to him. Jack's chin had slumped to his breast in sleep, the lad's hands still clutching his empty bowl. Hawker rubbed at Jack's mop of hair, rousing him gently.

'Enough of counsel. We need sleep,' he said to Maria. 'What are the arrangements?'

'Tokár will see that you are well served and bedded down.' She spoke to the gypsy and he in turn commanded his men. A few of

171

them rose and gestured for the westerners to follow. One of the Romani women even helped Jack up, leading him by the hand to one of the hovels. Hawker heard something like a short sharp bark of a laugh from Dieudonné and he watched as the Burgundian moved finally, slamming his empty wine beaker onto a nearby bench before following the Romani to find his bed. The Rascians looked at each other, said nothing, then got up and followed him.

Jacob stood close to the fire, staring at his liege lord. Hawker laid a hand on his shoulder but Jacob knocked it away.

'So this is this how you lead us? You have a death wish! You're nothing but a broken old man.'

The affront, so quick and so vehement, shook the fatigue from Hawker. With both hands, he shoved Jacob backwards, sending the Fleming stumbling.

'You dog! You dare speak to me so?'

Jacob recovered his balance and leaned forward, charging in like an ironclad bull. Hawker's arms flew up to fend him off but the clash of harness rang out in the night. For a moment, they grappled, scrabbling for a handhold on each other's shoulders and twisting to try and throw the other over.

Hawker grunted with the effort, his sudden rage overwhelming him. They were close in violent embrace and suddenly Hawker heard the Fleming sobbing and saw the tears streaming down the stubble of his cheeks. Hawker loosened his grip and Jacob's hands limply held on to his shoulders.

'You must lead!' Jacob sputtered. '*You* are my captain. You. Not that boy. What has happened, Sir John? How did we end up in this place?'

Hawker's heart was sick. He pulled Jacob in closer and wrapped his arms about him. 'I died in Venice, Jacob. Part of me died.'

He felt Jacob gently shake his shoulders. 'No, no, my lord. You're *alive* and you *are* our captain. You must lead us again. Damn you, God *wills* it… He wills it. If we are on a fool's errand then *you* must stop it.'

Hawker stepped back, letting his right hand slip down Jacob's breastplate. He patted it. 'A death wish, eh? Have I sunk so far? Sweet Jesus, Jacob, I am sorry.' He gripped the Fleming by both shoulders and gave him a gentle shake. 'I'll get us all through this, I swear it to you. But Sir Giles *must* lead. He can't always depend on me and he must learn. Learn by doing… and by commanding. His father led an army at sixteen. He is his father's son. I have seen it.'

Jacob exhaled loudly, blowing his cheeks. He lowered his head then looked up again and fixed Hawker in his gaze. 'Take command, Sir John, I beg you,' he said, voice soft but laced with urgency. 'Take command or else we will all most surely fall.'

Hawker shook his head slowly. 'I almost gave in to my pride. To take command again. At our halt that night east of Temesvár. But no, my old friend, I will not. I swore an oath to the king and then to his son. *You* swore an oath to me. And if it is God's will that we fall, then we shall all fall together.'

17

Each of the powerful guilds of Hermannstadt gave the money that built the tall stone towers guarding the town. And the wealthiest of these guilds – the goldsmiths, silversmiths, brewers, and the blacksmiths – administered their towers as their own private domains. They held court within their thick, tapestry-draped walls, cloaking their whispered secrets, alliances, and threats, all delivered behind a smile.

Lothar Bacher, grandmaster of the silversmiths and elected leader of the town council, pulled his cloak closer about him and leaned forward in his lushly cushioned chair, the better to gain the heat from the hearth. His private chambers in the tower would have elicited a nod of approval from any crowned head, so richly furnished were they with velvets and silks, fruitwood sideboards and chairs of ebony wood from far-off Serendip. The roaring flames of his fire danced reflections off the mirror-polished silver chargers that lined his sideboard. A row of twenty filigreed goblets arrayed like soldiers stood upon his long conference table, waiting for masters and craftsmen to grasp them and fill them with Rhenish wine.

But in this moment, Bacher sat with just three others around the hearth, discussing the contents of a message which had just arrived that morning, carried at speed from Temeschburg, called by the Hungarians Temesvár. It was a message that held as much promise as it did threat, and Bacher thought it prudent to summon the grandmasters of the blacksmiths and the goldsmiths, those who sat alongside him on the High Council of the town. He quickly rebalanced his huge, horn spectacles on the bridge of his nose and then again gently waved the folded parchment at his guests with a forest green kid-gloved hand.

'I told you I smelled something when that woman came before us, preening and demanding our indulgence. Her and that inconsequential Englishman she claims is her lawful husband. Most ludicrous.'

'We know all that,' whined the goldsmith. 'You keep saying you have intelligence about the woman but you haven't yet told us what it is. We sent her and her company away so what more is there of the matter?'

Bacher tapped the folded paper on his temple. 'Much, much more, I assure you.'

The blacksmith gave Bacher a stern look. 'You're not going to bring this to the full council, are you? Otherwise you would not have called us here. In secret.'

The man's squint annoyed Bacher. He was never quite sure which eye to address since they looked in different directions. He chose the one he thought the better chance. 'No, I will not address this matter to the full town council. It is far too important to be debated. Argued. Thinned out like watered wine.'

The blacksmith rolled his wayward eyes. 'Well… you've dragged us out here in the cold so tell us the matter. Just get on with it.'

Bacher sank back into the high-backed chair and reopened the parchment, scanning it again. 'The woman does appear to have some relation to the Hunyadi family – on her mother's side. Dubious and illicit it would appear, but nonetheless, most likely truthful. That does not mean she enjoys the full blessing of the king nor that of Duke Kinizsi in Temeschburg. You see, my spies have ferreted out some rather interesting information.'

The goldsmith nodded, eyes narrowing. He shot a self-satisfied smile, nodding sagely. 'So, my lord, I *was* right about her credentials being suspicious.'

'Yes, probably. Maria Hunyadi apparently left Buda under a cloud of suspicion before disappearing into Dalmatia or the

Venetian lands. Something about some bags of gold missing from the Exchequer while she was at the palace.'

'And now she has returned here, to raise a company of soldiers for the kingdom?' said the blacksmith. 'That rings no truer now than it did a few days ago. I could have told you that for nothing.'

Bacher plucked his spectacles from his nose and raised a palm towards his guests. 'My good lords both, I did not doubt you then but we had no real cause to lawfully arrest her. So we sent her away. But you may be interested in learning who her father was. The Impaler.'

The goldsmith's eyes widened. 'So, she is a daughter of the Dragon. And what is her business in the Siebenbürgen?'

Bacher smiled. 'She *claims* to be his daughter. But the more interesting fact is indeed, what is her business *here*. She believes that the Impaler still lives and that Prince Vlad Călugărul – the Monk – has had him imprisoned these last nine years.'

The blacksmith let out a throaty roar of laughter. 'Vlad Dracula is nothing but bones! We would have heard long ago if it was otherwise. Let her chase her ghosts!'

The grandmaster shifted his myopic gaze from man to man. 'Then why would she invest her own time and treasure, risking her life in the process, to find him? I think she possesses intelligence that the Impaler does indeed still live and she has raised a company of foreign adventurers to free him.'

'Free him? From where?' scoffed the goldsmith.

'The fortress on the other side of the Făgăraș mountains, just into Wallachia. Castle Argeș.'

'Ridiculous,' muttered the blacksmith. He looked around the room. 'Now then, where is the wine you promised when we arrived? Where is that apprentice servant of yours?'

Bacher looked down his long nose at the guildsman. 'She may well be right, my friend. As far-fetched as that may sound. And there is much more to her plans, as well.'

'And we should believe *your* intelligence?' said the goldsmith. 'Just who are your spies and where are they? Other than their words on that scrap of paper you're holding.'

176

The grandmaster shot his guest a tolerant, condescending smile. 'All in good time, my lord. But I ask you to indulge me for a moment. What if the Impaler *does* live? And what if she does manage to free him? Will he raise an army to confront the Monk? He had a sizeable following in his day.'

'That day is long over,' said the blacksmith. 'Besides, the Monk is secure on his throne with the backing of the sultan. *Our* king in Buda has other concerns at the moment fighting the Austrians and is content to let us sit here worrying behind our walls.'

'Very well,' continued Bacher. 'So if Dracula does *not* have an army, merely a few mercenaries who have freed him, would he not be a juicy prize to send back to Vlad the Monk with our compliments? Or perhaps even to Sultan Bayezid? Think of the good will the gift of the Impaler – alive or dead – would generate for us. The sultan is practically knocking at our door as things stand. What will next summer bring when his army marches again?'

Bacher replaced his spectacles and watched his guests frown as they digested his message. Silence followed for a minute or two until the goldsmith found his voice again.

'I see your point. It could offer us advantages and at the very least eliminate the possibility of Dracula regaining his throne. That was bad enough for us before and I would imagine nine years in a dungeon would not have improved his temperament.'

The blacksmith laughed. 'Kronstadt town have only just finished removing the last of Vlad's forest of stakes from the outlying villages. It would be a shame if they had to put them up again!'

'Still...' said the goldsmith, 'you offer no real proof about any of this. Just gossip from some shadow-crawling spy of yours. And what is it exactly that you propose we do? What do you want from either of us?'

Bacher laced his fingers together and rested his hands on his lap. 'I propose that we send a force of our own to Argeş, wait and see if this woman succeeds in storming the fortress, and then, afterwards, take them all. I would ask your guilds to join me in putting up the coin to make it so. For the good of Hermannstadt and the Siebenbürgen.'

'The proof?' said the goldsmith, tapping his fingers on the arm of his chair. 'Who is your spy?'

Bacher smiled and picked up a silver hand bell on the table next to him. It pealed twice and an apprentice scurried in wearing his white cap and cloak.

'Show him up now,' said Bacher to the youth, who bowed and exited.

The two other grandmasters exchanged quick glances, rapidly realising their bluff had been called.

A tall man strode into the room, the brass buckles of his thigh boots jangling as he entered. He walked to the large stone hearth, turning to warm his backside near the crackling logs. He faced the three and folded his arms across his long, narrow torso.

'Your antechamber is most inhospitable, grandmaster. Far too mean a room to keep your guests idling in. I am frozen to the bone.' His words were in perfect German.

The silver master gestured with his hand towards the man. 'My lords, this is Captain Bobik. Captain Milos Bobik.'

The man bowed forward, slowly, then recovered just as slowly. He left his fur hat firmly on his head though. He wore a wolf-trimmed black cloak which extended past his knees, fastened with a large silver brooch. Bacher pushed himself back into his velvet chair as he regarded the man. He was unusually tall and thin, yet retained an aura of strength even though he was as lean as a beanpole. His long face ended in a chin that was as sharp as the point of a sword. Bacher was instantly reminded of the old Wallachian legends of the *strigoi*, those undead ghouls who stalked the forests, preying on travellers.

'Captain,' said Bacher. 'If you would be so good as to relate to my companions what you discovered at Temeschburg concerning this mysterious woman. They would hear it from your own lips rather than mine.'

The captain smiled and adjusted his stance to better face the other two men. The hilt of his expensive arming sword flashed momentarily when he pushed back his cloak. Bacher could almost sense his friends tensing in their chairs.

'I am happy to tell what I have learned,' said Bobik. 'You're the one paying for my service.'

The blacksmith was the bolder of the guildsmen. 'Then tell me this, is the woman the Impaler's daughter? I heard he had sired two brats, both boys, by the king's cousin. Never heard of a daughter.'

The pale eyes of the captain fixed the blacksmith with intense interest. 'She is a bastard of the Impaler. That is clear. I have spoken with those in the duke's court, certain intelligencers who linger there.'

'You speak with a distinct accent, captain. Are you a Moravian perhaps?'

Bobik lowered his head slightly towards the blacksmith, lending a faint air of menace. 'I am from Bohemia, sir. A soldier of fortune with some experience. Long experience.'

The blacksmith shifted in his seat slightly. 'That would explain it. Continue.'

Bobik bowed facetiously with exaggerated drama. 'Thank you, my lord. The woman considers herself a Hunyadi as her mother was the daughter of the late King Jan's mistress in Hunedoara. For that reason, the court has tolerated her in Buda and Temeschburg. But she is not trusted for reasons that are unclear. Possibly she thieved at court. Accusation unproven.'

The goldsmith found his voice again. 'So why does she search out Vlad Țepeș? To what purpose?'

Bobik smiled. A thin razor-like cut across his pale face. 'Because she believes he is alive. And he may well be.'

The goldsmith barked out a short, sharp laugh which ended in a cough. 'Really? After all these years? Gossip from some old camp followers of his, begging in the streets?'

'A man we caught tried to conceal that information, my lord. But try as he might, I was able to get it out of him. That and a few other interesting things. This daughter of the Impaler employed a Greek servant, you see. Someone she left behind to run her house and look after the gypsy slaves. He had the appearance of a catamite but, my word, he was brave. Before we could lay hands on him he had shoved a stiletto into one of my men. Killed him stone dead. After we subdued the fellow, he still would not betray his mistress, despite what we did to him. I will spare you that bit of the tale, but in the end, *my word*! He poured forth a bounty. Alas, the fellow did not survive the experience.'

The goldsmith swallowed and shifted his weight again. 'Herr Bacher is proposing we hunt her and her foreigners down. Track them to Wallachia and to the fortress where you claim Dracula is held prisoner. That is a challenging scheme some would consider quite mad. But you would agree to undertake this?'

Bobik nodded solemnly. 'I would. For the right price.'

The blacksmiths' master turned to Bacher and gave a shrug. 'Seems a gamble for dubious reward if you ask me. We might capture the Impaler. Or an imposter. Or even just a bag of old bones.'

Bacher smiled knowingly and gestured to the Bohemian mercenary to speak again.

'My lords,' said Bobik, turning and grinning at the two guildsmen, 'I haven't yet told you the best part of all! Another little secret I've learned, a secret which will banish your reluctance.'

And the Bohemian began to tell them of the last confession of Theophilius the Greek.

Part IV

THE PRISONER OF ARGEŞ

18

By the second day, the rains came. Cold drizzle during the morning and changing to cruel, driving sleet in the afternoon. It was now the morning of the third day since the company had left the gypsy encampment south of Hermannstadt and the rain had not stopped once. Gaston Dieudonné, taking his turn as the rear guard once again, was beginning to doubt he had made the right choice after all. Something he was loath to admit even to himself.

He hunkered down in his saddle, the woollen cloak even heavier for being soaked. The Olt River, dirt brown, swollen, and tipped with white peaks of churning rapids, sped along to the left of the rutted road. The road itself was now slickly wet with terracotta-coloured mud and their progress was dismally slow. Either side of the gorge was brown and grey: denuded winter trees, rocky outcrops, and a few patches of hardy, dark pine. The steep walls rose up several hundred feet and to Dieudonné's eyes, they seemed impassable. The sky was curdled milk. Their path, treacherous as it was, was the only way in or out. Beyond the river, to the east, the snow-capped peaks of the Făgăraş shot up high. Dieudonné recalled their recent trek through the autumn Alpine passes down towards Brescia and Venice. He had hated that journey, too.

Worse yet, this morning he was riding next to Bartolo Faldi. The Milanese was torturing him with endless tales of his exploits the summer before, fighting for the House of Sforza and their allies. The droning – all in rather bad French – made it almost unbearable. His only consolation was observing the large blooms of orange rust on Faldi's once mirror-polished armour.

'The duke had ordered us all to remain manning the siege even with plague breaking out. Imagine! As if my pay was worth risking a fatal case of the shits while sitting in a trench with nothing but a broken pavise for cover. *Allora!*'

Dieudonné stopped listening and turned his thoughts inward again, the rain pelting down on his helm. Had his initial faith in the Hungarian lioness been misplaced? Given his options at the time, siding with her had seemed a good chance of gaining some riches, maybe even nobility if the gods of Fortune favoured them. But all he could see now was that their army consisted of ten gypsy brigands, a few ageing men-at-arms, and two youths. The latter turned his mind to Giles.

He was not going to give up on the young royal bastard. He knew part of it was his own base desire, true, but thinking like the mercenary he was, it still seemed the best gamble to attain future fortune. Giles needed saving from Maria. That was very clear to him now. He didn't trust her motives in this quest and it seemed to him that her filial love was a bit too rich to be fully believed. Hawker might accept that sentiment, but he most certainly did not.

Faldi had moved on to the weather. As if it wasn't obvious that they were being pissed down upon from on high. Bartolo Faldi was a cipher too, he mused. What would prompt a man like him to risk everything to help the Hungarian? Did he love her? Possibly, but he had not seen them steal away at any point on the journey. He seemed to dote on her but she did not reciprocate the affection. Perhaps he was just moonstruck. But he didn't believe that either. It was usually love of gold that drove men like Faldi to their profession. The more Faldi droned on, the more he thought about it, his suspicions mounted.

He lifted his head to see Giles guiding his horse towards him, an improbable smile on the youth's fair face.

'Gaston, you look half-drowned! How fares it back here?'

Dieudonné found himself smiling at the royal's sudden arrival and his heart gave a small flutter. A welcome respite from Faldi.

'My dear friend, it is a far cry from our Venetian hot baths of blessed memory! What news of the front?'

They both halted. The rear hoof of Giles's horse slipped on the edge of the road but the beast recovered quickly enough. Faldi stopped too, swinging his mount around to join them.

'The gypsy chieftain says we will cross the river later today, where it is safer. Once on the other side we follow another road that takes us eastwards. There lies a wide pass leading down into the valley. We'll be out of this blasted gorge finally. Into Wallachia!'

As jaded as he was, Dieudonné couldn't but help find the youth's pluck enamouring. He had been rebuffed before, but the pursuit was always what drove him. He would persevere with gentle insistence. 'I would settle just for the rain letting up,' he said, grinning. 'Perhaps a warming fire this evening in some little hamlet up ahead? Would that be too much to hope for?'

Giles nodded. 'I would pay a handsome price for just that, dear Gaston.'

'So would we all!' added Faldi in his booming voice. 'This downpour is soaking into my very soul – it's already made it through my braes! *Porca miseria!*'

Giles adjusted his reins and glanced behind him. 'I must return to the front. We shouldn't fall behind. I just wanted to see how you fared back here. My turn tomorrow I should think!'

Dieudonné laughed lightly. 'Yes, don't tarry back here with us. You should get back up front with the mistress. She will be missing you.'

Giles laughed in return and turned his horse around, carefully making his way to the front of the column again. Dieudonné vowed to himself that he would get Giles back to Flanders if their enterprise here failed. There was still a chance that the Hapsburg duchess dowager, Giles's paternal aunt, might take him in. With the right persuasion of course. One always needed to have choices.

Dieudonné flicked his reins, his horse moved unsteadily forward through the sucking mud, and the Milanese followed, resuming his dull commentary on Lombard and Venetian political intrigue and war. The road snaked along and soon was even closer to the roaring river's edge than before. Far up ahead and lagging behind Giles, Maria and her gypsy bodyguard, he caught sight of Hawker, riding alongside his dour Fleming man-at-arms. He couldn't quite decide whether the old knight was broken now after his defeat in Venice or if he was biding his time for some great *coup de puissance*. Either way, in the end he knew he could only depend upon himself if things went badly. He always had. The rain intensified and he rode on.

When Dieudonné saw the crack silently appear, for a moment he thought he was imagining it. His horse simply passed over it and then a groan sounded as a chasm opened behind him. A surging rush of water from down the side of the hill had undermined the road causing it to melt away in seconds. Dieudonné's mount went down, its rear legs sliding out when the road disappeared, and the Frenchman found himself flung out and crashing down. He rolled and scrambled forward, feeling no purchase under his feet. Digging in with his armoured knees he caught the remaining road surface and twisted to look back.

Neighing wildly, his horse had powered its way forward close to the hillside, reached the firmer road, and trotted after the company. Bartolo Faldi had not been so lucky. The Milanese was half submerged in the frothing torrent, clambering for a handhold but slipping further out into the raging current. The knight's horse was gone. Dieudonné scrambled down the bank, grabbed hold of a dead branch from the side of the road and gingerly made his way towards Faldi who, chest deep, was just managing to cling to a rock that had been revealed by the landslide. He had lost his helmet and had already been dunked fully, his long hair slick, face dripping.

Careful not to lose his own footing, the Frenchman eased his way, extending the branch towards Faldi. The Milanese was cursing and then calling for God's help in the same breath. When he saw Dieudonné and the tree branch, his eyes widened and he began to reach forward to try and catch it. Dieudonné rapidly shot a glance behind him: no one in the company had yet noticed what had happened.

He dangled the branch just outside Faldi's reach and then called to him over the sound of the rushing waters.

'What is her plan? Tell me! Now!'

Faldi's mouth gaped further. 'For the love of Christ! Help me!' His legs kicked frantically in an attempt to gain purchase on the rapidly dissolving roadside. It only made things worse: he lost his grip and slipped further down into the river. His hands clawed at another rock that had been exposed and the Milanese managed to hook a forearm around it. Still, the rushing waters pulled at him.

Dieudonné eased the branch back a little, further from his reach. 'Come now! What is she planning? What is your bargain? So help me, I will let you drown! Answer me!'

The answer, when it came, was half a scream of desperation.

'Treasure! Prince Vlad's treasure! Help me, you bastard!'

Dieudonné braced his feet again. The rushing water was beginning to take the ground out beneath him as well. He waved the branch of salvation teasingly. 'Cut me in! Cut me in on the treasure or you can swim!' Dieudonné moved the stick further out of Faldi's reach.

'Yes, yes! I swear it!'

The Frenchman moved the stick closer to Faldi. The Milanese gripped it first with one hand and then with the other. Dieudonné leaned back and grunted, pulling with all his might. Kicking for purchase in the slick mud, Faldi began to inch towards the road surface. When he reached Dieudonné, crawling on his stomach, the Frenchman hauled him in. Behind him he heard yells and hooves pounding. The others had finally realised something had happened. Turning, he saw three of the gypsies and Hawker closing in. Dieudonné scrambled onto his knees and leaned down over Faldi. He grasped a handful of the man's hair and yanked, forcing Faldi's head up. Dieudonné put his long nose close to Faldi's ear.

'Cut me in! Or I will tell Hawker your plan.'

'Don't tell her you know! I beg you!'

Dieudonné yanked a little harder. 'You tell her, or don't tell her. I don't care. But I wànt a piece of it when the time comes! Swear it or everyone will know your little secret!'

'*Si, si!*'

'Swear it!'

'I swear it! By the Virgin, I swear it!'

Dieudonné flipped him onto his back like a turtle, just as the gypsies dismounted to help them. 'We will speak later, my lord!' he said as the gypsies pulled Faldi to his feet.

Hawker sidestepped his way down towards them, careful to keep his footing. 'Is he alive?'

Dieudonné moved back and nodded. 'Yes, he is whole. I pulled him out before he was swept away.'

Hawker took Faldi's arm and helped bring him further up the road. The Milanese coughed and spluttered but said nothing.

'Lucky you were so quick to act,' said Hawker. 'He would have sunk like a stone out there.'

'It was God's will,' said Dieudonné. 'The Lord's heavenly grace gave me the means to save Ser Bartolo. That tree branch was already there. Close enough and long enough to allow me to reach him.'

Hawker raised an eyebrow. 'We must get him dried off somehow. We will have to make a halt to build a fire up ahead. The gypsies will know where.'

Dieudonné nodded again. But he wasn't really listening. He was congratulating himself on his suspicions, suspicions that had been proved correct. He still needed to know more, but Maria perhaps wasn't just the loyal daughter she wanted to be seen as. The Tears of Byzantium already in her possession had not been enough, it seemed. It then followed that the Milanese needed Dracula alive to learn where his treasure was hidden. Otherwise, they could have proceeded directly to where it lay, without dragging her old father along. What had Faldi offered her other than his sword arm and his empty closet of a head? Why had she trusted him this far? As soon as they dried out the fool, he would have to have another conversation. He hoped that Faldi wouldn't catch a chill and die before that could happen.

They got Faldi out of his armour and wrapped him in blankets that the gypsies had on their donkeys. Tokár was eager to continue for fear they wouldn't make the next halt before darkness. But at least the rain had ceased, leaving only an overcast sky of swirling grey and white. Maria consented and the company continued along the river. Dieudonné reclaimed his horse and this time, he rode closer to the front, the Fleming and the boy Jack taking up the rear.

From his vantage, Dieudonné was able to hear the conversation among the others. What struck him was the lack of any emotion from Maria Hunyadi at Faldi's plight. Some slight concern, even surprise about his misadventure, but nothing that smacked of relief for his deliverance. Nothing that spoke of affection and love. *That* intrigued the Frenchman. Though he had never experienced the emotion in any great way, he considered himself a master of seeing it in others. Maria did not love Faldi even if he worshipped her. There had to be something else at the heart of the matter.

Giles seemed to be doing his best to keep Faldi's spirits up as they rode along. Maria, too, encouraged the Milanese, but in an offhand way as if it was something with which to pass the time. Dieudonné could glimpse Faldi occasionally shiver under his woollen blankets and his replies – when he made them – were curt and sullen. The bombastic mercenary, far from the irate chattering from earlier, had become circumspect probably for both his near demise and the fact that his secret was no longer his and hers alone. Hawker seemed to take the event in his stride and had decided to ride at the lead with Tokár and the gypsy chieftain's men. That spoke volumes too: the old knight had concerns of his own.

By mid-afternoon, they had crossed the Olt where it narrowed, over an ancient bridge missing so many stones that it gave Dieudonné little confidence it would stand their passage.

They entered a small village, its solitary, shingle-domed wooden church sitting above it on the hillside like a mother hen looking down on her young. It looked to be prosperous for its situation along the trade road, its thatched cottages appearing well-looked after, with little garden plots alongside most of them. The road sliced the village in two, the east side gradually rising up from its grassy slopes to more uneven stony ground and eventually the mountains higher up. The west side contained more little houses with many willow trees and reed beds bleached like straw along the riverbank.

Faldi's new mount, a donkey, carrying his breastplate, back, pauldrons and vambraces strapped to its cruppers, sounded like a tinker's wagon as it trotted along and Dieudonné grinned at the sight of the Milanese wrapped up like an old woman. Tokár signalled a halt and trotted off with Maria and Hawker to arrange lodging at a two-storey hostelry that stood not far from the river. Peasants began to assemble, staring silently at them. They were, said Maria, Wallachians in the main with a few Magyars among them as well, hold-outs of earlier settlements. And although they were still within the jurisdiction of the Saxons of Hermannstadt, no one could be heard speaking the German tongue. They were now in a place where the Roman faith of the west bumped up against that of Greece and Byzantium.

Dieudonné edged his horse closer to Ellingham's. He was chilled to the bone as he too had been dunked up to his thighs. His boots squelched in his stirrups and he muttered an oath.

'How do you fare, Gaston?'

'In need of a fire and the sooner the better,' mumbled Dieudonné.

'Yes, and Ser Bartolo the most in need of it. You were lucky you didn't both wash away. We could never have saved you if the river had dragged you down.'

Faldi threw back the blanket from his head and shook his locks. 'I am still here, my lords. Not drowned and not ready to die. Just in need of a fire and a large goblet of wine.'

Giles laughed. 'Let's follow the mistress to the house. The quicker to get warm! What say you, Gaston?'

Dieudonné threw a knowing glance over to Faldi. 'Yes, why not? We all need a roaring fire and some drink. And some telling of tales... if any have a mind to.'

Giles waved to Jacob and Jack to call them forward from down the road where the village began. Faldi's eyes locked onto the Frenchman's, his newfound hatred shining brightly.

Dieudonné just smiled and gave a shrug. 'Let's get warm!'

–

The inn was large and squarely built of dark, pitch-stained timber. From the hay-strewn courtyard, wooden stairs ascended to a balustrade mezzanine off which several bedchambers were situated. The entire ground floor of the inn was the common room, a long, heavy oak table at its centre. The company, the only guests there, were gathered around a crackling fire which blazed away, smoke swirling lazily up towards the roof beams where openings gaped. The many flagstones of the floor were covered in more straw and dried river reeds, and this had not been refreshed in an age. Now, inside this space of rustic carved pillars and beams, the smell of damp woollens surpassed even the scent of the wood smoke. Jack's legs were so close to the flames of the hearth that steam could be seen rising from his hose and boots. Outside, the horses were stabled in a lean-to shelter while an old canvas pavilion, abandoned by the Ottomans after their last invasion a few years earlier, served as shelter for Tokár and his men.

Maria had been offered the best bedchamber by the innkeeper, but this time her 'husband' would not be sharing it with her. The need for that subterfuge was diminishing the further they travelled away from towns and Giles himself had belatedly realised, he admitted, the irritation the arrangement was causing among the company. The innkeeper, a ruddy and wrinkled man who had seen many winters, had set an iron tripod over the fire upon which a black cauldron of pottage bubbled away. He wobbled from guest to guest, ladling out the stuff laced with salt pork into wooden bowls. On a nearby stool, he had balanced a small keg of Moldovan wine for them to partake of.

Maria stood, still wrapped tightly in her voluminous cloak, watching them all with an approving look on her face. She thanked the innkeeper in the Wallachian tongue for his help and he smiled. She had earlier announced that she told the peasant she was on pilgrimage to the monastery of Snagov to seek a benediction and that the company were her protectors. Her poor handmaid had died of fever at Hermannstadt but she was continuing on alone but for her guard. Dieudonné had to admire her abilities to mould novel, heartfelt truths from the rough clay of lies. The man bowed low to her, probably thinking she was some wealthy noblewoman, and then left to check upon the gypsies and the two Rascians. Maria had admitted the man had not been happy with their presence but the addition of gold florins had persuaded him to forget his prejudices. Dieudonné thought that laughable – the old Wallachian had nothing worth stealing anyway.

'Tokár tells me,' said Maria, once the innkeeper had departed, 'we are but half a day's ride from the castle – if the weather holds out. We are on the edge of Wallachia. This country is not friendly to our cause. Not yet at least.'

'I didn't find the Saxon towns friendly to our cause much either,' remarked Dieudonné. 'Unless I missed something.'

Maria glared at him a second but continued on, turning to face Ellingham. 'I must now ask my captain...' She hesitated a moment and swivelled to face Hawker. '*Captains*... how we make our approach to the fortress.'

Faldi, hunched over close to the fire in his horse blanket, looked up briefly, his brow furrowing at the slight of being left out. Dieudonné supressed a grin. The Milanese seemed to have lost his favour as well as his horse. That might give him some influence over the man, currency he could later use.

Ellingham had sat upright at Maria's request, eyes widening slightly. He looked over to Hawker, uncertainly. 'My lady, Sir John has told us what he proposes... and I agree.'

Maria smiled. 'Yes, but we must decide the route we take to get up to the tunnel. Without being seen.'

Hawker gently placed his empty bowl on the trestle table and wiped his mouth. 'We will know that when we get there. It is something that I must see with mine own eyes first. And if Vilkas has been there as he says, then he will know where the cave lies. That rules where we must begin our ascent.'

Ellingham tapped his bowl with his spoon.

'But,' continued Hawker, 'if the hill is as steep and wooded as Vilkas says, then the horses will not be able to climb. We'll need to keep them further below – somewhere secluded – while the company scales the slope.'

Maria's dark eyebrows raised slightly. 'So, you are proposing to divide our force? Leave some men with the horses?'

'I am. We will need a camp first, so that we can observe the castle and its situation, its day-to-day life. And we must needs find the entrance to the cave in the daytime, explore it, and then return to the encampment. We would be foolish to rush in and find we have misjudged our enemies.'

Maria nodded. 'That is good counsel, Sir John. Do you agree, son of Richard?'

Ellingham looked up again. 'Yes, it's a sound plan. Scout things before we strike.'

Dieudonné watched the exchange, intrigued. It seemed that Giles was relinquishing some of his responsibilities back to Hawker, or that he had, at the very least, lost some of his earlier bravado. Dieudonné knew he had to shore up the youth's confidence somehow even if the veteran Hawker was the better to lead them into a fight. Giles would always be his path back to Flanders and some hope of obtaining favour or fortune. Of all of this company, it was really only the youth he had any affection for, even if that youth saw his friendship in only the most platonic of ways. He had not given up on winning Giles over and he was not about to let the blond noble belong to anyone else.

'Then Tokár and Vilkas will have to ride ahead and find where we may make an encampment off the road,' said Maria. 'It would do no good for all of us to blunder about on the mountainside looking for such a place.'

'I will go with Tokár,' said Hawker, a bit of quiet insistence in his voice. 'I would see for myself how the land lies.'

'I too will go with you,' said Ellingham.

Hawker nodded. 'Agreed. You should see the situation too.' He turned towards Faldi and the others. 'I think it better the rest of you stay together on the road. If you're surprised by any militia you will need every sword arm you have. We four will be enough to scout and I can at least understand the gypsy's twisted Venetian tongue. As for the Balt, let us hope he finds familiar ground.'

Dieudonné thought he caught sight of Giles's jaw tensing, as if the youth was clenching his teeth.

'Then it is decided,' announced Maria. 'I will take my leave of you and pray you manage to sleep well here.'

Faldi rose and bowed towards her and then went to refill his wine cup from the cask. The others nodded at her and valiant Jack stood to do so, copying Faldi.

Maria ascended the open staircase and disappeared upstairs. A heavy silence fell upon them.

Finally, Jack spoke up, in English. 'Is it nearly Christmas, Sir John?'

Hawker smiled. 'I expect it must nearly be. I suppose I have lost track of the days.'

'I would dearly love a feast. Maybe a fat goose and some pies. We did not have our goose at Michaelmas just passed. I can't even remember where we were then.'

Jacob laughed softly. 'We will do our best to find you a goose, boy. After we free the old prince of Wallachia.'

Faldi drained his wine and began pulling on his still slightly damp doublet, grimacing with the coldness of the touch. He then threw on his steaming cloak. 'I am going out for a piss.' It was said in a tone of deep reluctance.

Dieudonné smiled faintly. Faldi had yet to tell Maria that they had a new conspirator among them. That was no matter.

She did not have to know yet. But Faldi had already revealed to him that some of the Hungarian's little stash of ducats were his own. Mercenary earnings he had invested in her scheme which he hoped would lead to bigger riches once Dracula revealed his treasure. Dieudonné stood up, set down his mug upon the table and stretched. 'That is a good idea, Ser Bartolo. Before it gets much colder, I will join you.'

Faldi avoided his eye, mumbled something under his breath, and made for the door.

19

Hawker again checked the cinch strap of his mount. It was loose. The beast had bloated itself earlier to fool him into buckling it where he thought it tight but Hawker always checked twice. He gently scolded the horse as he moved the belt up another notch. 'You would have me riding underneath, would you? Not today my friend. Let's play nicely, shall we?'

The horse snorted and nodded, flanks twitching in irritation. Jack, holding the bridle, *cluck-clucked* at it and patted its neck.

The knight turned towards Ellingham who was already in his saddle and adjusting his reins. 'Are we ready then, Sir Giles, for our little reconnoitre?'

Giles pushed up the peak of his sallet helm with his gauntleted hand and gave a nod.

Hawker then turned to the rest of the company. Faldi stood impassive at Maria's side, ever her guardian. Behind them, Dieud-onné stood off to one side, arms folded, his expression inscrutable but Hawker sensing disappointment at his being told to stay behind. No such emotion seemed to affect Ser Bartolo Faldi. Hawker knew from past experience that the man was no coward, but Faldi had not said a word in protest at being left behind with Maria and the gypsy band. Indeed, he seemed to welcome it. Perhaps he wanted to stay close to her, and if she had insisted on joining the scouting expedition he would have bulled his way in as well. It was a loyalty that to Hawker's mind posed questions, questions he did not yet have the answers to.

'God go with you, my good knights,' said Maria, her voice carrying the regal tone she sometimes affected. 'We shall pray you quickly discover the castle's weakness and find a favourable route of attack. Tokár will not fail you.'

'If the cave still exists we shall find it, my lady,' said Ellingham.

Hawker smiled to himself. The besotted youth would do anything to please her. A day away from her charms – or her spell – might do him some good. Hawker took his sallet from Jacob's hands and buckled its chinstrap. 'We shall keep out of harm's way, my lady. Let our eyeballs do the work instead. Fear not.' Jacob finished attaching a wineskin and an additional woollen cloak to the back of Hawker's saddle. Hawker clapped Jacob on the shoulder and prepared to mount. But first he leaned into the Fleming and whispered in his own tongue, 'If we have not returned after two days, take Jack and get *out*. Back north. Go to the German lands.'

Jacob, grey-faced, nodded grimly but said nothing.

Hawker, sprang, grunted and threw his leg over the saddle to settle in. Jack kindly guided his toe into the other stirrup and Hawker adjusted his reins. Tokár, bare-headed and dressed in his pied cowhide jerkin, was already sitting in the saddle of the company's donkey, its cruppers piled with provisions and rope. A grim-looking Vilkas rode on a horse behind him, bleary-eyed. Tokár called over to the Englishmen.

'Andiamo? Si?'

Hawker flicked his reins and moved out. Jack stood back.

'Stay sharp… and practise, my boy!'

Jack gave him a nod and an uncertain smile.

Tokár and Vilkas led the way out on the road and the two knights followed.

–

They rode for some three hours without a stop, into a wide valley of undulating hills, the road gently descending before them. Tokár's broad-backed little donkey bounced its way along the rutted road without protest, setting a good pace. They travelled east, the land sloping away beneath them, down and down, as the foothills of the Făgăraş shrank away into rolling countryside, oak forests and pine copses scattered here and there. The land was sad, washed out in the grip of winter. Far away to their left, snow covered the high peaks, and swirling clouds of it could be clearly seen against the blue sky. Hawker suppressed a shudder, grateful they had survived the low pass and were spared the necessity of taking a higher route through the mountains.

They had yet to spy even a hamlet along the road. Although they were saluted by a few peasants who trudged along bearing wicker baskets, they saw no one else. The land seemed empty and wild but mercifully the weather had held and only a light wind blew at their backs from the west.

Hawker found himself staring at his companion's profile. For an instant he was transported back years, to Tewkesbury field and the great Yorkist victory he had helped to deliver. The youth that rode next to him was the very image of young King Richard. Ellingham's hair was fairer, yes, but nose, cheekbones, lips and chin, those were Richard Plantagenet, Duke of Gloucester as was. It was almost uncanny and he wondered why more people had not made mention of the resemblance. The duchess dowager of Burgundy might have had her suspicions. He remembered her stares at the youth as if trying to place him in her past. Just as well no one had remarked on it, for their paths might have taken an even more dangerous turn.

Ellingham caught him staring.

'You must think me a fool. For my arrogance these past days.'

'Explain.'

'That I thought I could be captain. To lead instead of you. I can do neither.'

Hawker smiled. 'You are leading us, Sir Giles. I am only... guiding.'

Ellingham moved his eyes to the gypsy riding ahead. 'That is mere word play. It is you with the experience. The skill. I should not have spoken out.'

'You don't lead by thinking about it. You lead by doing it. And that is what you're doing, with me at your side. You are the son of our king, not I. I will advise you on what I see and how I see it. But it is your decision as to what course we take.'

Ellingham let out a laugh. 'That simple, is it? Mayhaps my head has been turned by Maria Hunyadi, as you told me. I truly did believe I could take command. But now I'm unsure.'

'Don't blame the woman. It is your own doubt that holds you back. I've seen you in battle. Your judgement is sound. Half of success in war is luck anyway.' Hawker paused a moment. 'Did you tup her?'

Ellingham turned in the saddle and glared for a moment before softening. 'No, I did not… But I was sore tempted.'

Hawker nodded. 'Then you chose wisely. At the end of the day we are her mercenaries. Under contract. And becoming the lover of your paymaster seems to me the path to grand misfortune.'

'She would not have had me anyway, I suspect,' mumbled Ellingham.

'Just as well. If Vlad Dracula lives then we will deliver him to her. You may count on that. Then you can decide what we do next. My first bit of advice to you?' Hawker indicated Tokár up ahead. 'Watch and follow *his* lead. These people know the land and know the enemy. And I would wager that this gypsy and his comrades will be worth their weight in gold in the coming days.'

'I'll accept your good advice, Sir John. Gladly. And you will tell me when my head grows too large for my helm.'

A laugh rumbled up from Hawker's chest. He turned and smiled. 'Agreed, son of Richard!'

'And… I am sorry. For saying nothing these past weeks for your loss. Of Lady Chiara. It was wrong and selfish of me not to offer you even a few words of comfort. I was wallowing too deep in my own worries to see yours. Can you forgive me?'

Hawker kept his eyes ahead of him. 'You need not ask forgiveness of me, Giles. I bear what I must. We all do.'

There was silence between them, broken only by the dull thud of hooves on the pitted road. After a minute Giles spoke up again.

'I know not what awaits us ahead. But, if we yet live when all is done, know that I would go back with you, Sir John – to Venice. To find her again.'

Hawker glanced down at his saddlebow for a second then half turned to Ellingham. This time his smile was wan and fleeting. 'That is a most generous and loyal gesture. But I don't think my heart could bear what we might find there. No, Giles, that is gone now. We must look to you and your future. Not to my past.'

–

It was early afternoon when Tokár doubled back and reined in alongside the knights. 'We take different path here. Through woods. Too dangerous to stay on road this near to castle.'

They rode into a wide path among the bare trees, snaking its way eastwards. It was on an incline and difficult to negotiate, although Tokár's donkey had little trouble doing so. A few hundred yards below them, they could still just make out the road running in parallel. The forest was deathly quiet around them and Hawker was all too aware of the clamour their clanking armour made. The path swerved higher – they were ascending again. Vilkas would gesture frantically every so often leading Tokár to remonstrate with him. Their path turned again and again as the two argued about the way forward.

'Where in the name of hell are they taking us?' said Ellingham, urging his mount on.

'I imagine Tokár's trying to keep us out of sight. I just pray it is not much further.'

Tokár hissed and urged them onwards. The pace was slow now and the horses began to labour, their snorting breaths sounding loud on the chilled air. But they could handle the climb, allaying earlier fears. After half an hour, Tokár suddenly stopped, his head swivelling, looking and listening. Hawker could hear a fast-running stream somewhere nearby. He began to fear that the gypsy might have lost his way. But Tokár raised an arm and then turned to them. 'Dismount here.'

Tokár unhooked his canvas bucket and wandered off for a few minutes. He returned with it full to the brim and commenced to water the horses.

Ellingham tried his Venetian out on the gypsy. 'So we *walk* from here? How far?'

Tokár looked over to Hawker. 'We walk. Castle not far. Tie horses here.'

Ellingham shot Hawker a dubious glance. Hawker shrugged in turn and proceeded to dismount. The horses secured and given their nosebags to feed, Tokár and Vilkas led the knights onwards. The tall trees creaked, swaying gently with the breeze and they made their way along the slope. The gypsy's keen eyes had already made out a narrow footpath, well-worn and ancient, and was following it.

After a few minutes the forest became sparser, dotted with more old pine than oak and beech. They then came upon a curious clearing, one Hawker thought not made by man. A dead place where no trees grew, only scrub. It was no more than a hundred yards wide. It looked almost unnatural and could have been from a lightning strike years earlier. But there were no charred remains of trees to be seen. It was as if the forest had grown around it. Hawker looked at Ellingham and nodded thoughtfully. They had now found the company's camp site. Tokár carried on to the far side, halted and pointed through the trees. Vilkas, panting, stopped and turned, outstretched palms imploring the knights. 'Wein, *bitte!*'

Hawker shot Ellingham a glance and shook his head. 'We'd better give him a sip of something before he ends up in a fit,' said Ellingham.

Hawker gave Vilkas a wine flask but yanked it back after the Balt had taken a long swig. 'That's enough for now.'

Ahead a thousand yards, and slightly lower down the slope, a stone fortress squatted on the pinnacle of the ridge they had traversed. The castle of Argeş. Dracula's bolt-hole, built by the slave labour of his enemies and which now, ironically, was his own prison.

It was a narrow fortress, wedged along the spine of the mountain, and Hawker reckoned he could spit from one side to the other. At one end, the end closest to them, a squat square tower lay, topped with a tiled spire. Two tall turrets were built into the south wall which met the north wall at a third and final turret and spire. The footprint was but a small triangle balanced on the edge of a precipice overlooking the Argeş River far below. Its overlook was commanding, a veritable eagle's lair. Hawker grunted. If the tunnel had collapsed, and they were forced to take the gate, it would be a difficult nut to crack even with an army. A ruse to gain entry would be their only option.

'Why would the Monk even keep him alive?' Hawker mused aloud. He was surprised to hear Tokár answer him.

'It is a great evil to slay one's kin.' The gypsy's breath, condensing in the frosty air, rolled out in a cloud. 'They are brothers. Brothers who both want throne.'

'Shared blood hasn't stopped others from shedding it. It makes little sense to me. The Turkish princes slay each other with grim regularity. Why not the Wallachians?'

'We are in eastern lands, Sir John,' said Ellingham. 'We do not understand their ways. It is enough we know the prince is alive. In there.'

'Do we know that?' said Hawker, looking at the gypsy. 'Swear to me again you know the prince is alive.'

Tokár fixed Hawker with a gaze that could have turned others to stone. His words were slow, measured, and purposeful. 'I give you word. My word! You call me liar?'

Hawker drew himself up. 'You gave your word but you offered no proof. Have you seen him?'

The gypsy glared for a moment then looked towards the castle. 'I not see him. Others have. I believe them.'

Ellingham placed a hand on Hawker's shoulder. 'It will have to do, Sir John. We must throw the dice.'

Hawker switched to English. 'If his magic cave is not there then we will find ourselves in a gamble in which we will get only one throw.' He looked at Tokár and growled in Venetian, 'We must get closer. Get the Balt to find us that opening in the mountain.'

Tokár's head of long grey curls nodded, his anger having already receded. His jet-black eyes opened full. 'He will remember. I show you.'

Hawker turned again to look at the castle. There was no sign of life. No one upon the walls or on top of the wide square tower. But a long-tailed pennon flew there, snapping out in the swirling mountain winds. The place was inhabited – and defended. He grunted to himself.

'We should leave some of our harness here lest we make too much noise moving closer.'

Ellingham nodded. The knights helped each other undo their pauldrons, cannons and vambraces, then their leg armour, stacking it all near where the horses stood tied. Wearing just their arming doublets, breastplates and swordbelts, Vilkas led them forward through the trees, following the ridgeline towards the western wall of the castle. The Balt was more enlivened now with the dark, heavy wine infusing him. As they drew closer, Hawker could now see the castle gate and the narrow, steep road that led up to it. It looked barely wide enough for a two-wheeled tumbrel to pass. They kept low, hugging trees, fearful of every dead branch that cracked underfoot. The Balt was taking them down the steep left slope, heading towards the north face of the walls. Hawker noticed that the treeline and rocky ground seemed to suddenly disappear about twenty feet to their left. A sheer drop down to the Argeş River, a few hundred feet below.

Vilkas dropped down to a knee, watching the castle intently. He then raised an arm, his finger indicating an area below where the brick and stone of the castle footings ended. Hawker, leaning to look over Tokár's back, sighted down the Balt's arm. He could see what looked like a black space, darker than the surrounding rocky base, covered with brown saplings, briars, and evergreen gorse.

Hawker turned to Ellingham. 'It is an opening, a crevice below the walls. Not very large but it is there.'

'We need to go closer. We must learn if it is passable.'

Hawker nodded. 'Agreed. Without torches we won't be able to go in very far. But we must try.'

They hugged the outcrop, stepping carefully forward until they reached the opening. It was big enough for two men side by side. Tokár turned to the knights, grinning. Hawker rewarded him with a smile of his own. So far, the gypsy had been right. Even Vilkas was smiling, head nodding vigourously like some madman in the street. Hawker stepped inside and into the darkness. His nose was assailed by the acrid and foul stench of bats and other creatures that had made the cave their home. But he also felt a draught, a strong draught, blowing out from deeper inside. Moving forward warily, he found that the crevice grew wider still. He felt Ellingham at his back, eager to get his own look.

'The gypsy was right, Sir John. The old fool remembered after all.'

'We go no further. Not now,' whispered Hawker. 'It is enough to know it is here and that the Balt has passed through it before. We've got to get back while we still have light. And before we are seen or heard.'

They retraced their steps, fearful that at any moment they might hear a horn sounded behind them. A sally from the gate could catch them out as they made their way back up to where the horses were. But, looking back over their shoulders, the castle remained silent and dead to the world.

They donned their armour again, each playing squire to the other. Tokár chuckled, mumbling to himself and pleased with his success at finding the cave. Ellingham finished cinching Hawker's shoulders and looked over to the horses.

'We shall never make it back before midnight even if we leave now. Do we stay, wrap up in our cloaks, and take our chances with the cold?'

Hawker shook his head. 'We'd probably be dead by morning up here. No, we must ride back. Maybe find some small hamlet on the way that we missed. Tokár will know.'

Ellingham looked over to Vilkas and smiled. 'The old fellow is happy enough now. I think he surprised himself that he could find the cave. What is he saying?'

Hawker listened to the Balt's mutterings.

'Something about twenty and five years.'

He turned to Vilkas and spoke slowly in German. 'What are you saying? Twenty-five years ago?'

Vilkas wiped his drooping, snot-crusted moustache with thumb and forefinger and nodded. 'I help lead out the master from here. Through the cave. We escape his enemies – his brother Prince Radu and the Turks. They never know he gone!'

Hawker translated for Ellingham. Listening, the youth chewed his lip, brushed back his long blond hair, and pushed on his sallet helm. 'He makes it sound simple. But that was a long time ago. Ask him if there is a door where the cave ends and the castle begins.'

Hawker's brow elevated a little. He turned and posed it to Vilkas.

The Balt waved a hand dismissively and spoke.

'He says there is nought but a few wooden planks covering the hole. He says he remembers it well.'

'There is one thing that nags me,' said Ellingham.

Hawker gave him a little smile. 'And what would that be?'

'Dracula's been in that dungeon for nine years. And we're supposed to believe he hasn't had a single chance to find that cave again?'

20

For the first time since his beating and brief imprisonment in Hermannstadt, Pedja Jankovic was beginning to feel optimistic again. He knew that he and Orkan were riding through the closest thing to a friendly country. Wallachia paid tribute to the sultan – or at least he had heard that was so. Its ruler was the sultan's vassal. He remembered that Vlad Călugărul, the one they called the Monk, had even hosted a contingent of Turkish troops in the last two summers. Pedja might be a simple *martalos* with no mind for grand strategy but he knew enough to realise that he was probably on the safest ground he'd been on in weeks.

Orkan rode in silence next to him. They were on the road again south, hugging the foothills of the Carpathians. He had purposely fallen back to the rear, letting the gypsies on their ponies overtake him and the ursine Turk. The Burgundian had been loitering at the end of the company as well. He eyes had dwelt on Pedja a little too long for the Bosnian's comfort. The man was a suspicious sort. Pedja had picked up on that early on. He gave a nod of respect which was acknowledged, but without a smile by the Burgundian – the way with most Franks, thought Pedja. Dieudonné kicked his heels in and his mount trotted forward leaving them behind.

'I do not like that Frank,' said Orkan in his bad Slavic. 'How much further to this damned castle then? Up and down, down and up, I'm tired of this trek and my arse is rubbed raw.'

'Soon enough, my friend, just keep your grumbling down. We've only just had our reprieve.'

Orkan gave a short sharp laugh. 'Reprieve? It will be short-lived... like us, no doubt.'

'We're in *Wallachia* now, Orkan. If the worst comes to worst, we can ride off and find sanctuary. The prince of Wallachia, the one they call the Monk, he pays tribute to the sultan these days. Or we might even make it to Moldavia – to Chilia port – where the sultan's army camps. Remember how we heard that even before we left Zvornik?'

Orkan muttered a curse as his horse stumbled over a loose rock on the sloping ground. 'Old Kaziglu Bey had better be in that fortress once we get there. It's a miracle we've gotten this far with our heads still attached to our shoulders. And you still have to come up with a scheme to get the old man away from the Hungarian and her Franks once we spring him.'

Pedja frowned, stung a little by that truth. He didn't have the faintest idea how he would escape with the captive, even assuming the Impaler was still alive. 'I will find a way. You just stand by me with your beautiful iron mace.'

'Well, Tombik, I've come too far now to do anything else. My brains might be addled for all the shit we've been through in the last fortnight but I still can't figure why this Monk prince is keeping Kaziglu Bey in prison. He could have given him to the sultan as a great gift. The infidel who had bested his best. I reckon the Wallachian could have named his price from the sultan for his reward.'

It had preyed upon Pedja's mind as well for the past few days. Prince Călugărul hadn't executed his brother even though it was in his interest to do so. He could understand that himself having lost his own brother. And perhaps Călugărul had realised that if Vlad Dracula was turned over to the sultan, he would be beheaded on the spot. Maintaining a ruse that Dracula was dead also meant he could protect his brother from the sultan's reach as well. But how could he hope to know the motives of such men? As far as he himself was concerned, Pedja Jankovic would sell Dracula to the highest bidder – dead or alive.

'That matters no more, Orkan. We can take him to Târgovişte and gain our reward or bring him eastwards and hand him over to the sultan's beylerbey in camp on the Danube. Either way, we win.'

Orkan shook his head and smiled. 'Your definition of winning presumes a whole basket of good will on the part of others, Tombik.'

He wasn't about to let the *akinci* freebooter rob him of his optimism. So he let out a good-natured curse at the Turk, laughing. But he was angry. Not at Orkan, but at himself. This damned daughter of the Dragon, she who had slain his brother, had also saved his own life. Saved it even possibly by endangering those of her entire company. So how could he kill her in cold blood now that he owed her a blood debt? The more he thought about it the more he puzzled. He had not witnessed the slaughter at that Bosnian village where his brother fell. *Was* she the one who actually slew him by the sword? It was hard enough to believe that. Davud had been strong and fit. Was the old Croat just trying to goad him by saying a woman had killed his brother? He could never know.

He knew he had accomplished little in his life except to escape his father's farm. No great deeds, no great fortune either by theft or by reward. No great loves. No sons. Nothing. The promise of capturing the great enemy of the Ottoman sultans, a slim thread but a golden one, this was worth risking it all though. The Hungarian woman he would decide upon when the moment came. He might, in the end, decide to grant her life and pay back his blood debt, but if she stood in the way of his escape he would not hesitate to kill her.

The cowhide-clad *cigani* had now led the Franks off the road, continuing eastwards across open, hilly country. No bad thing, he thought. Road travel only attracted unwanted attention and they were a conspicuous band of rogues if ever there was one. They were strung out in a long single file and Pedja could just see Maria at the front alongside the Italian and her pet *cigan*, Tokár. After an hour they were still in a wilderness of scrub thorn, pine stands, and broken grassland, and although in the middle of nowhere, at least they were now out of view. The ground rose more steeply and the mountains to the north beckoned ominously. Pedja prayed that his escape route would not take him up there. It was obvious he had only two directions to choose from that would offer a chance: south and east.

Not long after, they entered a denser stretch of forest. The donkeys, sure-footed, coped far better than the horses, but it was still passable. His horse snorted with the exertion of the steady uphill climb, but it wasn't long before they entered a strange open patch of forest. The *cigani* signalled for a halt and Orkan looked over to Pedja, raising an eyebrow of suspicion.

The young *engleski* Frankish mercenary, the one they called Ellingham, shouted towards them. He watched the young man dismount and saw the older one, Hawker, do the same. Maria signalled that they should catch up.

'We are to make camp here!' she barked when they had trotted up to the rest of the company.

Pedja touched three fingers to his forehead and gave a little bow. 'Nobildonna, how far does the castle lie?'

She raised her arm and pointed to the far side of the barren field. 'You can nearly spit to it from here, my Rascian friend! See for yourself.'

He smiled and bowed a second time. Touching his heels to his horse's flanks he rode across to the edge of the circle where the trees began again. Orkan gave a sheepish grin to Maria, rubbed at the heavy black stubble of his beard, and followed Pedja.

Pedja reached the edge where skeletal beech trees covered the gently sloping ground, their naked branches reaching up as if in exhortation to the heavens. Through them in the distance he could see the castle perched on a mountain precipice. Orkan sidled up next to him, his eyes settled upon the fortress. A gruff noise issued from his throat as the Turk contemplated the ominous grey and black stone walls beyond. Pedja glanced back behind them and watched the Franks dismounting. The *cigani* were already leading the horses away to tie them to some trees on the opposite side of the field. A strange field, one which gave him a strange feeling. It seemed almost unnatural. No trees dared to grow in this circle on the mountainside, only hawthorn and gorse. Yet all around it, the ancient forest covered everything else.

'This place is bad, Orkan. I can feel it in my bones. The sort of place where drekavac dwell.'

'*Drekavac*? What do you speak of, Tombik?'

Pedja gave a shrug and turned to look at the castle again. 'Childhood monsters. Tall and spindly – like these trees. When I was a boy, Davud and I would scare each other in the woods. Listening for them. Around the winter holy days they screech in the night, looking to drink the souls of sinful men. Or unbaptised children.' He shot a glance over to Orkan. 'You know. Like you. Not baptised.'

Orkan chuckled. 'The Prophet looks after me well enough. I am not worried about *djinn* coming for me. But you, Tombik, you would provide a very filling meal.'

'What do you reckon, Orkan? Can we get in?' Pedja was staring out towards the castle again.

The Turk's brow furrowed. 'It isn't much bigger than a shit-house but unless that cave is there underneath... we're not getting in easy. The Franks have said as much. And they look like they know what they're doing.'

Pedja sucked in his cheek and chewed it. Doubt – self-doubt – was beginning to tug from within his chest. He wasn't afraid of a fight, he'd been in enough of them before. But he had never attacked a fortress and he had never had to swing a blade against Wallachians. By all the tales he had heard they were hard warriors. Staying alive from now on was going to take some effort. Taking the last money owed him by the Hungarian and buggering off, now that would be the wiser choice. One that Orkan would probably hug him for. But there was a dark, determined part of him, deep inside, that would not let that happen.

One of the *cigani*, a youth with a hunting knife shoved into his belt that was as long as his thigh, came over and looked up at them. He mimed 'eating' and gestured back towards the others.

Pedja could see Tokár and a few of his men, carrying the wicker baskets of provisions from the donkey over to where the makeshift camp was being set up.

Pedja gathered his reins and turned his mount back into the barren circle. 'Come on, you old fool, time to get our last meal while we may.'

Orkan laughed and nudged his own horse after Pedja. 'Food? I'm the one who needs to eat, Tombik, not you!'

-

Hawker, sitting cross-legged on the ground, chewed his dried sausage thoughtfully while the faint sun slowly disappeared. Whatever the meat was, it tasted better than anything he'd eaten in days. Maria told him the spice was *paprika*. The company ate in silence, so great was the hunger from the day's cold ride. They had dark Saxon rye, the crust of the loaves as hard as stone. Shared also were three great, round white balls of salty sheep's cheese which Tokár dutifully sliced for all with his single-edged, stag-handle dagger.

Hawker had permitted them a small fire, more for morale than heat, and they clustered around it. The gypsies had dug a shallow hole so that the flames would be less visible and they had gathered the oldest and driest dead wood to keep the smoke down. Hawker looked over to Ellingham. The youth looked tired. Understandably so, as they both had been in the saddle for two days running. His own bones ached and it would be no better up a mountain, catching just a few hours of sleep on rough ground, before they entered the cave at dawn.

Maria and Faldi sat next to each other, watching Hawker and Ellingham. She had her black leather armour and tall boots on, seated mannishly with her wrists resting on both knees. She had finished her food and was contemplating him and Ellingham eating theirs. Faldi looked nervous, staring at his hands and dismembering his chunk of bread with the intensity of a lunatic. Finally, Maria spoke.

'What is your final battle plan, Sir Giles?' she asked in her strangely lilted French. 'I've seen you in deep debate with Sir John but neither of you have shared your thoughts.'

Ellingham looked up, still chewing. He looked over to Hawker, who gave him a nod.

'We have a strategy, my lady. But it means we must divide our company.'

Faldi looked up, eyes large. 'That is madness! We are small enough as things stand, and you propose dividing us?'

Dieudonné, seated next to Ellingham, gave a sly smile, relishing the Italian's discomfort.

'If you hear me out, Ser Bartolo, I think you'll find it is the only way that will give us a chance of success.'

'Let the son of Richard speak, good sir,' said Maria quietly. Her dark green eyes stared straight at Ellingham.

'If we get through the cave and enter the dungeon, the garrison will discover us soon enough. They'll fight us. And then pursue us when we retreat out through the cave. That is a certainty. They won't just let us take the prince away.'

'Agreed,' said Maria, nodding.

'It's common sense that they'll undoubtedly send out for help through the main gate once we have escaped,' continued Ellingham. 'So... we will have our two crossbows ready to unhorse the riders who leave by that gate. It will be a small party to enter the cave and free your father. And Tokár's men can remain here with the horses and prepare to fight once the garrison follows us out. Which they will.'

'We can't kill them all inside,' added Hawker. 'We must get in and out as quickly as possible. If we stay inside and try to fight them all, then we might be trapped. And that would be the end of it.'

Faldi gave an explosion of exasperation and threw his bread crusts into the fire. '*Pazzo!*'

Maria looked at Hawker. 'You are right, Sir John. And... there can be no prisoners.' Her voice was calm but as cold as the stream that flowed nearby. 'We surprise them here. Where we now sit. An ambuscade. No one must escape to warn the Monk at Târgoviște.'

Faldi turned to Maria, his mouth still gaping. 'Then we die? In little groups?'

Hawker shook his head. 'Bartolo old friend, if we fight inside we could all be trapped there. This is the only way.'

'Killing all prisoners?' said Dieudonné, tut-tutting with a wry smile. 'That is not the way of an English belted knight... or is it?'

In a flash, Hawker's mind was suddenly filled with the memory of his task at Tewkesbury Abbey fourteen years earlier. Dragging defeated Lancastrian nobles out of sanctuary and putting them to death. A sin against God that he would never be able to wash from his soul. He wiped his thumb and forefinger rapidly across the corners of his mouth, not uttering a reply.

Jacob de Grood spoke up. 'Crossbowmen, Sir John?' He inclined his head towards Jack, the boy not following the fast-flowing French.

Hawker spoke in English. 'Jack Perry, you will watch the gate. If any try to leave, shoot them. You cannot let a single man escape to raise the alarm.'

Jack sat bolt upright then stuttered to reply. 'I... think I under-stood some of what was said, Sir John. But... stay at the gate? I should be with you. I'm your squire.'

'And I'm tasking my squire with a mission. And Jacob is to go with you. He knows well enough how to use a bow.'

Jacob's face darkened. 'My lord? You need me on the inside. You know this.'

Hawker leaned forward. 'I need you where I say I need you. And you can take one or two of Tokár's men in case you need to close with blades.'

'Ja, my lord,' muttered Jacob, giving a nod.

Jack gave Jacob's back a good-natured pat and the Fleming turned to give him a basilisk's glare.

'My lady,' said Ellingham, 'you can accompany us into the castle. Make sure the prisoner is the prince. Sir John and I will go with you. My lord Dieudonné and Ser Bartolo as well.' At his name being called, Dieudonné gave a dramatic flourish of respect. 'Tokár and – against my better judgement – Vilkas, to show us the way in. And the Rascians should come along as we may have to fight our way out again. You will have to inform them of that.'

The two in question were sitting off by themselves, conversing in low tones. Maria stood and called to them. Pedja rose first and Orkan, after a moment, followed.

She spoke in her usual commanding tone, in Slavic or Hungarian – Hawker wasn't quite sure which – and the two men nodded. The tall one who was a half-Turk seemed far less enthusiastic. The fat one called Pedja seemed to be smiling at the news of his joining the storming.

Ellingham turned to Hawker. 'It is like going to battle on the Tower of Babel!'

'That may be so, but we all speak the same tongue when it comes to saving one's skin.'

Maria came to Hawker and Ellingham and folded her arms across her chest. Hawker thought she had a renewed gleam in her eye. The talk of the raid had fired her up. Good, he thought, for she would need it on the morrow.

'Tokár will set the watch for the night,' she said. 'And he will prepare the men who will stay behind here when we set off.'

Hawker nodded. 'We leave at cockcrow. And tell Tokár to keep those tallow torches wrapped and dry tonight. We will be blind without them.'

Her piercing eyes, emerald green in the firelight, held him. 'He knows what to do. I pray that you two and your men-at-arms know likewise.'

Ellingham smiled. 'We serve *you*, my lady. We would not be here now if we thought we would fail at our task.'

She tittered at that. 'Son of Richard, you know full well we all serve ourselves. But I salute your chivalry.'

Hawker said nothing. Maria was made of stern stuff and he had no trouble believing the parentage she claimed. 'I suggest we get what sleep we can while we can. Into the treeline so we are less exposed to the deeper cold here in this field.'

Her eyes flitted from Hawker to Ellingham and lingered. 'Fare thee well and may your sleep be not troubled.' She turned and strode over to where the gypsies had begun to settle down, laying out their waxed ground-cloths and heavy woollen cloaks.

Ellingham let out a sigh and shivered involuntary as a gust blew past him. 'It will be a dice throw tomorrow, won't it, Sir John? No better than that to hope for.'

'The odds are against us, I won't lie. Pray that the Lord weights the dice in our favour.'

'It seems Ser Bartolo has more than a few doubts about our prospects. I have yet to untangle what his intentions are. Or how he even found his way into all this.'

'I remember him in battle. He's fought here in the eastern lands before. He'll fight like a lion when he has to.'

Ellingham put a gentle hand on the old knight's shoulder. 'Let us hope he still has his teeth and claws.' The youth moved away, drawing his cloak tighter across his chest.

Hawker looked across the barren circle and saw Dieudonné in conversation with Faldi. He had noticed that they were lately often in conversation, intense conversation without jests, ever since they had passed through the mountain gorge at Turnu Roşu. Gaston Dieudonné was still a cipher to him. Hawker had distrusted the Burgundian with good reason, but the man had ended up saving his life at the wharf in Venice. And he had stayed with the company. Still, he thought, what could the two have in common now? He could only put it down to the fact that Dieudonné had saved Faldi's life on the river. As he had saved his own in Venice. He was too tired to think any more of it. The fight on the morrow was enough to think about and he doubted any true, unburdened sleep would visit him this night.

He approached Jacob who was preparing bedding along with Jack. 'Walk with me, Jacob.'

De Grood, expressionless, moved off with Hawker and they walked to the centre of the barren, briar-strewn little field. Hawker stopped and turned to him.

'I know you would wish to join the assault inside. And I didn't ask you to guard the gate because you are a dead-eye crossbowman.'

De Grood sniffed and rubbed his nose with the back of his glove. His scarred cheek gave a twitch.

'It may go badly on the morrow. You know that full well. If it does, I need you to get Jack out of here. If we are not out of that cave in an hour's time, we won't coming out at all.'

De Grood looked at his boots.

'The boy deserves better than a death here. You take him back to Flanders. Follow the path we took here, back through the Saxon lands, and head west to Austria. Get yourselves home.'

De Grood looked up again. 'I have been sworn in your service these many years, Sir John. I should stand by you now.'

'You do me honour by obeying my command. And that command is to save Jack Perry... and yourself.' Hawker paused a moment. 'That boy is the closest I have to a son.'

Jacob's voice was gravel. 'I know that, my lord. And what of Sir Giles?'

Hawker put a hand on de Grood's rusty spaulder. 'If God wills it, the son of the king will die with me. His father would expect no less.'

21

When they roused themselves at dawn, their world was covered in white, wet, drifting fog. Thick as an overhead cloud, it obscured all vision, then just as quickly dissipated before drifting in again. Hawker stood up, his body feeling clammy and chilled from sleeping in his doublet and armour. Aching and stiff as well. But that was to be expected. At least the mountain had not grown too cold, they might never have awoken again.

De Grood was already up. He emerged out of the murk, bearing both crossbows.

'A good morrow to you, my lord.'

Hawker nodded. 'The crossbows?'

The Fleming pulled a face and shook his head. 'The rawhide bindings are wet through. I should have thought of that. They're so stretched we'll be lucky to get any range out of them at all now.'

'You won't be at any great range. You will be in their faces.'

De Grood chuckled. 'Aye, hadn't thought about that either.'

Jack came up to them, bearing a leather flask. 'Water, Sir John. From the stream.'

He was dressed ready for battle, and had even already put on his head his open-faced helm. Hawker accepted the flask and saw that Jack's hand trembled a bit. He drank deeply, the ice-cold water invigorating him. He then splashed some on his face before handing it back. 'This fog will aid us if it holds a bit longer. They won't be able to see us make our approach.'

'We won't be able to see our approach either, my lord,' grinned de Grood. 'I don't want a tumble down the mountainside.'

'You're an old Flemish goat and just as sure-footed. Don't whinge.'

Jack was staring at the crossbows that Jacob still held in each hand. Hawker could see the trepidation in the lad's eyes.

'Which one is for me, Jacob?'

'Eh? Oh, aye, whichever one takes your fancy, boy. Both the same by my reckoning. Good for birds and hare but we'll see how they fare against Wallachians.'

Jack took one of the bows and cradled it. 'Bolts?'

De Grood smiled. 'Bag is slung over your horse's saddlebow. If you can find your horse again in this.' And he waved his hand at the swirling mist.

Jack looked blank.

De Grood frowned. 'It's a jest, boy! Be glad in your heart! We finally get to do something.'

Hawker put a hand on Jack's spaulder and rattled it. 'You know what you must do. Fear not. Once it begins you won't have time to think – or be afraid.'

Jack nodded and threw the knight a nervous smile. 'I'm not afraid, Sir John. I swear.'

Hawker looked over to Jacob. 'Take up your position as close as you dare to the gates. There is only one narrow track leading down so you should be able to cover any attempt they make to leave. But no one must get out to warn anyone below.'

'The lad and I will shoot every bastard that comes out of there.'

Hawker turned to the cleft in the large beech he had sheltered in and bent to retrieve his bastard sword. Jack beat him to it. 'Let me, my lord!'

He placed the crossbow on the ground and unwrapped the sword belt from around the scabbard. Standing in front of his knight, he wrapped the belt around Hawker's breastplate and back, reaching around the front again to do up the buckle. Casting about, Jack spotted Hawker's sallet helm nearby and hefted it.

'My lord,' he said, offering up the helm.

Hawker accepted it and placed it on, his gnarled fingers struggling a bit with the chinstrap for a moment. 'I reckon the enemy

218

will send out for help once they realise we're inside. Stay on that gate. We break our fast once the morning's work is done!'

Tokár approached them, agitated. 'You must come! Now!'

Hawker and the others joined him as he led them to the edge of the encampment. Maria stood, hands on hips, looking down at a figure on the ground. It was Vilkas. Tokár rolled the Balt over and revealed an empty wine flask. Somehow, he had filched it in secret and had drunk it in the night.

'Is he alive?' Hawker asked, his voice pinched in anger.

'Tokár says he is just drunk,' replied Maria. 'But very drunk.'

'Get him on his feet. And fetch some water from the stream to douse him.'

—

Single file and led by Tokár, the company wended their way through the trees along a gently sloping deer track towards the castle walls. Tokár was in front by a few paces, choosing the ground carefully. Hawker came next, Maria after him, Faldi, Ellingham, Dieudonné, the Rascians and Bartolo Faldi at the rear, prodding Vilkas forward with the tip of his blade. Tokár wore nothing to turn an enemy's blade except his heavy pied cowhide, a wide belt, leather gorget and a simple boiled-leather skullcap with iron cross-bands.

All had drawn their weapons: a mix of arming swords, bastard swords, short single-edged hunting swords, and the half-Turk's short iron mace. Hawker became aware of his heavy breathing even as branches crunched beneath his boots. The climb had taken the wind from his lungs the previous day and his body had yet to find it again. The fog was now lifting, the grey stone walls clear in the dawn's faint but growing light. Another bank of fog, a low grey cloud, drifted across from their left and rolled up against the stones. Tokár turned left, as Hawker remembered from their scouting, and they made their way towards the north side. Thank God that Vilkas had shown them the way beforehand: his usefulness was probably at an end now. Hawker's eyes anxiously scanned the tops of the walls but no one stirred. After a few minutes of scrambling in a half-crouch, they made it to the great gash in the granite hillside.

Tokár nodded towards Hawker, drew two torches from his belt, and went inside the cave. Hawker turned to the others and motioned for them to halt and to move to their knees. They waited, their breath condensing and rolling out in little clouds of their own. Hawker took in the company behind him: a young knight, a woman in a soldier's harness, a Burgundian captain, a Milanese *condottiere*, a pair of dubious Rascian mercenaries, and a drunken executioner. A more unlikely lance he had never commanded.

His gaze settled on Maria. Her large eyes were larger still and Hawker for the first time thought he saw fear in them. She, alone among them, wore no helm. Her long, raven tresses uncombed and frizzy in the moist air cascaded over her leather breastplate and back. Her long delicate face, normally olive in tone, was now much paler. She had barely spoken to him since they had risen. Either she was frightened of dying in the next hour or she worried about something else: whether her father still lived and whether he still was here. Hawker noticed that Ellingham was watching her, too.

Tokár re-emerged, holding the two tallow torches he had lit with flint and stone inside the mouth of the cave. He gave a nod of reassurance. Hawker signalled to Ellingham. They stood again, Ellingham casting a nervous glance upwards to the parapet over their heads. Hawker entered the cave. Instantly, his nostrils were assailed by the stench of dead animals. Rising above that even, was the pungent, acrid and stomach-turning smell of bat turds which littered the floor of the narrow cave. He could feel them slick and slippery under his soles. His eyes moved upward to the low ceiling, illuminated by the gypsy's torch. Dozens of small furry bodies huddled in the crevices, occasionally jostling each other.

Tokár handed a torch to Hawker who in turn handed it back to Ellingham. Tokár began to move forward again, leading the way. The cave was tunnel-like but natural, just wide enough for two abreast but with no room to swing a blade. Carefully, they made their way through, the cave gradually turning and rising.

Hawker heard Dieudonné's muffled French from further back. 'We are walking into hell, no? Maybe we should have brought a gift for the Devil!'

'Gaston!' chided Ellingham. 'Enough!'

The Burgundian's cynical cackle followed the admonition. Hawker gritted his teeth. They kept moving forward, now perhaps a hundred feet inside. Tokár suddenly halted and indicated the walls. They were now lined in brick. Overhead as well. Hawker turned and signalled to the others to not speak by placing his gloved hand flat across his mouth and tapping it twice. They moved forward again.

Hawker heard a soft exclamation from Tokár and then saw for himself the cause. A few feet in front of them was an iron grating comprised of flat, riveted bands and held in place at four corners. It spanned the width of the tunnel and went from floor to ceiling. Hawker's sword tip lowered to the floor. His sigh was muffled by the close quarters. Tokár mumbled something and approached the grate. His torchlight illuminated a chamber on the other side. It was filled with wooden casks and coils of rope, a room about twenty feet deep. The gypsy rattled the grate, lowered his head and turned to Hawker.

'Not here before,' he said, disbelievingly, eyes wide. From somewhere further back in the darkness, Hawker could hear the wheezing, besotted laugh of Vilkas.

Maria moved forward and wrapped her fingers around the rusted iron bands. Her lips moved, silently, as if in prayer. Her forehead touched the grating.

Ellingham pushed forward and taking her by the shoulders moved her back. 'My lady,' he said quietly.

Hawker winced in frustration, eyeing up where the grate had been mortared into the surrounding brick and stonework of the tunnel. He then seized one corner with both gloved hands and yanked. The grating moved a little but was still held fast. Falling brick dust rattled the iron bands.

'It's loose, but still holds fast,' said Hawker, frustrated. His head was now filled with an image of them all trying to force their way in through the main gate. Ellingham moved next to Hawker and also tried wresting the grating. His hand probed where it had been dug into the tunnel wall and cemented.

He turned to Hawker and whispered, 'We can smash the wall.'

Hawker exhaled and rubbed his mouth with the back of his glove. 'With what? We'd need a ram.'

'The Turk. He has an iron mace. We might be able to break enough of the brick work to prise out the grating.'

The tallow torch in Tokár's hand sputtered loudly as if a sign. Hawker squinted and again felt the wall where the strip of iron was held fast. 'Aye. It will wake the dead, but we have no choice. Get the Rascian up here!'

Maria pulled Ellingham back by his arm. 'What do you speak of? Tell me.'

'We can try and hammer the wall and break the mortar. Pull off the grating. But we need that Rascian and his mace.'

She pushed past him and retreated back into the tunnel, elbowing past Dieudonné and Faldi who were engaged in a vehement exchange of whispers, eyes flashing. She was back in an instant, propelling a sputtering Orkan in front of her, crushing Dieudonné against the tunnel wall.

Hawker and Ellingham moved to the opposite side of the grating and Maria hurriedly explained to Orkan what needed to be done.

The Turk's fuzzy brows became one. 'It will be loud. Very loud.'

'It matters not. You must strike true and break the joint! Strike many times!'

Hawker raised his sword up and gripped the first unsharpened third of the blade in his left hand. 'Pray that he shifts this iron before the noise brings them down here.'

Ellingham pulled Maria back and to his side. 'Give him room to swing, my lady.'

Orkan took a pace back, sized up his target and gripped the short iron mace in both hands. The black pomegranate was lifted, poised, and then brought down with all the force the Turk could muster. The iron rang out dully, only half as loud as Hawker had thought. It crunched into the brickwork and bounced back off the grating. Orkan struck it again and again, small chunks of brick and stone ricocheting off onto him and Hawker.

The knight grasped Orkan by the shoulder, warning him to halt. They listened. There was no sound or voices from the other side to tell them any alarm had been raised. Hawker tapped the Turk twice and Orkan braced himself, ready to hammer the mortar again. He let out a grunt and the swing was rewarded with a huge chunk of stone falling with a thud to the earthen floor of the tunnel. Hawker seized the grate in both hands, Orkan at his left doing the same, and they heaved as hard as they could, pulling the iron grating. It resisted with a terrible screeching sound and then gave way, bowling them backwards into Ellingham and Maria.

'We're through!' cried Ellingham.

Even as the grating fell away, Hawker saw light pour into the chamber. A man entered, torch high, steps hesitant. When he set his eyes upon the armoured men, he froze, not comprehending what his senses were showing him. He was unarmoured, wearing a filthy brown tunic and quilted hood, green hose and splay-footed leather shoes. His jaw went slack as the sight of Hawker and Ellingham. The cry was about to leave his mouth when Hawker's sudden rush, followed by the thrust of his bastard sword, took the man in the throat, shoving him backwards until the blade scraped and fractured the man's neck bones. The man gurgled and dropped his torch, clutching at his ripped throat. He sank to his knees, then toppled over.

Hawker recovered his guard and moved into the chamber, ready for the next man to enter. The company followed him in, and Ellingham moved up to his side.

'Gaoler?'

Hawker glanced down. 'See if he bears a ring of keys.'

A voice carried down from a short stone staircase at the end of the chamber. 'Ion? Ce este?'

Ellingham raised his sword, point forward, and chanced a glance back at Maria. She was shaking her head slowly, urging quiet. No one said a word. Torchlight began to spill into the chamber. Hawker and Ellingham pushed against the wall. As soon as the man's feet had left the last stair, Hawker bulled into him, sending him sprawling. Ellingham leapt forward and half-swording, as Hawker had done, gave a short sharp jab with his blade, severing the man's windpipe. It was a garrison soldier, grey-haired and moustachioed, wearing an old leather and plate brigandine. His eyes were wide with agony but he was unable to scream. Ellingham stepped back, seemingly hesitatant to move in again with a killing blow. But Tokár was already there, shoving his long dagger deep into the guard's eye and killing him instantly.

Tokár pointed at the man's wide leather belt. A leather thong bearing three keys was wrapped around it. Maria, quick as a cat, squatted down on the paving stones which were becoming slick with blood. She ripped the thong away, grasped the keys and stood again.

'We must find the cells while we still have stealth on our side!'

The company barely fit into the storeroom, jostling one another while they awaited the word to move further into the cellars. Faldi wobbled one of the casks next to him. It made a sloshing sound.

'Wine.' He released it.

Dieudonné chuckled. 'Hoping for something else, Ser Bartolo? Some treasure?'

The Milanese glared and mumbled a low curse.

Maria hissed at the both of them. 'Silence! We must move while there is still time.'

Hawker looked at each of them and then Ellingham. 'You and I take the lead. If we are challenged pray that the passage remains narrow that we may hold the garrison off.'

Ellingham nodded, swallowing, but not answering. Hawker could tell the youth was embarrassed for his moment of hesitation in not finishing off the fallen guard. This was not as battle was fought. They were like robbers murdering in the night. These two had been unarmed.

Maria signalled for Tokár to take up his torch again and then she hefted her slender single-edged Ottoman blade and took up position behind Hawker and Ellingham. 'We should move now.'

Hawker gave her a nod and they ascended the four steps that led to the passage. The corridor was wider here and a torch set into the wall at the far end cast its glare, illuminating two vaulted, crypt-like cells, each with a heavy oak-planked door. An archway at the far end led up a few more steps and Hawker thought he could just make out the white glow of daylight playing on the stones. Without waiting, Maria went to the first door and peered through the round observation hole. A moment later she pressed her face against the grate in the second door.

'Here! Sir John, here. Open it!'

Orkan grasped Pedja by his shoulder and squeezed. The two stood back, letting the Franks and the gypsy take charge. Dieudonné went to the far end and positioned himself at the short flight of stairs, listening for new arrivals. There was a heavy, studded oak door at the top and Dieudonné darted up, peered outside, and then slowly closed it. He dropped the bar into place and came back down and called over to the others.

'I've barred the door to the yard. They won't get in easily now.'

Tokár stood at Maria's side and raised up the torch to the cell door and its massive box lock. Hawker fumbled with the keys he held but Ellingham had already pulled off his gauntlets. Bartolo Faldi leaned in, trying to get a look for himself through the little iron grating at the occupant within.

'Be it him?' he asked, his voice dripping with anxiety.

Maria didn't answer.

Ellingham whispered close to Hawker. 'Let me, Sir John.'

Hawker looked at him for second and then handed the rawhide and keys to him. The youth's fingers would be nimbler than his, still gloved as they were with his plated gauntlets. Ellingham tried the first of the large iron keys. The lock did not move.

Ellingham's hand shook, fumbling with getting the second key into the oversized iron lock. But the key finally turned with dull clunk.

'Ser Bartolo,' said Maria, turning to the Milanese, 'wait outside.'

Faldi stepped back, mouth opening wordlessly. Before Hawker could warn her off, Maria had shouldered past him, thrown back the bolt and pushed open the door. Without a pause she rushed inside the cell. Hawker glimpsed a figure standing in the corner, half in shadow. Muttering a curse, he followed Maria inside.

Tokár raised his torch to illuminate the cell. There was a shaft overhead, set at an angle which let in daylight from above, but it was too early and grey outside to penetrate the dank chamber. The floor was strewn with rushes. A small wooden-framed bed and mattress, a chamber stool, a Turkish rug on a low table and a clay drinking vessel, these were the only furnishings. Maria took a step towards the cloaked figure in the corner. The man had not moved nor even flinched when they had burst in. He was still in shadow now, unmoving.

Maria called back to Hawker and Ellingham. 'Do not come closer!'

She then softly spoke to the shadowy figure in the Romanian tongue. The man stepped forward out of the gloom and Hawker could now just about make out the contours of the prisoner's face. It was a man his own age. He was not tall, but he was broad shouldered if not barrel-chested. His long face was sallow for the most part, but bluish-grey around the eye sockets for want of good fare or adequate light. His hair, frizzy and streaked with grey, fell about his shoulders. A drooping moustache likewise was wiry and grey. The nose, beaklike and proud, could have been Hawker's own. But the eyes, almost preternaturally large and hazel-green, were arresting for their power.

'My lady, is this the prince? Your father?'

She seemed afraid to move closer or to reach out to the man. And for his part, the man said nothing but just stood there looking back, an expression of curiosity and even disdain mixed on his face. He made no move to defend himself or to attack.

Maria spoke to him again, just as softly as the first time. Still, the man would not reply.

'It is he. It is my father.'

Tokár muttered something in his tongue and took the knee, bowing his head towards the prisoner.

Maria again spoke to the old man. She tapped her chest and Hawker assumed she was telling him who she was. There was no sign of recognition or even understanding from him. Tokár rose up and spoke softly, imploring as well.

Hawker's eyes caught on something on the floor near where the light well illuminated the paving stones.

Something disturbing.

Half a dozen rats impaled on sticks were arrayed against the wall. Each had been impaled from the bottom up, the carefully shaved sticks protruding out of their mouths.

There was no doubt, now.

They had freed Vlad, son of the Dragon. Dracula.

Hawker became aware of raised voices outside the cell. An instant later Dieudonné burst in, pausing with surprise when he saw the strange figure before him. He spoke quietly. 'That drunken fool Vilkas has opened the door and run outside. They'll be on to us now!'

'Sweet Christ!' Hawker ran to the short stone steps leading up to the heavy oak door which was now ajar. The Rascians were there, just staring outside at whatever was unfolding. Faldi and Ellingham pushed in behind Hawker. Hawker stepped forward over the threshold, bastard sword in hand, and stopped immediately. There was Vilkas, in the centre of the long, narrow courtyard, ranting at the top of his lungs.

'Where are you, my prince?' he shouted. 'I'm here! Vilkas is here for you!' He staggered around, tracing a circle of uncertain steps. By now, the garrison was rousted, like a nest of angry hornets, men poured out from the other quarters, half-dressed but carrying swords and spears. Two came at Vilkas warily, uncertain as to who he was. Vilkas howled and flew at them swinging a plank of wood he had picked up somewhere. He bashed the first man, spun around with a speed Hawker thought impossible for one so innebriated, and launched a crushing blow on the second Wallachian.

'Perkunas!' He invoked the name of his ancient unforgotten god in a strangled half-scream. 'Perkunas!'

Ellingham pushed past Hawker. 'We've got to save him!'

Hawker yanked back the youth and thrust him behind. 'No! Inside, Giles! He's lost!'

More than a dozen Wallachians had poured forth, surrounding the Balt. Hawker pushed Faldi back too, the Milanese standing transfixed by the unbelievable scene before them. Hawker caught sight of a spear being thrust into Vilkas's unarmoured stomach, stopping him still. The Balt looked up for a moment, eyes rolling, long grey mane shaking furiously like an enraged wolf in a bear fight. A moment later a sword blow cleaved his head.

Hawker slammed shut the iron-studded door and leaned against it. His eyes searched the landing around him. 'Where is the bar? Where is it?'

Dieudonné looked at Hawker. His lips parted in a grim smile. 'That is what the old fool was swinging outside.'

Hawker felt the door shake under him as someone had thown their weight behind it from the other side. 'All of you! Get your backs behind this!' The door pushed inward a crack and a spear shaft came through low, trying to leverage it open further. Hawker called for Dieudonné, then let the door open a bit further. The spear wielder fell forward and the Burgundian neatly thrust him through the narrow opening and pushed him backwards. The door slammed again.

All of the company piled on, feet braced, holding back the shoving from the other side which came on like waves pounding a shore. Ellingham found the discarded sword of the gaoler and rammed it into the iron supports. They watched it bend precariously with the next bashing of the door. 'Keep bracing it! All of you!'

He ran down the steps and back into Vlad's cell. 'My lady, you will have to get him moving. We can't wait. Take to the cave. We'll hold them off a bit and then join you.'

Ellingham's voice sounded from behind him on the stairs. 'Sir John! I'll stand with Gaston and the others. You go back with Maria.'

Hawker turned and called back. 'Nay, we'll need every blade we have if they force their way.'

Maria glared for a moment then moved forward, gently taking the arm of the man she claimed was her father. She tugged at him, guiding, and the man followed without a sound of protest. With Maria pulling and Tokár behind the old man with a gentle hand on his shoulder, they guided him out of the cell and down towards the storeroom and the tunnel entrance.

Shouts came from the stairwell followed by the rattle of iron-ware and then another loud thud as the door slammed into its frame again.

Dieudonne's voice, a tone higher than normal, echoed down to the cells. 'Hawker!'

Part V

PRINCES AND THIEVES

22

Jack Perry watched Jacob de Grood carefully and then repeated the Fleming's exact moves: arse on the bare ground, feet lodged either side upon the thick prod of the bow, and both gloved hands gripping the strings. De Grood leaned back, pulling the strings and pushing with his feet and the string bundle dropped into place behind the bow's catch. Jack strained with the load, his biceps stinging with complaint, but he managed to cock the crossbow even though it took more effort than it had for the Fleming. They both got to their feet again, their armour jangling.

De Grood reached in and pulled out a crossbow bolt from his pouch and held it up, smiling. He lodged it into the stock of the bow and nodded. Jack copied him. And then they waited.

De Grood had positioned them and two gypsies just into the treeline, on the slope that led down to the narrow track, the castle's only gate off to their left. On the opposite side of the track, a road not even wide enough for a donkey cart, the ground sloped off again, very steeply to where the river swirled two hundred feet below. The track doubled on itself as it snaked up to the gate. Jacob had told him that made it difficult for attackers trying to make an assault but it also exposed anyone leaving the castle as well. And they were depending on that.

Jack was a shaking a bit. It wasn't fear, it was a damp gambeson and only a crust of bread to break his fast that accounted for his shivers. But it *was* cold. He stood there, rocking from one foot to the other, the wind whistling into his barbute helm. The gypsies were stone-faced and passive, saying nothing. It wouldn't have mattered if they had spoken, as he didn't understand their tongue.

Jacob stood next to him, his crossbow cradled in his arms, his eyes locked onto the great double gate no more than a stone's throw away. It seemed an age had passed. Yet there had been no movement or sound from the keep. The light grew stronger even though it was suffused in grey cloud. The morning had come.

At first it was one shout, then quiet. And then many were shouting behind the walls. Jacob moved back and gestured for Jack to do the same. Sir John had launched his assault and they could know nothing of how their company were faring. But whatever surprise they had had on their side, it was clearly gone now. A head popped up on the parapet over the gate and Jack instinctively retreated further into the trees. The head bobbed and then disappeared again.

'Stand ready, lad!' de Grood hissed at him. After a few moments they heard the bar being lifted, and the doors began to sway a little. Jack prayed it would be just a few running out and not a sally by the whole garrison. He raised up the crossbow, heart pounding faster.

'Don't you dare loose that bolt before I tell you to!'

Jack nodded and shifted his weight, watching. One of the doors opened and a bare-headed soldier emerged dressed in a studded brigandine, baggy woollen hose and boots. He led out a shaggy pony and then another soldier followed him out, barking orders, before retreating inside the castle gates. The other led the pony down the sloping path, his head swivelling all the while, looking for danger.

'I will take this one,' whispered de Grood. 'You save your shot for now.'

Jack now saw two heads pop up on the parapets, the soldiers watching the progress of their comrade. All the while, the sounds of alarm were carrying up and over the walls. Sir John and Sir Giles were now fighting for their lives while he stood outside, still as a statue, unable to aid his knight.

The soldier gripped the pony's bridle, coaxing it down the slope. De Grood waited until the man had reached level ground and had mounted the beast, before breaking cover. Jack moved forward, following in his footsteps to provide support. The Fleming walked briskly ahead as if he was approaching an old friend. The soldiers on the walls cried out but the soldier had already spotted the armoured man coming towards him and he drew his blade even as he kicked the pony into motion.

De Grood calmly brought the crossbow to his cheek and pulled the lever. There was a gentle snap of the releasing strings and the soldier fell back, shot through the face. The pony slowed and walked on for a few feet before the man tumbled out of his saddle and over the precipice on the far side. The pony shook itself and carried on before one of the gypsies broke cover and went to retrieve it, dragging it up the slope and into the treeline.

De Grood raised up his bow and taunted the Monk's garrison men in Flemish before returning to the cover of the treeline. He reached Jack's spot and broke into a grin.

'Now it is their move. We want them to think we have an army out here.'

They did not have to wait for long. The gates opened again and this time four soldiers in brigandines and helms armed with swords and spears came out. One carried a great pavise to shield his comrades. Jacob whistled and then stuck his foot into the stirrup of the spent crossbow and spanned it again almost effortlessly with one heave. Jack found he was shaking again, unable to take his eyes from the soldiers making their way down the slope towards them.

'Come lad, move forward! We've got to get closer to stand a chance of getting through their armour.'

They were a dozen paces from the Wallachians who, now seeing there were two crossbowmen, decided to hold their position. They stood in single file, sheltering behind the large wooden pavise. Jack found he was staring at the colourful picture painted upon it: some haloed saint slaying a dragon. His feet kept moving but he felt as if someone else was directing him, some invisible puppeteer. Jacob sidestepped, and the soldiers did the same to keep behind the shield.

A cry sounded from the woods as two gypsies ran forward across de Grood's and Jack's position and straight into the Wallachians. The soldiers broke their cover to take on the new threat and in that instant de Grood rushed to within practically swinging distance, made his target and pulled his trigger. A Wallachian dropped his sword and collapsed, the quarrel protruding from his chest. Jack struggled to get a clear target amidst the swirling mass, worried for hitting the gypsies or Jacob who had now dropped his bow and drawn his sword.

Beyond their little deadly scrabble, Jack saw the gates open again. More soldiers. De Grood had now chopped another Wallachian to the ground. The soldier with the pavise flung it and ran back up the slope. Menaced by the two gypsies, the other followed suit. It was then that Jack noticed that the soldiers outside the gate had a great dog with them. They unleashed the mastiff and sent it down, snarling as it came. Everything was happening so quickly and he had yet to even loose his crossbow. He wasn't sure whether to just take his shot or drop it and draw his blade.

The mastiff leapt and de Grood went down, bowled over by the momentum of the creature. The Fleming cried out and tried beating it with his hands. The beast's huge dripping jaws kept lunging for Jacob's face and throat. And then, Jack Perry woke. He rushed forward, took a bead on the mastiff's ribcage and sent the bolt on its way. He heard one shrill howl from the beast as it tumbled over Jacob and then lay still. He turned, instinctively, the crossbow raised up to shoulder level. A swinging blade ripped it from his hands but missed his head. Jack fell back and scrambled for his sword hilt.

He drew it from the scabbard even as a second blow came raining down on him. He just managed to deflect it, his wrist high, sword-point down. He looked into the eyes of the man he fought and saw it was a boy, a boy his own age. He was clean-shaven with brown eyes and a nose that had been broken long before, mashed flat upon the Wallachian's face. And he saw no fear in those eyes. Steel rang out as Jack parried a second vicious cut to his head. He was in a fight to the death, this time on foot, and he felt very much alone.

They circled each other, feinting blows. Jack from the corner of his eye was aware that the other Wallachian soldiers had descended, three in total. He heard Jacob's voice boom out.

'Kill him, boy, and be done with it!'

Jack's jaw was clenched tight. He *was* trying to kill his man. It just wasn't working. He swung a side-cut which was parried and then felt his opponent's blade strike the side of his helm with a glancing blow. It was then that de Grood rammed the Wallachian from the side, knocking him off balance. Jack raised his blade and brought it down, biting into the youth's brigandine and into the collarbone. His opponent dropped to his knees, raised his blade weakly, and then Jack saw fear in the boy's eyes. It was terrible to behold. Something he did not want to have to see. Something that the later memory of, coming unbidden, would make him ashamed. Jack thrust his sword into the boy's throat, ending him.

De Grood was on his feet again, crossbow in hand. Jack saw the gypsies shield him, their single-edged blades waving, while the Fleming spanned the crossbow again. A spearman rushed in towards de Grood, but Jack was there, deflecting the haft away with a chop of his blade. De Grood backtracked, fumbling in his pouch for another quarrel. He laid it, raised the bow, and shot the spearman in the face, dropping him like a sack of flour. That left three Wallachians who decided that the castle walls were a better idea. They retreated, shouting defiance all the while.

'Let them go!' shouted de Grood. 'We'll get back up into the treeline. Let them think we're laying a siege. Fetch your bow!'

Jack did as he was told. But the two gypsies harried the Wallachians to the bottom of the earthen ramp, then realised that the two Franks were not pursuing. They looked slightly confused but withdrew, following de Grood back up the hillside.

They climbed, chests heaving, back into the denser wood a hundred feet from the castle gate. The Fleming paused, leaning on a tree. He looked over to Jack and smiled. 'I used to like dogs,' he said. 'I've changed my mind now.' He waggled his sword towards Jack. 'You did well, jongen. Very well.' He looked down at his rusty sabatons for a moment then looked up and gave a thoughtful nod to the youth. 'And you saved my life.'

But Jack was looking past the Fleming, down to the path below and the bodies that lay sprawled there. 'And you... saved mine.'

De Grood nodded again. 'That is how it works, my young friend.'

They waited, watching the gates. There was no sign of another sally, nor could they hear the shouting that they had earlier.

'It's quiet now. We should go back,' said de Grood. 'The company has either fallen or pulled back out of the castle.'

He signalled wordlessly to the gypsies and one of them untied the pony he had earlier retrieved. De Grood let out a chuckle. 'Christ. The spoils of the battle. Come, Jack Perry, more fighting to be done elsewhere, I think.'

–

Hawker made sure that Maria and Tokár, their charge in tow, had made it down to the storeroom.

'Tell the others to prepare!' he called to her. 'We'll be drawing the garrison out and they will be right behind us! Godspeed!'

She did not turn back or shout a reply. Hawker, his heart pounding, hefted his blade and dashed back up to the dungeon chamber. The sound of the door crashing, again and again, told him the enemy had not yet forced entry. He arrived at the bottom of the short stairwell to find the Rascians and the knights straining to hold the Wallachians. The door cracked open again and the blade of a rusty bill was shoved through as someone tried to lever the opening wider. Ellingham's eyes were as large as silver chargers and Hawker saw that he was frozen in indecision. There was not enough space for Giles to add his weight against the door and the youth stood, poised, as if willing all his strength to the Rascians.

'What say you, Giles?' called Hawker. 'What's your plan?'

The door squealed again, splinters of wood flying from the clawing pole-arm. 'Are you testing me, my lord?' shouted Ellingham angrily.

'I am, sir!'

'You bastard!' Ellingham snapped back. 'There *is* only one choice. We let them in. Fight backwards.'

Hawker nodded grimly. 'Aye. That is the only way.'

Dieudonné, bent low, below Orkan's belly and leaning against the shuddering door, gave a harsh bark of a laugh. 'But *you* are the bastard, my friend!'

'Gaston, pull back to the bottom of the stairs!' Ellingham tapped the others and gestured for them to follow.

The door crashed inwards, carrying the first two Wallachians with it and sending them sprawling. Orkan clubbed one of them, Pedja hacked the other's hand off. This was the bill man and Dieudonné snatched up the dropped pole-arm, far better for fending off the rest. Six more Wallachian guards poured through the door. The narrow stairwell funnelled them and only two could fight abreast, and even that with difficulty.

The company pulled back, forming a line shoulder to shoulder, Dieudonné wielding the bill to keep the enemy at bay. The whole company moved backwards carefully, jabbing and thrusting as the Wallachians came on. Faldi, seeing an opportunity, leapt forward and chopped down a Wallachian guard who had edged too far out in front of the others. In an instant, Faldi stepped backwards into the company again, sword raised in a guard.

Once they had regained the dungeon, step by backwards step, the Rascians were now in the second line, behind the knights. They made it to the entrance of the storeroom and from the grinning, gaping faces of the garrison soldiers, Hawker could tell they thought they were backing them into a dead end at the storeroom. They would be in for a surprise.

Holding just past the threshold, Ellingham barked over his shoulder for Pedja and Orkan to go to the tunnel. After a moment of confusion, Pedja elbowed his comrade and signalled to retreat. It was now only Ellingham, Faldi, and Dieudonné to support Hawker in menacing the wary Wallachians. A spearman arrived, bellowing, and Dieudonné engaged, blocking a spear thrust towards Ellingham with a parry of his bill.

Hawker was already thanking the Lord that the garrison were an undisciplined, ill-led rabble. They would not have even got this far if the enemy had been proper men-at-arms. Dieudonné feinted a high jab at the Wallachian spearman, then followed up again, striking the man in the face and dropping him.

'Move!' cried Dieudonné, seeing the hesitation of the Wallachians, who were frozen in disbelief. None seemed particularly eager to die to regain the momentum. Their indecision gave the company the precious time needed to get to the storeroom. They dashed for their escape. Once Faldi and Ellingham had turned into the tunnel, Hawker backtracked alone, his bastard sword pointed menacingly. He knocked and kicked over casks as he went, creating more obstacles.

'Hawker, enough!' cried Ellingham. 'Get out of there!'

The knight turned and made the last few feet to the hole in the wall. Once through, he and Ellingham wedged the iron grating into place as best they could, then scuttled deeper into the cave. They could just see light ahead from the torch one of the others had retrieved from the floor. The jangle of the enemy's weapons and armour could be heard back in the storeroom. They were coming on again.

'It's *him*, isn't it?' said Ellingham breathlessly, his armour rasping against the walls as they bounced through the stinking, narrow confines.

Hawker kept propelling Giles forward with a hand on his back. 'I don't know,' he lied.

23

Ellingham's feet snagged and caught in the ground-hugging ivy as if it was a writhing nest of serpents. He nearly tripped and tumbled twice. They were out of the cave now and climbing as best they could back up the slope, knowing the enemy was not far behind. Did those fools not know that the cave they had blocked with iron and mortar was another way out? And in? He heard Hawker behind him, wheezing loudly as he trudged, the man's armour clanking as loudly as his own. But stealth mattered no more.

They reached the crest and pushed on through the wind-deformed bare trees until they gained the circular clearing again. The gypsies had fanned out either side, weapons drawn. Ellingham spotted both Jacob and Jack Perry off to the left and whispered a short prayer of thanks. He felt physically drained after the short fight in the fortress, sick in his stomach, and chilled in his bones. Now, they were to fight a melee in the forest.

He turned to check on Hawker. The knight was slowing, falling behind, and he returned to him.

'Sir John! How do you fare?'

Hawker looked at him, scowling. 'Not as spent as I might sound. Keep moving!'

In the distance, Ellingham saw men through the trees below, coming from where they had just climbed. The garrison was following them out as they had hoped. He didn't dare offer to pull along Hawker, so he redoubled his own pace. Faldi and Dieudonné seemed to be shouting to Tokár and gesticulating towards his band of men, no doubt trying to gain some semblance of a formation. He could not yet spy Maria and the old one they had freed. He reached Dieudonné who smiled and rushed to him, clapping him on the shoulder.

'Well done!' he said in French. 'Where is Hawker?'

Ellingham pointed down the slope.

'Ah, well, let's hope he makes it here before the enemy does. This Milanese pirate and I are trying to make ourselves understood to the old gypsy. We need his men ready to fight here, not spread around like will o' the wisps!'

Jacob and Jack reached them. Jacob was spattered in blood but Ellingham could tell it was not his. 'My lord Giles, I am glad you fared well. Do we have our prisoner?'

'We have him,' replied Ellingham. 'Though we are none the wiser for it.'

'Here comes Sir John. I hope he is whole.'

Ellingham nodded. 'He is.' He wasn't sure though.

'Jack Perry!' exclaimed Hawker, waddling forward. He clapped the lad on both spaulders, beaming at him. 'How was your fight, my boy?'

Jack didn't answer but instead tried to form a smile on reluctant lips.

'He accounted himself very well, Sir John. We drove the bastards back. By bow and by sword point!'

Hawker smiled again. 'I have no doubt of that. You two will need to span your bows again. We have but a few minutes before they'll be upon us.'

'And what of the old drunk? I don't see him yet.'

'He fell… fighting inside the keep.'

Jacob nodded as if unsurprised. 'A blessing perhaps.'

Hawker turned to Ellingham, his breaths still coming hard. 'My lord… will you command the line?'

He had expected that. Hawker, ever the mentor, fulfilling his promise to a dead king. 'I shall, Sir John.'

Dieudonné smiled and made an exaggerated bow. 'My prince!'

Faldi's brows knit together in anger and confusion. 'Wait!' he spat in Venetian for Hawker's benefit. 'We are to be led by this… *boy*? Who has decided *he* is to command? And where is the lady Maria?'

Hawker closed the distance between them. Though half a head shorter, he pushed himself right up to Faldi's breastplate. 'Are you a prince of the blood? No. You are nothing. Like me. A mercenary and nothing more. The youth will command *all* of us.' He had spoken in slow, measured French, so that all of them might understand.

Faldi growled, stepping back one pace. 'So be it,' he replied, also in French. 'It matters not who commands. Without the grace of God we are all going to die.'

'Sir John!' Jacob pointed towards where the fortress lay below them. Ellingham turned and saw at least a dozen men some two hundred yards away. They were being corralled by one man, pointing with his sword and guiding them into their places. The garrison had apparently found their captain. More were pouring in to join them as they watched.

'Sir John, tell Tokár we need his men to assemble along this line.' Ellingham indicated a small rise that they might defend better. 'We will form a line in front of them. When we make contact, we need Tokár's men to break and run to the ends to harry the enemy. We shall keep our line together as best we can. That way we can better defend each other. If we're flanked, we can fight back to back.'

Hawker bowed, a trace of a smile on his face. 'As you command.'

Faldi walked away, pushing past Dieudonné. 'He has a death wish. *Pazzo!*'

'My lord,' said Jacob, nodding to Ellingham. 'Where do you want your crossbowmen?'

'You and Jack, together, on the left flank. If either of you get a clear shot at their captain, take him down. He's probably the only one who knows what he's doing.'

Jacob nodded and shifted the crossbow in his arms.

Tokár called to his men, and quickly got them formed into line. They were not soldiers, nor had ever been, they were herders and traders. But they were all hardened, many having fought to the death before.

'Where are the Rascians?' said Ellingham, casting an eye.

'They are there,' replied Hawker. 'Up on the other side of the field where Maria is. And her father.'

'We need her to order them down here. We'll need every sword we've got.'

When Ellingham approached he saw Maria standing over the old man who had thrown his heavy cloak up over his head, hiding himself. Pedja and Orkan stood near her, apparently keeping guard and looking nervous.

'We need the Rascians, my lady. To finish the task.'

She looked at Ellingham, and he could see her once-fair face was now deathly pale and twisted with worry.

'They have said they wish to keep me from harm.'

Ellingham turned to the one called Pedja. 'We need you both in the line.' The Bosnian shook his head and raised his shoulders to signify his lack of understanding.

Ellingham groaned and turned to face Maria again. 'You won't have need of a guard if we're overwhelmed down there,' he said. 'Tell them to stand with us, my lady!'

She scowled at him, not enjoying being told what to do. She spoke to them in Hungarian and Ellingham saw that Pedja was apparently resisting. Ellingham took a few steps back and raised his blade into a guard, ready to force the Slavs to fight. Maria barked at them again and like scolded curs they gave ground. Glaring at Ellingham, they walked past and down to where the most unlikely lance ever formed was taking shape. Tokár came running up, even as the Rascians moved sullenly towards the skirmish line that was forming. The old gypsy bowed before her and she spoke to him quietly but firmly. He acknowledged her order with another bow.

She hefted her light sword.

'Tokár will stand by me here. We shall defend my father if needs be, son of Richard. Do not fail me.'

'We will stand and fight. For you.'

She threw a glance down to the forlorn creature at her feet. 'My knights still hold my trust. God go with you.'

Ellingham swallowed hard. 'You once spoke of a bond between us, my lady. I pray you still believe in it? For what it matters, I still do.' He did not know his true heart's desire any longer. Whether it was lust, the foolish infatuation of a moon-calf fool, or a burgeoning love within him, he no longer knew. He was lost.

She reached out and touched his forearm. Her eyes began to well up, glistening. 'I do, Giles. God protect you.'

He covered her hand with his. He glanced down at the old man. 'Is he... is he your father?'

Maria looked full into Ellingham's eyes and the young knight saw her anguish. 'He was.'

-

There wasn't even a parley.

The garrison's soldiers trotted forward, in a rough semblance of order, bearing small square-shaped shields, swords and some with pole weapons following in their second line. The Wallachian captain bellowed from behind, wearing a pointed Ottoman-style helmet of fluted steel and horsehair plumes. With his wide-bladed sword held over his head he waved his fighters on. There were some twenty or more, double the number of Hawker's force. The garrison soldiers, enraged at their losses thus far, became emboldened upon seeing the true number they now faced. Roaring defiance, they came on across the clearing.

But Jack Perry had stopped shaking. He was strangely calm, his mind at ease, fixed upon shooting that Wallachian captain. As soon as the lines met, he'd seen the more lightly armed gypsies surge around either flank, splitting up, trying to harass the enemy from behind. They darted in and out, drawing the Wallachians back and away from their line, swarming like angry wasps. Jack balanced on the balls of his feet, ready to move. Jacob stood just to his right and further forward, already taking a bead with his crossbow. He waited until Jacob had loosed. The quarrel missed the Wallachian commander but struck the man next to him in the shoulder, dropping him.

Jacob immediately dropped back to draw the bow again. But a swordsman was already charging him. Jack raised his crossbow to his shoulder, took aim, and pulled the trigger. A swishing noise followed and he was rewarded with the sight of the Wallachian falling to his knees and then forward on his face. By now Jacob had managed to reload moving forward again.

Jack dropped the nose of the crossbow, stuck his toe into its stirrup, and grasped the strings and pulled with all his might. He missed hooking the nut and the strings slid from his grasp. A heavy grunting sound made him raise his head. A bearded Wallachian was already swinging at him. He rolled to the ground and then scrambled to his feet, struggling to draw his sword. He just managed to deflect the second blow but the man's blade carried on, sliding up and glancing off his helm. The blow staggered him and his guard fell.

Hawker's sword swung in a high arc, striking the Wallachian's shoulder, forcing the man to turn and defend himself. Jack, flooding with rage now, raised his blade and brought it down on the man's head, crushing the light helm he wore.

'Fetch the crossbow!' yelled Hawker before he had to turn to face another.

Jack scrambled again and picked up the bow and then ran back, outside the melee. He sheathed his sword and again attempted to span the crossbow, this time on his backside. It clicked into place and he was again on his feet. For the first time he noticed a black and red banner flying where Tokár stood guard, sword drawn, over the old mad prince. It was the same as Maria had flown on her galley when they fled Venice: a dragon with its tail coiled about its own neck, a cross carved across its folded wings. Tokár had somehow mounted it on a long dead branch and hoisted this up to catch the wind. It rippled and snapped, the dragon dancing upon it. Jack tore his eyes from the sight and brought them back onto the confused fight in front of him, once again searching for the Wallachian commander. He sighted him, placed a quarrel in the stock, and began walking forward again, skirting the melee wide.

It was a scene of chaos now; whatever skirmish lines Sir Giles had intended had disintegrated into a series of deadly brawls. He caught sight of Maria, now fighting next to Giles, and beside her was the Italian, swinging gustily at a probing spear. They were still badly outnumbered and already Jack could see the bodies of at least three gypsies scattered across the clearing. The two Rascians fought back to back, circling and lashing out at their antagonists. He could hear Sir Giles shouting, trying to call to Hawker and the others. He had seen few battles but he knew this one was not going well.

He could feel his heart pounding away, the jingle of his armour sounding with every step he took. He kept his eyes on the captain, circling wide. Any moment now, a Wallachian would charge him. He had to make a charge himself. He raised his crossbow and trotted straight for the captain. There would not be a second chance. Ten feet away, he saw the captain finally catch sight of him, eyes widening at the impending danger. At the same moment another Wallachian began to rush him. Jack put his left leg forward, leaned in, took aim, and pulled the trigger.

He had only time to see the captain drop his sword and raise his hands to his breast. Jack had caught him just at the armpit where his brigandine jerkin did not cover. In the same moment Jack instinctively raised his crossbow up in front of him. It was chopped out of his hands by a garrison soldier, broken and spinning, and Jack back-pedalled furiously to avoid the next blow. Without thinking, he twisted his body round and ran away as fast as he could.

The Wallachian gave up and returned to the melee which Jack now saw was growing tighter, bodies scattered about the clearing. The knights, with Maria, the Italian, and the Rascians, had formed a tight half circle, bending in upon itself. They were holding their own. Jacob was reloading on the far side of the clearing. Jack drew his sword and skirted wide again to rejoin the company. It was then he saw Sir John fall.

Even as he spurred himself on, he felt deep pain in the pit of his stomach, dread rising up within him, instantly anguished that he had not been by his side – as he should have been – protecting his knight.

But in that moment, he also saw that what remained of the Wallachian garrison seemed to be melting away and falling back, confused. His crossbow bolt had taken down their captain and without him, the enemy had lost their will. He knelt down as Hawker was dragged in behind Ellingham and Faldi by Tokár and one of his surviving men.

Jack managed to pull up the chinstrap from the knight's sallet helm and gently eased it off his head. It was creased where the edge of a blade had struck it full on.

'God, please, don't take him!'

Hawker stirred, eyes opening and rolling in his sockets. 'What… what are you pestering me about, boy? Sweet Christ, head ringing… minster bells.'

Jack rolled him onto his side and Hawker's near-empty stomach spewed up a little bile. He coughed and gagged, then muttered a low curse. Standing over them, Orkan swung his iron mace again at a sword and shield man who had yet to notice his comrades had pulled back. The painted shield buckled and splintered, and the Wallachian fell back a few steps, realised he was out in front of what was left of his line, and turned and ran. The remaining Wallachians made a half-hearted attempt to form a line again but many, seeing their dead captain, the fletchings of a crossbow bolt protruding from his side, thought better of it. They continued to fall back until they reached the treeline and then they made for the fortress gate at a full tilt.

He heard Maria shouting at them all but he could not understand her. Ellingham took a few steps forward, balancing his sword, making sure all the enemy had flown. The rest of the company seemed unhurt. De Grood came and also knelt by Hawker.

'Here, let me raise him up a little, boy!'

248

'He spoke, Jacob! I swear it. He must live.'

De Grood's hands pored over Hawker's scalp. 'Bruised, not broken. Thank the Virgin. We must get him up to the trees. Get him covered up with a cloak.'

Ellingham was now shouting at Faldi, the Rascians seemed to be eyeing a retreat, and Maria had begun walking back to the encampment, her eyes glazed and cheek bloody.

Jacob had Hawker on his feet again but the old knight was barely conscious and almost unable to stand. 'Help me get him over there!' ordered Jacob. Jack threw an arm around Hawker's backplate and gripped his right elbow to steady him.

'What are Sir Giles and the Italian arguing about?' said Jack, straining under the weight of the stumbling knight. 'We've won, for Christ's sake!'

'We didn't kill them all,' replied Jacob, grunting. 'Faldi is saying they'll fetch help and come after us. Sir Giles told the woman he would never have murdered prisoners anyway.'

Jacob's grip slipped and Hawker went to his knees. 'Shit! Help me, boy! Get him on his feet again.'

They got him up again, Hawker now rambling incoherently.

'His brains are addled, Jacob. I fear for him.'

'*Ach*, he was thumped harder in Mechelen a few months afore. He'll come around.'

They made it to a little crest just where they had made camp the night before. They set down Hawker and kept him on his side. Jack looked back to the far side of the circle. Tokár and his surviving band were pulling the bodies of their dead back. The Wallachians had melted away and Jack once again keenly felt the cold wind blowing right through his sweat-soaked gambeson down to the skin. A hand still on Hawker's chest, his eyes scanned the encampment. He then turned to the Fleming.

'Jacob, where is the old prince?'

24

Ellingham tore through the waist-high growth of laurel and young oak, searching for the man who was the fallen prince of Wallachia. Bartolo Faldi was fifty yards to his right, loudly cursing as he too cast about, searching for the old man. Ellingham reasoned that Vlad might make for the horses and donkeys, but none had been taken. Vlad had not passed by them, making for the fortress path, so he must have wandered west the way they had arrived. The company had come all this way only to lose their prize the moment they had attained it. More than that, there was every reason to believe they could face a counter-attack the longer that they lingered on the mountain. He could feel the anxiety welling up inside him, threatening to lock him again into agonising indecision. And now, at the worst possible time, Hawker had been wounded.

The surviving gypsy band had fanned out, too, combing the wind-blasted wilderness around the encampment. Ellingham watched Faldi, shouting and cutting through the briar with his sword. The Milanese had already challenged him in the last few minutes, demanding that as soon as they found the prince they should immediately make for the town of Sighişoara which lay back over the Făgăraş and deep into the Siebenbürgen. When Ellingham had demanded why, he replied because it was the prince's place of birth. That alone seemed a poor reason. As for Maria, she was frantic and making no sense. She had rushed into the forest along with Tokár before he could even stop her.

Ellingham heard Maria's shouts, coming from off to his left and close by. He rushed to follow her voice. She was calling his name. Clearing a small pine copse, he saw her. She was not alone. Tokár, visibly upset, was on her right and in between them was Vlad. Ellingham reached her and threw up his arms.

'Thanks be to God! You have him, my lady.'

'Tokár left him alone – unwatched – when he joined us in the fight, when it looked bad for us,' said Maria, her voice weary. 'Tokár spied him first, westwards along the trail we came in on. He had suspected that was the way he had wandered. He's greatly ashamed for abandoning the prince. I told him he is forgiven.'

Ellingham for the first time was able to get a good look at Vlad. Less old than he had first thought, the man looked stocky even in his weakened condition. Hawker had said he was once a powerful and feared swordsman. There was still a trace of that and he stood unbowed by age. He looked up at Ellingham's approach. Large, dark green eyes, almost protruding ones, dominated the man's face. Long, drooping mustachios the colour of burnt ashes draped below the aquiline nose, laying along his cheeks down to his chin. The rest of his face, a perfect oval, was shaven; he had then at least had some comforts provided in his captivity. The look he gave Ellingham was one of distrust, the wariness of a caged animal looking out on its captor.

Faldi now approached noisily and Vlad inclined his head slightly to take in the new arrival.

'By the blessed Virgin!' Faldi exclaimed.

'We must get back to the encampment while we still have time,' said Maria flatly. 'There is much to discuss.'

Ellingham couldn't decide if the prince could even understand what they were saying. He had not uttered a word. He showed no sign of fear or even confusion at his situation. But equally, he showed no sign of caring about it either. It was as if he really wasn't aware of anything. And it dawned on him that even if he was who Maria believed him to be, this man, a prisoner for some nine years, might truly be mad.

They walked back to the clearing, Faldi jabbering at him the entire way about the urgency of their situation and how exposed they were.

'If Hawker worsens, we'll have no choice but to leave him. We can't all die because of his ill luck.'

Ellingham rounded on him. 'You're a base dog and it is a wonder that he ever called you friend and comrade! Hawker will ride if I have to strap him into his saddle! Enough of your prattling.'

Faldi went for his sword and Maria stepped forward and stopped him. 'Ser Bartolo! You remain in my service! Remember your place!'

The Milanese gave a low laugh and moved his hand away from his hilt. 'This boy, though son of a king he may be, needs to learn respect.' He moved off, doubling his pace, making for the encampment.

Dieudonné, his sword still drawn, met them there once they reached it.

'I was just coming to find you, Giles. You had me worried. But I see you've found our reluctant captive.'

Ellingham swept up the Burgundian by the arm, walking him away. 'Is there any sign of the Wallachians coming back?'

Dieudonné shook his head and shrugged. 'They have fled. I doubt they'll try a foray again this day. The question is what will *we* do?'

'How fares Sir John?'

'He will live. The boy and the Fleming are looking after him. He speaks, if a little bit slurred.'

Ellingham let out a long breath. 'Can he ride?'

'The Fleming would know better than I.'

'The Milanese is testing me. Trying to take command now with Sir John down. I need you to stand by me, Gaston.'

Dieudonné raised an eyebrow. 'Mutiny? We're but an ill-stitched company of mercenaries so I'm not surprised, given our situation.'

Ellingham grabbed Dieudonné's forearm. 'You haven't answered my question. Can I depend on you?'

Dieudonné smiled, his fine teeth showing. 'That you even must ask that, my friend! I stand by you. Always. I told you that a long time ago. But it's the Hungarian who has turned your head.'

The last curt words were like the snick of a finely honed dagger. 'Careful, if you value that friendship. And whether you approve or not I've decided that Maria must decide our next destination. Given what we have just done here, I'll urge her to return whence we came. Hermannstadt is closed to us now but there are other towns in the Saxon lands.'

Dieudonné looked away a moment. 'Forgive me. I stand by you, always. But we must not alienate Faldi, my friend. We are short on numbers and he does have his uses. I would urge diplomacy to keep his disposition sweet.'

Ellingham chewed the inside of his cheek. 'I must tend to Sir John.'

Reaching him on the other side of the clearing, he found the knight propped up against the trunk of a young beech, a rolled cloak behind his neck and another draped over him. Ellingham could clearly see the lump on the top left side of his head. Jack was squatting next to him, fussing like a mother hen.

'How does he fare?' whispered Ellingham.

Hawker's eyelids raised. 'He fares goddamn vile. Bastard slipped my guard. Got through.'

Ellingham smiled. The old knight still had vinegar running in his veins. 'We can't tarry here long, Sir John. Will you be well enough to ride?'

Hawker shifted himself, winced, and swore an oath that would have made a Britanny corsair blush. 'Give me an hour and some more wine. I can ride. Who did we lose?'

'Four of Tokár's men. The others, a few bruises at worst.'

Hawker made a growling noise of acknowledgement. 'Poor bastards. But Fortuna favoured us. What of Prince Vlad? Grateful?'

Ellingham pursed his lips a second, looking down. 'I believe he has lost his mind. He's not spoken a word. Doesn't seem to recognise Maria.'

Hawker let out a long breath, his head lolling. 'To have come all this way for such meagre reward. I'm sorry, my lad.'

'It was my choice, Sir John. And the prince may yet rally his sense again. I must see what the lady now wishes to do.'

'The fortress will have sent out a rider to fetch help by now.' Hawker paused with the effort to speak. 'Get the company fed while there's time. And the gypsy will want to bury his dead.'

Ellingham nodded. Behind him he could hear the carrion crows already cawing and screeching as they fought over the bodies that lay strewn about. 'Jack, see that Sir John gets his wine. I will return shortly.' He looked up and for the first time caught sight of the dragon banner flying proudly at the edge of the clearing. It looked sadly insignificant, a reminder of a time long past and now forgotten.

-

Gaston Dieudonné stood with folded arms, listening as best he could to the cacophony of speech around him and growing ever more frustrated as he did so. He prided himself on his knowledge of foreign tongues, a skill which had served him well over the past years in his many deceptions, but Hungarian and Wallachian had never gained his ear. He did not like not being in control or being deprived of intelligence. It made him irritable and prone to overreactions, often ending in blood being spilt.

Seated on the ground in front of him was Maria and her supposed father as well as Tokár and Faldi. The two Rascians – whom he trusted about as much as he would a grinning street pedlar – stood on the opposite side within hearing distance. The short, stocky one appeared to have the brains, the other the muscle. They were listening and occasionally speaking in hushed tones. Conspiracy, perhaps. He didn't like having competition for his plotting. And he really only knew half of what Faldi was planning in his empty, moth-blown skull.

He watched the old Wallachian warlord who sat in the middle, hunched, with shoulders draped in a russet red woollen cloak. His eyes followed whomever was speaking but neither could Maria's entreaties nor the gypsy's heartfelt pleas convince him to open his mouth in reply. At length, Faldi spoke to Maria in Italian. It could have been Venetian or Lombard – he wouldn't have been able to tell the difference – and Maria answered him back. It was then that the old man spoke, also in Italian.

'Who is this man? Is he from the Republic?'

All the others fell silent. Dieudonné smiled.

'He is from Milan,' said Maria in the same tongue, leaning forward and eager to draw him out. 'He is in my service, a friend.'

'I know no Lombards who are friends,' replied Vlad. He looked hard at Maria. 'I do not know you either, woman. Or what it is you want of me.'

Dieudonné had acquired enough Tuscan over the years and Venetian from the misadventures of the summer just past to understand what the old man was saying. He was now all ears to hear more.

Maria reached over and touched Vlad upon his wrist. 'Do you know who you are?'

Prince Vlad looked at her again and blinked slowly. 'I am of no consequence. And you have taken me from my chamber. Against my will.'

Maria looked away to Faldi. Her face had fallen, bereft. Dieudonné thought he heard a muffled sob emanate from the gypsy, still prostrate at the feet of the one they believed to be Vlad Dracula. Face on the ground, the gypsy had grasped the prince's ankles in obeisance. Vlad slowly pulled his feet back under his cloak.

Maria reached into her large leather belt pouch and slowly withdrew the ruby cross that lay within. The Tears of Byzantium. She held it up to Vlad.

'Father, I have found them again. Brought them home. To redeem us.'

Dieudonné saw Dracula blink twice rapidly, while the rest of his gaunt face remained the same. He said nothing.

'We must get out of here,' said Faldi, impatient with the pace. 'His enemies will return and they'll not be taking any prisoners.

We should go back. Back to the Saxon lands and seek out a physician for him.'

Maria's eyes had begun to well up. She stood, with effort, and Dieudonné leaned over to assist her. 'We will go where I have always intended. We make for Sighişoara. What the Saxons call Schässburg.' She placed the ruby cross back into her pouch.

Dieudonné saw Vlad's eyes dart upwards at the name of the town. The Frenchman suppressed a grin. The sly old fox was no madder than he was. He would swear it. Far from mad, in fact. The old man, not knowing for certain who his new captors were and what they wanted, was playing the fool to gain time. To learn who it was that had freed him. It was clever, and in Dracula's place he might have used the same ruse. But it did raise a question. Had the old man truly rejected his own blood? Or did he recognise Maria and just not trust her – yet. Was her tale of paternity just a lie? Her sadness and surprise seemed unfeigned. But Vlad had reacted to the jewels as if he had seen a long-lost friend. Or a ghost.

Maria turned to Tokár. 'Get him food and drink. Keep him warm. And do not let him out of your sight again! If we must, we will bind him.'

The gypsy bowed, and again to Prince Vlad, and moved off.

'Where are my English?' Maria said, turning to Dieudonné. She had found her steel again. 'I want us back down the hillside inside the hour. See to the horses and take your meat while you can!'

Dieudonné locked eyes with Faldi and beckoned him with a head motion. The Milanese returned a stony look but followed him to where the horses and donkeys were tied.

Leaning his arms over the saddle of his mount, he smiled at Faldi standing a few yards on the opposite side. 'So... where does that leave your clever little plan? You need the old man to tell you the exact location of his treasure. He isn't interested in playing your game though.'

'I told you already. I know the town where it lies.' Faldi tried hard not to sound desperate.

'And you are certain it does not lie here in Wallachia? Because we have fewer friends here than a one-handed leper. And about as many friends in the Saxon lands as a two-handed leper. Vlad would have been more likely to hide his treasure here where he ruled – maybe even in this castle – than leaving it among the same folk he impaled when the fancy took him.'

Faldi shook his head slowly. 'Don't talk of things you don't know. Or understand. Frenchman.'

Dieudonné scowled. 'Burgundian.'

'All the same. I was in the Saxon lands when Vlad launched his last campaign. He had friends there. Noblemen, Saxons who supported him. And several houses. It was a Wallachian servant who told me where the hoard was buried. Vlad wanted it safe knowing he was embarking on this great attempt to regain his throne. Others who had helped conceal it were killed on Vlad's orders. He alone escaped. Said he was the only one to know. He told me the name of the town but not the house. Said it was one of Vlad's little manors. He wanted me to take him there and that he would recognise it. All he asked for was protection and a small share.'

Dieudonné rested his pointy chin on the saddle and gave a little laugh. 'And I have no difficulty in believing you swallowed every word of it.'

Faldi cursed and took a step closer. 'You fool! Maria had already hired me to look for the prince. And she had told me of his treasure. A casket of many gems. The same hoard from which the Tears of Byzantium came. That servant's story was the clue I needed.'

'So where is your little slave?'

Faldi frowned. 'He was killed. The half-wit got into a fight and was knifed before I could stop him.'

Dieudonné's smile widened further, showing all his gleaming teeth. 'So, you know the town but not the house itself. Let us hope it is not a *big* town.'

'The fool told me what it looks like. That it lies in the northern neighbourhood. I can find it.'

Dieudonné's finger wagged. 'And let me hazard a guess. You have not told the lady which town this is. That is to keep her sweet upon your continued presence. That is your bargain, is it not? A share of the treasure if you lead her to it.'

Faldi cast a quick look over his shoulder and moved to the flank of Dieudonné's mount. 'It is my insurance, so she will not cross me.'

'Then why the need to free the prince? Come all this way and risk death? Something else tells me you need him too to solve the puzzle.'

Faldi's voice was barely above a whisper. 'She would set him up again. To rule. She believes the stories. Believes many will flock to his standard again. The treasure would be needed to gain support. Allies. Mercenaries.'

Dieudonné lowered his chin further, looking down his nose. 'My dear fellow, my mother did not find me in a cabbage patch. *You* need Vlad, too. You can't search every house in – where did you say it was?'

It was Faldi's turn to give a little laugh.

Dieudonné shrugged. 'I saved you. And you swore an oath. I would only ask you to tell me the town. Nothing more. If you won't tell me then I have nothing to lose by telling the English there is more here than a daughter's fealty to her father.'

Faldi hesitated a moment, then spat out the answer in a hiss. 'Thorenburg. It is Thorenburg. Near—'

'Near Schässburg?'

'No. That is the place where Dracula was born. This town lies some twenty or more leagues to the north.'

Dieudonné now realised its significance to the old prince and why he had reacted to its name. 'So you've convinced her to journey first to Schässburg and then move on north. And why will she do that?'

'Because she *knows* the place, you fool. That is where she last saw her father. When he raised his standard for his last campaign. I will reveal that is the true destination once we are in Schässburg and not before then. She has agreed. She only knows the treasure lies in one of the great towns, not which one.'

Dieudonné shook his head disdainfully. 'You assume much, my friend. The prince has lost his wits. Indeed, all his reason it would seem. He will be of no help to you.'

'Maybe. Maybe not.' Faldi moved to the thin horse he had acquired in the last village they had rested in and began preparing the old and dilapidated saddle for the ride out. 'And you would do well to keep your mouth shut until the time is right.'

Perhaps Faldi thought Prince Vlad's madness a ruse as well. If it was a ruse then three men knew where the treasure lay. For Gaston Dieudonné, that was two too many.

'Tell me,' said Dieudonné, his voice as soft as silk, 'what did you and the fair lady thieve in Buda from the king of Hungary? And who silenced the witness?' Hawker had let slip some of the story but now was the time to squeeze more of it from Faldi.

The Milanese paused his fiddling with saddle straps and smiled at him, a grin laced with subtle menace. 'You are a meddlesome creature, Burgundian. Careful, or you will find your long nose in a steel trap.'

'Let me hazard a guess. She charmed some poor devil in the king's counting house into parting with a few sacks of *ducati* and once she had those, she spurned him. He threatened to confess the thievery. But *you* took care of that problem. That was when she made for Venice to pursue the ruby cross and you went east to ready the ground for this hare-brained adventure we're all on. My long nose – and your face – tells me I'm close enough.'

Faldi let out a derisive grunt of a laugh. 'You blind fool. She's a Drăculeşti! She doesn't need me to cover her tracks. She was a common whore in Hunedoara, a courtesan in Buda, and a noblewoman in Venice. A nimble-fingered thief, too. She is a fire salamander who changes again and again and again. Believe me, Burgundian, she's as skilled with a stiletto as she is with any sword. Our lady, our employer, is every inch a murderer. Just like you and me.'

Pedja Jankovic was cold and hungry. Being hungry was the worse of the two. Bad enough he and Orkan had been tasked to help the *cigani* bury their dead. They could barely scratch out even a shallow grave in the cold, hard earth and ended up having to cover the bodies with rocks.

Gathering rocks.

He seethed with anger and with self-loathing for having gotten himself into it all.

The train of horses and donkeys was moving now and they were leaving the cursed place. No monsters, no *drekavac* to be faced down. But death had come anyway. They had brought it with them. He was still incredulous he had survived the little battle with him being only a garrison rat like those that had attacked. They were not skilled warriors and had paid the price. He and Orkan had been battered and bruised but not stabbed to death. That was something to be grateful for.

'What are you worrying about now, Tombik?' Orkan had closed the distance and come up behind him. He spoke Turkish to him, not caring who overheard the tongue. They were riding amidst the surviving *cigani* and Pedja doubted they knew anything other than their own language.

'My stomach.'

'It was ever thus, Tombik. Proves you're still in the game with me.' His horse's chest brushed the flank of Pedja's mount and the Turk leaned forward in the saddle. 'Do you believe it truly is he? Kaziglu Bey? Why is he being treated like, like a… *captive*?'

Pedja leaned to his left and spoke over his shoulder. 'It's him. But he may be broken in mind. And body.'

'I thought he would be taller.'

'And I thought he'd be happier for being freed by his daughter.'

Pedja looked up ahead and could see Prince Vlad being pulled along on a donkey, tied to Tokár's own. The Impaler was wrapped up tightly in a hooded woollen cloak and hunched over. His body bobbed and weaved as the donkey negotiated the sloping terrain.

Pedja thought it looked as if he might be strapped to the saddle. The Impaler was just baggage, not a rider.

'Tombik, my friend, you realise we're going back west? We're moving further away from those who might... might be favourable to what we would be offering. We're travelling back into Hungarian lands. They're not well disposed to my people, in case you've forgotten.'

Pedja didn't reply.

'We've spent so much time in the company of these Franks maybe you *have* forgotten.'

Pedja gritted his teeth. His scheme was unravelling, he knew it, and it irked him to have Orkan reminding him of it. 'We need the right moment. You know that. And this is not it. We need patience. Then we seize the moment when it arises. At least it looks as if the Impaler has no fight left in him.'

Orkan Ozdemir let out a loud sigh of exhausted resignation. 'Ah, Tombik, I have all the patience in the world.'

25

Hawker's head throbbed, the pain arcing from his crown down to the back of his neck. He could not bear the weight of his helm and so wore only his rust-stained quilted arming cap. The line of riders followed the undulating treeline of the slopes, remaining just inside the first few trees to avoid detection while keeping an eye on the winding road below them. It was tortuous and bone cold.

He was still angry for allowing himself to suffer a blow full on the head. He wanted to put it down to lack of sleep and food, but Hawker knew in his heart it was more than that. He was getting slower. Anticipation was what distinguished a good swordsman from a poor one. Knowing where the next blow might come from, being aware of danger on the flanks, these were all skills that made the difference. The difference between victory and death. While he rode in silence, the realisation was sinking in that his next skirmish might be his last.

His eyes settled on Jack. He hardly recognised the boy now. Big for his age, he was now more muscular and leaner than before, the wispy red down of his chin beard growing faster. Jack had rigged a rope sling for the remaining crossbow which now swung gently across the lad's backplate as he rode. He recalled how Jack had regaled him with his slaying of the Wallachian commander, the act that precipitated the flight of the enemy. And through the whole of the lad's animated retelling, Hawker knew it had all turned out as he had predicted: the boy had accepted the life of a man-at-arms. And killing.

He bowed his head and made a promise to himself. A promise that if God would grant him the strength, he would see them all returned to Flanders, a place where their chances of finding a good life – and perhaps a longer one – would be the better. Where the search for a worthy employer and subsequent beneficence might be easier. And, God willing, perhaps it might just be time for Giles to reveal himself to his aunt, King Richard's sister, the duchess dowager of Burgundy. Her protection would serve the youth well long after he himself was gone.

By the time they returned to the Olt Valley it was late afternoon and almost dark, a light, dry snow blowing around them. Tokár had guided them back to the same little village that lay on the eastern bank of the great river, the place where they had stayed a few days earlier. Approaching along the undulating roadway, they could just make out two or three lanterns burning among the collection of peasant dwellings, waypoints for those hurrying to their homes in the early nightfall of winter. Hawker felt strangely relieved to be back to the place again. It seemed a peaceful place, and a welcoming one to travellers. And he was so very tired.

The entire company was ragged and worn from the fight of the morning and the cold, long ride of the afternoon. Most had barely eaten all day. The little innkeeper grinned widely at the sight of Maria when she entered the hostelry, arm in arm with a hooded Vlad, his face obscured.

'My lady! God has delivered you just in time! The wolves would have had you and your party had you remained out in the countryside. A large pack has been seen here in the valley.'

Maria threw back her hood and guided her father to the fire. 'Please see to my retainers outside and to our horses.'

'As you wish. Would have thought you might have remained in Wallachia – at Snagov – for the Feast of the Nativity,' said the innkeeper, already curious as to her companion.

Maria, her face drawn, hair dirty and bedraggled, managed to break into an insincere smile. 'My retainers here,' and she motioned to Hawker, Ellingham, and Faldi, 'they are from the west and so fall under the Pope's protective and generous cloak. Snagov holds little for their creed.'

'Well, let me see…' The man counted on his fingers. 'It is five days since the Feast of Saint Ignatius so tomorrow is the Nativity in the Catholic Church, my lady. Your knights can celebrate Christmas here this night! The pig is slaughtered and there is meat aplenty. And you have brought me another guest?' The man lowered his head as if trying to peer under the prince's hood.

'A fellow companion of the road,' she replied, turning Vlad towards the fire and away from the innkeeper. 'He was travelling on his own and being an elder I wished to give him protection. I will pay.'

The innkeeper grinned broadly again, the promise of gold no doubt upon his mind. 'I will see to your party's needs in the courtyard first. Still have your Rascians and gypsy servants I take it? And your room I will ready upstairs, my lady, once I return.' He gave her an obsequious bow and went outside.

Maria quickly translated their exchange for Hawker.

'Christmas?' he sighed. 'By the Rood, I confess I'd forgotten.' He thought of Jack and his fat Christmas goose. 'If you will allow your company a bit of respite, my lady, I am sure we will ably meet our duty to you afterwards.' The thought of roast pig made his stomach growl and the reflected heat of the roaring fire lifted his fatigue. Perhaps a meal would set his aching head to rights.

Jacob plodded inside, an avuncular arm around Jack's shoulders. He shivered dramatically and then propelled Jack towards the crackling log fire. 'Warm your bones, jongen!' he said. 'You did well this day.'

Gaston Dieudonné entered the room, brushing a dusting of snow from his vambraces and gloves. He nodded at Hawker and then walked to the edge of the stone circle of the fire. He propped the toe of his boot up on the stones until the snow upon it hissed and steamed.

Maria found a bench for her father near the fire and sat with him, the pain of her estrangement plainly there on her comely face. Hawker approached her and pulled another short bench near.

'Will he be recognised in this place?' he asked her.

She shook her head, not looking at the knight. 'I don't know, but I fear to take the chance of revealing him.'

'And is his mind still addled? He still does not seem to know you.'

She didn't reply. Ellingham and Faldi joined them but remained standing. Faldi had a look of pure disgust on his face, directed towards the former prince of Wallachia. Ellingham, on the other hand, was watching Maria, his compassion for her suffering writ clear upon his face.

'My lady,' he said quietly in French, 'the prince has been through a long ordeal. We do not know what he was subjected to all these years past in that place. He needs time for his mind to heal.'

She looked up at Ellingham. 'I pray that seeing the place of his birth will help him remember all. There is nothing more I can do.'

Hawker saw Faldi's lips begin to purse tightly as he listened to her words. It was a reaction he could not quite fathom.

Maria looked over to Hawker. 'Schässburg is two days ride from here, maybe less. If you are well enough, Sir John, I suggest we rest here tomorrow and then set off the day after. I will feel more confident of support once we reach that place. Here... I am not so sure of friends.'

Hawker smiled. 'My head is as hard as an anvil and is used to being struck like one. I'll be ready to ride with you when you give the word.'

'The company stands with you,' added Ellingham, nodding. 'We will protect the prince as we protect you.'

Dieudonné, listening intently, tapped the stone of the hearth a few times with his toe.

The innkeeper returned with his servants and beckoned them to the long oak table on the far side of the room. Maria sat her father at one end of the table and took a place next to him. The others of the company joined; Hawker on Vlad's elbow and

Ellingham next to Maria. Faldi and Dieudonné took seats halfway down while Jacob and Jack took the opposite end closest to the door. Before sitting, Jacob angled the bench outwards, facing the door, and drew his blade. He motioned for Jack to do the same.

Wine in clay pots arrived, some wooden plates too, and soon after a large pewter trencher of carved roast pig, boiled onions and parsnips and covered in sprigs of rosemary. Before any had helped themselves to the fare, Vlad slowly pulled back the hood of his cloak and fixed his eyes on the heaping platter before him. And then he spoke.

The high French poured from him as if he was the dauphin himself. 'Here is a bounty I have long been unaccustomed to. I am grateful.'

All eyes turned to him. Dracula pulled the platter towards himself and began piling chunks of meat on his plate. He then proceeded to begin eating while the others watched, something he no doubt had been long accustomed to years before. He paused to slake his thirst with a deep draught of Moldovan spiced wine.

He put his cup down and looked to Hawker and then to the others. 'You have my leave to join me.'

Hawker caught a spark of hope in Maria's eyes. Was Vlad regaining his memory? If anything was to be salvaged from this adventure other than a handful of gold it would depend on just that. Vladislav Dracula was of no use to the House of York if he remained in dotage. It was clear that imprisonment for nine years had taken its toll but Hawker could not fathom why that would rob a man of the memory of his very identity.

Hawker had seen the prince a few times from fairly close distance when he served in the expedition to Bosnia as part of the Venetian contingent. The proud nose, large eyes and full lips he was seeing now were indeed the same. He was in no doubt it was Dracula. And despite the weathering and wrinkles of his sallow skin, the calculating gaze of the Impaler remained as ever. What he had seen on the floor in the castle cell took away any lingering doubts. What was not answered was the question of whether Maria was truly his daughter.

'My lord,' said Hawker, without introducing himself, 'we have set you free from your captors. This woman is your daughter, Maria. Do you not recognise her?'

Maria drew back, his direct address taking her by surprise. Before she could intervene though Vlad spoke again.

'I have had many children. Do you expect me to remember them all?'

'I might expect you to remember one who has risked all to free you from your enemies.'

Maria slapped her palm flat upon the table. 'Hawker! Enough.'

Vlad shut his eyes for a moment, opened them again, and slowly pushed his plate forward a little. He turned to Hawker. 'And who are you, sir, to make demands of me?'

'I am Sir John Hawker, an English knight and condottiere. My company is in the service of this woman, Maria Hunyadi. She is your daughter. Born at Hunedoara.'

Vlad swivelled his head around to look upon Maria again. He wiped some meat juice from his mouth. 'She is indeed fair and could be one of mine. But I do not remember her.' He picked up his cup and drank again.

Maria's eyes were hard but Hawker saw the tears welling in the candlelight.

Hawker persisted. 'Then tell me, sir, who *you* are?'

'Hawker!' exploded Faldi, seated next to him. 'For the love of Christ! Keep your tongue!'

Vlad raised his hand to silence the Italian. He looked at Hawker again. 'You are very bold, sir. Very bold. For you know full well who I am.' He raised his chin and gazed down the table. 'As do you all.'

The prince's face had suffused red and his demeanour had suddenly regained vigour. Hawker now noticed that the innkeeper had been lurking near the stairs. The look on the man was one of both wonder and fear mixed. He had recognised the old man. A man thought long dead. He moved sideways towards the door and Hawker motioned for Jacob to stop him. Jacob's large hand firmly on his shoulder, the Fleming gently guided the innkeeper to the table.

Maria addressed him in Wallachian and Hawker could guess the gist. The promise of more money for his silence accompanied by the promise of death if he spoke to anyone. As she spoke, a sly smile appeared on Vlad's purplish lips. He leaned on his right forearm, inclining towards Hawker, his wild, matted hair and protruding eyes yet giving him the air of a madman.

'Perhaps she *is* my daughter.'

The shaking innkeeper was quickly on his knees next to the prince, head bowed. Vlad laid a hand of benediction on the man and whispered something in Wallachian. The innkeeper scuttled away, hands clasped in front of him.

The company exchanged looks and a tense silence fell across the table. Dieudonné maintained his sardonic smile of knowing, Jacob and Jack gawped, Faldi simmered, and Ellingham and Maria both looked anxious. For Hawker, Ellingham's worry seemed to be focused on her; the youth could not take his eyes from her, watching her as she in turn stared at her father.

The prince pulled his plate back in and resumed eating, tearing at the fatty pork with the fervour of a starving man before popping a small roasted onion whole into his mouth.

Maria broke the silence, her voice soft but determined. 'I was with you at Torda, when you raised your standard. The day you left to regain the throne from that Turk lickspittle Basarab. I was sixteen. And you say you do not know me?'

Vlad wiped a long, grubby-nailed finger underneath his nose. He looked over to her and his heavy lips parted slightly in what might be a smile. He then nodded a little in recognition of her assertion.

'Maria *Hunyadi*.'

'My mother was the bastard child of King John's mistress. You *know* that. She was *your* mistress.'

Vlad took a sip of wine, all the while studying her with his bulging eyes. 'What I don't know, Maria Hunyadi, is why I am here. Why you have freed me. Or what you intend for me.'

His court French was perfect, thought Hawker. He saw that Faldi was eyeing Maria with a cool eagerness, waiting to hear her response.

Maria leaned forward. 'Why? Why to *restore* you. Take you to a place where you will be safe. Where you will find new allies. That is what I wish.'

Vlad chuckled and wiped his mouth with the back of his hand. 'Woman, that is a mountain higher than even those around us. One I will not be climbing again. And why should I? I was betrayed by everyone I trusted.'

She didn't respond, and silence fell heavy again. It was a strange feast, with all except the prince still clad in their armour, begrimed from the road. Hawker observed poor Jack at the far end, hardly understanding what was going on around him and still far too young to feel the import.

At length, Vlad turned to Maria again. 'Bring me that old gypsy who attended upon me earlier today. Him I do remember.'

Hawker narrowed his eyes. Watching Maria, he sensed she was unsure whether or not to comply. She must have decided it was worth the gamble, hoping it might bring her father out of his aggressive and defensive sulk. She went to the door and called out.

Poor Tokár came into the inn, wrapped up tightly in his cloak against the cold. He and his men were in the stables as before, taking turns to feed the fire they had begun outside the timber lean-to. Vlad beckoned him closer.

Tokár knelt on one knee while the prince addressed him softly, placing a hand upon his shoulder. Maria looked on, hanging upon every word. Tokár replied, nodding, and the prince smiled a little, the man's fiery eyes incongruous against the toothy grin. He then whispered something very quietly to his old servant and sent him on his way, the gypsy bowing respectfully before he left.

Vlad looked at them all. 'He was one of my finest armaşi. Never failed me and never failed to obey an order.' The prince smiled again. 'His axe was always sharp, his knives so keen he could flay a man as one would gently peel the skin from a plum.' He seemed to briefly have a faraway look in his eye and then reached again for his wine.

Faldi let out a laugh to humour the prince but Hawker did not, nor any of the others.

'He created the armași to be his loyal followers because the boyar nobility could not be trusted to remain loyal,' said Maria. 'My father empowered the less fortunate to be his most trusted – free peasants, gypsies, Magyars, Serbs, and Tatars.'

'Yet even they could not save him from defeat and imprisonment.' Hawker spoke, unafraid, as if Dracula was not sitting next to him.

The prince pretended not to hear but Maria bristled slightly. 'My father would raise those from low station because of their loyalty, not solely because they were high-born. His defeat was because he was betrayed. Betrayed by the nobility.'

Dracula sat back a little, hefted his cup and beheld Hawker with a steady gaze.

'My lord,' said Ellingham addressing the prince, 'we are sworn to conduct you to a safe place. That is our agreement with this brave lady, a woman who has risked her life and spent much treasure to see you set free. It is for both of you now to decide upon the destination.'

Maria forced a smile. 'This knight speaks the truth, my lord. We will take you back north. Where you still have friends.'

The prince looked down his nose as she spoke the words. He set down his cup and pushed it away. 'Friends? You took me from my castle without my leave. My brother *gave* it to me, gave me solitude. Gave me life when I was hunted like an animal. God told me that I was never to rule again and I became content. Content in mine own company.'

Maria's face, suffusing red, dissolved into confusion. '*You* are of the royal bone… ruler of Wallachia, Făgăraș and Amlaș. Together… we can…' Her voice trailed off into a deafening silence.

Hawker now began to understand. It was Vlad Dracula who had rejected the world and become a monk, not his half-brother Călugărul.

Dracula raised his cup to his lips again and took another sip of the sickly-sweet wine. 'I have ordered Tokár to find a tall paling and sharpen it well. It will be interesting to see which one of you ends up dancing upon it.' He turned towards Hawker and smiled. 'But I think I have already guessed who it will be.'

—

The light snow still continued to swirl about the courtyard of the inn, small delicate crystals which vanished on contact. Ellingham had stripped off his armour but remained in his quilted doublet, sword belt strapped about his waist. The light of the brazier fire outside the stable lean-to cast an orange glow across the front of the hostelry. Beyond this, and looking towards the road and the other few houses of the village, it was near pitch black. The clouds above obscured moon and stars.

He had helped Jack Perry assist Sir John in preparing for bed. The grizzled knight was worn out, that was clear to him, and he sorely needed rest after his knock to the head. Jack walked with him now, the hour late, but sleep far from both of them.

'Will he be whole again, Sir Giles? He seems so terribly old to me now.'

'We have all been tested these last days. None more than he. And it was his misfortune to take a blow full to the head. He is lucky his helm was not cleaved through.'

'It was a mighty dent. I tried knocking it out. Deep as a plough's furrow. When I saw it my stomach wambled some it did.'

'Aye, it could have killed him but he's made of sterner stuff. He will recover.' Ellingham stopped and faced Jack. 'Now that Sir John is abed, I need to ask you to sit guard on the old prince this night. Outside his chamber. Jacob will relieve you later. Will you do that?'

Jack blinked a few times in the reflected firelight. 'I do guess I can do that, Sir Giles. Are you afeard he may be attacked by someone?'

'I am afeard he may run away. And I will ask my lord Gaston to keep a keen eye on the gypsies and Rascians too.'

When Ellingham had climbed the steps up to the exposed mezzanine of the inn he noticed the door at the end was ajar. In the near darkness he could just make out the figure who stood on the threshold half-exposed to the firelight. It was Maria.

When he reached her she made no move to close it upon him. The heavy black oak door, set deeply with crudely carved fretwork, remained only half open. Ellingham bowed his head to her.

'My lady, the guard is set. Tokár has a few of his men at the ready, if needed. We have all earned our sleep this day.'

He could not see her face, partially obscured by the darkness of the chamber. When she replied her voice was small.

'Is it over? Our quest? I had not thought enough these past months about how captivity might have scarred him. His mind... his *reason*. I don't know who it is I am bringing back with us to the Siebenbürgen.'

Ellingham swallowed. 'I cannot judge it, only you can. But he refuses to acknowledge you. That is a hard blow to take and I sorrow for you. I sorrow mightily.'

'It shames me to say... I have not felt this alone before. I'm believing it was all just a confection, a sweet comfit melting in my mouth to leave only the bitter seed behind.' She leaned on the doorframe. 'What have I done, son of Richard?' she whispered, reaching out to grasp his forearm.

Ellingham reached over and placed his hand over hers. 'You have freed him,' he said softly. 'As was your desire. Do not scourge yourself over what you could not have known. Tomorrow is Christmas Day. And the day after we will go wherever you tell us to take you.'

Her hand remained firmly upon his forearm. 'Călugărul's men will hunt us if we remain here in the Făgăraş. We *must* return north. To the Saxon lands.'

'We will defend you. Until you release us and the quest is complete. Do not despair, my lady.'

She stepped back into the chamber, slowly, and he felt her pulling him along with her. The room seemed colder to him than the outside air. A single candle on a table next to the bed shuddered in the draught. Maria closed the door and then turned to him, embracing him tightly. She said nothing but lifted her chin to his face. Ellingham leaned in, their lips touching tentatively. The gentle brushing of her lips and her honeyed breath blew up the embers that had been long glowing in his heart, stoking the fire anew.

He crushed her to his breast, ardour building. Maria returned it, her mouth searching his, her hands rising to cup his head as they kissed. Ellingham sensed the need in her for him, as if he was an anchor for her grief and all her fears. It made her more mortal to him for the first time, no longer the fearless and haughty Hippolyta, the Amazon queen, who had first charmed and held him at arm's length these past weeks. The admonishments of Hawker faded fast away, scattered by the passion of the moment such that he was no longer conscious of the dangers that hovered around them. Forgotten were the fortunes of the company, Hawker's health, even his own future. His entire body desired her, and hers him.

She broke their kiss and fumbled with the cloth ties of the front of his padded flaxen doublet, her shaking fingers pulling at the bow knots, plucking each undone. He, eyes becoming accustomed to the room, pushed her cloak from off her shoulders. He pulled the tapes of her chemise, revealing her, and she shrugged the gauzy linen off so that it fell around her feet. He drank in her beauty in the glow of the single candle. Her teeth flashed in a smile, instantly bringing forth a smile in him, and Maria loosened his sword belt to the floor then lifted his doublet from off his shoulders, pushing it down and rolling it off his arms until it dropped to the planks of the floor. Ellingham, not waiting, pulled his shirt up over his head and tossed it down.

They fell upon the bed in an entangled embrace. She was flawless, he thought, eyes wide drinking in the sight of her, lithe-limbed and golden in the candlelight. His mouth moved from her neck down to her breasts. She pulled down his hose and he somehow managed to unlace one side of his braes so that they too pulled away. She wrapped her legs around his pale thighs, pulling him into her. They made love as if it might be the only time they would, with abandon and with intensity. But it was brief, Ellingham only realising after he was spent that his boots remained firmly on his feet. He rolled to her side and swept her into his arms, pulling the coverlet over the both of them.

She hugged him tightly.

'My lady,' he said, 'A knight should not wear his shoes in bed. Forgive me, but I couldn't be bothered trying to unbuckle them.'

Maria smiled. 'You made the right decision. As you always do, son of Richard.'

They became silent for a while, holding each other, he listening to her steady breaths. He began to grow more aware of the chill in the chamber and sought to draw the coverlet further to warm them. Ellingham let out a long exhalation.

'Why have you never told me of your upbringing? Your life before. I know nothing about you. About Hunedoara… your family.'

He felt her body shift a little in his arms. It seemed more than a moment passed before she gave answer. 'There is little to tell… and still less a reason for the telling. I live in the moment, not the past. Not even my past.'

'My past was a delusion. Until Sir John revealed the truth to me, who I really am. I am still trying to understand what that means; to be who I am.'

He felt her arms tighten around his chest. 'You are who you choose to be. Let no one tell you otherwise. That is how I live. That is all one needs.'

274

He let her words sink in and decided not to press her for more, for what she was shielding from him. He would wait.

'What will happen when we go back to the Saxon lands? Will your father find supporters? So much time has passed. I already fear what may become of you if all goes ill.'

She turned her head to him, the stiff straw-filled pillow crunching underneath. 'I have to believe. Who else will save these lands from the enemy? My uncle Matthias has lost the taste for crusading and would rather sheath his sword in Christian soldiers from Austria, not the Ottomans. Wallachia will sink further into the sultan's grasp if nothing changes.'

Ellingham leaned in closer. 'And what of Bartolo Faldi? Where does he fit into all this? He has the look of a fellow who knows more than he is willing to say. He boasts to distract and play the clown.'

She didn't answer him straight away. He heard her swallow and she then looked up to the ceiling rafters. 'You are right. And I would have revealed all, given time. To raise an army requires more than fine, brave words. It requires gold. Faldi holds information regarding my father's treasure, knowledge that I don't have. I need him.'

Ellingham rolled her back towards him, their noses touching. 'But the Tears of Byzantium? You have those already.'

She pulled her arm from underneath the coverlet and stroked his hair and cheek. 'They're hardly enough to win over the nobility and the burghers. And not enough to pay for all the soldiers to challenge Călugărul and the sultan. If this treasure still exists, I must convince my father to reveal it. If not, Faldi alone knows in which town it lies hidden.'

Ellingham felt a chill seep into him. 'I thought you wanted to free your father. Not find his gold.'

Her face scrunched in hurt as if he had stabbed her. 'Is that what you think? That I hunt his fortune? Do you not believe me when I tell you only Vlad can save Wallachia – and maybe Hungary too?'

He stroked her cheek. 'I only wish you had trusted me and Sir John with this secret. If others find out what we seek we'll soon be fighting off everyone – not just a garrison full of ill-led militia.'

Her dark green eyes searched his face. 'I *always* intended to tell you. But not before we found and freed my father. We've done that. The next leg of the quest will be just as dangerous. I need you to stand with me.'

'I will stand by you, Maria. I swear it.'

She kissed him again, deeply, and he returned it. 'Will you tell Sir John?' he asked.

'You may tell him. But it must remain with you both, for now. Do not speak with Faldi.'

Ellingham nodded and then, awkwardly, became aware of his woollen hose about his calves, his boots rubbing on the mattress. 'I cannot stay the night here. It would not be right.' He arose and dressed himself hurriedly, Maria sitting up and watching him as he did so.

'I've wanted to lie with you many days now, Giles,' she said. 'But I knew – you know – that it was not right or chaste to do so. But I could no longer deny myself. I need you in more than body. I need you in spirit. To stand by me now more than ever.' She left the bed, retrieved her cloak and covered herself. 'You are right. You cannot stay here and I don't know when we may be together again. But I will pray it will not be the last time.'

She opened the door just a little, peered out, and then opened it wider for him to pass. A lone crow called out nearby, its cawing mournful and raspy. 'I have heard only the voices of crows for days now. How I long to hear the call of a nightjar... or a robin by day. We must hold faith that these times will come again.'

He gave her a wistful smile, unsure that she could even see it through the darkness, and stroked her hair before kissing her once again on the lips. 'Sleep well. Tomorrow is the first day of Christmas.'

Ellingham walked along the mezzanine balcony as softly as his boots would allow, his head once again filling with worry and now a sense of shame as well. He had gone against his wiser conscience and Hawker's wisdom too. His heart had won that struggle in the end, spurred on by lust. That she felt the same for him gave some solace, told him there was more than base desire at play. There was the spark of something deeper between them.

He reached the last door along, the room where Prince Vlad was. A gypsy and Jack stood outside, both silent and wrapped tightly. Had they taken notice of his tryst? Jack looked away when he passed.

As Ellingham descended the steps, he thought again on Maria's words about the crow. Surely she knew that the call of a crow in the night was a harbinger of impending misfortune?

26

Hawker awoke to the sound of a cock crowing and some shouting in the Wallachian tongue. He barely remembered falling into bed but he was awake now, blinking and sore. When he rolled over to climb out of the rope-strung bedframe, his felt the crick in his neck. No doubt he was now an inch shorter too after the hammering he had taken the day before. He sat on the edge of the bed wearing only his braes and rubbed the nape of his neck. His breath condensed in a cloud before him. Hawker pulled up the coverlet from behind and wrapped it around himself as he huddled. Light poured through the wide cracks in the window shutters and he took in the surroundings of the small room which he'd been unaware of the evening before.

His armour lay stacked neatly in a corner, his sword, scabbard, and dented helm alongside. His shirt, hose and arming doublet had been folded and placed on a small bench near the bed. Next to it flopped his long boots, side by side. He smiled at that. Jack playing the squire again. He looked down to his left and saw the hilt and handle of his *cinquedea* dagger protruding from under his pillow. Jack was indeed showing that he was learning the trade.

He remembered the previous evening: the erratic haughtiness of Prince Vlad, Maria's distress, the drink he threw back to ease his pains. His memory ended with being helped out of the main hall and up the stairs to the bedchambers by Jacob and Jack. But he could not remember them stripping him or leaving. It was as if he was already in his dotage, some ancient grandsire waiting to breathe his last. He was filled with melancholy at the thought of his strength fading and muscles weakening with each passing year. Half a dozen broken bones leave their reminders: twinges and aches, winter throbs and occasional limps. He rubbed his face with both hands and then remembered that it was the first day of Christmas. They were all lucky to witness it after the past few weeks.

He wasn't going to live for ever. And Hawker felt that Christmas was as good a time as any to tell some truths that needed to be told while he could still do so. Giles had a right to know that which he had neglected to tell the youth before. He hoped that it would be taken as a gift of sorts, but such was his news that he was quite unsure of the spirit in which it would be received. Steeling himself against the frigid air, he rose and pulled on his clothes, then saw his portmanteau lying at the foot of the bed. He retrieved a clean linen shirt and exchanged it for the soiled one he had thrown on. It was a holy day.

Hawker entered the courtyard wearing his quilted arming doublet and sword belt, his woollen cloak now keeping out the worst of the morning chill. The gypsies were cooking something over the brazier on a spit, a rabbit by the look of it. They looked miserable still for the loss of the others in their band. Tokár was not among them and Hawker guessed that the old *armaşi* was with his former master. Hawker still was not sure if the prince wasn't mad but Tokár had sealed his bond anew with the Wallachian lord. Hawker scanned the courtyard and beyond. Peasants went about their tasks, hauling brushwood, water from the well, taking their cows out to the hillside pastures that lay at the foot of the mountains. He saw the two Rascians sitting by themselves, hunched and in deep conversation under the lean-to. Those of his own company, however, he did not spy. He made for the entrance to the hall.

Ellingham emerged before he reached the great studded oak door and seeing Hawker, broke into a grin.

'Sir John, you look the better this day!'

Hawker laughed a little and clapped him upon the shoulder. 'Looks are deceiving. My neck creaks more than a mill wheel. Where is the rest of the company?'

'Jacob and Jack are still abed. I set them to guarding the prince during the night. Gaston has wandered off somewhere. Faldi and Maria break their fast inside. Come, there is good fare to be had and beer besides.'

Hawker nodded. 'Soon, Giles. First, come walk with me. I need to stretch my legs and shake the sleep from my head.'

–

Ellingham knew Hawker had something weighing upon his mind even as they left the hostelry. The old knight seemed almost distracted by whatever it was. They walked out onto the road and followed a smaller rutted one up a slope past two ramshackle cottages. Just beyond, they came to a small church, stone-built and cruciform, topped with a dome of wood shingle and a simple cross at its pinacle.

'It is the first day of Christmas,' said Hawker, half to himself.

'You wish to pray?' replied Ellingham, only half-serious, gesturing towards the church.

'It's no doubt of the Byzantine communion. I doubt their priest would be happy with us darkening his threshold. Besides, it's not yet Christmas in their confession. That is weeks away.' Hawker stopped and stared for a bit at the door. 'I don't think he would begrudge us the use of his steps though. Come, I wish to speak with you.'

They sat next to each other, Hawker leaning his elbows upon his knees. The swirling clouds and winds of the previous day and evening had given way to bright sunshine. From where they sat, looking eastwards, they could see the still-verdant lower slopes of the hills and scattered specks that were grazing sheep. Higher up, the forest reigned, rising steeply until it joined the snow-capped peaks of the Făgăraş mountains, pale schist and limestone glinting in the light. Despite December's frosty mantle, it was growing warmer by the blessings of the bright sun. Hawker inhaled deeply.

'Puts me in a mind of our journey through the Alpine passes,' said Ellingham, reflectively.

'Less mud, though,' replied Hawker, smiling. 'And no Flemish merchants this time.'

Ellingham smiled, too. Then he remembered the savagery of Dieudonné after the company had been ambushed by brigands. The killing of those who had yielded to them. He could still see the starving Bavarian soldier pleading for his life before the Burgundian had hacked him down. Ellingham's smile faded quickly.

'Aye, memories I could happily trade for others.'

'There is something I must tell you, Giles.'

Ellingham looked into the heavily lined face of his mentor. Hawker's great beak of a nose, a slight bump on the bridge where it had been broken years before, stood proud in profile. His eyes were looking into the middle distance, and Ellingham knew the man was trying to find the words with which to convey some heavy thought.

'I am listening, Sir John. From your look it seems grave news.'

Hawker leaned back and looked at him. 'Ah, no, Giles! Indeed, I'm hoping you will see it as good news, hopeful even. Something worthy of hearing on Christmas Day. It's a bit of something I had meant to share long ago but for which the time and moment never seemed right.'

Ellingham threw him a quizzical look. 'So why now, my lord?'

Hawker pursed his lips a moment. 'Because I forgot I was mortal. Assumed I would go on from contratto to contratto, battle to battle, until the last trumpet of the angels was blown. It was a foolish, prideful conceit, my lad.'

'You're a veritable ox, Sir John. You will endure.' Ellingham had come to believe this as he could not conceive of any service without the knight by his side, his only link to a world now denied to them all.

'Maybe so, maybe so. But I will not challenge God again on that score. I've been struck down now twice in the space of a few months. The next time I might not get up again. That is why I must unburden myself to you... now... in this place.'

Ellingham nodded and swallowed. 'I am listening.'

'You have a brother. A half-brother to be exact. And as far as I know he yet lives.'

Ellingham's lips parted but nothing came out. He looked out towards the mountains, his eyes squinting in the bright sun. 'But… the young prince Edward died over a year ago…' Then, an instant later, he understood. 'Another bastard then.'

'He is John. Called John of Gloucester. He was recognised by your father and a year ago appointed captain of the Calais garrison. If he's there still, I do not know. He won't keep his station under Henry Tudor. He may have already fled. It was a hotbed of traitors even a year ago.'

Ellingham dropped his head and stared at his boots. Was his heart lightened to hear that he was not alone in blood, that he had a sibling? It was a curious feeling. He was no longer alone in a way. He had a brother now, one who was alive, but the chances of ever meeting him were slim. And would this John of Gloucester even care? Other thoughts flew into his head. Why had his father denied *him* but recognised his other bastard? It was a question that would never find an answer.

'There is more,' said Hawker, 'though by your silence I am not sure you might wish to hear.'

'Tell me.'

'You have a half-sister too. You never mentioned her when I revealed your parentage so I took it you were unaware of her existence too. Her name is Katherine. Mayhaps a year younger than you.'

Ellingham felt his family was growing each time the old knight opened his mouth. He couldn't help frowning with the surprise of it all. 'My father was ploughing many fields it seems.'

'I believe all of them in his bachelorhood. Including you.'

'Tell me of my sister, then.'

'She was wed to the Earl of Huntingdon, William Herbert. One year ago.'

Ellingham turned to Hawker again. 'And is she acknowledged too? As a royal bastard?'

Hawker nodded. 'She is. She was Katherine Plantagenet the day she was wed.'

'Sweet Christ... I have family... *blood*. I'm not sure how to take this gift of yours, Sir John. It is one bittersweet.'

Hawker put an arm around his shoulders and squeezed. 'I believe, had he lived, your father would have acknowledged you as well. But we can none of us choose our fates. I thought it better that you know your kin survive – even in these dire times.'

'It will take some time for me to measure what lies in my heart. Time to think upon it.'

'If God grants us a return to England, I will ride with you, if that is what you wish, to seek them out.'

He could not think that far ahead. Not with the uncertainty that swirled about the company. And not with the memory of Maria Hunyadi's passion still fresh in his mind. It was truly in God's hands. He and Hawker had more immediate challenges.

'I can return the favour, Sir John. With intelligence of my own.'

Hawker's sunken eyes grew a bit larger.

'Maria has revealed that Prince Vlad may have secreted a large treasure. One that lies back in the Saxon lands. And only he and Faldi know where it lies. She wants to find it to buy support for her father with the nobility. And Faldi isn't telling where, to leverage her and seek a share of it.'

Hawker swore under this breath. 'You have told no one else?'

Ellingham shook his head. 'And she begged me not to challenge Faldi.'

'Aye. His loyalty to her cause was always a mystery to me. As was his dismissing his lance of men when we could have used more swords. That made little sense. Now it makes more. He'll dismiss us too, given half the chance. A bigger share for him.'

'What shall we do?'

Hawker brushed his palms on his thighs and arose, knees cracking loudly. 'Hold firm. Get the prince back to the Sieben-bürgen towns and pray he regains what is left of his wits. I don't like remaining in Wallachia any longer than we must. The current prince of this land will not stand for his brother running loose. Mad or not.'

'Let us grant the company this day at least,' said Ellingham, rising. 'To gather strength if not to celebrate.'

Hawker looked at him. 'It carries risk. We're naked here.'

'We stayed off the road. Took the higher ground most of the way here. How will they know we came this way?

'But we are squarely on the road now, in this place.' He was quiet a moment. 'You truly think that Wallachian innkeeper will throw a feast for us?'

'He now lives in fear of Vlad Ţepeş – Dracula – and his sharp-tongued daughter. I would wager he'll lay on a banquet worthy of a king if he is but asked!'

Hawker rubbed his lip with a forefinger and thumb. 'I fear…' he growled, 'I fear that you won't find the patronage that was promised to you. Not here. And a share of Vlad's mystical treasure will not make up for that even if it is to be found. It will be enough just to leave this land with our heads still on our shoulders. I wonder which it is that spurs the lady on – her father's throne or his gold.'

Ellingham could not look Hawker in the eye. But he knew Maria's faith in her father was not feigned. The promise of patronage or not, he seemed to already be held in a trap, a prisoner of his heart. He could not now even imagine abandoning Maria, no matter what lay ahead.

27

Ellingham's lips formed the trace of a smile. For Bartolo Faldi now shone like the sun itself. He had paid some silver coins to a peasant to scrub and burnish his rusty Milanese harness and now he strutted about the yard of the inn like a rooster, hand on sword pommel. The polished steel glinted as he pranced and a song was on his lips in between gulps from his cup of Moldovan wine. Faldi urged on the others of the company to take up his song but with no success as probably only he knew the words or the tune.

Ellingham sat at the long trestle table that the servants had set up in the yard. The innkeeper said that he had not known of a day this warm in December for more than ten years. The snow of the previous day had melted away completely, revealing still-green grass. The birdsong that Maria had wished for had now come to pass. Robins and starlings argued ferociously over the breadcrumbs that Jack Perry tossed out to them from where he sat. The innkeeper had done his guests good service. Knowing they were of the Latin Church he had indeed thrown a modest feast for them just after the hour of sext, the sun at its low zenith of the short day. Roast pig, a few broiled chickens, onion and offal pie, boiled cabbage, dark breads and hard sheep's cheese all spread across the length of a rickety tabletop set upon barrels.

Ellingham felt the heat of Maria's thigh against his own so close together did they sit. She was again dressed as a man: hose, boots, a curious sort of short houppelande gown and black leather breastplate. He watched her as she ate, daintily placing the food in her mouth, sometimes turning to bestow a sly smile upon him. His chest fluttered when she looked at him. Hoping his affection wasn't too obvious to Hawker and Gaston, he hurriedly swigged some more wine. Indeed, all of the company had been imbibing deeply while they gorged themselves on the best fare they'd eaten in days.

Hawker sat at one end, more contemplative than the others.

'Is he recovered of his wound?' whispered Maria.

'I do not know,' replied Ellingham. 'I pray it is so. And how does your father fare? He stays in his chamber.'

'He will only speak with Tokár. Demands that he stay with him. He still doesn't trust you, or even me. I'm hoping that with each day he will recover his sense, but I do not hold my breath. I can think of nothing else to do but to take him to where he was born. He will still be safer there than here.'

Ellingham set down his cup. 'And we will see that you get him there.' He looked over to Faldi who was capering about with a serving girl. 'And you still trust *him* to hold to his bargain?'

She looked at her trencher and picked at a chicken wing. 'What choice do I have? And I must ask you: does Sir John still believe in my cause? He has said little to me this day.'

'He worries. That the prince is mad. That we're still pursued. Maybe even that your dream for your father to regain his throne will never be realised. Nor the treasure you speak of.'

He felt her hand reach down and touch his leg. 'But you do not doubt me... do you?'

Ellingham leaned over and spoke into her ear, his lips brushing her raven hair. 'I am yours, my lady. And I'll fight to keep you safe.'

'And the others?'

'They will stand by me. As will Sir John. We're all going back to the Saxon lands. Together.'

He felt her hand squeeze tight, the only signal she could give in present company. She nodded a little. 'I will reach my father. Give me time.'

The innkeeper scurried about, bringing more wine and smiling. He rattled on in the Wallachian tongue, encouraging

Ellingham to drink as soon as he had refilled his cup. 'That man still has faith in the prince,' said Ellingham.

'Some remember. Others will have been told of those days. The embers still burn just waiting for a fresh wind to stir them into flame again. The son of the Dragon will return to his people.'

He wanted to believe it. Wanted to believe that Prince Vlad would rule again and bestow favour and wealth upon him such that he might return west with a force of his own to offer to the Yorkist cause. But what he had seen thus far was a broken man who had no desire to fight the Ottomans or anyone else. There only remained a husk of arrogance and entitlement. Vlad, though he lived, was more a relic than a ruler.

'What runs through your mind, dear Giles?' shouted Gaston Dieudonné from the other end of the table. 'I see you have a more comely dining companion than I do,' he said, patting Jack Perry upon the head like a pet dog. The lad scowled and knocked away Dieudonné's hand. The Burgundian laughed and Jack got up and left, returning to the inn in a fit of anger for the insult.

Hawker had observed it all. 'Careful, my lord Gaston,' he said, his face dark. 'You might wake to find a dagger at your throat. One held by that boy.'

Dieudonné shrugged. 'It was only a jest, a jest among comrades. The lad is too soft-skinned.'

Jacob de Grood, who had been silent for some time, refilled Dieudonné's cup, slammed down the near-empty clay jug, and shoved the sloshing vessel towards him. 'Drink up, my lord. And shut up.'

The Burgundian's mirth suddenly froze, replaced by a sullen glare.

Ellingham's eye wandered to the stable lean-to, where the large bell tent still stood pegged and where the six surviving gypsies gathered around their burning brazier. The two Rascians sat on benches nearby. They devoured their food greedily in between their muttered conversation, but seemed to drink little. They were, he thought, neither in the company nor outside of it, yet always obedient when asked to do something. The one called Pedja seemed respectful enough, bowing and smiling whenever she addressed him. The half-Turk, fathered by some Ottoman invader, fought like a lion with his mace of iron. Indeed, they had both fought well and fought hard upon the road and at the fortress, but even now, days after their paths had first crossed, he still did not know why they stayed. They were far from their homeland, had claimed to have left one war, but then had decided to join theirs. Perhaps that was the way of these eastern mercenaries, no cause too insignificant if there was coin to be gained.

Once, he had thought their company driven by a noble cause. The company of the White Rose. That sentiment he felt to be waning, replaced by his own madness: his increasing passion for a woman, maybe at the cost of their lives. And part of him, a large part, did not care anymore.

Faldi struck up another song, his deep voice ringing around them. Maria even laughed a little at the comedy of it. Ellingham was now feeling warm and a little flushed from the wine. His worry was slowly fading into some half-imagined past, even if Hawker's still seemed to cling heavy on the old knight's shoulders.

Ellingham leaned in close again to Maria. 'Will the prince not come down and raise up a cup of wine with us to celebrate the first day of Christmas?'

She half-turned towards him, her voice equally low. 'I begged him to come down to break bread with me. I told him what day it is. Reminded him that he is of the Latin confession. He said he had no wish for his Orthodox subjects to see him cavort with Franks such as you.'

Ellingham snickered. 'Franks?'

'An archaic epithet. It's what the Turks call the men of the western kingdoms.' She shook her head. 'There is a black cloud that surrounds him. One I cannot dispel despite my entreaties. I pray that the Saxon lands will revive his spirit. But that may not be possible. Not once King Matthias learns of him.'

'What do you mean?' said Ellingham, his head and reason beginning to cloud a little.

'I suspect that the king of Hungary prefers my father dead to the world. Worse, my father's supposed widow, Ilona Szilágy, cousin to the king, has married *again*. To one of the great nobles of the kingdom. She is unknowingly guilty of bigamy and Vlad Dracula's resurrection would be more than an embarrassment to the king. You see, I believe the king has plans for her son – my half-brother – who is young and malleable.'

Ellingham shook his head slowly. 'Your family's line is a puzzlement that I confess I may never understand.'

'My uncle uses relatives like pieces on a chessboard, Giles. The son of Dracula may, someday, be of use to him. A future puppet for the throne of Wallachia. A thorn under the seat of the sultan perhaps. My father would never let himself be used so.'

'Ah, that is why Sir John said that King Matthias let your father be captured all those years ago.'

'He held off his relieving army, waiting. Waiting until my father's force had overextended against the Turks and their minions, waiting until it was too late to save him. Matthias abandoned my father to his fate.' Maria's green eyes glowed with anger as she spoke.

Ellingham wrapped his fingers around his cup, now understanding how alone they really were. 'If Prince Vlad is to regain the throne he can expect no help from the crown of Hungary. He must do it on his own.'

Maria gripped his wrist. 'There are *others* who might help. The king of the Poles for one. But first, we must win over the Saxon towns. To do that we need to find the hoard of my father.'

Ellingham looked about them. Eight men-at-arms a long way from home and seven gypsies. It was hardly the beginnings of an army. And now their quest had turned into a hunt for some buried fortune. Even half in his cups, Ellingham saw what a thin, cruel thread they hung by. He raised his vessel to his lips again and drank deeply of the sweet, heavy wine.

–

The wine made Hawker morose. Far from enlivening him in spirit, he felt as tired as when he had arisen, cold and shivering. There was now no doubt in his mind that young Ellingham was besotted by more than the wine. Maria Hunyadi *cum* Drăculeşti, the Impaler's daughter, had well and truly ensnared him. He knew that all his words of admonishment would do no good for they would not be heeded. As for Maria, he believed her faith in her father was heartfelt – he had witnessed her tears – but it was clouded in judgement. Their chances were slim at best. Part of him felt that they should cut and run rather than play out the quest to its bitter end. But that would not happen. His own honour was at stake, and he had sworn to protect the son of his king come what may.

The sun had sunk lower now and though it was still warm he pulled up his cloak and let his shoulders round into it. The chill of winter seemed to single him out. Faldi was standing again and singing. Hawker gritted his teeth and watched the Milanese clown. The man had his own scheme all along and all his talk of comradeship of old was nothing but empty words to placate an old companion in battle harness.

'*Hawker! Come sta?* Your face is as long as an overworked mule! Drink up!'

Hawker grimaced and Faldi laughed. 'Sir John, we have freed the good lady's father, fought off a company of the Monk's militia, and now we are heading north. It is Christmas today, my friend!'

Hawker thought at first it was a starling, diving to raid the trestle. There was a swish of feathers, a streak of black. And then, Bartolo Faldi tipped forward, head and chest falling flat and sending platters and vessels flying. His head lay on the planks, his body resting on his knees, the trestle shoved forward. Hawker got up slowly, his eyes fixed upon the shaft and fletchings of a crossbow bolt protruding from the back of Faldi's head.

Maria cried out in shock and the others were all on their feet in the same instant. Hawker froze, waiting for the next bolt to strike one of them. But no further death followed. A movement to the left and Hawker saw five men-at-arms walk into the courtyard supported by two crossbowmen at the ready. From the opposite side entered another half a dozen and a further crossbowman. Ellingham looked at Hawker, eyes wide, asking if they should draw their arms. Hawker looked at him calmly and just shook his head. They had been taken.

The innkeeper had run for his life, dashing out towards the village, his two servants hot on his heels. Hawker could hear shouting out in the road afterwards.

The two crossbowmen aimed their weapons at the gypsies and the Rascians, while the fully armoured men-at-arms followed, swords drawn. The company stood frozen in place, all eyes turned to the newcomers. From the opposite side, the other soldiers walked calmly forward, the archer gently swinging his spanned bow from Hawker to Ellingham and the others. Behind them came a lone soldier, sword drawn, his exquisitely fluted Bavarian harness shining as brightly as Faldi's. He wore a heavy-looking black cloak trimmed with silver-grey fur which had been thrown back over his shoulder to free up his right arm. Upon his head was a sleek sallet helm, brightly polished, its raised visor giving the man an illusion of even greater height.

Hawker caught Jacob's eye. The Fleming had already moved his hand to his hilt, his body tensing. Hawker shook his head and held out his palm flat, low above the trestle. Jacob squinted and swallowed, his hand falling to his side. At his side, Dieudonné focused on the new arrival, his face devoid of any emotion.

The lone soldier was tall, taller than Ellingham, middle-aged and gaunt of face. His pale eyes, washed of colour, scanned each of the company and then focused on the body of Bartolo Faldi. He gestured with his sword, gently tapping the dead man's backplate.

He spoke something in the German tongue and smiled. When no one responded he switched to French.

'The captain always wears the best harness. Did I guess correctly?'

Maria leaned forward, gripping the table with both hands. She was flushed, eyes flashing at the stranger who had just taken them all without a fight. 'Who are you?' she demanded, her voice slightly strained. 'You are no Wallachians.'

The man didn't immediately give her an answer. He addressed the rest of the company, still as statues, except for their eyes, all searching each other's for what to do next. 'Unbuckle your sword belts! All of you!'

Ellingham looked to Hawker. Hawker felt his jaw tense so tight, it might not open again. He nodded to Ellingham slowly. He then looked at Jacob and Dieudonné at the table's far end. 'Do as he commands.'

Slowly, reluctantly, the company disarmed themselves, scabbards and belts clanking to the ground. Behind him, Hawker heard the sound of boots crashing up the outside staircase to the bedchambers.

The stranger took a few steps back, his naked arming sword cradled in the crook of his arm. 'I am Captain Bobik. I am currently in the service of—' He stopped himself, then smiled at them. 'My employers are of no concern to you. But you have something they are very much interested in.'

'You are a dog sent from Hermannstadt, aren't you?' spat Maria.

'And you,' said Bobik, inclining his head in a court bow, 'are the lady who claims blood to the Hunyadis… and to another family. It is the latter which is of interest to me.' His attention focused on Ellingham next. 'Another supposed noble here, haven't we? An Englishman who says he is a prince.' He cast an eye towards Hawker and then gestured towards Jacob. 'And his men-at-arms. But not very many it seems. It is all very strange to me.'

Bobik's lifted blade pointed to where the gypsies sat glaring, under guard. 'And why in God's name are you making company with these filthy Romani? All very strange.'

He walked slowly around the table, behind Hawker and continuing on until he stood behind Maria. 'Such lovely hair of jet. Perhaps a touch of Romani blood in you, my lady?'

Hawker saw Ellingham inhale deeply, body tensing.

'Giles,' growled Hawker in English, 'hold. Bide your time.'

Bobik took a half step back. 'Ah, an *English* man-at-arms... and one long in the tooth. Stranger still.' He continued walking, now towards the opposite end where Jacob and Dieudonné stood. 'I am interested in another prince. Not the bastard one I see before me.'

Maria laughed. 'You're a brigand and murderer. Fit for the king's gallows which you will no doubt see soon enough. And you cannot disguise your Bohemian peasant's accent even if you speak the German and French tongues. If you truly know who I am, you and your rabble would leave now.'

Bobik made a *tut-tutting* noise. 'Boldness becomes you, my lady. But it is an empty threat. I *may* let some of you live. The blond princeling might fetch a good ransom. You may have some value yourself. Possibly.'

Hawker had no recollection of ever meeting the mercenary before, despite his own service in the Habsburg lands. The man looked neither old nor young, just cadaverous – a creature who knew war and knew it to his advantage. The finely worked and fluted armour Bobik wore attested to some success. But if cruelty wore a face then it was his: a bleached parchment palour, high cheekbones and a long, pointed chin. Eyes the colour of sea fog which harboured neither warmth nor compassion and probably had never done so.

Hawker prayed that Jack had made good an escape, grateful though that he had not had to witness the ignobility that had just befallen the rest of them. Prayed that the lad would be wise enough to run back north. But in his heart, he doubted Jack would have the knowledge and sense to get very far. He had failed him. He had failed all of them.

'Now,' said Bobik, 'you may all get down upon your knees. The lady may remain where she is though. I enjoy seeing her in her armour. She is like the celebrated Maid of Orleans from the time of our grandsires, is she not Englishman?'

Ellingham spat on the table and a soldier yanked him backwards and forced him down upon his knees.

'The rest of you! Down!'

Slowly, Jacob and Dieudonné backed away and then sank down, one knee at a time. Hawker watched. Jacob's face twisted into a mask of anguish and frustration but the Burgundian looked like a cat waiting to pounce, a coiled intensity shining from his eyes. Hawker felt a large hand clap his shoulder and push him down. He had felt such humiliation before when he was a young soldier, captured, waiting to be slaughtered. He survived that and he vowed now that he would survive this insult too. The stones of the yard ground into his knees when he shifted his weight and he gritted his teeth, all the time watching the mercenary captain.

One of Bobik's men called down from the railings above. Hawker knew enough of the German tongue to understand what was shouted: *We've found him!*

The soldier held his prisoner roughly, lifting him under an armpit and pushing him in front, marching him down the staircase. Hawker recognised the colour and hem of the tunic, the boots, even if a heavy cloak and hood obscured the face. Maria made to move but Ellingham reached up and grabbed her wrist.

The soldier hauled the prisoner over to Bobik, the mercenary towering over the cloaked figure. He knocked back the hood and tilted his head. 'So... the last ruler of this land, the once-feared Impaler. Feared no more.' He nodded to the soldier and gave an order. The prisoner's hands were tied behind his back.

Tokár looked up into his captor's face and blew out a weighty gobbet of phlegm, spattering Bobik's gorget. Bobik grabbed a fistful of Tokár's grey curls in his left hand and jerked the gypsy's head backwards, exposing Tokár's throat while his raised sword pulled back level to his ear.

'Have a care, my prince,' he said, his thin lips creasing into a smile. 'We might find a stake nearby to shove up your arse. God knows, you deserve no less.' He released Tokár's head with a disdainful wave. 'Sadly, I cannot do that. It is for my paymasters to

294

decide who will eventually receive the pleasure of your company. Something about trussing you up as a gift to the sultan.'

Hawker watched Maria. Was she thinking how to play along, to buy time for her father's escape? Tokár continued to glare at Bobik, probably not having understood a word of what was said. He didn't have to. He only had to do this one service for his master, one task to play out even if it meant his own death.

Across the yard, the six gypsies and the two Rascians still sat, tense and restless. One tried to rise and was knocked back down with a sword pommel to the back. Two more of Bobik's men waded in to cow them, punching with their steel gauntlets. Hawker swivelled his head, trying to count the number of the enemy. There looked to be about a dozen. He was for the moment unbound, as were the others. His sword lay just in reach.

But a glance told him the crossbowmen were still poised and ready, on their guards. At this range, he would be dead as soon as he rose up with his blade. Three crossbowmen shooting their bolts at close range meant three of the company dead or wounded. He would have to wait until the conditions changed. If the gypsy's ruse was discovered though, the Bohemian's rage might tip him into more killing. Faldi's sightless eyes stared at him down the length of the feasting board, the Italian's head lying against the table edge, holding his body up.

'Now, my lady, we know from your brave little Greek servant that there is more to tell. Much more. He did tell me – finally – but sadly the lad was in no condition afterwards to join us on the journey.'

Maria's face fell, her thick eyebrows bunching up. Her hands gripped the table but she said nothing in return.

Bobik manhandled Tokár by the scruff of his neck, making him face Maria from across the table. He lowered his face into the gypsy's ear. 'Now, you are to tell me where you have left your gold, my lord. I would rather take my share of it *before* the guild master sees the lovely, decorated casket in which I am sure it safely slumbers.'

Bobik snarled something in German at one of his men-at-arms. The man grinned, sheathed his sword, and walked to where Maria stood.

'Your daughter is a beautiful woman,' said Bobik to the gypsy, wrapping an arm around his neck. 'A maiden? Well, on that score I truly have no idea. Now, my lord, you will tell me where the treasure lies or you will witness her deflowering. Perhaps though, not for the first time, no?'

The man-at-arms pushed Maria, splaying her flat on the table and lifting the skirts of her heavy gown. She fought back, scratching at her attacker, and Ellingham twisted around and leapt up at the man but was pommelled to the ground by another. Hawker started forward, his stomach churning at his own impotence – and his carelessness. A hand from behind pushed him back down, the plates of the soldier's gauntlet biting into his neck.

Bobik gave Tokár a good-natured grasp of the shoulders. The gypsy tried shaking him off to no avail, his eyes glistening with tears. 'And, my lord, after my banner man has taken his pleasure... if you *still* haven't named the place... then you shall watch me slit her throat.'

28

Jack Perry was proud of his harness. It was not as shiny, as fine or as expensive as Bartolo Faldi's, but it was his. His first proper armour. And he had equipped himself early that morning at the inn, dressing, fastening straps, buckling on breastplate and then sword belt. Donning it all while the others had not. Now he was in hiding, still wearing it while his knight and his comrades suffered capture and death. It now sat heavy on his shoulders. He was scared, and he was ashamed.

His anger at being teased by Dieudonné had made him storm off in pique and embarrassment. But it had brought him to this. By the time he heard the commotion in the yard and looked out to see the matter, it was too late. Sir John and the others were already disarmed and he could clearly see the body of the dead Italian sprawled on the table, his bright armour having done nothing to save his life. Even in his fear, Jack's mind raced, ideas tumbling about. Could he dash out and attack? Could he run for help? From whom? These soldiers would no doubt search the inn. He had to get out before they did so.

He picked up the crossbow Jacob had readily gifted him earlier, grasped the pouch with his last remaining quarrels, and went to the window of the bedchamber. There was a sloping tiled roof, small, but something that would let him get a bit closer to the ground before he had to jump. Somehow, he managed to squeeze through the window frame, rattling like an ostler's wagon of ironware, and then he slid down to the end of the roof. The final leap was about ten feet to the ground. He hit it, rolling to the leaf-strewn ground, and then regained his feet. He had to get away from the inn, maybe into one of the village houses.

He ran. Frightened that his jangling armour would alert the soldiers. He kept looking back over his shoulder. No one pursued. Pushing through brush and saplings around the back of the inn, he worked his way wide until he came to a cluster of small cottages, whitewashed and with thatched conical roofs. A few villagers had already gathered there, jabbering excitedly and carrying hand scythes and bill hooks. As soon as they saw Jack they raised their implements and started for him.

Jack raised his hands, shouting he was a friend. His strange tongue made them pause and then the innkeeper came out of one of the houses, red-faced and sweating. He must have recognised Jack because he intercepted the others and stopped them. Jack approached, his heart pumping wildly. He tried to tell the innkeeper they had been surprised but it was useless. Desperate hand gestures on all sides could not convey reason or intent. Jack felt tears begin to roll down his cheeks. He had no idea how to escape on his own. He spoke no foreign tongues, knew no allies, and didn't even know in which direction to flee. He wiped a gloved hand angrily across his face, drying it. The innkeeper spoke to him in a low tone, called to the others, and then pushed Jack inside one of the houses.

The Wallachian began peppering him with questions but all Jack could do was shake his head. He was still gripping the crossbow and he now looked at it. It was a weapon like the one he had first taken a man's life with all those months ago back in England. He had pulled the lever out of fear that John Hawker would be killed. So, he had killed first. He opened the pouch containing the crossbow bolts. Three remained. Then he remembered what he had accomplished the day before, outside the fortress.

Dieudonné had once called him their little assassin. He had to ask Sir John what that even meant. Now he knew. He lifted the crossbow in his hands, hefted it, and looked at the innkeeper. The innkeeper stared back at him hard for a moment. The Wallachian then picked up a threshing flail that lay propped up near the doorway. He nodded at Jack. They went outside and the innkeeper started speaking intently to the other men; more were joining while two kept an eye out for the invaders. The only words Jack heard that he thought he recognised were 'Vladislav' and 'Dracula'. At one point the innkeeper pointed to Jack and his bow. There was arguing, it grew louder and one of the others angrily hushed them. More men came, a few of the village women too.

Jack, still afraid, was also becoming angry. He could see it in the faces of the peasants who surrounded him. Men whose village had been violated, their hospitality trampled. His anger was beginning to overtake the fear and hesitancy which had washed over him earlier. He realised, too, that he had stopped shaking. He knew he had to steel himself to approach the courtyard again to see what was happening. To find the enemy's captain. And then kill him.

Jack looked at the innkeeper, pointed to himself, and then pointed in the direction of the inn. He raised the crossbow in both hands. The innkeeper nodded and then looked to the others. Agreement spread amongst them, a rippling wave of determination.

Jack placed the stirrup of the crossbow to the earth, put his toe in, and hauled on the string bundle with all his might until the bow was spanned. Reaching into his pouch he pulled out a quarrel and placed it into the channel on the stock. And then he began inching towards the inn, slowly and cautiously, house by house.

Peering from around the corner of a woodpile, he found a line of sight to the inn. He could see soldiers spread out, his comrades kneeling on the ground, and one tall soldier – an officer – barking commands and wearing fine plate armour and a dark cloak. The man held the gypsy chieftain in his grasp, shaking him. Jack knew he would get but one shot. He saw that the enemy had bowmen arrayed and at least a dozen men-at-arms. But all except the captain were facing *away* from him. God had granted him that at least. He remembered being back in Stamford, in his days of thieving across the streets of the town. He was as a ferret in a warren, nimble and fast. Sometimes stealthy as a rat, fading into stillness flat against a wall such that no one would notice him. He'd never been caught.

He started forward again, bow stock tight against his shoulder. A crossbowman was in front of him, his weapon trained on Sir Giles and Sir John. He saw Maria in the grip of another soldier, being pushed forward, his hand gripping her long black hair. Jack moved forward, slowly, closing the distance with the archer. He willed himself to fit in, to blend.

I am one of you. You see me, but you don't.

He saw the archer's helmet turn a little at his approach, almost alongside. But the archer quickly refocused on his targets, assuming Jack was one of his own. Jack was just half a pace behind the man, flanking him to the side. He raised the crossbow and took aim at the tall soldier. He was the one giving orders. He had to be the captain. Jack pressed the stock again into his shoulder, sighting down the tip of the quarrel.

Maybe twenty-five yards. Plate armour… only chance… head shot.

Jack squeezed the lever and the bolt flew with a whisking snap.

–

Hawker whispered the quickest *Pater Noster* he had ever managed. Maria was fighting with all her might but failing to stop her attacker from raping her. Hawker reckoned he might end up with a crossbow bolt in him, but if he didn't, then he might just have time to grab his sword, and make a lunge at the soldier. He tensed, ready to spring. At the same moment, Ellingham was beat down again for the second time, pounded by one of Bobik's men.

And then, Bobik's sword dropped from his hand. The Bohemian staggered away from Tokár, clutching at his throat. There was an instant of disbelief from them all, and then Hawker had rolled to retrieve his blade. He heard the swish of a quarrel flying past him and saw that Ellingham had now tackled Maria's attacker, grappling him to the ground. Hawker rushed the nearest of Bobik's men, beat away the soldier's blade and followed up with a two-handed downward stroke that bit into the man's coat-of-plates where neck joined shoulder, dropping him.

It was all a whirl of motion. Hawker caught sight of Jack wrestling with a crossbowman, and behind him, rushing into the fray, some two dozen armed peasants bellowing for vengeance. The remaining crossbowmen fired into the surging peasants but as soon as they had done so, Jacob and Dieudonné were upon them, beating them down and then stabbing them. A screaming Wallachian farmer staggered across Hawker's path, a crossbow bolt protruding from his thigh. Hawker made for his next opponent, a mercenary in rusty harness. He engaged, feinted a chopping blow, and then thrust to the face, killing the man.

A few of the peasants had fallen to bow and blade, but their numbers told. They mobbed the last of Bobik's squadron, bringing the Bohemian's mercenaries down like a pack of hunting dogs. Hawker saw a huge Wallachian with a great threshing flail swing it to knock a soldier off his feet and then swing it up and down again to smash into the man's bare head, exploding it to pulp.

It was over in moments. Every single one of Bobik's band was dead. No quarter was offered nor given. Jacob and Dieudonné floated about the courtyard, angels of death, despatching all of the thrashing, moaning mercenaries who clung to life. Captain Milos Bobik, gasping and choking from his mortal throat wound, they left to suffer.

Hawker, bloodied sword in hand, watched as Maria, her shoulders hunching in shame, pushed away Ellingham's embrace and walked to where Bobik lay in the yard. Her gaze lingered on Faldi's body as she passed where he lay crumpled. Tokár stood over Bobik, relishing the mercenary's agonies. Maria knelt down, one knee on the Bohemian's breastplate. He had been struck in the windpipe, missing the artery but still filling his ruined throat with blood, slowly choking the life from him. He tried to speak despite his voice box having a quarrel protruding from it. Maria put a finger to her lips and leaned over him.

'Did you think Vladislav Dracula – or his daughter – would be taken so easily? I will make sure you return to your paymasters in Hermannstadt. Or at least part of you will.'

She reached up and took the rondel dagger which Ellingham was proffering her. Twisting it into a blade-down grip, her thumb on the pommel, she poised it over one of Bobik's pale eyes. The man tried to raise an arm to fend her off but Ellingham placed his boot upon it, pinning it to the ground. Slowly, Maria pierced the eye, popping it. A muffled gurgle and a half-formed scream erupted from her antagonist, accompanied by a spray of blood from his shattered throat. She pushed the blade in further until she met resistance and then shoved it with force, piercing his brain.

Plucking out the dagger she stood up again, leaning on Ellingham a moment to steady herself. She turned to Tokár. 'Take his head.'

Hawker approached the body of Bartolo Faldi, still lying sprawled, face-forward against the trestle table. He placed a hand on the man's pauldron and let it rest a moment, angry with himself that the preening coxcomb Milanese had to die because he stood out from the rest of them – and because of Hawker's own incompetence about setting the watch.

'Giles, help me move him.'

They hauled him up and laid him out near the door to the inn. Ellingham fetched a discarded cloak and covered the mercenary.

'I am sorry, Sir John. You were right that we should have moved on.'

'Right?' Hawker growled. 'If I was right, why didn't I do as I said? This day is cursed now.'

They became aware of Maria standing behind them. She was staring at the body, her face leaden. But she said nothing.

'Sir John!' Jack Perry stumbled towards them, slightly wobbly, the crossbow dangling at his side. Hawker embraced him in a bear hug. He gripped the lad's head, looked into his flushed face and spoke softly. 'You found your mark, my boy. You found it. God be praised.'

Jack returned a weary smile, wiping sweat from his eyes. 'You taught me, Sir John. I swore to you I would make you proud.'

Hawker hugged him again and nodded. 'I am. As if you were mine own blood.'

'My lord Dieudonné told me it is always best to take the head from the snake. So, that is what I did. Did I do right?'

Hawker stepped away, grasping him by both shoulders. 'That you did. And for the second time in as many days.'

'So, it was your arrow that saved my virtue.' Maria stepped forward and cradled Jack's chin with both hands. 'I owe you much, young one. And you paid that bastard in kind for Ser Bartolo.'

Jack looked quizzically at Hawker, not comprehending all her French. Hawker smiled again. 'She says you did well. Very well. And she gives you her thanks.'

Ellingham spoke up. 'We all owe you, Jack Perry. I don't know how you managed to get so close but you saved our hides.'

A few of the villagers approached, led by the innkeeper. Still carrying their bloodied farming tools or swords they had taken, the innkeeper stepped forward and bowed to Maria. He spoke reverently to her and then stepped back again.

'He says they would all gladly offer their lives to save the warlord from his enemies,' said Maria, smiling. She called over to Tokár who immediately ran for the stairs to the inn. She turned to Hawker. 'And it was Tokár's quick thinking which has saved my father's life. He must have left my father hiding in one of the chambers before taking his place.'

'It was a brave deed,' said Hawker. 'He is a loyal servant.'

Jacob approached, wiping his blade down with a torn piece of cloak. 'Sir John, I can't find the two Rascians. They might have run off.'

Even as the words left his mouth, the gypsy chieftain emerged at the balustrade above them, shouting, his face twisted in distress.

Maria grabbed Ellingham's arm. 'My father! He's gone!'

Part VI

DRACO OUROBOUROS

29

Pedja Jankovic climbed. His light Ottoman chainmail hauberk felt heavier than ever before. He gently prodded his new prisoner in front of him to keep moving. He still only half believed their fortune: surviving this far and now snatching the most infamous enemy the Ottoman Empire of the Sublime Porte had ever known. *Kaziglu Bey*. He poked Vlad in the backside with the tip of his blade.

'Hurry up, there!'

'Are you talking to me?' bellowed a wheezing Orkan Ozdemir from up ahead. 'I don't even know where we're going, Tombik! Now you tell me to hurry up this damned mountain.'

The light was fading faster than Pedja had hoped. The beautiful blue sky had now darkened to bright purple, a scattered orange sunset spread out like roaring flames, lighting up the entire horizon. It was also growing much colder.

'Stop complaining and save your strength for your bandy legs! Look up there! No, to your left! See that white square tower up there? That's where we're going.'

Pedja had spotted the monastery high up on the mountain when they had first arrived at the village. And when the attack by the Saxons on the company happened, he knew in an instant it might be their only and best chance to carry out their plan. They'd had no trouble circling around the unfolding melee and gaining entrance to the back of the inn. They had found the old prince in a large chest in the kitchen and taken him without a fight. The Wallachian had looked daggers at them but he didn't say a word and did as he was ordered. They fled the village unopposed, it seeming that every peasant had joined the fight against the attackers. They herded their captive before them, running across the low pastures and then began climbing a well-trodden path that led upwards to higher ground.

'We could be riding south right now!' complained Orkan, grunting. 'Instead you spook our horses and send them careening off down the road! Without us!'

'For the love of Christ! They would have caught us up within an hour. Either those Saxons or the Franks if they manage to live. We want them to *think* we've fled south, you big fool. We wait it out in the monastery and then we come back down once the others have left the village.'

Orkan let out a laugh of derision. 'And the monks will welcome us, will they?'

'They'll have no choice. Just look at it! It's a small place. Won't be more than a dozen there.'

Orkan shook his head, not even bothering to look back over his shoulder. 'And you didn't get to kill her, did you? Changed your mind?'

Pedja chafed at the dig. His personal sense of honour had sapped his need for blood revenge. She had saved *his* life. The debt was annulled. 'Maybe the Saxons will,' he said, half-heartedly. 'We have bigger concerns.'

'Like staying alive? I'm still having those dreams I told you of, Tombik. The ones where I strangle you in your sleep.'

They kept ascending. The path had ancient steps of stone at points where it grew steeper, making it slightly easier to climb. A raw wind had picked up, blowing across the tumbling cliffs and stands of pine trees, piercing them through cloak and armour. Pedja bent over further in a forlorn effort to shield himself. The monastery seemed just as far away as before. He swore under his breath. He could feel the icy fingers of self-doubt entering him, every bit as penetrating as the biting winds.

Hubris. Arrogance. They will be your undoing, boy!

His father's words of long ago came back to him. Mocking him across the years. They buzzed inside his head now and he found he could not banish them. For in his heart, he knew they were true. Orkan, his only friend, knew it too. The pain stabbed at him. And then, behind him and below, he thought he heard shouts. He stopped, turning.

'Orkan, hold up here. I want to make sure we're not being pursued.'

The Turk turned around, hefting his iron mace. 'So *now* we can stop and have a rest? Maybe we should ask the Impaler here what he would like to do, too?'

'I thought I heard shouting on the trail below. I just want to make sure. Stay here!'

Dracula turned around and looked at Pedja from under his hooded cloak. He could have been a *cigani*, as he was now dressed like one. The large dark eyes and chiselled features, drooping moustache. A thieving killer if given half the chance. But not a prince. Not the great *Kaziglu Bey*.

'We two will have a little rest,' said Orkan, gently laying his mace on Dracula's shoulder. The old prince pulled his cloak around himself and then sat down on a stone step. Pedja thought he caught a glimpse of a smile underneath the hood.

'You do that then,' said Pedja. 'But I'll be back before you can nod off,' he added, pointing a finger at his friend.

Orkan grinned. 'The bey and me, we will get to know each other.'

—

Orkan, arms folded across his chest, stood over the figure before him. Dracula had pulled his long and wide cloak about him, fashioning a tent against the elements. Orkan leaned forward.

'You. Of all the people in this world,' said Orkan in his broken Slavic, 'Allah put me on this mountain with *you*. Did you know – you probably did – that mothers in my village would frighten us with stories about you? You were our djinn, our monster. Something to scare us into being good. Something to make us learn our verses.'

Dracula raised his head, the hood falling back a little. Orkan thought the man looked like any other peasant he had seen across the Balkans. Maybe even a little less hale than most. He found the reality of it almost amusing. The *Kaziglu Bey* looked up at him, and Orkan thought that he too was amused by the same thought. A bogeyman in the tales, but in the flesh a weak and ageing despot who ruled nothing at all anymore.

'The stories of your mothers were true.' Perfect Turkish flew from the Dracula's tongue. 'All of them. I feasted on their fear. I made a forest of your countrymen, impaled on the road north of Bucharest. A thousand of them. Your sultan saw them. He wept. Then he went home. Do you think I am in fear of *you*?'

Orkan sneered. 'You bastard. You'll be sitting not upon a throne but upon a stake of your own before a fortnight has passed. We'll deliver you to Sultan Bayezid. And to your death. Mark me well.'

Dracula shook his head slowly, as if reprimanding a child dullard. 'You have helped me escape those who held me. And I've come with you of my own free will. Did you not think that perhaps this is the outcome I have waited for?'

Orkan's brow furrowed, not quite believing the obstinacy and arrogance combined. He squatted down to eye level with him. 'You old fool,' he said, the disgust dripping, 'I'm not afraid of you. You are no longer the demon of my nightmares.'

Dracula smiled at him, his deeply lined face creasing, dark eyes full of glinting fire. And then he pounced.

–

Pedja found nothing below and realised he had probably heard the screams of foxes. He scrambled back up the path. The flame-red mackerel sky had now turned to a dark pink in the dying light. They would have to redouble their efforts to make the monastery before night fully descended. He hoped they might inveigle their way inside without bloodshed, posing as pilgrims or lost travellers.

But he had come too far now to give up. If it meant the blood of holy men being spilt, then so be it.

He reached the spot where he had left his comrade and his heart leapt into his mouth. There was a crumpled form on the stone stairs. It was Orkan. Dracula was gone.

Pedja cursed and rolled Orkan over. He was still alive. Pedja's hand came away covered in blood. It was from a stab wound to the gut which had pierced Orkan's jerkin. The Bosnian lifted the Turk's head and then saw blood oozing steadily from a neck wound. Orkan's eyelids fluttered as he fought to remain conscious. The wounds were deep. Even in the failing light Pedja could see the stomach wound pulsing with blood, pouring out and soaking Orkan's baggy Ottoman breeches. It was mortal.

The Turk opened his eyes. 'Tombik.' It was barely above a rasp and Orkan's face was contorted in pain. 'Tombik… you stupid dhimmi. I told you… you'd be the death of me.' It was all in Turkish now, Orkan too far gone to speak in his bad Slavic.

Pedja hugged him close and rocked a little.

'I can't strangle you now, Tombik. He was fast as the Devil. Caught me out. Had a knife.'

Pedja swallowed hard. 'Forgive me, my friend. Forgive me.'

Orkan seemed to shrink even as he held him tight. Pedja felt the great bear of a man begin to melt away in his arms.

'Tombik… go. Kill him.' Orkan's eyes fluttered and then shut. After a moment Pedja heard him mumble, 'I'm dreaming.'

Pedja eased his comrade back down on the steps and grasped his blade again. He had to catch Dracula before the Wallachian reached the monastery. He leapt up the steps and then onto the rain-eroded and rutted path, running as fast as he dared. His eyes he kept raised up, looking to spot his quarry, and this cost him a few stumbles over the broken ground. But he saw the Impaler silhouetted against the sky, ascending a hundred yards ahead. The monastery was still at some distance. He knew he could catch him if his lungs held out.

Dracula turned at his approach, pausing to assess his adversary, and then turned off the path heading into broken rock-strewn ground slick with wet and patchy snow. Pedja saw that he wielded Orkan's iron mace. The Bosnian swore and redoubled his pace, breaths coming fast and laboured. He cursed again, wondering how the old Wallachian could manage such a climb. But he closed the distance in a few moments and Dracula turned again, this time to face him down.

They found themselves on a stony escarpment bare of all trees and covered by a few scraggly misshapen gorse bushes. Behind the old prince, the sky was purple with a thin streak of blood red running along the horizon. Pedja could see they were above a gorge, a sheer drop just a few feet from them. He saw Dracula's gaze move past him and upwards. He was assessing the distance to the monastery which was close enough to see in detail. There was lantern light casting a warm glow on the outer walls. And Pedja Jankovic, a *martalos* of the Ottoman Bey of Zvornik, was now barring his way to sanctuary. Dracula moved sideways to a patch of level terrain, the mountain schist crunching under his boots. He opened his arms, cloak falling back, and took up an open stance: iron mace in one hand and a long, single-edged gypsy dagger in the other.

Pedja felt his long quest coming to an end. And it would not end in glory in Târgovişte. It would end not in the sultan's gaily bannered camp, nor his shining turquoise palace. It would not end in reward or riches. But it would end here. He would slay the Impaler and avenge his only friend.

-

Dieudonné was unconvinced by what he heard and by what he saw.

The company had argued while hurriedly donning armour, Hawker and Ellingham trading accusations, the mad Hungarian woman railing at both of them for lack of foresight. For his part, he had never trusted the Rascians. He knew plotters when he saw them, recognising in them what he was in himself. Yes, there *were* horses missing. An old trick. But he could not believe the two would be so foolish as to try and outride the rest of them on an open road with the winter night descending. And with a reluctant prisoner in tow.

Hawker and Ellingham had mounted up along with the woman and her gypsy chief to chase the Rascians down before the remaining light failed. He himself had volunteered to stay at the inn along with de Grood and the boy squire in case the Rascians blundered back again or more Saxons showed up. But he had no intention of preparing some new defence.

He saw the little church on the far side of the village, the path that led upwards from there, and much higher up among the slopes and just below the bare stone and snow-capped peaks, a monastery. Already lamplight shone up there, the brothers preparing for a cosy evening around the hearth, screwing each other or doing whatever else monks did at night – all of them either slackers or fools in the first place.

Dieudonné confessed the need for a shit and instead set out on foot, alone. His cloak fastened tightly and wearing only his breastplate, back and helm, he loped his way past the little church and kept moving up the rutted path. Even in the failing light he could make out boot marks in the mud, greater gouges where feet had slid out from under their owners on the treacherous ground. He moved higher, reaching stone steps set out on the steeper slopes. Pausing to look and listen, his sword rasped from its scabbard. He could practically smell his quarry.

After no more than half an hour, he came across a body slumped on the path. He made sure there was no one else nearby and then pulled back the cloak which covered the man. It was the bastard half-Turk, for whom a belly wound had proven his undoing. Dieudonné's boot toe turned Orkan's head. His throat had been stabbed too. A falling out between the two? The Frenchman hefted his sword as he considered the situation. At any rate, now he only had to worry about the portly one – and the old prince.

He kept climbing, feeling the increasing cold despite his exertions. After a few minutes he heard the clash of steel upon steel. It then became clear in his head: Vlad Dracula had made his move. Dieudonné pushed through the low vegetation and off the path, heading in the direction of the fight. He spotted the two once he rounded an outcrop. They were on a piece of near-level ground, the monastery not much further up above them. He lost sight of them though just as he approached and only a moment later the sounds of steel ceased.

There was one man down in front of Dieudonné, and another standing ten feet further wielding a sword and a dagger. It was the prince of Wallachia. Dieudonné stepped around the body of the fallen Rascian, keeping his blade outstretched. The Turk's mace lay next to the body of Pedja, it appeared that Dracula had fancied the man's sword after he had slain him by clubbing him to death.

'Well met, my lord,' said Dieudonné in French, smiling. He could barely see the prince's face, shadowed by the setting rays. 'It seems that our Rascian friends were trying to take you on a little journey somewhere and you had no wish to join them.'

Dracula raised Pedja's curved blade into a high guard, keeping his dagger hand low. 'Declare your interest, Frenchman,' he replied in his perfect French.

'Burgundian,' said Dieudonné with a flourish of his sword. 'And my interests are yours, my lord. Come back down with me. The Saxon brigands are slain. All of them. Your daughter will be relieved to see you safe.'

'Blood carries no loyalty. I have learned that many times. The woman is no different, even if she is my kin. But I have watched *you* this past day. Observing all. Whom do you trust? I saw your nature from the beginning. You trust only yourself.'

Dieudonné nodded. 'You speak the truth, my lord. And with wisdom. But do not let your distrust spurn opportunity. She means to put you upon the throne you once held. Even if she seeks her own fortune through yours. Come with me!'

'She is like all the others! *This* is all she seeks.' He pulled something from his belt and tossed it at Dieudonné's feet. It was the cross of rubies. 'She seeks whatever else I hold besides. Just as my half-brother has stolen my crown. She seeks what she thinks still lies hidden.'

'My lord, she seeks what will return the throne to you! Crafty she may be, but I believe her. She searches for your fortune to serve you with it!'

Vlad Dracula let out a throaty laugh which echoed along the escarpment. 'Flatterer!'

Dieudonné inched forward and the prince brandished the point of his sword. 'I once commanded armies. Thousands swore their fealty to me. I drove the Turk from these lands not once, but twice.'

'Do so again!'

This time Dracula's laugh was scornful. 'All princes are false! I stood *alone*. Not the Pope, not the Hungarians, not the Poles, not the Venetians, no one came to my aid! Nor will they next time.'

Dieudonné watched the prince's guard drop a little and saw him shake his head. His voice became softer, the anger dissipating on the icy wind.

'I tell you Frenchman… for her mother's sake and soul. I will give her what she seeks. It lies in the White City – in the arms of Saint Michael. She may seek it there. If she's of my blood she will understand.'

Dieudonné sensed the old man's wish to believe was there, behind the bitterness. 'Then we will take you there, my lord! You will raise your banner once again.'

This time there was no laughter from the prince. He moved as if to flank Dieudonné. 'You're a tempting devil, sir. Your words are honeyed but there's nothing behind them. My kingdom did not like my justice. My law. They betrayed me. They would do so again. Now they can kneel to the Ottoman and drink of that bitter cup. As the king of Hungary soon will. I have seen it in my dreams!'

Dieudonné gritted his teeth. If they lost the prince then the road to fortune – his and Giles's – would be at an end. Having travelled and fought across Hungary's sprawling empire, they'd end up empty-handed, bereft of noble patronage and with an embittered woman hanging on the young Plantagenet like a succubus. The Frenchman weighed up whether Prince Vlad would fight, or return with him. If the former, he knew the Wallachian would fight hard and fight well. Dracula had been feigning frailty and madness all along. He was still formidable and had just killed two men far younger than himself. The Frenchman stepped to his right, preventing Dracula from getting past. If he could not convince him to return, then he would have to kill him. Or be killed.

'My prince, Maria already knows where your treasure lies. In Torda. She does not need you to obtain it. It is you she wants. On your rightful throne once again.'

'There is no treasure in Torda.' Dracula smiled wanly, his blade swishing. 'All that I treasure lies in the White City. There's nothing more. And she may have it.'

Dieudonné's mind swirled. Faldi was wrong. Had always been wrong. Dracula had now revealed the truth. *Possibly*. He crouched and laid his sword on the ground, then rose and clasped his hands. 'My prince, *believe* her! Our company – the Englishmen – a royal prince among them, they seek to serve you, too. You do not realise how many yearn for your rule again.'

He still needed the old man. Until they actually found his hoard.

Dracula's sword tip sank a little further. His chin lowered while he contemplated the words of the man standing in supplication before him. 'You say things I thought never to hear again. Would that I might believe you. And her. You swear there is support? Across the mountains?'

Dieudonné bowed his head. 'I do, my prince. Come down with me.' He could hear the hope, the yearning, in the old man's voice.

Suddenly, he saw Dracula spring into a guard again, blade raised high. Dieudonné ducked down, scrambling to retrieve his blade. But the force of a blow upon his back from behind sent the air rushing from his lungs, knocking him to his knees. The second blow, full upon his pauldron, then deflecting into the side of his helm, sent him to the ground. His eyes saw a thousand sparks dancing before him, his head spinning.

Rolling himself onto his side he saw the Rascian, magically arisen, swinging the iron mace at Dracula with the fury of a demon. The prince fought back, catching the blows as they rained down, the Rascian screaming out his rage. Dracula caught the mace haft on its hilt and simultaneously swiped his dagger across the Rascian's neck. A spray of blood erupted from the man and Dracula released his sword bind, raising the blade on high to follow with a straight edge blow that would cleave the Rascian's head in two.

But Pedja Jankovic leaned forward and ploughed into Dracula with a high-pitched cry, the mace spinning away from his hand, and both of them propelled across the escarpment in an embrace of death. There were no cries or curses. Dieudonné watched as together they tumbled over the edge in silence.

Cheekbone pressed against jagged gravel and ears still ringing, Gaston Dieudonné let out a long breath. 'Merde.'

His unsteady gaze was caught on the golden cross of rubies lying a few feet away – the Tears of Byzantium. And he began to crawl to them.

30

The arguing ceased the moment they saw Dieudonné stumble through the door of the inn.

Ellingham started forward and Hawker, still agitated, drew himself up and put his hands on his hips. They'd debated whether the Burgundian had flown, ditching the company to pursue his own ends.

'Christ's nails!' said Hawker, shaking his head.

Jacob de Grood threw up his hands. 'Seems I've lost my wager! He's back.'

Ellingham was relieved beyond words. He had been alone in defending the missing Burgundian. He approached Dieudonné, grinning. 'I knew you wouldn't abandon us.' He only then saw the pain etched on Dieudonné's face and how his right pauldron was dented and twisted. Indeed, the Burgundian was bent forward, wounded. 'Jack! Help me get his harness off!'

They eased him down on a bench and stripped off the twisted shoulder armour. Jack saw a large dent on the man's rusty back plate and whistled. Dieudonné let them take it off and he then leaned forward on his elbows with a groan.

'Give me a drink.'

Jack set a wooden mug of mulled wine into his hand and the Burgundian drank deeply.

'There's no blood,' remarked Jack, standing back as Hawker approached.

'*That* would be the Turk's mace,' said Dieudonné sardonically.

'Explain,' said Hawker, his voice little more than a hoarse rasp.

Dieudonné looked up at Hawker and then over to Ellingham. He ran his hand over his damp, lank hair, smoothing it back. Maria joined Ellingham, looping her arm in his but her eyes focused like a falcon's on Dieudonné.

'I thought they might have made a run up the mountain.' He flicked his pointy chin towards the door. 'To take refuge at the monastery up there. I was right.'

'My God! You found the prince?' said Ellingham.

Dieudonné nodded, took another swig, and wiped his mouth. 'I did. But it did not go well.'

'Speak up, Burgundian!' said Maria, sharply. 'Where is my father?'

'My lady… the Rascians did take him. Probably to ransom him to the highest bidder. They didn't make it to the monastery. The prince turned on them. Fought them. And he slew them. But he fell, too.'

'You lie!' she broke away from Ellingham and sent her palm slamming into Dieudonné's face. 'Where is he?'

His cheek instantly blossomed bright red. Dieudonné spread wide the fingers of both hands and then slowly reached down to his right boot. He pulled forth the cross of rubies and placed it upon the table behind him.

Maria's rage vanished and her face turned to stone. She seemed to sink a little and Ellingham moved to her side.

'I found the half-Turk lying on the path, dead,' continued Dieudonné. 'The prince and the other Rascian were not there so I gave chase. I heard the ring of steel and when I got there your father had already slain the other – or so I thought.'

Maria's hands were at her stomach now, one pushed into the other, fists turning white.

'I tried to tell him to come back with me. He was distrustful. Said you only wanted his gold. That you were all false. He threw away the cross. I did everything I could to convince him we were sworn to his honour.'

'So where is he?' she spat.

Dieudonné raised his head again, looking Maria in the eye. 'The other Rascian wasn't dead. Your father had clubbed him but not killed him. He was behind me. Got up and struck me down before I could defend myself. He and the prince fought, the Rascian was stabbed, but then he rushed the prince.' The Burgundian paused and shook his head, shutting his eyes. 'They were on a precipice... grappling. They both fell... fell away.'

'And you did not try and find him!' Maria's words were sharp and accusing. Ellingham put a restraining hand on her shoulder, fearful she might leap upon Dieudonné like some enraged leopardess.

'My lord Gaston,' he said. 'Did you see where he lies?'

Dieudonné shook his head. 'I peered over the edge. It was a sheer drop. No one could have survived such a fall. It was so great a height I could see nothing below. I swear, my lady, I could have won him over... if the Rascian hadn't struck again. I am lucky I made it back down alive... to deliver you *that*.' He pointed to the gleaming cross lying on the table.

'We will ascend tomorrow at first light,' said Ellingham, turning to Maria, trying to console her, knowing it would do nothing. 'We'll bring him back.'

She looked at the young knight, a hint of her haughtiness returning again. 'No. He is dead. And the quest is at an end.'

Hawker said nothing, his face an unreadable mask.

'Sir John,' protested Ellingham, 'surely we must recover his body and bury him.'

'We cannot stay here,' growled Hawker. 'You know it's too dangerous. We must go back north. Tomorrow.'

Ellingham looked at Maria, frowning with consternation. 'Why?'

'Because the Lord has delivered his judgement. And my father now will rest in the mountains that were his.' She moved to the table and picked up the cross. Each ruby lay in a cage of wrought gold wire, interconnecting with the others. She snapped one of the seven stones off the foot of the cross and handed it to a bemused Dieudonné.

'Your bounty, Burgundian.'

She then set about snapping one off of each arm and placed them on the table, thrusting the truncated cross of red and gold into her chemise. Ellingham winced, seeing a welt of blood instantly arise where the broken armature had scratched her breast.

'One for my lord Sir John, and one for Sir Giles.'

Neither knight moved to retrieve them.

'Fear not,' she said, 'if they were ever cursed it is now lifted. The prince of Wallachia is dead.'

There was silence across the hall. Dieudonné twisted the gem between his thumb and forefinger. 'My lady, there is but one more thing for me to tell. The prince told me – for the sake of your mother's soul – where you can find what he held most precious. That which Faldi knew.'

Hawker looked over to Ellingham, his eyes offering neither encouragement nor disuasion.

However, Maria's face transformed at hearing the Burgundian's words. Her jaw tensed, eyes looking into the middle distance. 'Well, my knights, I will hold you to your promise until that final task is done. And now, I demand the Burgundian tell me where this treasure lies.'

Gaston Dieudonné nodded respectfully. 'He said what you seek lies in the White City. In the arms of Saint Michael.'

Maria's lips parted at the words, her tongue darting out to moisten them. She seemed to whisper it to herself again. 'The white city is Weissenburg. Gyulafehérvár in our tongue. The seat of the holy bishopric. He concealed it in the cathedral!'

–

Ellingham pulled up the sweat-soaked shirt from Dieudonné's back and arms, peeling it off. The Burgundian lay down on the bedstead upon his stomach, cursing at his pain. His body was as lean and muscular as a well-bred whippet. A great bruise spread out across his back and shoulders, yellowish-brown and purple at the centre.

'Christ, Gaston, your back looks like a purple cabbage – and is just as big. But the shoulder is only reddened over the top – more of a glancing blow I reckon.'

'One should never underestimate a mace,' he replied, tucking up the pillow under his throat and chest. 'And I should not have walked past a corpse without ensuring it was truly dead. I never trusted that fat bastard.'

'The innkeeper promised to send a healing woman up with a poultice. You have to be fit enough to ride out on the morrow.'

'Ah, my friend, no physic will mend this that quickly. I just pray my sword arm isn't lost for good and that we're not jumped by more Saxons… or damned Wallachians.'

'You said you almost convinced the old prince to return to us. Would he have?'

Dieudonné shrugged then winced from the movement. 'He was half-mad anyway. Who knows? But I could tell he was weighing it up. Trusting me more. Alas.'

'But he told you of his hoard.'

'And I have now told her. His dying wish, as it turns out.'

There was silence between them for a moment or two, the only sound the hissing of the tallow candle that burned on the little table next to the small bed.

'Do you go to her now?' asked Dieudonné, turning a little towards Ellingham.

'I must. She is grieving. And she has lost her purpose.'

'Have you forgotten yours? This adventure was undertaken to gain *you* preference. Patronage. To lay a path for *your* return. That won't happen now. Vladislav Dracula is as dead as the world always believed. And all you have is a single ruby for your trouble.'

Ellingham said nothing. Dieudonné spoke the truth and it burned his heart.

The Burgundian reached out and grasped his wrist tightly. 'My friend – *my* prince – do not be deceived by her charms and soothing promises of fortune. Find out what she plans after we find this treasure in this White City. We don't belong in this land anymore. It holds nothing for us but our deaths.'

'I am sworn to her, Gaston. Until the quest is complete.'

Dieudonné groaned. 'This quest is dead, my prince. And the love of the moonstruck is no substitute for it. I won't let you be taken down a path that leads to your doom.' He paused, then turned his head up again to look at Ellingham. 'But... know this. I will stand by you come what may. On that you may depend.'

Ellingham looked away, stung by Dieudonné's dismissal of his love for Maria. He regretted that his affections had been so transparent to them all. He felt like a fool. He folded his arms across his chest. 'I will leave you now... see where that cunning woman is with your physic.'

But he went to see Maria instead. Tokár, his face still puffy from his earlier copious tears of mourning, stood guard at the door to her bedchamber, bundled against the cold. He eyed Ellingham warily, blocking the entrance. Ellingham glared back and reached over the gypsy's shoulder to knock, once.

She opened the door and spoke quietly to Tokár who then moved slowly out of the way, the whole time his eyes boring into the young knight. Ellingham entered the room.

'He blames himself for what has befallen us,' she said softly, closing the door. 'For letting my father be taken.'

'There's more than enough blame to be shared amongst us. We are the ones who failed you. We should have set a watch. It might have bought us enough time to defend ourselves.'

She approached him and took both his hands in hers. 'Sir John's boy did well to gather the villagers. He was brave. But it was you who fought like a lion when the Saxons were set upon. You and your company. We live yet.'

She released him and sat down on the edge of the bed. 'I grieve. Grieve that I have come this far, this close, only to lose him. Lose him forever but a day after he was free.'

Ellingham, not knowing if he should sit next to her, remained standing. She sat in her kirtle and chemise, a rough cloak thrown over her shoulders, hands clasped in her lap. It seemed that the untamed wildness of her spirit had vanished altogether. She was now as any lady of any noble house: demure and penitent, wistful and slightly vulnerable. His heart ached for her.

'I do grieve,' she said quietly, 'but so too am I angry. With him. Angry that he could not tell me I was his daughter. After what we have risked to free him. Humiliating me in front of all of you. And he enjoyed it! Freed from the very castle he had built and *still* he couldn't accept me. Part of me *hates* him.'

Ellingham pushed down the pommel of his sword, moving it behind him. He knelt at her feet. 'Maria... my father never acknowledged me as his own. And I've only just discovered that I am not his only bastard son. The other he did acknowledge as his. I keep asking myself why I was not so favoured. And I know I will never get an answer to that.'

She managed a twisted smile. 'We, two unloved bastards of great men. It is a curse, no?'

Ellingham put his hand on hers. 'Curse? No. But it is a burden. One we must always carry. And we both shall do so.'

She looked at him thoughtfully for a moment, as if trying to read his mind. 'We two shall do great things yet.' She then looked down. 'I am tired. So much death this day, this holy day. And we must be ready on the morrow. We will bury Ser Bartolo and then we'll ride north where there is more to be done. Leave me now, son of Richard.'

He hadn't expected to lie with her again. Not that night and not in consolation of her grief. He ached from the fight and his head was still too distracted with worry for what might happen to them all next.

'My lady, sleep well.'

He left her without a kiss, an invisible curtain seeming to fall between them.

Tokár resumed his watch and Ellingham returned to the hall of the inn where Hawker, Jacob, and Jack had bedded down upon wool sacks near the fire, all of them in battle harness. Outside, Tokár's remaining men stood guard, Hawker agreeing to a change of the watch in the night. Ellingham sat down near Hawker, his sword scabbard scraping the flagstones as he did so. He stretched out his long legs towards the hearth and set his back against a wool bale.

Jack Perry's head was thrown back, mouth gaping as he snored. Jacob's chin was down on his chest, eyes shut. Ellingham could not tell whether the wily Fleming slumbered or not.

'Gaston's back is bruised brown like a rotten apple. Might have broken a rib or two,' said Ellingham quietly.

'And how fares the lady?' replied Hawker. 'You have spent some time with her as well.' It was delivered without sarcasm but Ellingham knew Hawker's reticence lingered.

'Hurt. Pained by her loss. But she still speaks of going on… recovering the other treasure.'

Hawker raised a gloved hand and pointed towards the corpse of Bartolo Faldi, laid out on the floor and wrapped up in a shroud of raw linen.

'That is where her quest leads those who follow,' he said. 'The rest of us sit vigil on those who have fallen first.'

A wooden bowl of water sat at Faldi's head, placed by the village women to offer his soul refreshment, a single candle burned at his feet to light his way. Fragrant rosemary sprigs covered Faldi's chest.

'We all knew the risks, didn't we?'

Hawker nodded. 'We did. Though I wonder what Faldi would make of his armour and his last ducats being given over to the innkeeper and the menfolk here for his burial – and in compensation for what our stay has wrought upon them.'

Ellingham turned his eyes away from the corpse across the room. Hawker was again playing the master of the training yard and he the squire. Letting him decide whether remaining with Maria was worth the candle – or their lives. Just as Gaston had done with him. It rankled.

'We must see this through,' he said, turning to the old knight. 'We bury Faldi in the morning, make ready, and ride north again.'

Hawker's head fell back on his wool bale and he seemed to be contemplating the ceiling beams. 'Well… the Milanese might be spending a little more time with these villagers than he planned. If the ground proves too hard they'll put him in the dead house for the winter and bury him in the spring. At least he has well and truly paid them the rent.'

31

Hawker and Jacob sat mounted, side by side, watching as Dracula's sworn retainer and *armaşi* Tokár trotted off on his donkey towards the walls of Hermannstadt. Bouncing and swinging from his saddlebow was a rust-red bloodstained canvas sack.

'I would give half a florin to be there when the guild master opens that Christmas gift,' said Jacob, with barely concealed mirth.

Hawker nodded. 'Perhaps it will put the fear of God into them that Vladislav Dracula still lives. That will make them shake as they lie in their winter beds.'

They had bid goodbye to the gypsies with little ceremony. Tokár had spoken with Maria and then bowed, touching fingers to forehead in obeisance. The gypsy had vowed to deliver the head of Captain Bobik to the south gate with the note Maria had written and shoved into the mouth of the dead mercenary. Having been released from service by her, he and his men would ride south again to rejoin their camp and ready their families for a trek eastward. For Tokár, his loyalties must have died with his master. He had made no objection when Maria released him. His sworn purpose was at an end with the death of the warlord of Wallachia.

Hawker made his farewells more informally. A quick exchange in Venetian, wishing each other good fortune and health, and the two greying warriors each had nodded curtly to the other. Hawker admired the gypsy's cunning, boldness, and his willingness to risk his life to save the old prince. Tokár's last ruse had been a gamble that was nearly won but for the treachery of the Rascians. And many fortunes had hung upon that outcome.

The much-diminished company waited until the gypsies had grown small in the distance and then set off again on the road, north by north-west, bound for Weissenburg beyond the Mureş river. Hawker and Jacob took the vanguard, Ellingham and Maria followed behind, and bringing up the rear was a rather subdued Burgundian and a more talkative young squire who pestered him with questions of battle. The sun shone down, and along with an azure sky came the first true crisp and biting cold of the season, something they had been spared from in the mountains.

Hawker rode a short distance out in front of the others, Jacob at his side. He wanted the distance to keep eyes on the road ahead, his bastard sword eased two fingers'-width out of its scabbard in case trouble appeared. Carts carrying barrels and baskets rolled by them occasionally and they were hailed with good cheer on the feast days. At other times, small groups of riders, mainly merchants bundled up from the cold and their outriding servants, passed them with wary glances. The company must have seemed to them nothing more than a noblewoman and her armed guards on pilgrimage in the height of the Christmas feast. Some travellers, drunk, grinning and red-faced, wealthy for their tall felted hats, velvet bonnets and pheasant plumes, shouted jibes and admonishments. Hawker grunted with satisfaction. Drunken men seldom fight well or long. He prayed the company's luck would hold until they made their destination. But even this was doubtful as he did not know how many knew of Maria and her quest. One motley band of Bohemian mercenaries had been dealt with, but what if there were others who had similarly been hired?

Jacob's voice brought him round again.

'What do you make of this last try for the Wallachian's treasure? All on the word of the Burgundian and his last exchange with the prince. It is likely just a will o' the wisp, my lord.'

'We are still in her employ. We go there. Then we decide.'

'Ja, my lord, we are sworn. But I worry that Sir Giles is more sworn to her than we are.'

Hawker's eyes narrowed. 'We have settled that score have we not, my friend?'

Jacob laughed, good-naturedly and devoid of any challenge. 'I am sworn to *you* no matter who you place in command. Come, you know that! I speak of the lad's future. Not mine. We followed because it might bring us fortune for the cause – *his* cause – not for any damned coin or rubies.'

Hawker turned his eyes back to the road. 'Then why do you carp on, Jacob? There is still one task to be done.'

Jacob's reply was hesitant. 'Because my lord… I fear that Sir Giles may have lost sight of who he is. We're a long way from what is familiar. What we believe. Over time we can forget that, no?'

Hawker shifted in the saddle. He had to believe that Giles would find his way. The confidence he would need in the coming years could only come from trial and through free will. That was something that he could never dictate to the youth. He was sworn to give this Plantagenet foundling not just what was needed to survive, but to triumph. Triumph to restore the glory of the House of York. And on that path would lie many traps and temptations, successes and failures. A path that could only be taken by pressing on. By living through it.

'I have faith in him, Jacob. If I lose that, then I no longer have faith in anything.'

–

They rode at a trot most of the day, bypassing the square towers and walls of the Saxon town of Mühlbach and pushing on through the valley until they crossed the Mureş river as the sun dipped low on the horizon. Maria announced with her usual sense of airy confidence that a good inn lay in the town whose walls were now coming into view.

Ellingham beheld her with not a small sense of awe: the confidence, the bravado which had steel behind it, her beauty, all of these things bewitched him. Gone now was the vulnerable creature he had glimpsed the evening before.

The red-roofed towers of Weissenburg were of whitewashed stone, a high wall encircling the place. Maria had wisely discarded her leather breastplate and wore only her brocaded houppelande coat, her raven hair tied up and concealed in a twisted turban of white silk and pearls. They went unchallenged as they entered the gates, the purple sky forewarning the rapid descent of nightfall. And none too soon, thought Ellingham, hearing his mount's laboured huffing. The horses were nearly spent.

Ellingham smiled to himself as Maria led them through the twisting narrow streets to the little inn without a single wrong turn. How many times had she visited this place before? Her knowledge of the Saxon lands, the Rascian territories, Wallachia, and even Venice seemed vast for someone who was but only a few years older than he. They were received warmly at the stone and brick-built hostelry, or rather, she was. The innkeeper gave her a chamber befitting her station while the company took the large bedchamber used for most travellers. This held a dozen low, creaking, rope bedsteads with mattresses thin as communion wafers. Ellingham stacked his harness next to one of them, rebuckling his sword belt and purse over his rather ripe arming doublet. Jack helped Hawker do the same while Dieudonné felt content enough to don a doublet and hose that had been rammed deep in his portmanteau. Jacob de Grood remained in armour, flinging his barbute helm onto his chosen bedstead.

'I must lie abed,' said Hawker, the weariness in his voice obvious. 'Far too long a time to spend in the saddle at my age. And by the Christ, I have little devils hammering away in my skull. I will come down later.'

Jack pushed Hawker's leather bag up under his ankles to elevate them. 'I'll stay with you, Sir John.'

'And I,' added Jacob, looking fed up with the world.

'You should both take some food and drink,' said Hawker, running his hands through his hair and leaning back on the stained pillowcase.

'I can wait,' said Jack crossing his arms. Jacob grunted, signalling assent, and lay down on the bed with a jangling of metal.

'I will join you for some wine and food, my friend,' said Dieudonné to Ellingham, halfway finished buttoning his doublet. 'I need something to kill this cursed backache.'

Ellingham nodded to them all. 'Very well. I'll go find Maria.'

Jacob grunted again. Unimpressed.

Ellingham found her in a stuccoed alcove at the back of the crypt-like tap room, no more than a cellar, waiting for him. She had already procured a jug of wine and beakers. The rising din around them bespoke of the season of cheer and the serving boys and girls darted from alcove to alcove and to the main trestle where the barrels and taps were racked. Candles burned everywhere, giving the room a warm glow, black wispy smoke from the tallow stained the low ceiling. Ellingham saw tradesmen, whores, merchants, and a soldier or two. More topers were arriving every few minutes. At the hearth, a cauldron of something bubbling sent its smell wafting about the place.

'Take your seat here, next to me, son of Richard.' Her voice was soft – mischievous even – he thought. He squeezed in and sat on her bench, their bodies close.

'You seem better in yourself, my lady,' said Ellingham, smiling. 'Is the wine that good?'

'I see the future ahead of us,' she replied, pushing a filled vessel towards him. 'And it is full of promise.'

Ellingham drank long of the cup. It was warming and tasted of spice. 'And what you seek… do you really expect to find it there? Or that they will simply give it to you if you demand it?'

'I don't know what my father secreted away. But if he did, it must have been of great value.' She turned and looked at him intently. 'And I will convince them to give it to me. I am his daughter.'

Ellingham frowned a little. 'And if you can't convince them?'

'I have my knights with me. Steel makes a good argument with clergymen.'

Somehow, he didn't find either comfort or certainty in that.

She reached over and placed her hand over his. 'I will take you to Hunedoara, to the greatest fortress in the empire. Where

I was born and raised. I will present you to my Hunyadi kin, the castellan, everyone! And we will thrive. You will gain a post, of that I am most certain.'

Ellingham smiled again, but this time more wanly. 'And what of Buda? King Matthias. You are his kin also, are you not?'

She laughed a little and inclined her head, teasingly. 'Perhaps not best to journey there until we are established. Wealthier. The court is a treacherous place, fickle towards newcomers. But we will go there someday, I promise you. With you as my English prince.'

Ellingham took another sip of wine, rolling it in his mouth. The royal court at Buda held appeal. He might find a captaincy there or better, fighting for the Hungarian crown. If Maria could inveigle her uncle, then who knew what favours might come his way. Had not Dieudonné counselled him the same advice just weeks before? Seek advancement here and only then return west to join the Yorkist struggle against the Welsh pretender. Could this still be accomplished now that Maria's father, the prince of Wallachia, was no more? Or perhaps the path to Buda and the king there was the better plan after all. She was formidable.

Ellingham set his cup down and placed his other hand over hers. She smiled at him, her large eyes shining with eagerness, eagerness for her plans and eagerness for him.

Dieudonné silently glided into the alcove, and wincing, squeezed himself between a wall and a wine-stained oak bench before straddling it in order to take a seat. He bowed his head to Maria. 'My lady.' He then turned to Ellingham, 'Pray, give me some wine, dear Giles. Between my back being pounded by a mace and my arse bounced in a saddle all day, I fear I may not recover without it.'

Ellingham pursed his lips and slowly pushed the cup over to him.

Dieudonné grinned at Maria. 'Tell me, my lady, how do you propose to charm the treasure from whomever holds it at the cathedral? With respect, what proof can you present to them that you are who you say?'

332

It pained Ellingham to hear Dieudonné voice his doubts, just as he had to Maria in private. And he knew that Hawker probably felt the same. Ellingham swallowed, choking back his embarrassment over the lack of a strategy.

Maria's eyes went hard but she matched Dieudonné's smile. 'Does my Burgundian doubt my abilities?'

'Not at all. I just think it unlikely that the priests will give up what they hold. In my experience of the Holy Church they rarely ever do.' He raised his eyebrows and then took a drink of wine.

'My lord, if my words do not persuade them, I always have you to offer something else. Something more pointed.'

Dieudonné chuckled. 'If it came to that we might be excommunicated – assuming we ever get out of this city afterwards. But, alas, I suppose we must try. I would think your bag of ducats must be lighter by now, no? And we must be paid for our service – one ruby notwithstanding.' He inclined his head in a bow of respect.

'You will see your pay, Burgundian. Do not forget we have the son of the king of England with us,' she replied, nodding at Ellingham. 'We will not be refused. We will have an audience with the bishop – or the dean – and demand to see my father's legacy. How things go afterwards, well that is up to them.' She hefted her cup towards the Burgundian with a mock salute.

Ellingham said nothing but waved to a servant to bring another cup. He was the son of a *dead* king of England. And Dieudonné's casual effrontery still had the ring of truth to it.

–

Music wafted to their ears, reverberating off the close quarters of the narrow streets and tall dwellings. Shortly after, a procession of mummers pranced by, costumed in motley colours, riding brightly caparisoned hobby-horses, blowing horns and pounding tabor drums. It was the third day of Christmas. Maria and her companions waited on the edge of the cathedral, close until the parade and its throng of followers had passed by. The last man, already drunk though it was still morning, thumbed his nose at them and laughed, before turning to catch up the rest of his companions.

Hawker looked up at the Romanesque edifice before him. The cathedral of Saint Michael was ancient by the looks of it and easily as long as Saint Paul's back home. His sleep had done him good and now he felt well enough to face what the day would bring. If the bishop knew of any treasure Hawker doubted deeply that he would hand it over. And just what had been Dracula's instructions to the church when he had left it with them? It was a fool's errand no doubt, but he would hold his peace and see what played out. Maria was a persuasive woman, but this time, her hand was weak. He knew it and he hoped that Sir Giles did as well.

Ellingham stood next to Maria, conversing in low tones. Dieudonné had come along as well, inviting himself. Maria had assented and now the Burgundian stood, hands on hips, surveying the cathedral. He walked to either side, eyeing the lengths of both sides. Hawker smiled grimly to himself. He knew what the Burgundian was looking for: escape routes and entry points. All of them had dressed as well as they could, but their clothes were shabby from their travels, crumpled and smelling of leather and horse. And all of them – except Maria – wore their steel. Hawker's thumb played on the hilt of his *cinquedea* dagger, its presence on his hip comforting.

Maria turned to Hawker. 'We go to the chapter house, Sir John.'

Hawker nodded and gestured for her to lead on.

They walked halfway down the length of the cathedral until they came to a side building and a large, studded door of dark oak. Ellingham knocked and they were received by a black-robed priest who ushered them inside. Maria spoke in the Magyar tongue, making her request for an audience. The young priest's eyebrows elevated. He said a few quiet words to Maria, bowed, and then left them standing on the tessellated tiles of the great hall as he left. They waited.

'The bishop is away to Torda,' Maria announced to them in French. 'He will ask if the dean will grant us an audience.'

334

Dieudonné continued to survey the surroundings, studying the carved corbels and ornately painted ceiling. 'Oh, I'm sure his curiosity won't let him miss this opportunity.'

Ellingham scowled and then turned to Maria. 'My lady, we must be patient with them. This priest may not even know of what you speak. We catch more flies with honey than vinegar.'

'They'll get more than honey if they do not open their vaults,' said Maria darkly.

Hawker groaned inwardly. If they invoked violence, the militia would be upon them in minutes. He'd seen soldiers just beyond the cathedral close, at station upon the gate. Short of slitting throats, Maria had nothing with which to coerce the church to give her what she sought.

The young priest returned, spoke and then beckoned them to follow deeper into the chapter house. He brought them to a private closet, richly adorned, where there sat an older priest in white robes on a golden chair and wearing a four-square black biretta. As they entered, the dean pulled close his fox-fur mantle. They bowed low, Maria in front, and she began her address.

The dean listened in silence, his face giving no indication of his disposition. He occasionally shifted his considerable bulk, putting weight on one side or the other and then leaning on his elbow, thumb and forefinger tucked under his chin. And although Hawker could not understand the language, he could see what lay in the cleric's eyes. It was distrust.

At length, the dean gave her his answer. His tone was measured, soft, but insistent. From time to time his eyes moved from Maria to Ellingham and then Hawker. Maria answered him back, her voice raising higher, irritation mounting. Finally, she began to move closer to the dean, her tongue pouring forth. Ellingham reached out and gently pulled her back.

The dean reached over to a side table and lifted a large brass hand bell. He shook it with angry intensity until the door opened and the young priest entered again. The audience was at an end. Maria began to boil, eyes flashing, but Ellingham pulled her away.

Hawker looked over to Dieudonné who in return gave a shrug and then stuck out his lower lip in a pout. Two other priests entered bringing along a burly stonemason, still wearing his apron and bearing a maul. Behind him came yet another workman, trowel in hand. It was made clear it was time for them to leave.

'*Andiamo!*' shouted Maria, throwing off Ellingham's grasp. She shoved a smirking Dieudonné and pushed past through the doorway.

Maria stormed through the hall of the chapter house, muttering curses in Italian and Magyar. Hawker kept an eye on the clerics and the masons, taking up a position behind the others as they were herded out.

'Maria!' said Ellingham, catching her up. 'This will do no good. Tell me what he said.'

The great oak door slammed behind them all and they stood together, mocked loudly by the cawing of the crows that strutted past, pecking at the paving stones of the close.

Maria turned, her eyes wet with tears of rage and frustration. 'He called me a madwoman! The fat prick! Said that the lord of Wallachia had never left anything with the cathedral. That I had been led by the tales and lies of others. Played for a fool!'

Ellingham reached for her arm but she batted him away.

'So what is your wish now, my lady?' said Hawker quietly. 'And do not ask me to lay siege to a holy church. I've done that before and it did not end well.'

Maria opened her mouth to respond but words would not come. She looked down and then up to the sky. Lost.

The door to the chapter house opened, creaking slowly on its ancient hinges. A priest emerged, one of the older ones that had brought the stonemasons in to protect the dean. His black woollen vestments were worn and mud-stained, and his oversized cowl made his bald head look like a pea in a pod. He opened the door only enough to squeeze out, closing it behind him with a nervous glance behind.

'My lady!' came the words in Venetian. 'I do believe you are who you say. And I know what you seek.' He looked past them all like a frightened fugitive and then began walking past the white walls of the chapter house towards the chancel end of the cathedral, sandals slapping on the stones. He turned, his baggy black sleeve flapping wildly as he waved them forward, urgently beckoning them. 'Come, come! We have little time!'

They followed him around the side of the cathedral, past the uninhabited stonemasons' timber lean-to, chiselled pediments and corbels lying strewn about.

'I am Father de Lucia,' he said, pulling a ring of keys from a large pocket of his vestments and opening a side door to the transept. Hawker drew his dagger out by an inch, ready to defend any treachery. He shot Ellingham a look and gave a nod towards the youth's scabbarded weapon. Ellingham nodded in return, gripping his hilt. The priest led them inside and immediately down a flight of narrow stone steps, illuminated by torchlight.

Hawker sneezed; the mustiness of the place was strong. There were three arches each with iron gratings and locked doors. The old priest shuffled to one of them and fiddled to find the right key. Hawker could see golden chalices, crucifixes, candelabra, and metal caskets of different sizes scattered across the damp and green mould-strewn floor.

The Father began mumbling, half to himself. 'They will miss me if I am away long. But, you have a right, my lady. I have heard the rumours from Venice. Of a noblewoman who took the Tears of Byzantium from under the Doge's nose. You are the one from Hunedoara. His child.' He turned one of the heavy, ornate iron keys in the lock and yanked open the door. 'We keep reliquaries and other things in here. This is where it has lain since...' He trailed off, struggling with the hinges of the grating.

Ellingham stepped forward and helped him open it fully with a retched squeal, as if reluctant to reveal its secrets.

The company waited while the priest went inside and began moving the coffers, caskets, and jars. He then lifted a small, tarnished silver coffret in his hands and carried it out. 'Here! This is it!'

337

He clasped it to his chest and stood in front of Maria. 'This is what your father held most dear. He was a true soldier of Christ. His instructions to the bishop were to keep it until he returned from his campaign against the Ottomans. But he never did, as you know well, my lady.'

He opened the lid and Maria lifted out the only thing it contained. It was an enamelled pendant the size of a large coin, a winged dragon crouching with its tail passing under its claws and encircling its own neck. An *ourobouros* of gold. Upon its back was a cross, enamelled in bright carmine red. She blinked a few times, holding it up to her face.

'There was a gold collar with it,' said Father de Lucia, embarrased. 'But it was pilfered a few years ago.' He shook his head with disgust. 'An itinerant Franciscan who visited us. I am sorry.'

Maria looked to the priest, her face scrunched up in disbelief. 'The Order of the Dragon? That is all?'

The priest's countenance changed to one of solace, of the sort given out to grieving parishioners. 'There was nothing more, my lady.'

Laughter sounded, starting as a restrained burst of breath then building to an outright cackle. It was Dieudonné.

Hawker moved forward and grabbed the front of his doublet, hauling him close. He thrust Dieudonné backwards, a forefinger pointing out warning. 'You would do well to heel, my lord.'

Dieudonné spread the fingers of both outstretched hands. 'I yield, Sir John. Mea culpa.' But the trace of a smirk still was on his lips.

Ellingham stood next to Maria, peering at the pendant. He put his hand to her shoulder and addressed the priest. 'That is *all* of the prince's treasure?'

The old man's sadness visibly deepened, eyebrows falling. 'I was here then. The prince said that this bestowal was what mattered most to him in the whole world. He was a Dragonist… like his father before him. It is a great and ancient noble order. And the crusade against the infidels was his life's work. He knew he might fall in battle but wanted *this* kept safe.' He proffered a shaking hand towards the pendant she held. 'You may take it, my lady. You are of the blood.'

Maria said nothing. She rubbed the golden dragon with her thumb as if gently stroking it. She then reverently placed it back into the silver coffret which the priest still clutched to his chest. She shut the lid, her hands trembling.

'I have not even my father's bones to give proper burial to. So then, let this be in his memory... and let it be his resting place.'

32

Jacob de Grood, wooden spoon in his fist, attacked the stringy parsnip with an intensity he usually reserved for an enemy on the field. He shook his head then scratched at his burgeoning black beard, now flecked with even more grey.

'My old sire would be spitting venom if he could see us now. A right tongue-lashing. We've made it to the edge of the world with nothing to show for it but a few coins. And a ruby. The same one you were sworn to deliver to somebody else, I seem to remember.'

The inn seemed nearly empty even though it was mid-afternoon. Raucous Christmas revels echoed in the town's squares. Hawker shovelled in another mouthful of lukewarm *gulyás*. 'We did what we were bade. And Fortuna can't be bargained with. She gives. And she takes.'

'So, *are* we finished here with our business? Seems to me that we have fulfilled our contract.'

Hawker wiped his mouth with the back of his hand. 'I thought you and I were of one mind upon that, Jacob. I give counsel but it is for the son of my king to decide where his future lies. I will follow. And so will you.'

Jacob bisected a black-spotted potato with a jab. 'Aye, my lord. That I will.'

Jack Perry had kept his head down during the exchange, having finished his meal already in a series of gulped mouthfuls.

'Sir John,' he began, looking down with some uncertainty before meeting the knight's eye. 'Will you let me keep the crossbow?'

Hawker tilted his head to one side. 'The crossbow? You can be a squire – or a bowman – but you cannot be both.'

Jack looked down again, seemingly torn by the choice. 'I'm *good* with it. You know that. And I've killed two captains with it so far.'

Jacob chuckled. 'If that's to be your profession, knights who love a bowman are few and far between. Get captured and they're sure to chop off your fingers. The Burgundian here can tell you that!'

Deep down, a part of Hawker worried the lad was beginning to enjoy it all a little too much. He leaned forward. 'Killing from afar is easy. I give you that. Makes you feel invincible. And you have done well, my boy. But killing should never be an easy thing, done thoughtlessly, even if that is what we must do.'

Jack's brow furrowed as he took in the knight's words. 'But… I know I'm good.' He said it half to himself.

'I think young Jack knows his weapon of choice,' said Dieud-onné quietly from his corner, in his broken English. 'But sometime… he shoot back. The enemy. Then *you* see what it like.' He winked.

Jack's lips twisted in clear annoyance.

'You need to keep training with the blade, my boy,' said Hawker. 'For that is what will keep you alive at the end of the day. But, God forgive me… you may keep the crossbow for now. Might come in handy for hunting fowl and hares in the coming days.' He smiled and gave Jack a gentle push on the shoulder.

Jacob looked up. 'Oh, here now,' he mumbled. 'Looks like we are about to hear our fate.'

Ellingham and Maria Hunyadi approached the alcove, he leading her by the touch of a raised hand. She was wearing a gown that they had not yet seen before, dark wine trimmed in white lace. A fur mantle of black pine marten covered her shoulders. Her hair was coifed and draped with a shawl of fine cambric. Hawker tried to decipher her expression. Still that air of confidence, but perhaps something more besides. She stopped at the table and gave a nod of acknowledgement while Ellingham found her a bench and moved it underneath her. An incongruous seat in an incongruous place for such a woman of noble birth. Hawker could see the eagerness in the youth's eye, but whether it was for her or her plans he could not tell.

'My brave company!' she said, smiling at Hawker. 'We have come far and you have stood by me these many weeks. I grieve for my loss, a loss for my kingdom, but in my heart, I know there is much more we can do. And your service has not been in vain.'

Hawker leaned back, slowly, pushing the remains of his stew away.

'I have discussed with Sir Giles what may be salvaged from our quest,' she said, nodding to the youth who stood over her shoulder. 'And he has consented to give my proposal his full consideration.'

Dieudonné shifted on his bench and sat up straight, eyes riveted onto the woman, eager to hear her next words.

Hawker looked up at Ellingham. 'The root of the bargain we sealed at Venice was to see your future secured, my lord. I trust that is still uppermost in your mind.'

Ellingham's response came quickly. 'It is, Sir John. And I would sleep upon a decision before committing us to it. My lady proposes we make for the castle at Hunedoara. It is her family seat – on her Hunyadi side,' he added, looking at her. 'The castellan there will receive us warmly.'

'And then?' asked Hawker, this time directing his response to Maria.

'The son of King Richard will indeed be received well there,' she replied. 'We may winter there, build the company strength, and from there seek the court of the king of Poland. To further the cause of my lord's house and to build an army.'

Hawker raised his eyebrows. 'I see… an army. And what of the king of Hungary? Were we not told that Buda was where Sir Giles would find patronage? Matthias is your uncle, is he not?'

She laughed, brushing it aside as if yesterday's concern evaporated in the light of the new day. 'One goes where the reward is the greater. And it is in the east that the struggle continues against the infidels. Where one can gain fortune. And respect.'

Hawker glanced over to Jacob, who stirred his now-cold stew with intent, not looking up. Dieudonné's face was devoid of any emotion, a faint benign smile on his lips. And unusually, thought Hawker, he seemed in no hurry to poke a finger through the joyous picture she was painting for them. He looked over again to Ellingham, but this time the youth seemed unable to hold his gaze.

'And you would give consideration to this offer?' he asked.

Ellingham broke into a wide smile, smacking more of bravado than conviction. 'We need more than our little company now, Sir John. To gain respect we need two hundred or even five hundred men with us. A hundred lances under our command! King Matthias's war against Austria is over and won. But the Poles fight on in the east.'

'And your decision?'

Ellingham folded his arms across his chest and watched Maria as he spoke. 'I've listened well to her... and to your wise counsel, Sir John. And I will weigh it all tonight. Sleep upon it. And in the morning, I will tell you what I propose we do.'

Jacob rubbed a forefinger under his nose and remained silent, staring into his bowl. Dieudonné ran his hand over the well-worn table as if admiring the wood, attentive but also remaining in silence. Jack Perry looked from one to another.

'Is there any more stew?'

—

She ran her hands down the front of his arming doublet, fingers toying with the points and lacing. 'Go now, my lord. It is late and we both need rest.' Ellingham stood over the threshold of the small bedchamber, reluctant to leave.

'I would stay the whole of the night with you.'

She smiled, tolerating his boyish libido. 'And you would fall out of the saddle on the ride tomorrow. You need sleep, my lord. Go now, before you are seen.'

He stroked her lean face, disappointed. 'Very well. Sleep well, my lady.'

She shut and bolted her door. She was tired. Tired of having to salvage her dreams and plans each time fate intervened to thwart her. But she was not finished yet. And a Plantagenet prince would do no harm in whatever royal court they ended up in. She hugged herself in the chill of the room and pulled the coverlet up from the floor where it had fallen, wrapping herself in it while she pondered what would come on the morrow.

The knock made her smile. He was insistent and eager to please.

Cracking open the door she was surprised to see the serving boy of the inn standing there and brandishing a small letter. She accepted it, shooed him away, and shut the door again. It was written in French, a crabbed hand.

> *My dear lady,*
>
> *Come to me as soon as this is delivered to your hand and with all speed. Meet me by the entrance to the Chapter House. I have more news but for your ears only! Do not bring the others for they will alert the guard.*
>
> *De Lucia*

She hurriedly dressed, putting her gown over her chemise and then pulling on her woollen socks and the riding boots she always wore. Her fur mantle she threw about her shoulders before peeking out the door to see if anyone lurked. The inn was quiet, and with the tin oil lamp from her room she made her way down the hall and then outside into the cold.

The dark alley gave way to the wider street and she could see the cathedral's bulk illuminated in the sinking moonlight. There were no folk about at the hour, only stray dogs which slunk away in front of her. She made it to the chapter house without seeing a soul, but there was no one there to meet her. She carried around to the side where the heavy stone buttresses jutted outwards. Perhaps the priest had a change of heart, she thought. He seemed a timid old man, even if a loyal one.

The force of the bear hug from behind propelled her forward, and the lamp flew to the pavement, extinguishing. She reached behind her to find an eye to poke or hair to pull but she was lifted off her feet and carried behind the first buttress. Her assailant's hand flew to cover her mouth and then she was yanked around to face them. Even in the faint moonlight she could see it was the Burgundian. He held her close, nodded once, and then slowly removed his hand from her mouth.

She did not cry out. Her response was quiet and laced with venom. 'You vile dog,' she said, raising her chin with defiance. 'What is your game?'

Dieudonné glared without his usual smirk. 'No game, my lady. An ultimatum.'

She made to thrust him back. 'Let me go, you insolent bastard!'

He pushed her against the large square stones of the wall, pinioning both arms. 'I am here to give you a choice. Leave before the sun rises and take your precious rubies with you. Otherwise, I will tell Giles that you are a whore, a murderess and a thief. Faldi confessed all to me. You cannot return to Buda. Ever. You've latched on to our young prince like a beautiful serpent but you never cozened me as you have him.'

She hissed back at him, her rage stoking. 'He would not believe you!'

Dieudonné tilted his head, a small smile forming on his lips. He pulled back a little and released her wrists. 'Would you roll those dice? He *will* believe me. And more importantly, so will Hawker. He already suspects your motives. All we need do is return to Temesvár to find the proof. Count Kinizsi will provide it. A day's ride, no?' Dieudonné wagged his long, gloved finger at her. 'And I never – *ever* – believed the house we stayed in was actually yours. Who did you pay to rent it? No, my lady, this company has honoured its contract, but it is now over.'

Her dark olive eyes danced with hatred for him. 'I have *your* measure, Burgundian. Well and truly. You think I have not seen how you look at him? The desire you fail to hide. You are a lustful, unnatural beast and you want him for your own ambitions! *Your* future fortune!'

Dieudonné's hand darted out and seized her throat. She glared back even as he squeezed, not a drop of fear in her eyes. And then, just in time, his other hand caught her wrist. She had already drawn a stiletto from her gown, the point at his belly. He pushed it down just as it began penetrating into his doublet, releasing her throat as he defended himself. She let out a muffled squeal of frustration and tried to break and run. He pinioned her against the wall again, the stiletto clattering to the stones.

'Do not tempt me to kill you! I rarely need an excuse. But I'm giving you *this* chance because you and I have much in common. I see in you what I see in myself. But you've lost this game. It's time to find another. Giles is mine.'

33

The horses pawed in frustration, heads tossing. They'd been saddled and loaded for some time and they were eager to move, raring to throw off the gnawing cold which had settled on the courtyard and into their hides. Jacob and Jack, fully armoured and holding the reins of their own mounts as well as Hawker's, did their best to calm the beasts. There was tension in the air besides.

'A pouch of ducats! And not even a goddamned note!' Ellingham launched his boot toe against a wooden bucket and sent it spinning away across the paving stones. He cursed and ran his hand through his long, lank hair. 'Why? What did we do to make her flee?'

'We've waited long enough. She's not coming back.' Hawker's voice was devoid of emotion. He wasn't about to offer a salve to the youth when what was needed was what the lad had already received: a hogshead of icy water poured over him. 'Maria Hunyadi has made her decision. Now is the time we must make ours.'

Ellingham looked at Hawker and then over to Dieudonné, who was watching with a studied detachment while he fiddled with his bridle. The young knight cursed, pulled his dagger from his girdle, and strode back into the hall of the inn.

'Sweet Christ!' muttered Hawker, dashing after him. Dieudonné followed.

They found Ellingham gripping the Saxon innkeeper by the collar of his leather jerkin, the dagger already drawing a drop of blood under the man's quivering chin. The youth had made his demands in English and then French but the innkeeper had merely begged for mercy. Dieudonné slowly reached for Ellingham's forearm, wrapped his hand around it, and spoke quietly.

'Come, my friend This avails you nothing. Would you get us all killed?'

Ellingham released the innkeeper and took a step back. The poor man touched his chin and then stared at his red-stained fingers, shaking his head in disbelief.

'Ask him!' demanded Ellingham. 'Where did she go?'

Hawker handed a coin to the innkeeper and spoke in broken German. The innkeeper blurted out something angrily then followed this up with words more measured, his eyes still set upon the blond youth whose cheekbones were blown bright red.

'He says that she told him she was journeying to Hunedoara. She made it clear that she wasn't returning here. She left no other word.'

'That's all? By Christ's blood, why? And why bother telling him *where* she was bound? Unless she expects us − *me* − to join her!'

Dieudonné placed his hand on Ellingham's shoulder. 'Because, my friend, she had finally realised that the contract was done. That the quest ended along with her father. She slept upon the matter too. Like you did. Something the rest of us already knew. I am sorry.'

Ellingham's shoulders fell a little and he held his hand over his heart, shaking his head at the Saxon. The foolhardiness of his outburst had suddenly dawned on him. He looked over to Dieudonné, his eyes beginning to well up.

'Was I really so blind, Gaston?'

Dieudonné gave him a smile full of brotherly understanding. 'She was convincing, my friend. And brave, for I will give her that. But her path lies elsewhere. Yours lies west. And we ride there with you.'

Ellingham cleared his throat and sheathed his dagger. 'Let's go,' he said. He walked past them and back outside.

348

Hawker's boot tips touched Dieudonné's. They stood nose to nose. His words were delivered with an intensity belying their softness. 'Clever, my lord. Very clever. You don't like what the cards say… so you slip in one of your own. If he ever learns of the truth… I will kill you.'

The Burgundian stood motionless, his eyes locked with Hawker's. 'I understand. It will not come from my lips. But tell me… tell me you're displeased by the outcome, Sir John.'

'I will tell you one thing. If you ever attempt treachery against him, I will be there. The Lord's Angel of Death. Coming for you.'

Hawker took two steps back, still quietly simmering, and then wheeled and went outside. Dieudonné followed, chastised, but biting his tongue. He put boot to stirrup and mounted his roan palfrey, adjusting his reins with a jerk, born of pique. He did not like being caught out. It was a sign of sloppiness. He would need to keep an even sharper eye on Hawker from now on. Jacob threw a quick, hopeful expression to Hawker, one that spoke of relief, and handed the reins over before signalling to Jack to mount up as well. But Ellingham stood, frozen, hand on the pommel of his saddle, staring at his boots. The old knight sighed and went to him, laying both hands upon the shoulders of a bastard son of a fallen king.

'Giles, she knew your destiny was elsewhere. If she'd made her choice clear, said her goodbyes, would you have accepted it? Truly, this is the better way. If the weather holds – and the Austrians behave themselves – we'll be in Flanders by Candlemas. Three Tears of Byzantium should more than pay our way. And then you'll see that the fires of rebellion are kindled well and truly. And we shall serve the cause with all our strength. There was an oath we both took. An oath to your father.'

Ellingham turned his head and held him in his gaze. Hawker saw a coldness there he'd not glimpsed before. But it was the true countenance of a Plantagenet in all its hellfire and power. The look of a prince of the blood.

'She *betrayed* me. Betrayed my trust and affection.'

'We're going home. Set your mind's eye upon that, and let your heart go there too.'

Sir Giles Ellingham nodded slowly, taking in Hawker's words. 'Yes. I have a brother and a sister to find. My blood.'

The young knight mounted and Hawker gripped the bridle. 'And I will help you find them.'

'But first, to Trieste.'

Hawker frowned. 'Trieste?'

'A quick sail to Venice from there. You've stood by me. It's time for me to stand by you. If you want to find her again – Chiara – I will go with you.'

The older knight's hand slid from the bridle and he took half a step back. His wrinkled brow furrowed even deeper. An inelegant, stuttering confusion rushed over him with the surprise of Ellingham's offer. The guilt and sorrow he had borne with him over the fate of Chiara Contanto, the woman he had loved and left, had never been concealed well. That he knew. It was a weight that grew heavier with each passing week. 'Giles, the generosity of your offer... it has cut me to the quick... but I would not put your life in danger in Venice again. It is the past now.'

Sir Giles Ellingham shook his head slowly, staring at his saddle. He turned to face Hawker. 'Sir John, I know you well enough now. Well enough to know that your grief will kill you in the end as sure as any arrow or sword. You must learn her fate. Save her if she yet lives. You will need a few blades besides your own if you are to challenge the Serene Republic again. I give you mine.' His lips formed a wan smile that made him look older and wiser than his years.

Sir John Hawker tilted his head, face lighting up, all weariness vanished. His hand reached out for the youth's armoured shoulder. 'Good my lord! Know thee well, I would never have asked such a thing of you, but you've seen the true wish of my heart! If this is your wish too – given freely – then Giles, God give us speed!'

350

Historical Note

The Real Dracula

Born in Transylvania in 1431, Vlad Dracula, son of Vlad Dracul, gained and lost the throne of medieval Wallachia not once but three times during his tempestuous life. Wallachia, a fractious principality of the kingdom of Hungary in what is now Romania, was a geopolitical cauldron for much of its existence. Caught between the rising Ottoman Empire in the south-east and its western overlords in Hungary, Wallachian rulers had to employ skilful diplomacy as well as force of arms just to survive. Dracula had come from a long line of rulers or *voivodes* (a Slavonic word for 'warlord' or 'prince'). His father had been inducted into the knightly Order of the Dragon in Nuremburg, hence the adoption of Dracul, meaning dragon in the Romanian tongue (from the Latin *Draco*). Its second translation – devil – would later be employed by Dracula's detractors and enemies, of which there were many.

Infamous in his lifetime as 'the Impaler', Vlad's sadistic cruelties were legend. Although the horrific punishment of impalement had already been in use in the Ottoman world and Eastern Europe before Dracula's arrival on the scene, Vlad made it his signature as part of his campaign to secure loyalty among the fractious *boyar* nobility of Wallachia and the ethnic German merchant-class of Transylvania, as well as to intimidate the Turks pressing on the southern and eastern borders of the country. Tales of his mass impalements of rebellious noblemen and their wives as well as Ottoman prisoners were spread by both the Germans and the king of Hungary, Matthias Corvinus, as part of geopolitical manoeuvrings and constituted some of the first mass broadsheet print propaganda campaigns in western history.

Much has been speculated about Dracula's state of mind given the number and depravity of executions during his reigns, remarkable even for such an age of general cruelty. But Vlad had been brought up in a world where death was frequent, violent and sudden. His older brother, Mircea, and his father were both murdered: Mircea being buried alive, while Vlad Dracul was assassinated in marshland near Bucharest days later. Vlad Dracula and his younger brother Radu had in boyhood been made hostages at the court of the Ottoman sultan in Istanbul in order to secure the loyalty of their father. There they had witnessed execution and torture. In the Ottoman court, mercy was rarely rewarded and it was common practice for sultans to have siblings strangled to preserve their own hold on power. Dracula, a prince on familiar terms with Sultan Murad and later with Murad's son, his near-contemporary Mehmed 'the Conqueror', saw first-hand how survival often depended upon striking first.

His boyhood years at the Imperial court gave him an understanding of Ottoman mentality and the Ottoman way of war. This was knowledge he would exploit in the defence of Wallachia years later. Medieval Wallachia's *voivodes* found themselves having to carefully balance loyalties. Ostensibly owing fealty to the crown of Hungary, they would often pay tribute to the sultan to avoid occupation. Swinging back and forth between these power centres – even promising 'loyalty' to both at the same time – was a dangerous game. In 1456, Dracula took the throne from the rival who had slain his father, killing that *voivode* in combat. He then threw all his support behind the king of Hungary. Burning all his bridges with the Ottomans, his campaign to free Wallachia from Turkish influence and occupation was about to begin in earnest. He would soon capture the attention of all Europe and gain papal sanction with his new crusade in the east.

Securing his rule within Wallachia, Dracula used terror against those who challenged him, both the Saxon merchants of Transylvania and rebellious *boyars*. According to accounts by both enemies and allies, Dracula's opponents were impaled, boiled alive, flayed, beheaded or disembowelled, with punishment inflicted regardless of gender or age. Dracula's military campaigns against the Turks were equally bloody, ruthless, and effective. Working in conjunction with the Hungarians, gains were made against the Ottomans in Bosnia, Serbia, and Wallachia. A major counter-offensive by Sultan Mehmed in 1462 drove deep into Wallachia but was halted by a masterful lightning attack from Dracula's army in the dead of night, sowing confusion and chaos in the very camp of the sultan. Withdrawing northwards in the face of the larger Ottoman force, Dracula employed a scorched earth strategy to deny the Turks forage and water. Plague entered their ranks and soldiers began to sicken. The final straw for Sultan Mehmed was the sight of thousands of impaled Turkish soldiers on the road before the gates of Târgoviște, the Wallachian capital. The so-called 'forest of the impaled' comprised Turkish captives earlier executed, their bodies in an advanced state of decomposition in the summer heat, ravaged by crows and magpies. Seeing the corpse of his emissary Hamza Pasha on the highest stake garbed in silken vestments, the sultan admitted defeat. He withdrew his army to the coast to take ships home.

Dracula's victory was short-lived. His younger brother Radu had remained loyal to the sultan and managed to win over loyalties in Wallachia. Vlad found himself having to take flight westwards with the small rump of a force that remained his. His plan was to be rescued by his royal benefactor Matthias, arriving with a large force from Buda. Holing up in the Carpathians, he waited to join the king so that he could regain his throne. But the pendulum of great power politics was swinging against him. Matthias had decided to let Radu take the throne in order to keep the peace with the Ottomans while he attended to more urgent matters regarding Hungary and the Hapsburg Empire. Vlad Dracula had become a liability. In a stunning betrayal, King Matthias arrested Dracula in Transylvania and had him transported to confinement outside Buda where he was held for more than ten years. Most of these were probably in relative comfort in what today would be termed 'house arrest'. But as the geopolitical pendulum in the region swung again, King Matthias saw that Dracula might yet have purpose.

Dracula was released, given the hand of a cousin of the king in marriage, and appointed as Captain General to lead an expedition against the Turks in Bosnia in the winter of 1475–76. Vlad and his army triumphed, tales of his ruthless treatment of captives being carried back west by the papal legate and cementing his notoriety in Europe. With Hungarian support and that of King Stephen of neighbouring Moldavia, Vlad extended his campaign into Wallachia and in November regained the throne, driving out the Turks and their puppet *voivode*, Basarab Laiota, thus enabling him to again take the throne of Wallachia in November.

But within weeks, conflicting reports of his death began to leak out to the wider world. Some said he and a small party had been ambushed by Wallachian enemies outside of Bucharest. Others claimed a raid on an Ottoman camp made by Dracula had gone disastrously wrong, leading to him being overwhelmed and killed. A third claimed he had been assassinated by stealth. By the end of January 1477, ten Moldavian soldiers of King Stephen who had been seconded as Dracula's bodyguard made it home to say they had been overwhelmed by a Turkish force and that Dracula had indeed fallen.

For a ruler of his notoriety and renown, there was never any confirmation of his identity or whereabouts by a definitive source after his death. According to popular folklore, Dracula's headless body was interred at the monastery of Snagov but there is no evidence for this. His tomb has never been found. In all likelihood, Vlad Dracula indeed met his fate south of Bucharest that December at the hands of the Turks. The court historian to King Matthias, Antonio Bonfini, wrote that Dracula's head was sent to Sultan Mehmed. If so, Ottoman records of its arrival are lacking. But I've used the vagueness surrounding his death and the conflicting stories about what became of his mortal remains to build a plausible fiction: that he survived in secret, a prisoner of his ruling half-brother Vlad Călugărul.

And what of Vlad's descendants? Vlad Dracula had two legitimate children and an unknown number of illegitimate ones. Ilona Szilági, the Hungarian noblewoman and cousin to the king, bore him two sons: one died young and the other stayed close at the court of King Matthias, no doubt as a possible 'spoiler' should Matthias choose to intervene again in Wallachian politics. In any event, this son never did. A third son of the Impaler, born to a mistress of Dracula's around 1460, was named Mihnea. He eventually rose to the throne but ruled for only two years before being assassinated in 1510. His children and grandchildren, however, also reached the thrones of Wallachia and Moldavia, ruling sporadically, briefly and ironically, under Turkish suzerainty. According to Romanian historian Alexandru Simon, Mihnea's mother may have herself been an illegitimate daughter of Hungarian king John Hunyadi and a courtesan. I have based the character of Maria Hunyadi-Drăculeşti – who is fictitious – on this union of Dracula's. We shall never know for certain how many illegitimate children Vlad Dracula sired and therefore, who carries on his bloodline today.

In English, there are two comprehensive biographies of Vlad Dracula worthy of note. I recommend *Dracula, Prince of Many Faces* by Radu R. Florescu and Raymond T. McNally (1989) and *Vlad III, Dracula* by Kurt W. Treptow (2020). Alexandru Simon's *In the World of Vlad* (2021) also delves deeply into the political realities and challenges of the time.

Acknowledgements

First and foremost, I would like to thank my editor at Canelo, Craig Lye, for his guidance, insight, and helpful nudges, all of which assisted me to craft this novel. I must also tip my hat to the rest of the team at Canelo who've worked hard to produce and promote the adventures of Sir John Hawker and his unlikely company of cast-offs. The team at Black Sheep deserve high praise for their beautiful and haunting covers for the novels, and they have my thanks also. The Richard III Society (www.richardiii.net) has proved a wonderful resource to me in researching the series, for which I am hugely grateful. Lastly, I would like to thank all my readers who have come along with me on this journey through the fifteenth century and the final days of the Wars of the Roses. *Vivat!*